SUNRAYS AMONG SHADOWS

THE ANIM • BOOK ONE

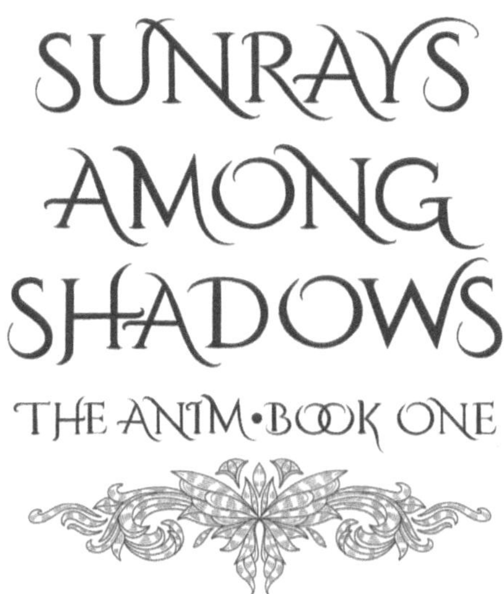

H. Dawn Hunter

ISBN: 979-8-9875335-0-5

Cover, book design, and illustrations by H. Dawn Hunter

An early version of this story was published in 2012 by Mirror Publishing as "Risin' Sun" under the name H. D. Hunter.

hdawnhunter.com

CONTENT WARNING

This book contains depictions of and references to content that may be troubling to some readers. Please be mindful of this while reading and visit hdawnhunter.com for a full list of possible triggers.

If you or someone you know is experiencing a crisis, please seek assistance.

Dial 911 for Emergencies
Dial 988 for the 988 Suicide and Crisis Lifeline
Text HOME to 741741 for the Crisis Text Line

For Shawnee and Kyle

MIDRON
INN
BYRNE CLINIC
ERISILON
GIMLON
TONLON

TRIGON
EGALDON
VRODON
DWILON
N
W
E
S

APRIL 1912

PART ONE
SILENCE

LILY

My stomach turned to stone first. It weighed me down, anchoring me to the solitary chair in front of the window. I waited for the rest of my body to petrify, but instead, I seemed to grow, my shadow bleeding from my feet, slowly dragging itself across the room.

I couldn't seem to make up my mind, and it was a painstaking affair. Every breath fought its way in through my teeth. Every exhale seemed a labour to expel. Perhaps my lungs had frozen, too, sometime during the hours I'd spent staring at the rope on the floor, coiled like a serpent. But it wouldn't strike without my help—without my nimble fingers to twist it into the right shape.

What a strange thing.

How dull the rope seemed, a frayed pile on slats of old wood, glowing in a stream of dusty lamplight, not yet devoured by my flickering shadow. And yet, how tragic a device it could be with just a few twists and a knot and some high place to hang it from. How easily something so ordinary could be made a weapon.

Anything could, I supposed. That candlestick or that broken

vase. The loft was full to the brim with items waiting for their time and their use, and what a use that could be—a grand entrance for them and an exit for me.

I almost smiled. Perhaps I would have if my cheeks weren't so tired from faking them. What a chore and a bore and a devilish thing it was to pretend, especially for a woman grown, who felt more like a statue than a person. But it was a great deal easier to hide away and pretend to turn to stone than it was to face another day with people but alone.

The air felt brittle as if, trapped up here, it had aged and soured. It had gone unbreathed so long that it didn't seem capable of sustaining life, inviting a silence so deep, I had almost convinced myself that I could hear my own shadow straining across the floorboards like some foul creature splintering its fingernails trying to crawl away from the light. Even the cobwebs in the corners were so heavy with dust that they stretched down the walls, no longer holding shape.

A slow exhale rattled through my lips, and abruptly, I stood, determined to stir the dreaded quiet. I unstuck my bare feet from the floor, whirled around, and slapped the window with both hands. My shuddering breath fogged the glass, a bead of condensation trailing down, drawing a line through the cloud. I pushed it open, shoved myself half out, and gulped the night air, where it felt clean to breathe because the dust outside was far more dispersed than it was in a musty old attic.

There were sounds and shadows of life—fluttering shapes of bats and bugs and wind-tousled trees under a waning crescent moon—and they were far more welcome than my own.

Carefully, I ducked my head back in, my hair catching on the latch but only for a playful tug. I pretended it was the night's way of telling me to stay—to keep breathing its air and savouring its sounds. I stared through the opening as the wind gusted in. First, one great push of coldness that drew gooseflesh on my arms and nearly blew out my candle. Then, just a breath —an apology soft as a kiss—and the night stilled.

I turned from the world outside to the one within, where there was still a chair and a coiled rope among the crates and trunks and forgotten things—where there was still an opportunity.

But now, my fingers felt stiff from the cold, and the rope was no more pliable than before.

I abandoned them both, extinguishing the lamp and retrieving my chamberstick. I turned, cupping my hand around the tiny flame, dousing the room in shadow as I reached the stairs to begin my descent, but I left the window ajar.

Silently, I wished the rope really was a serpent. Perhaps then, it could find its own way out—slip through the window and fade into the night—and when I returned with this hollow feeling, there would no longer be a weapon to tempt me. There would be only a smudge and a line drawn in the dust, one that would be covered by more soon anyway.

LILY

I took the steps two at a time when I heard the familiar knock, rounding the corner in time to intercept John before he admitted the visitor.

"Wait!" I waved from the landing. "Let me!"

The man turned, eyes darting, searching for the source of the voice, and when he saw me leaning over the railing, he blanched.

"B-But—" he sputtered as I hurried down the remaining steps.

"Please, let me. It's Mr. Ramey," I told him. "I know that knock."

He found his voice at last. "But madam, you're not properly dressed."

A downward glance exposed the alleged impropriety. In my haste, I'd forgotten to fasten my robe—or even put it on correctly. One sleeve had fallen into the crook of my elbow, while the sash dragged on the floor. I raised my head again, flushing when I met John's gaze, which bore a look that felt like a scolding.

Yanking the sleeve up onto my shoulder, I closed the

garment over my nightgown with one hand and shooed him from the entryway with the other. "Never you mind. I'll get the door please."

Scratching his cheek, he opened his mouth like he had more to say but closed it again without a word. With a slight bow—and one last scrutinous glance—he sighed deeply and retreated.

I waited for another knock and flung the door open, revealing a surprised Sladen Ramey with one fist still hanging in the air. His eyes travelled up my figure with a mixture of disapproval and awe.

"Miss Lily, how ... underdressed you are this morning."

I frowned. Surely, at some point in our acquaintance, he'd seen me with so dishevelled an appearance. John, too, had served us long enough to have borne witness. Neither had any reason to act shocked, and I found their shared reaction a little offensive, even if it was meant in jest.

"Are you quite finished?" I asked. He turned away, rosy-cheeked, stuttering, and directing his gaze anywhere but my person. "Oh, just a gander? Is that all? Very well. A good morning to you then, sir." I rolled my eyes and made to close the door.

"Wait! Miss Lily!"

I paused. "Yes? What d'you want?"

Recovered from his initial embarrassment, he drew himself up importantly and, with a theatric sweep of his arms, said, "I am here again to bask in the glory of your company."

I closed the door another inch, but he slipped his hand in the way to stop me from securing it fully. I thinned my eyes. "I'm on my way to have breakfast with my family, and you're interrupting."

His face fell. "I must say, the shrewd look you're giving me is rather unbecoming. You were so elegant when we met; I almost feel cheated."

I forced my lips into an apologetic smile. "Well, I'm terribly sorry to have shattered the illusion. You must be devastated. I completely understand if you never want to see me again."

He grinned. "Come now, Lily, I said I felt cheated, not put off. If I'm being entirely honest, I think I could get used to this fresh-out-of-bed look."

"Mr. Ramey! Your tireless persistence is terribly bothersome, and quite frankly, it ruins my mood to see you every day. So, if you don't mind, kindly take your wares—" I gestured toward his belt with a flick of my wrist. "—and peddle them elsewhere."

"Lily ..."

"Look, there's a brothel on the other side of town, and you've money. I'm sure they'd take you. I'm willing to bet they'd even stay with you 'til morning for the right price." When he didn't back down, I added, "I should warn you, sir, I'm not above crushing a few fingers to get what I want, and presently, I would like nothing more than to shut this door in your face."

"How discourteous of you."

"Courtesy is reserved for *gentlemen*."

But he was dismayingly accustomed to my taunts. He feigned disbelief. "How wicked you must think me! You've not even given me a chance to state my business."

"If you've come to ask for my hand again, I must assure you that I've no intention of ever becoming Mrs. Sladen Ramey, and if you've no other objective than that, I would very much like for you to leave."

"Lily, that's unfair." Folding his arms behind his back, he leaned forward, poked his head in the opening, and winked. "At least let me ask before you reject me."

I recoiled, tsking. "Haven't you some other business to attend?"

"At present, I do not, so if you'd be so kind ..."

It injured me to yield to his advances, but I knew he wouldn't leave until he asked. Immediately, I began plotting his defeat.

How should I deliver my answer today? The tearful rejection of a woman scorned, heartbroken and unwilling to love another? Or perhaps a shy young maiden unready to part with her family to become a bride?

The fun of it was to decide in the moment.

Sighing, I released the door, letting it ease open with a low groan. "Fine," I said dully, careful not to betray my amusement. "Get it over with."

It was his turn to roll his eyes. "Your enthusiasm is overwhelming."

"Isn't it always?"

Flashing me a reproachful look, he took a step back, placed a hand over his heart, and knelt on one knee. With a deep breath, he said, "Miss Lilith Howell, would you please do me the honour of becoming my wife?"

In the same way I changed my answers, Sladen always had new phrasing or a new posture or location. I wondered if each proposal was premeditated or if he let himself be guided by the moment as I did. Last week, the prospect of marrying me had been an 'immense honour.' I decided to take the downgrade as an insult.

I looked at his extended hand, then at his ardent expression, opting for something simple today, given that I was already late for breakfast.

"No," I replied and shut the door in his face.

LIAM

I sat at the table, opening the Herald as my sister ambled into the room. She took the seat opposite me without a word, nodding at Sophie and smiling a wide grin at little Colin, which he returned with a chunk of ham clenched in his teeth. I tutted and returned to the paper. Without looking up from it, I gave the page a shake to get Lily's attention and asked, "Was that Sladen?"

She answered, "It was."

"Did you invite him in?"

"No."

I resisted the urge to chastise my sister and called for the maid. "Marie, would you please receive my guest? Lily's tried to send him off again."

No further explanation was needed. The young woman hurried through the door and returned a minute later with Sladen beside her. "A Mr. Ramey for you, sir," she said and bowed.

Sophie and I stood to greet him, and when I gestured to the spot beside me, Marie pulled the chair out. "Welcome. Allow me to apologise for the state and behaviour of my sister. Please sit.”

“The pleasure is mine, William.” Lily remained seated, and noticing, Sladen chuckled, took his own seat, and added, “I was merely receiving my usual rejection.”

We both glanced Lily’s way, and although I knew she was listening, she refused to meet either gaze.

“How many is that now?” I asked to harass her. Her deliberate show of indifference annoyed me ... or perhaps it was her complete disregard for traditions or propriety. In fairness, nearly everything about my sister irritated me, but at present, it was most notably her refusal to accept a perfectly kind and capable man like Sladen.

He smirked, eyeing Lily when he answered. “Honestly, I’ve lost count.”

She snorted from across the table, and I cleared my throat to suppress a chuckle. She could never resist the bait for long.

“It’s a wonder you’ve not given up yet, Mr. Ramey,” she said. “Your persistence is impressive if nothing else.”

“Persistence gets results,” he countered.

Although his voice held the playful cadence of a joke, she met it with dismissal. “Persistence is merely an inability to accept defeat in this case.”

“Ignore her,” I said before either could speak again. Our harassment had to have its limits, or she’d retaliate with a vengeance. To change the subject, I asked my sister, “Were you up the loft last night?”

Her returning silence surprised me. When I glanced up to see if she’d heard, she was facing me, but her eyes were focused on the wall above my head.

“This morning.”

“Why?”

A soft smile touched her lips as she poured herself tea, and her eyes lowered to meet mine. "Making friends." She flicked her brows. "There're all sorts up there you know. Bats and spiders and snakes." She raised her teacup, breathed in the steam rising from it. Then her voice dropped, her gaze drifting again. "I'm rather fond of snakes."

I huffed, returning to the paper as the kitchen staff entered to place new dishes on the table. After they'd gone and Lily and Sladen had been served, it was Colin who broke the silence.

"Aunt Lily, I'm going to visit Uncle Jacque today!" he said, beaming at her.

"Tomorrow," I corrected from behind the paper.

My son didn't skip a beat. "Yes, tomorrow!" Excitedly, he bounced and scooted his chair closer to Lily's, nearly impaling himself on the corner of the table.

"Colin, sit still," I told him. He acted as if he didn't hear me, but when Lily hunched down to meet him face to face, his seat scraped to a stop.

"Sorry," he murmured, immediately responding to his aunt's disciplinary expression.

"Not to me," she said, her voice ringing out softly despite the firm set of her jaw. But then, she relaxed her brow and rubbed his back. "Your father's suggestion came from a place of worry; he doesn't want you injured. You understand that, don't you?" It always surprised me how mild she could be when she spoke to him.

Sheepishly, the boy said, "I do."

"And next time, you'll listen and take it into consideration, isn't that right?" She smiled, and nodding, he grinned back, picking up his utensil again.

"Your ability to inspire obedience in him is astounding as always." I didn't intend for my voice to come out as cynically as it did, but I didn't offer an apology, nor did I acknowledge Lily's returning stare. I lifted the paper higher, though it may as well have been a blank page. I'd already read most of it, but it served as an easy barrier. She may have been mild with children, but that wasn't the case for adults, including (if not especially) me.

Her voice was low but lighthearted. "I had a lot of practise inspiring obedience in you when we were young."

"There's a difference between inspiring and manipulating."

Lily sipped her tea. "You were rather an impressionable child, weren't you?"

I folded the corner of the paper down so she could see me roll my eyes, but she took it as an opening and wasted no time.

"Liam, do you remember when Father returned?"

This time, I lowered the paper altogether. No one had called me Liam in years, and that surprised me more than her question. Our eyes met briefly before I ducked behind my shield again. "Which time?"

"The last time."

I swallowed. "I hardly think that's an appropriate conversation to have over breakfast," I muttered, though Colin didn't appear to be listening. He was thoroughly inspecting his beans as he ate them individually speared on one prong of his fork.

"You've already finished," she pointed out.

I turned the page. I'd spent long enough on the last section; she'd know I couldn't still be reading it. "Yes, I remember. You used to call me Liam all the time then."

"Everyone did. I think we should start again. It suits you better." She turned to Sladen. "Don't you think, Mr. Ramey?"

"It's a child's name, Lily," I said before he had a chance to answer. "We aren't children anymore."

She smiled thinly as the maid approached to remove her empty plate.

"More tea for you, ma'am?"

Lily shook her head.

Sophie noticed my sister's dead stare and excused herself

and our son. "Viens, mon fils," she said to Colin. "We must go and prepare for the journey tomorrow."

He considered the three beans left on his plate, seeming reluctant, but he didn't object. "Ah oui, Maman," he mumbled and climbed down from his chair.

Sophie stooped to kiss my cheek as she passed, ushering Colin in front of her. The boy peeked around his mother to wave at Lily, and as soon as the door closed behind them, I dropped the newspaper, flattening it on the table and, at last, admitting my defeat.

"Go on then," I said, training my eyes on Lily's face.

"You're not gonna hide anymore?"

"I've been holding it too long."

"And what should I be going on about, Liam?"

"Whatever it is you've chosen to debate with me this morning." She stared back silently, but the slight curl to her lips hinted that she already knew exactly what she wanted to say. I sighed. "Well, it always ends up at the same place, so we may as well skip the pleasantries. We're going to talk about how you're jealous of my son."

She tilted her head. "Jealous?"

"Colin gets to remember every bit of his childhood, and we don't," I said. Still, she remained stoic. Nothing in her expression changed to reveal her thoughts. "Is that where this is going, Lily?"

"Should we move this to the parlour?" Sladen suggested, but I waved him away, my gaze locked with my sister's.

"Here's fine."

Lily matched the intensity of my stare, but her voice was unemotional when she finally responded. "You're not wrong." She propped her elbows up on the edge of the table and rested her chin on her hands. "I am a little envious of it."

"A little?" I scoffed. "You haven't shut up about it for

months, but it's only bothering you *a little*?" I had no patience for it anymore. It was the same conversation on a different day, and her uncaring attitude frustrated me to no end. "Well, we don't get to remember. It's as simple as that." I leaned back in my chair, folding my hands behind my head. "Besides, there's nothing to remember. I don't understand your obsession with this after all these years."

"Just because we can't recall it doesn't mean the time didn't pass. Something happened. Don't you want to know what?"

"No."

"Liam ..."

"Look, you're right. Time *has* passed. So, move on."

Her voice shot up, her face at last producing an honest expression. "It was a year out of our lives!"

"One year? Ha!" I threw my arms down, slapping my thighs in jest. Sladen shot me a cautionary look, but I persisted, unwilling to submit to Lily so easily. "That's practically no time at all. It's been twenty since then, and we've got on fine. It doesn't matter anymore."

"It does matter!" She lurched forward, bringing a fist down hard on the table, rattling our cups on their saucers. Sladen touched her shoulder, and glancing at his hand, she exhaled loudly and sat back again. But I'd already pushed her over the line, and the bite didn't leave her voice. "People are born in minutes and die in seconds. A lot can happen in a day, let alone a year."

Don't give in, William. Don't admit defeat.

"Well, we're clearly not missing anything. Our lives haven't been hindered by—"

"What if we've lost something important, and we just don't realise it?"

"It still doesn't matter because we don't *know*."

"Yes, but ..."

It was the tone of her voice.

It was that small, pitiful, pleading voice.

I bowed my head so I wouldn't have to see the expression that accompanied it because I knew it would shake my resolve. But when she said my name, my gaze automatically lifted to her face, and I saw a fresh sheen of moisture in her eyes.

"But Liam ... don't we owe it to ourselves to try?" Her voice hitched slightly. "I just want to talk. That's all."

I gulped, unsure if I should believe the emotion on her face was genuine. My sister was a very accomplished liar and, therefore, exceptionally good at *inspiring obedience* in me.

Don't do it, William.

But my voice betrayed the warning in my head. "Fine," I muttered. "What d'you want to say?"

I picked up the paper again, embarrassed by my concession, but with a sudden fervor, she flung herself over the table and slapped her hand down the centre of it, tearing the page.

"Don't! Don't you hide from me, Liam! Oh, don't give me that look; you've already finished it. You'd already read the whole bloody paper before I even came downstairs."

Gritting my teeth, I sucked in a long breath through my nose and exhaled just as slowly, laying the two halves of the newspaper on top of each other. I waited for her to return to her seat, staring at her coldly for a few seconds, watching her hardness shed the longer I drew out my response. Her hands started to move anxiously, one thumb kneading the back of the other hand. It was a habit of hers, tracing an absent pattern as if easing a pain that lingered there in the space between her thumb and forefinger, but I knew as soon as she started, it would calm her.

Now was the time to surrender.

"Have it your way. Go on," I prompted. Then, with a little reluctance: "I'll listen."

But the moment I agreed, she relaxed into her seat, and I watched a smile build on her face with displeasure. There was no need for her to keep up her passionate act once she'd chained me to the conversation by the moral obligation of my agreement.

"You certainly recovered quickly just now," I said. "You couldn't pretend a little longer?"

She wiped her eyes, and her smile only grew. "I always did win the arguments when we were children."

I sneered right back. "Did you? I can't remember."

SETH

My feet had brought me to Earth again, despite the bitter resistance my mind had fought against my heart. I never quite knew what to do when I arrived, but I was careful never to overstay my welcome, never to be seen or heard, never to leave any trace of my existence on a world that had long forgotten mine.

I folded myself into a nook of trees at the edge of the lawn, wrapping my cape more tightly about me as I settled into my usual spot. This was the best vantage point from which I could survey all the windows and grounds, while the position of the garden hid me from anyone who might wander out onto the terrace. But they never ventured far, and their predictability served me well.

For years, I'd watched their lives unfold from this very spot, keeping them safely at arm's length as if they lived on the pages of a treasured book. Somehow, the feelings were the same—that of a close kinship that would forever be unreciprocated with both the characters and the world they occupied.

But although they were not fictional and this world was as real as my own, there could be no acknowledgement, no conversation, no happy reunions or embraces. We simply weren't the same people.

Seth Atwood no longer existed in the Howell family's world.

Three seasons had passed since last I'd come, but I couldn't bring myself to sever our acquaintance completely, despite the number of times I'd endeavoured to. Instead, religiously, I arrived at this place with a terrible longing to see to them, like a drunkard seeking the numbness of another round, which was the comfort of their smiles and their ignorance.

The trees had grown taller over the years and the house, more weathered, but the estate was largely unchanged. It was soothing—the resilience of an object compared to that of a human being—and so, since I could not abandon them entirely, I resigned myself to a view of the house with only accidental sightings of Lily and Liam. Because every time I saw that they had aged more, I felt an unsettling tug in my heart for the children they still were in my memory.

And how profoundly I felt that disquiet today.

My capacity for comfort seemed not to exist, and the possibility of seeing them felt guilty and awkward and intrusive. I feared that my coming would one day be noticed, and I couldn't stomach the thought of what might happen if it were.

Today, I could not stay; I should never have come in the first place.

I lowered my gaze from the house to the garden fence in front of me, mentally preparing myself to leave this place yet again. And then—

I froze.

An eye probed through the pickets, staring unblinkingly at me.

The child must already have been outside when I arrived. He must already have been hidden within the confines of the garden, and I must've been too lost in my reveries to notice. Regardless, there would be no veiling myself from him now.

"H-hello," I said, unsure what else to say because, in all these years, I'd never actually encountered another being in this world, despite how populous Earth had become.

The boy popped up, stretching on his tiptoes to peer over the fence, and then, huffing, he disappeared only to reappear at the gate a few seconds later. Carefully, he secured it but halted when he noticed me watching him.

"Rabbits will get in and eat the vegetables if I don't lock up properly," he said, and I nodded, not wanting to belittle his efforts by informing him that, even with my limited knowledge on the subject, I suspected that a rabbit could burrow under it quite easily. I followed him with my eyes until he planted himself a couple yards in front of me.

He was a small child with reddish hair, a furrowed brow, and a frown, and I nearly smiled because his manner reminded me of my younger brother when he was that age. This was Liam's son, of course; I'd seen him before. I'd watched him grow, too, from my place in the shadows of the trees, and now he stood before me with that brooding look and arms crossed in expectation.

"How d'you do?" I politely bowed my head, though his scowl remained.

He contemplated, looking me up and down, and finally, with a tut, he answered simply, "I am well."

"That is a fine way to be, young master."

"Who are you?" he demanded to know, though I knew his haughtiness was mostly bravado. He glimpsed my smirk and pinched his lips tighter. "Why are you here?"

"It matters not," I replied smoothly, hoping the tone of my voice would ease him. Liam had often told me it had a calming effect. "I am a person of little consequence."

"You look strange."

"Are you scared?"

Again, he considered my question very seriously, then relaxing his face, he answered, "No, I don't think so. You do look quite strange though. Are you ill?"

"Afflicted," I corrected with a chuckle, though he did not understand the humour. I asked, "What're you doing out here by yourself?"

Although he seemed, at first, reluctant, he answered rather quickly. "Maman said to prepare to go see Uncle Jacque, but I only get in the way when Marie is packing."

"Still, children should not wander alone."

"I'm not though," he said and took one big step closer to me. "Besides, Aunt Lily is the only one who'll come out to the garden with me, and she's busy."

My chest tightened at the mention of her. I wrung my hands. "How fortunate," I whispered.

He agreed with me and said, "Well, it is today because I get to speak with you, mister."

"Should you be so keen to speak to a stranger?"

"But Aunt Lily said strangers have a lot of potential. With time, they can easily become friends or loved ones ..." He leaned closer to whisper, his hand arched around his mouth. "...or even enemies. But we should try our best to avoid making those."

A laugh left my lips before I could stop it. "Lily said that?" I patted the boy's shoulder. "How wise she's become, and how wise you are to remember it. She's taught you well, hasn't she?"

He studied me, a brow quirked in inquiry, perhaps noticing how familiarly I'd addressed his aunt. I wondered what I should say when he questioned the nature of my relationship with her, but he didn't.

"Why're you here?" he asked again instead, and in less than

a second, I felt the mirth between us disintegrate, the carefree smile that had found its way onto my lips faltering.

I'd stayed too long and let my guard down too much.

With a wearied sigh, I ruffled his hair, gathering my cloak. "Fret not, young one. You shan't see me again after this, for I am only passing through."

But then the boy's frown deepened, and he peeked over his shoulder at the house again to check if we were alone before speaking. He stepped closer, shook his head, and said in a hushed voice, "No, you're not."

"Pardon?"

His next words dealt me a blow: "I've seen you before."

My eyes widened, and he seemed amused by my astonishment. But while the child gloated his skills of observation, I felt my insides lurch and twist as if a great wave had crashed through my body.

Breathless, I said, "Surely, you haven't," but the triumphant grin didn't leave his face.

"I have though," the boy insisted. "I remember because you never come to the door, and you look strange. Are you one of Father's acquaintances? Or Aunt Lily's?"

I managed the shadow of a smile but couldn't keep it, overlooking his question to ask, "Is your father at home?"

He nodded, ignorant of my internal panic. "He's talking with Aunt Lily and Mr. Ramey. They always have a chat after breakfast, but Mother never lets me stay for it." Then, a sudden delight lit his face, and excitedly, he asked, "D'you want me to go fetch him? If you're his friend, I'm sure he'll be happy to see you!"

"No, no!" I caught his wrist before he fled, the urgency in my voice stopping his feet.

"Why? You've been coming all this time. Don't you want to see him?"

"Have you ... told your father about me?"

He spun around to face me again, shaking his head, standing tall and proud as if he were a tiny soldier saluting his commander. "I thought you might want to surprise him since you're always so sneaky."

I laughed airily, surprised indeed by the boy's cunning. "How observant you are ..." He really did remind me of my brother.

Noticing my solemn expression, he shrank where he stood and anxiously asked, "H-have I done wrong?"

"No, you've done well," I assured him, replacing my hand on his shoulder. Then I gripped it as firmly as I dared—enough to make him pay attention but not enough to hurt. "You cannot tell him," I said gravely. "I'm not ready to meet him yet, you understand?"

His nod was immediate, and it was clear his assent had been driven by my sudden severity. I bit my lip, wondering how I might assure his cooperation. Then, lowering my voice and relaxing my grip, I asked, "Can you keep a secret, young master?"

His face brightened at the prospect, and grinning, he thrust his hand out. "I'm Colin," he said. "What're you called?"

Taken aback by how quickly his mood shifted, I stared at his hand until he wiggled his fingers impatiently.

"I can't keep a secret unless we shake on it," he said.

Hesitantly, I complied, and when I took the boy's hand, he flinched.

"Your hand is cold, mister."

I nodded.

"Isn't it because you're always sitting in the dark? The sun will keep you warm, you know?"

"I don't mind the dark or the cold." Then brusquely, I released him and stood, automatically combing my hand through the grass to revive the blades that had flattened beneath me.

Don't leave a trace, I thought and nearly rolled my eyes. My mantra seemed superfluous now.

"I must go, Colin."

"But, sir, what's your name? It's rude not to introduce yourself when someone else has done it; Aunt Lily told me so." He scratched his chin. "Actually, I think we should've done it at the start."

Perhaps I should have given an alias to keep my anonymity, but he reminded me so much of Jasper that I couldn't bring myself to lie.

"Seth," I answered, drawing my hood.

"Will you come again tomorrow?"

I glanced back at him and saw the same youthful optimism that had graced Liam's face long before. It was an expression that grasped my very heart. How many years had it been since I saw such a perfect display of naivety? It was an echo of his father's face—an expression I'd once vowed to protect, not only for Liam but for Lily and my brother as well. How motivating the innocence of a child was ...

But I clenched my fists beneath my cloak, reminding myself how misplaced that motivation had been—how I'd used that vow as an excuse for actions I could never reverse.

No, there could be no more empty promises, despite how deeply I desired to watch Colin's face light up as I assured him that I would arrive again to mold our strangeness into kinship.

I could only answer with the ambiguity of silence, and I left the boy with his ignorant hope, knowing very well that I would not return.

Quade emerged from the library, starting down the hall as I turned the corner, but when he heard my footsteps, he smiled over his shoulder. "You're back," he said, abandoning his course to greet me. Weakly, I nodded, and sensing my mood, he asked, "What's wrong?"

He followed me into our suite and then the bed chambers, closing the door behind us as I found a chair and lowered myself into it. He knelt in front of me, touching my knee. I could hear the concern in his voice. "Seth? Is everything all right?"

I exhaled, glancing behind me at the far door. "Any changes?"

He didn't have to follow my gaze to know what I meant. Lowering his eyes, Quade shook his head. "Nothing." But his worry was persistent. "What's wrong? Did you go to Earth? Did you see them today?"

Slowly, I lifted my hands, steepling them in front of my mouth. "I fear I may have just made a terrible mistake."

LILY

Despite his acquiescence, my brother still resisted.

"Get on with it already. Mother's gone, too. Do you want to talk about her as well?" He raised his hands, gesturing as if inquiring of an audience. "In fact, why don't we just rename breakfast altogether? We can call it the Dead Parent Conference."

I held my head higher, reluctant to waste an opportunity, despite his tasteless quip. Clearing my throat, I opened my mouth to begin, but already, he was unenthusiastically picking at his cuticle. I sighed. "Can you indulge me just a little?"

But I bit my tongue when his eyes slid back to my face. How cold that look was, and I wondered then when the innocence had left him. Surely, the Liam of our youth could never have produced so dark an expression. But when had it gone, and why hadn't I seen it happening? Had it been snuffed out in a single forgotten moment? Or had it been a steady metamorphosis—a slow burn that went unnoticed until all that remained was a puddle of melted wax with too little wick left to call it a candle.

"Lily," my brother prompted. "I'm not gonna sit here all morning while you lose yourself in daydreams."

"I wasn't lost," I murmured.

"I think you're always lost, wishing you were far away in some place you'll never remember because it isn't real."

"You don't know that."

"Get to the point."

"You don't know that."

For a moment, I felt his eyes on me, and I could all but see the scrutiny in them. But instead of trying to convince me that no such place existed outside of my head, he asked, "Why ask about Father? Because he went missing, too?"

I could tell by the tone of his voice that he didn't think it relevant—that he already had some argument against it—but I nodded anyway because his assumption was correct.

"We've been down this road before."

"Even you have to admit those circumstances weren't exactly normal."

Sladen's hand brushed my arm again, reminding me that he was there. "What was abnormal about it?" he asked, leaning forward so that his face obscured my view of my brother.

But to my surprise, Liam didn't respond to his friend's attempt to civilise us. "What is your definition of normal, Lily? A woman in her thirties still living at home, unmarried?"

I narrowed my eyes, peering past Mr. Ramey's head. "Turn me out if it bothers you."

Liam snorted. "As if you've anywhere to go." The corners of his mouth twisted up snobbishly. "Anywhere that you remember, at least."

"William, please," Sladen warned, and my brother held his hands up in surrender.

I slipped my own hands off the table onto my lap so they couldn't see me tremble. I'd improved my ability to manage my emotions over the years, but Liam wasn't usually so relentlessly sardonic.

Quietly, I said, "You haven't travelled beyond the market-place in 20 years. Is that normal?"

Liam tapped a finger on the table. "It's not unthinkable. I'd say it's a conditioned response from someone who felt abandoned as a child because their father left and didn't return until he was ready to die. I'd rather stay here and remain present for my son."

"Afraid you'll be whisked away with the twilight if you go any farther?" Then, studying my brother's face, I asked, "You think Father only returned to die?"

He sat back in his chair, uncrossing and recrossing his legs. "Don't you?" When I didn't answer, Liam groaned. "With the state he was in, it would've been folly not to entertain the possibility. It doesn't really matter. It was a sickness, not a mystery. You want everything to be dramatic and interesting, but the reality is quite simple. I mean, honestly, don't you think you'd be the same?"

"What d'you mean?"

"I mean, if you thought you were gonna die, who would you reach for? Who would you want to see before you did? Your family?"

The question made me feel guilty. I had to remind myself that it was purely hypothetical. Liam didn't know about the serpent in the attic.

I opened my mouth to answer, then paused when I realised that to agree would be wrong and not because of the nights I'd spent contemplating it. I felt a clinch in my stomach, and my fingertips found their way to the little scar beside my navel, feeling the bumpy ridge through my nightgown. But Liam didn't know about that either, and to be fair, neither did I—not how I'd gotten it, at least. What I *did* know was that it hadn't been the face of any immediate family that had formed in my mind then, nor their hands I'd reached for with that ripping pain in my gut. It had been someone else entirely, some other name I'd called.

But because I didn't know whose it was, softly, I said, "I don't know; I've never died," which felt like a lie as it passed through my lips. When I looked up again, Liam and Sladen were both watching me warily. I averted my eyes, wondering if my expression exposed the nature of my thoughts without my realising it.

Mr. Ramey addressed my brother. "Your father died of an illness then?"

Liam nodded.

Before I could think to stop it, I laughed, and both men gawked at me.

"An illness? Don't lie to Mr. Ramey."

Liam arched a brow. "He was sick, Lily."

"Not enough to succumb to it."

"He was in an awful state. You were there. You saw."

"I did, but ..." My brother's face showed no sign of understanding. "I told you," I said. "I know I told you."

I watched his throat move as he swallowed, and although his voice stayed calm, I could see the faint line drawn between his eyes. "Told me what?"

"It had to have been you ..."

"Told me what?" he pressed, leaning forward in his seat.

"C'mon, Liam, be serious. It was a secret then, but it doesn't matter anymore."

"He—Which secret, Lily?"

I pushed my tongue into the roof of my mouth to avoid answering too quickly and gazed back at him—at the confusion and quiet desperation in his eyes. His lips pursed and then relaxed like he was resisting the urge to reiterate his question.

Maybe he *didn't* know.

Slowly, I shook my head. "If you don't know already," I whispered, glancing down into my empty teacup, "I'll keep it."

His chest expanded with a deep breath then sank inward as he dragged his hands down his face. "Do you want to talk about this or not?"

I made to answer but stopped myself. I could've sworn I'd told someone, and who would I tell besides Liam? Of course, I knew I couldn't fully trust my memories of that time. I tried to backpedal. "I only mean to say that I spent a lot of time with him after he returned."

"I know you did. So?"

"He told me all manner of things—all sorts of mysteries and secrets, history and promises. Mostly, it was just rubbish." I rubbed my hand, pulling my thumb in an arc across the back of it. "And then when he died, it was very sudden."

Liam's face reddened, and I knew my weak explanation had done nothing to ease his agitation at my having mentioned a *secret*. He cleared his throat, his voice sharpening again. "Yes, I'm well aware how much it affected you, Lily, but that doesn't make the circumstances abnormal."

"But he went missing, too, just like we did. Don't you think it's possible that—"

"No, I don't."

"Can you at least let me—"

"They were completely separate events! Father didn't go missing; he chose to leave. There's no link between them, so stop trying to create one."

"But he was found the same way we were! And he never did say what happened to him. Maybe he just didn't remember, and—"

"Lily, please ..." He gritted his teeth, and I could almost see it on his face—how he stacked the bricks of the wall he would use to separate us, how he would barricade in his own mind to shield himself from the artillery of my argument.

My face burned. "There are similarities, Liam! You're just choosing to ignore them!" Exasperated, I shouted, "God, why're you so okay with not knowing? Don't you understand this is killing me?"

Liam's stony expression didn't break. Slowly, his eyes lowered to my hands, which were clenched into fists on the table. He waited for me to relax my grip before speaking in a measured voice—waited for the echo of my words to dissipate.

"I don't know what fever-mad stories he fed you, but he wasn't long for this world when he returned that day. I think he knew. I think that was the only reason he returned at all— because he knew his time was ending."

I didn't even try to suppress my scoff. "Oh, he most certainly did."

Liam frowned, eyeing me pointedly before continuing, "Look, I get that you want some closure, but that may not be possible." He rubbed the back of his neck. "I know how much Father's death affected you. I know that image is etched into your brain. I remember months later when—"

But the moment that word left his lips, a spark of anger flared in me and loosened my tongue. "What does that even mean?"

"What?"

"You can't remember, then you can?" I laughed bitterly. "How can I take your word for anything? If you're never truthful when we talk about this, how can we—" But I'd said too much. I'd ruined my own chances for the day. I saw his fists tighten and knew our conversation was over. He would entertain me no longer.

And yet, the expression that greeted me when I looked up wasn't cross but solemn. Tiredly, he peered sideways, his eyes fixing on the doorknob—a too obvious display of just how badly he wanted to escape.

His voice was low. "Father's death was an unfortunate circumstance; that's it. Do you really think I haven't thought about it over the years? About how he abandoned us? Of course, I have. He's the reason I haven't gone beyond the market." He swallowed. "But he wasn't some great adventurer or hero who was spirited away. He was just a man that couldn't sit idle. Maybe he finally realised that he may not have a home to return to much longer. Maybe he just wanted to be with his family one last time. I would, too, if I felt my days were numbered and feared the end."

If we'd been outside, I would've spat at his feet—anything to release the ire that seemed to bubble up my throat. "He didn't fear death," I hissed. "He looked it in the eye and embraced it."

Immediately, I crossed my arms and sank down in my seat, prepared for my brother's reproach, though none came. Liam furrowed his brow, his lips parting only slightly to whisper, "Say that again."

"What?"

Then louder: "What you just said. Say it again."

Gulping, I observed the alarm on his face and said slowly, trying to repeat my exact phrasing, "He didn't fear death; he looked it in the eye and embraced it."

The crease between his brows deepened, and again, I could see the inner workings of his mind shadowed on his face. Something had entered it just then—some thought or memory. I knew because I'd seen it before. I knew because I'd experienced the very same thing myself.

And I knew that next, he would flee.

But I didn't interrupt his process. I wanted him to remember as much as he could, and I wanted him to realise that

I knew exactly what was happening. Even Mr. Ramey, though confused, seemed to notice my intentions and remained silent.

When, at last, my brother looked up and found us watching him, he scooted his chair back. "I'm done with this."

I stood when he did, leaning forward on the table. "Why?" I asked.

For a moment, we stared at each other in defiant silence. There was something hollow there in his eyes—hollow and sombre and just … tired. For a moment, I felt as if a hand had pressed through my chest and squeezed my heart.

I hadn't expected to see the same emotions I felt on my brother's face.

Then Liam took a breath and turned away. "The doctors told us back then that it was likely some type of dissociative amnesia caused by events so traumatic that we struck them from our own minds. Please stop trying to romanticise our past when there can't be anything worth remembering."

What did you just see? What memory did you recover? Why are you rejecting it? Why are you rejecting me?

I felt a lump slowly growing in my throat. I had to fight through the ache to whisper, "You're wrong. I know you're wrong. You must be." Then, even more softly, begging him to look at me again: "Please, Liam, I—I need this. I need to know."

He couldn't know how desperately I meant it.

There was no apology in his voice. "You already have an explanation, Lily; you're just choosing to ignore it." He stood, facing the door. "Don't bring this up to me again. I won't hear of it."

My brother disappeared into the hall. As I dropped back into my seat, gently, Sladen placed his hand on top of mine. I glanced down at it. His palm was warm and a little clammy.

"Lily …"

I slid my hand out from under his, my eyes returning to the doorway.

"If ..." Sladen hesitated, but it only took a second for him to gather his courage. "If you did know, could you move on with your life?"

"By 'move on' do you mean get married, have children, tend a home ... embrace the life that was always expected of me?" I peered upward and inhaled, blinking to dry my eyes. "I don't know. Perhaps I could be content with that."

"Maybe I can talk him round," he said, too eagerly, and I chuckled.

"For my sake or yours?"

"Maybe both."

I turned away to roll my eyes so he couldn't see it, though I knew he still watched me; he always watched me.

"What?" I asked when I thought his gaze had lingered too long for a simple gander.

Again, he delayed.

"What is it, Mr. Ramey?"

"Why now? Why are you so adamant? It's been ... Five? Six months? And before that, you never brought up your childhood at all."

I swallowed, leaning back in my chair. "Liam said himself that nothing would change until one of us remembered."

"He says that every day."

I exhaled, my eyes drifting over to the window.

"Lily?"

But I didn't answer, and Sladen retreated, aware that I'd shut the door between us once again. The comfort I desired couldn't come from him. The only person who could feel these feelings with me was my brother. The only person who could validate them and help me feel like a whole person again—help us both.

Nothing would change until one of us remembered something.

Six months ago, I remembered something. And so did he.

He just had to be willing to admit it.

I needed him to admit it.

LIAM

I'd managed to hold it in until I was in the hall—the trembling of my hands, the shudder that wracked my whole body at the reemergence of that memory. I slipped into my study and pressed my back against the door to close it, fearing that Lily might've followed me—that she would see how my expression contradicted what I'd said.

I groped behind me for the lock, and only when I heard the click assuring my solitude did I release the breath I'd been holding, allowing a soft whimper to escape my lips.

I lifted my tremoring hand, observed it and tucked it safely in my pocket.

'I do not fear death, Liam, nor will I; I will embrace it. I will cross that vast ocean and greet it, not as a spectre, but as an old friend.'

I pushed myself off the door and crossed the room to my armchair.

'...embrace it ...'

I couldn't place the man's voice, though I knew the words had been uttered to me before. To have told me such a thing— to have called me Liam—we must have been well-acquainted, and yet ...

I hung my head.

Lily's secret was easy to guess. Try as she might, my sister was anything but subtle. I'd long been aware of our father's suicide and of how desperately Lily had tried to protect me from that knowledge, though it seemed silly now that we were grown.

What I feared were the other secrets she kept—the ones *I* kept, hidden away somewhere in my brain. What I feared was their reemergence. What I feared was the unknown.

I knew she'd remembered something. She'd never be so persistent if she hadn't. And—another shiver passed through me—I suspected she knew I had as well.

I folded over my knees, burying my face in my hands.

What secrets are you keeping from me?

I closed my eyes, exhaling through my fingers.

What ghosts are waiting to haunt us, Lily, and why are you so keen for them to find us again?

MARCH 1892

PART TWO
FAIRIES & FALSEHOODS

In the spring of 1887, Mr Roderick Howell, a native of London, left his home in the Kent countryside on a business venture. Regular travel was not uncommon for Mr Howell, but this time would be different. This time, he would not return, and his family would be left to wonder: what on Earth happened to Roderick Howell that fateful day?

Left to the public's speculation, I sought answers from the last person to have seen him alive and well: Mr Howell's beloved wife, Mrs Elizabeth Howell. She claims her husband had been travelling west to Hampshire but never arrived at his destination, though the poor woman was so awash with emotion that she could barely comment.

Mrs Howell expressed that herself and her children miss him dearly and pray everyday for his safe return or even simply word to say that he's alive and well.

But during my visit to the family's manor, I was reminded of another tale well-known to this region, and now I, myself, am left to wonder: could this be a reoccurrence of the infamous Atwood mystery? In fact, the remnants of the old Atwood House abut the Howell estate.

As the tale goes, Miss Alvah Atwood, only daughter of well-known nobleman Somer Atwood, was spirited from her bed while her father was away. No signs or struggle, the doors and gate still safely locked. The girl had simply vanished.

Her father, driven mad by her absence, disappeared shortly thereafter, and neither were ever seen or heard from again.

Now, only a stone's throw from that seemingly cursed place, yet another individual has gone missing, and he isn't the only one. Mr. Howell is among a dozen or so residents of this region that have gone missing over

LILY

I crumpled the newspaper without finishing the article and marched down the hall with it smashed in my fist. My face felt hot. I swung my arms and stamped my feet. I huffed and loudly clicked my tongue, mumbling curses under my breath because I wanted someone else to share my aggravation. But my tantrum was ignored by the single maid I passed in the corridor.

I charged straight into the drawing room. Finding Mother on the sofa, I inhaled a deep breath and slapped the paper on the table in front of her.

"What is this?"

Unalarmed, she looked up from her embroidery, her hands stopping for only a moment before they returned to stitching. "A publication," she replied simply.

"Did you speak to them?"

This time, she wouldn't even spare me a glance. Impassively, she asked, "Lilith, is there some unfathomable reason you feel the need to address me so harshly this morning?"

"Did you speak to these people?"

"What else would you have me do, child?"

"I'd rather you not fuel rumours about our family! This isn't a news article; it's opinionated rubbish! How can anyone even read this?"

The inflection of her voice wasn't altered by my anger. It remained calm, almost detached. "It's a new publication from a man who didn't know what to do with his wealth, so he started a paper. He writes in such a fanciful way. I rather like it."

"Do you?" I scoffed. "This isn't news!"

"I'm doing what I can, Lilith. I can't very well go out and search for him, can I?"

"You'd rather exploit our family?"

With a disparaging sigh, she set aside her stitching and, at last, gave me her attention. "I just want him found safe."

"Don't talk to me like I'm one of them!"

"Are you not interviewing me?" She folded her hands, her elbows sticking out in perfect right angles. Her face barely moved when she spoke, her posture strict, unerring as if she were but another piece of furniture in the manicured room.

I chewed my lip, suppressing the urge to throw my hands up and stir the air that had settled around her. If it was an interview she wanted, then it was an interview she'd get. "Why d'you want him back? He's already dealt us a blow."

"He's gone missing, Lilith; he didn't abandon us." She spoke the words as if she'd rehearsed them, though whether for others or herself, I couldn't be sure.

"What's the difference?"

She straightened her spine. "A matter of choice."

"He walked out the front door of his own accord. *That* was his choice."

"You don't know what may have happened to him after." Delicately, she placed a hand over her heart—another practised gesture—though there was little emotion in her voice. "We can patch it up if he returns, or if he's found dead—" Her eyes flicked over to the window. "—we'll gain sympathy as the victims of a terrible misfortune."

I gaped at her, the cap I'd placed on my anger bursting. "Listen to yourself, for God's sake!" But that pushed me over the line. She shot to her feet, her index finger stabbing the air in front of my face.

"Don't you *dare* speak to me in such a way."

Why? I thought. *You don't listen if I speak normally.*

But I bit my tongue.

How quickly that measured indifference fled her eyes, only to be replaced with ire. My stomach tightened with anxiety, but I didn't know how else to make her communicate. I wanted to draw some kind of emotion from her, and anger was the easiest to produce.

When I said nothing, she glanced past me at the grandfather clock. She lowered her hand, and even that movement was made with careful restraint. Her exhale hissed through her teeth. "Get out. Your governess is waiting for you, and I haven't the time to entertain your nonsense."

I couldn't help myself.

"My nonsense? This." I snatched the paper from the table and shook it between us. "This is nonsense—this rubbish. The Atwood House? Really? That's what you're doing? Creating fear and mystery to soften the scandal, turning it into a tragic end?"

I watched her jaw clench and unclench. Then, she sat back down and picked up her embroidery, the furniture-stillness returning to her face, though her voice lost none of its venom. "With your father gone, until your brother comes of age, I am the head of this household. Do you know what that means, you insolent child? It means I will do what I can for the sake of your father's good name—and for yours. Now get out."

JASPER

I drummed my fingers on my thigh one tap at a time, thumb to pinky, pinky to thumb, silently counting as I leaned back against a wide oak. I crossed my arms, pressing them down against my ribcage and squeezing, holding the tension until my fingertips tingled, but then I felt too constricted. I unfolded my arms, shaking them out, flexing my fingers.

"C'mon, Bridget, don't be late." I pinched the bridge of my nose. "Not today."

Then suddenly: a noise.

I dropped my hand, my eyes darting, though I stood still, waiting, listening.

A twig snapping underfoot. A rustle of leaves from afar.

I dashed forward a few strides and peered across the grassy field, but as soon as I was out of the oak's shadow, my palms began to sweat, an alarming thought slipping into my mind: *what if it isn't her?*

I tensed, my chest collapsing as the breath fled my lungs. Swallowing, I turned my head slowly from side to side, my hands closing into fists as the wind moved the grass in a wave across the meadow.

Then came a realisation: I was out in the open. Visible. Vulnerable. An easy target. When the wind gusted again, every blade of grass seemed to be directed at me, thousands of little hands pointing and crying out, *'Him! Here! He's over here!'*

Panic urged my feet backward, stumbled step after stumbled step, until I hit the oak's trunk and was forced to halt. Immediately, I ducked down, bracing myself, waiting for an attack, waiting for—

Stop it, Jasper. There's no one out to get you; there can't be. No one on Earth knows what you're doing, and no one elsewhere would care. Take a deep breath. Relax. You're safe.

Who was I hiding from? I wondered, but the answer came easily: myself. *I* was the only enemy here. *I* was the only one to be feared.

Peeking up through leaves and branches, I checked Aurisol's position and nearly laughed, though without humour. The Auric Sun hadn't yet begun its westward descent, and noon had been our chosen hour.

Bridget wasn't late; I was early.

Sit back, wait, and stop fearing when you ought to be celebrating the fact that everything is still going as it should.

My plan had been successful many times before, so I couldn't help distrusting every new moment. That was the problem with having a *perfect* plan. It couldn't stay perfect forever, and the possibility of it failing grew with every execution.

Don't worry. Bridget isn't even late yet!

I inhaled and relaxed against the tree again, closing my eyes.

Everything is perfect, Jasper ...

The corners of my lips turned up as I wet them, excitement

stealing the place of discomfort, which I welcomed. Noah once told me in one of his tiresome lectures that it's impossible not to smile while watching a plan unfold in exactly the way it was imagined. It seemed I was no exception, and although he could know nothing of my assignment, I thought it would please him to see that I'd taken initiative and planned something for once in my life. Then again, I doubted he'd support this particular plan. I hardly approved of it myself.

Capturing and imprisoning foreign children wasn't exactly a notable accomplishment by most standards. Though ashamed as I was to admit it, I couldn't help feeling proud. Could anyone after succeeding in so delicate an undertaking? I'd probably be embarrassed by the grin spreading on my face if there was anyone around to see it, but there wasn't.

Not yet.

But she would be here soon. They both would be, and if Bridget was timely, I would only have seconds left to wait—seconds left to collect myself enough to put on a decent show.

The Auric Sun hung almost directly above me in the sky; noon was here.

The clothes I wore were restricting, but I managed to hoist myself up onto a low-hanging branch. I scanned the tree line beyond the field, searching for movement. My heart rate spiked when I saw them.

Materialising near the forest's edge was the child—a young girl, perhaps ten or eleven—running doggedly after the fairy, her eyes glued to those soft blue wings. I sat on the bough and adjusted my collar, my smile broadening. I couldn't help it; this was almost too easy.

I stuck my neck out, squinting to find Bridget. The tiny woman balled her fists as she sped toward me, her arms swinging back and forth, increasing her efforts until she swooped up and around and disappeared under the oak's cover.

"Bridget!" I whispered, directing her to me.

She slowed, and when I held out my hands, she dropped into them with an exhausted huff, appreciatively patting my palm. She rubbed her eyes and flattened her wind-blown hair before turning to face me, but her accompanying smile was almost immediately swapped with a frown.

Had I forgotten something? My hair was neatly parted, my jacket fastened, my sleeves rolled down and buttoned at the cuffs ... I'd even asked a maid to steam my clothes so they'd look nice and proper. There wasn't a wrinkle on me.

With puffed cheeks, Bridget stood, marched across my hands, and used her tiny fist to rub a smudge of dirt off my chin. She inspected me a moment longer, her hands on her little hips, and when she seemed satisfied with my cleanliness, she gave a final contented nod and returned to her seat at my fingertips.

"Thanks ..." I muttered. She glanced over her shoulder, and her wink met my eye roll.

When the girl finally approached, I drew my feet up and took a deep breath, mentally preparing myself for the encounter. She stopped fully a few yards away, panting but smiling as she searched for the fairy. She was scrawny for a clergyman's daughter with dark hair and eyes—pretty enough, I decided, but unremarkable.

I sighed, prepared with a greeting, but when I opened my mouth, the words held in my throat. All at once, the nervous discomfort came sweeping back through me. I closed my eyes, squeezing until I could see splotches of white across my eyelids, wishing I could vanquish the unwanted feelings with sheer force of will, but—

She looks so happy.

A shiver shook my body, though the air wasn't cold, and I couldn't stop the thought from forming: *This is wrong, isn't it?*

No, I told myself, *No, it's fine. Just do it. Don't think about it.*

You're overanalyzing again. Everyone does things they aren't proud of to get what they want. Everyone. You aren't exempt.

A prick on my finger opened my eyes, and Bridget stared up at me expectantly. She tossed her head, motioning toward the girl, lifting her shoulders and giving me a look as if to say, *'What're you waiting for?'*

I swallowed thickly. What *was* I waiting for? There was no one here to judge my indiscretions, no one to stop me from taking advantage of the perfection this day afforded. Everything was fine, so why hesitate?

Bridget was right. If I were going to have doubts, I should've had them the first time. My integrity had long since been sullied, so these moments of uncertainty didn't matter. What mattered was that my plan would work. At the end of the day, the job would be done, and if I came out the victor, everything would be fine ...

I lifted my chin again to look at the girl, masterfully composing my face within a breath of time.

"Hello," I said loudly, scooting forward on the branch. I cupped my hands around Bridget as I slid off, careful not to jostle her too much when I landed. "It's a lovely morning, is it not?"

The girl whipped around, panic flashing in her widening eyes as I stepped out of the oak's shadow and into the Auric sunlight. But I was careful to keep my distance. If I'd learned anything from encounters with my previous quarry, it was to always expect a wait, and although it was almost a mandatory occurrence, it still felt awkward.

This was the moment where she made her decision—where silence loomed as she weighed the options in her head: to run and hide, to remain at a distance, to approach a stranger and his mythical pet ...

Which to choose? Desire or logic? Which is safest? Which is smartest?

I licked my lips, waiting, but she only stared, brown eyes bulging without so much as a blink.

I shifted my weight from one foot to the other, holding the smile.

She stared.

I swallowed and rolled my shoulders back.

I curled my toes in my boots.

And still, she stared.

I clenched my jaw, sucked in a big breath through my teeth, and squared my shoulders. If she wouldn't speak, I may as well begin introductions.

"I'm Gabriel," I announced, pushing my chest out, trying to mimic my eldest brother's confident stance. Apparently, *'confidence is key when establishing an air of authority,'* but as far as I could tell, Noah only said things like that to justify being such a pompous arse all the time. "Gabriel Atwood."

She didn't answer.

I drew in another long breath, trying to relax my face, and wearing what I hoped was an inviting expression, I nodded toward the fairy, raising my hands.

"I see you've met my friend here," I said with an even wider smile. Voice low and smooth. Polite. Believable.

Timidly, she nodded, and I exhaled in relief, glad for some acknowledgement at last. I'd taken care with my appearance today. I'd washed, combed my hair, and even dressed myself in a ghastly mess of silk and tassels. I didn't always appear particularly royal, but I didn't think I was *that* unfortunate-looking. I was approachable, at least.

I held my breath, the smile frozen in place on my face.

"Y-yes, I have," she said softly, her eyes peeking up through her lashes and then dropping to her feet again. "Bridget, isn't it?"

Finally.

Bridget nodded exaggeratedly, used to inflating her movements when talking to humans. I tossed my hands, flinging her into the air. The fairy's wings caught in the breeze, and she easily corrected herself, swooping around the girl's head. Relaxing enough to grin and giggle, the girl followed the little woman with her eyes for a moment before returning her attention to me.

"Who are you?" she asked, still smiling as Bridget lifted a lock of her hair.

"Gabriel," I repeated, bending into a formal bow, one arm behind my back, the other folded across my chest with my hand over my heart as was customary. "At your service, milady," I added as I straightened up again. "Might I ask your name?"

Her eyes widened. "M-Maple," she answered, twisting a handful of her skirt in her fingers, a light pink blush blossoming on her cheeks. "My name is Maple B-Burdock."

"It is a pleasure, Miss Burdock," I said and bowed again, this time reaching out to take her hand delicately in mine. I kissed the top of it, and she flushed a deeper shade of red.

Her reaction was perfect—exactly the one I'd hoped for.

Let your flighty little heart fall for me, Maple; it makes my job so much easier.

Young hearts are so quick to feel enamoured. A few more meetings and she'd go with me anywhere. She'd followed Bridget this far into the wild after only seeing her twice, and my lures were vastly more tempting. I could promise her more than fairies. There were other creatures—other worlds!—to see. Adventure. Magnificence. Romance. I would build her expectations until they reached the sky.

She wouldn't be able to resist so grand a temptation, and by the time she realised her error, she'd already be my captive. It would be her own fault for believing me.

Expectations never did anyone any favours.

When Maple took another cautious step toward me, I relaxed a little, standing tall but not too; I didn't want to intimidate. I wanted her to feel at ease while I set my trap. All she needed to do was ask the right questions, and I could spin her a tale of magic and intrigue—a tale she would want proof to believe, and proof was something I could give her. I just needed an opening.

But it seemed that I remained in the Spirits' favour. Just as I opened my mouth to speak, she asked, "Where did you come from, Mr. Atwood? Are you from the same place Bridget came from?"

I could feel the nervous flutter in my stomach again.

"Yes," I said, licking my lips. "We're from a place called Iraxhar."

Her eyes widened a hair, enough to show her interest without making a scene of it, but her voice betrayed her fervour with her next question, which flew from her lips only a second after I'd answered: "What's Iraxhar?"

My brother had been right after all.

The smile was on my face again, but this time, I didn't care that there was someone here to see me. Because everything was perfect, and it's impossible not to smile when success is already within grasp.

LILY

I crept around the fence, peeking through the pickets at my brother, who squatted in the garden between two rows of vegetables. I watched him in wonder. Liam was a peculiar creature, though his irregularities often skirted the line between entertaining and concerning.

Today, there was the scraggly top of a carrot in one of his hands, and he waved it about as if in heated conversation. I lowered my brow, craning my neck to see his audience, but there was only Liam. Honestly, I was more surprised that he'd pulled a carrot so prematurely than by the fact that he was talking to himself.

I straightened my dress as I rose to my feet, rearranging my hair and patting a little colour back into my cheeks. Both of those behaviours needed to be stopped, and I had to present myself properly or my reprimand wouldn't be taken seriously. I sucked in a deep breath.

"Liam!" I shouted, and immediately, he started. "What're you doing?"

He whirled around, bug-eyed and gulping like a fish out of

water, though he didn't manage to produce a reply, only stuttered sounds that I guessed were an attempt at my name.

"Yes, yes, it's me," I said. His reactions were always so dramatic. "Are you gonna answer me? What're you doing over there?" I let my body fall forward and caught myself on the side of the fence.

Glancing from me to the meagre carrot tops, he forced a chuckle, though his expression held more tension than humour. "Me? Well ..." He slid his tongue over his teeth. Then, as if suddenly realising that he still held that underdeveloped root, he said, "I-I'm not eating this!"

I arched a brow.

"I-I was just holding it," he assured me. "I pulled it accidentally. You know carrots don't agree with me."

I tapped a finger on the fencepost, waiting for him to continue, and when he didn't, I said, "Liam, here I am taking time out of my busy schedule to fetch you, so I expect a proper explanation."

He was acting more peculiar than usual, but his nervous demeanour deflated long enough for him to frown and mumble, "Since when're you busy?"

I clicked my tongue. "I'm always busy, especially when I have to get rid of those grubby kids from town you like so much. Fortunately, I don't today, so that saves time."

Liam's frown expanded into a full-faced grimace. "They aren't grubby ..."

"Liam, you can't be serious. They're gross."

"They're my friends."

"Is that supposed to magically nullify the grossness of commoners?"

"Lily, that's unkind ..."

"Honesty is often mistaken for unkindness."

Groaning, he dropped his head back. "Lily, I really don't—"

"Let me explain it to you," I began. Liam sighed heavily, but my resulting stare silenced him. "Look, I know it annoys you when I shoo them off—"

"And yet, you continue to do so."

My glare strengthened. "Let's keep the interruptions to a minimum, shall we?" I waited for his unenthusiastic nod before continuing. "Now, I know it bothers you, but someone needs to maintain our family's good name. Those low-class brats aren't worth the scandal, and after all that's happened, I, for one, would like to dodge any more blows to the family's reputation."

"Having friends isn't scandalous, Lily; it's healthy," he said, then turned away to mutter, "Maybe if you'd actually get some of your own, you'd understand."

My face fell. "I don't appreciate your sarcasm, Liam."

"I'm serious. Socialising is important when you're young."

I rolled my eyes, leaning on the fence. "Then socialise, Liam. I've no objection to it, but the people you're doing it with ..."

"My friends are fine the way they are, Lily. If you'd just give them a chance—"

"You're not listening." I breathed in. I needed to talk loud and fast so he'd be forced to listen to my whole argument before dismissing it. "You said before that having friends was healthy right? Maybe so, but you need to pick them properly. It's a well-known fact that poor people die much sooner than people like us. They're far more susceptible to murder and disease." I saw his face redden and raised my voice. "Who catches plague first? Poor people. It's in all the history books. Now, I don't think it's particularly healthy to be so near to someone who's likely disease-ridden."

My brother's face puckered. "Lily, you're being ridiculous! That's just—"

"Regardless of the cause, the truth of the matter remains that they will die before me, and the emotional stress of it would be horribly exhausting. Can you imagine having to find new friends so often to replace the ones lost?"

"Lily, honestly—"

"I, for one, haven't the time for such nonsense, and anyway," I said, "I'm not here to argue with you, especially on a topic about which I am clearly right, and you are clearly wrong. I came all the way out here—"

"The walk takes two minutes. *Maybe.*"

"—in this dreadfully hot weather without my parasol entirely for your sake. Do you know what this exposure is doing to my complexion?" He rolled his eyes, but I didn't give him the chance to answer. "I will not be reduced to looking like some common street peasant, so make haste with your explanation. Every second of my time wasted is carving an avoidable injury to my appeal as a prospective wife."

Liam stared back at me without a word.

"*Well?* Time's wasting."

Exhaling, he dropped his shoulders. "Lily, you never even use a parasol ..."

"I do, too!"

"There's an unopened package with a parasol in it that's collecting dust in your wardrobe."

"Yes, well, Mr. Howell gave that one to me, and I've no desire to use it."

He sighed. "Lily, you can call him Father."

"He's been demoted," I said, "and anyway, this isn't about me. This is about you avoiding what should be a very simple explanation." I inclined my body, leaning my chest over the top of the fence. "What. Are. You. Doing?"

He lifted the carrot stem, looked at it with hard eyes, and then set it on his lap. "Um ..." He swallowed tightly. "Well ..."

"Well, what?" I'd gotten rather good at pressuring him into telling me things, though I still wasn't sure whether that was a talent I should favour. One of Miss Sawyer's speeches about morals made it seem a bit indecorous, but another of her lectures had said I should practise what I was good at. I liked to think the second negated the first.

Liam picked up the carrot again, passing it back and forth in his hands. "D-do you promise you won't laugh?"

"Of course," I replied, shrugging, though I knew I most certainly would if the occasion called for it ... and it usually did when Liam tried to be serious.

He shrank where he sat, his shoulders hunching. With one last peek at me, he turned away and mumbled, "T-the fairy was hungry."

For a moment, I watched him in silence, allowing him ample time to declare that he was joking and give me his actual answer. But when he didn't offer one, I realised that *was* the actual answer. I pinched my lips together, fighting to keep a straight face, but I couldn't help it. I laughed.

"Lily!" Liam cried, gawking at me as though he couldn't believe I'd do such a thing. Honestly, he should've known me better.

"A fairy? Is that really the best you've got?"

"You promised!"

"Yes, and we both know my word isn't worth anything. Come on, listen to what you're saying. A fairy, Liam? *Really?*"

"B-but—" His bottom lip bulged out in an exaggerated pout.

"Liam," I said, dangling my arms over the fence, snapping my fingers to make sure I had his full attention before continuing. "It's nonsense. You're daft."

"I am not! Stop teasing me!"

"Then stop talking about ridiculous things like fairies, you ninny!" I frowned. "And while you're at it, stop talking to yourself all the time, otherwise Mum and Miss Sawyer are gonna haul you off to London and have you locked in a madhouse."

He glared, and I scowled right back.

"They wouldn't."

I shrugged. "Well, obviously anything's possible if you believe in fairies, right?"

"It's not ridiculous because I'm perfectly serious! There's a fairy in our garden, her name's Bridget, and she's right here!" Dropping the carrot, he reached into the plants beside him and drew back with cupped hands. He lifted his chin, triumphant.

He seemed to be going all out with this one.

One brow raised, I crossed my arms and shifted my weight back onto one foot. "Fine," I said with a smirk. "Let's see it then."

He hesitated. It appeared he needed some encouragement, so I tried again.

"Y'know, Liam, it would be a shame if Mum found out you were in the carrots since they always make you ill. She'd have Madame Renoir all a fuss, wouldn't she? Unless you like medicine crammed down your throat. It's not exactly my cup of tea, but you are a bit odd."

Liam's lips pinched, his nose scrunching, and then his chin dropped to his chest. I could see it; he was almost defeated.

"Look," I said, twisting my hands in the air. "I want to believe in fairies as much as anyone, but without any actual proof ..."

"All right, fine," he agreed at last, softly, perhaps hoping I wouldn't hear. I waited. His voice stayed meek, but it gained a little volume when he added, "I-I guess I'll see if she wants to meet you."

I grinned with my success.

JASPER

I sat up to attention.

Something was wrong. That noise—that horrible, wailing shriek!

Scrambling to get my feet under me, I peered around the tree trunk, scanning the surrounding forest.

It was the scream of a fairy—a defence mechanism. Faint as it was, there was no mistaking that awful sound. Even from afar, it left my ears ringing.

"Bridget?" I said, quietly at first. If something had gone wrong, she would be headed back to me. She should be on her way already. I raised my voice. "Bridget!"

Nothing stirred. Only the soft echo of my voice answered.

My heart pounded.

What if she were caught? What if someone other than the boy had seen her?

This is it, I thought. *It's all over. The plan failed.*

But then I saw it: a flash of blue in the distance.

"Bridget," I breathed, rushing toward her. She barely slowed before she hit me, slapping against my chest. She hung there, gripping the collar of my shirt until I grabbed her around the waist and held her in front of me.

"Are you okay?" I asked, thankful when she nodded. Exhaling, I dropped into a squat, opening my hand so she could sit on my palm, looking her up and down just to make sure. "You scared me. Why'd you scream? Did someone else see you?"

She shook her head.

"Almost?"

She nodded.

"But everything's okay? The plan could still work?"

Hesitant this time, she scrunched her face and then, finally, nodded.

"You're sure?"

Her next nod was more resolute.

Sighing, I lifted her to my shoulder, and she climbed into the little space between my neck and my collar, slipping her legs under the fabric like a blanket. "Let's go get some rest. We'll lay low for a while ..."

She scooted closer, nestling her tiny head against my neck. I smiled, my skin warming with her touch.

"I'm glad you're okay."

LILY

"Lily! Lily, wake up!"

Who? Liam?

"Lily!"

His voice sounded distant, but through blinking eyes, I saw him leaning over me. I raised my head. Everything spun. I looked one way, then the other, but I couldn't tell which was right or left. I saw only the fence stretching out on either side of me, rocking like the rails of a ship on the open sea. Shapes blurred. I closed my eyes and inhaled through my nose, lowering my head again.

"I'm seasick," I mumbled.

"Seasick? Lily, you've never been on the sea."

I opened my eyes and peered up at my brother. "What?"

"Are you—?"

"Shh!" I hissed, squishing a finger on his cheek, his nose, and at last, his lips where I meant it to go. I blinked, giving my head a little shake, but there were still three of him hovering over me. "Stop."

"Stop what?"

"Stop yellin' please. I can 'ear yah," But the words came out slurred and lazy. They didn't sound right. I opened my mouth wide, trying to relieve some of the pressure in my ears. "What is it?" I asked. "What d'you want, Liam?" That sounded better.

"A-are you all right?"

I ignored his question, trying to sit up again but teetering. I leaned back on one arm and pressed the opposite hand to my forehead. "Oh, for goodness' sake."

"Lily?"

"What on Earth is wrong with me?" I squeezed my eyes closed and opened them, waiting for the swaying of the world to lessen. Then, I faced my brother. "Liam?"

He gulped.

"What is bloody wrong with me?"

"I-I—" he sputtered.

"Liam!"

"I-I don't know what—it's just—Bridget was frightened, and sh-she made a sound a-a-and ..." He leaned toward me, arms extended, but I shoved him back.

"You liar!" I heaved myself up on wobbly legs, holding the fence and glaring down at him. "There was no fairy! There wasn't anything at all, was there? What did you do?"

"Nothing! Lily, I didn't do anything, and I didn't lie!" he cried. "You have to believe me!"

"Oh, really? I *have* to?" I slapped a hand onto my hip. "And why in the world would I want to do something like that?"

His expression slackened, and for a moment, he just sat, dumbfounded. "Because ... because I'm telling the truth," he said as if there were no alternative—as if he couldn't possibly be lying.

I stood rooted to the spot, waiting for him to give me a reason that was actually worth hearing because, quite frankly, I didn't care that he was *telling the truth*. I wanted an explanation, and I would stare him down until I got it.

"B-Bridget was there, okay? She *was*," he began, waving his arms as he spoke. "I think she was scared and flew off. There was this sound. It was loud, and I blacked out. That's all I remember, I swear! I really don't know what happened. I—" Pausing to breathe, he dropped his arms, exasperated. "Lily, please ..." he hung his head. "Just please believe me, all right?"

I watched his body jump with a little hiccough and felt a twinge of guilt for yelling at him but only momentarily. He couldn't be telling the truth. He *couldn't.* How could we both faint at the same time?

"Liam," I snarled, bending to grab the collar of his shirt, forcing him to look at me. "What happened?"

His lips trembled around words. "I—Bridget, she ..."

"Liam!"

"It was Bridget! She—"

"Don't lie to me!"

"I'm not!" he cried, and ... he wasn't.

His posture was loose. He wasn't avoiding eye contact. He stared directly at me with big watery blue eyes. They would betray him. They always did. They silently spoke every emotion he felt, but there was no lie in the eyes that returned my gaze. And when he spoke, it made too much sense to be ignored.

"Lily, I couldn't have done anything from where I was. You were all the way out here."

He was right. We'd been several yards apart and separated by the fence.

I released him, leaning back on one of the posts, my eyes focusing inward, trying to see some flaw that would yield an explanation. "Then ... Then what happened?"

"I told you," my brother whispered.

"It wasn't a fairy, Liam!"

Quietly, he asked, "Why can't you just believe me?"

"Because you're lying; you have to be."

"I'm not," he asserted.

"You—" But I froze with my mouth open.

It was his earnestness that frightened me. It was the possibility that he *was* telling the truth—that he wasn't at fault for me fainting—that made me so uncomfortable. Because if it wasn't him, then what was it? He was right that he couldn't have done anything from so far. There was no way, but ...

"Okay, fine," I said, holding out my palms in surrender, forcing myself to relent before my mind could put together a fitting explanation for such an absurdity. I was fully awake now and uninjured, so really, there was no harm done, right? "Let's say you are telling the truth, and this fairy ran off." I swallowed hard. "I guess I can believe you ... for now." Liam's face brightened. "But—" It fell again almost instantly. I cleared my throat, drawing myself up importantly. "I want proof. You absolutely must introduce us the next time you see her."

"Yes, of course!" Liam jumped to his feet, beaming.

I tried to match his gaiety, flashing him a half-hearted smile, but the unease of not knowing still knotted my stomach.

Then again, perhaps it was simply the clouds moving in and the humidity in the air that stirred the little storm inside of me.

LIAM

I watched Lily watch Mother. I could tell she wanted to say something. She kept glancing down at her plate and picking up her fork and putting it down again. Then she would lean forward a little and open her mouth and close it. She couldn't seem to spit it out. I suspected it was something she thought might create a dispute, so she simply sat, battling with her indecision, at first certain and then timid, over and over until—

"Say what's on your mind, Lilith," Mother said. "It's impolite to let your food go cold."

But even with Mother's permission, my sister wavered.

"Your reluctance is boorish. You had no trouble speaking your mind when you confronted me in the drawing room." She sliced her vegetables into smaller bites. "Has my daughter suddenly learned some manners?"

From anyone else, the words would seem teasing, but from Mother, they were harsh.

"I—" Lily began, but when Mother lifted her gaze, she gulped and bowed her head. "I simply wished to apologise for my behaviour the other day. I'm sorry, Mother. My words and actions were out of line."

"Good," Mother replied, took a bite, and chewed it before continuing. "You would do well to remember your place in the future."

From where I sat, I could see Lily's hand tighten into a fist on her lap. Then breathing out, she let the tension relax and said softly, "Forgive me."

Mother resumed eating without responding, so Lily and I followed her example, though the tense atmosphere didn't lift. I chewed quietly, stealing glances at Lily, who'd somehow managed to mask the agitation I knew she still felt. I reached over to touch her hand reassuringly, but the clang of silverware made me jump.

When I looked up, Mother had a hand pressed to her forehead, her dinner fork teetering on the edge of her plate.

"Mother, is something the matter?"

She pinched her lips together, shaking her head as she lowered her hand and retrieved her utensil. Perhaps embarrassed, she ignored our curious stares and simply answered, "It's nothing. My ears just won't stop ringing today."

I met Lily's gaze for the briefest moment, peeked through the centrepiece at our mother, and the three of us finished our meal in silence.

JASPER

I stepped lightly, asking Animgeo to guide my feet to avoid disturbing any new growth on the trail. Trees arched over me, looming on either side of the narrow road, and there at the end of it was Aurisol's last light silhouetting the Gate.

It still stood after all these years, preserved, perhaps, by some form of magic, though the space around it hadn't fared so well. The walls extending from it crumbled, the whole estate ripe with the decay of abandonment, but in an odd, dreamy sort of way, I liked it like this. Surely, it couldn't compare to the home's former glory, but it let the light in. The Auric Sun set behind it and could now shine through the rubble and illuminate what was left.

I paused to watch the light wane and the shadows grow. There was something peaceful about an Auric sunset. The colours burned between the trees and on the horizon beyond, strips of different hues stacked on top of each other like paint strokes on a canvas. The clouds above them glowed and then slowly darkened as Aurisol sank behind the tree line, and the Gate's shadows stretched toward my feet, beckoning me. Although the sky held its vivid shades, the light from them dimmed and eerie semi-darkness set upon the world around me, leaving all but that little strip of colour in shadow.

Prompted by the twilight, I moved toward the Gate again, which seemed ominous without Aurisol's glow.

I peered through bars—the rubble of the house, the crumbled brick, the courtyard that had been cracked and broken by the roots of steadfast plants … No matter how many years passed, the Gate of the Atwood House would remain. It had been here long before me, and I was certain it would endure beyond my death. I smiled to myself, wondering how much history flowed from this very spot.

I touched the bronze, feeling the warmth it had absorbed from the Auric Sun's rays, though the clouds above me heralded rain. Within the hour, the Gate would be cold to the touch.

I rocked on my heels, pondering whether I should pass through or risk the storm. I sighed and stepped forward, lamenting but knowing it was the right decision.

"Home, it is …"

PART THREE
A FATHER'S LOVE

LILY

I woke to sounds of fear—to a woman's hysterical scream, followed by cries of, "Oh my God!" and hastened footsteps. People rushed out of rooms and raced down the halls with no regard at all for others who may be sleeping, their feet stomping and doors banging shut behind them.

In seconds, I was on my feet, the shouts driving me out of bed in a fluster. I grabbed my quilt and wrapped it around me, hurrying to the door to find the source of emergency. But when I flung it open, I nearly collided with a maid, who continued her flight down the corridor without even an utterance of apology.

Glancing to my right, I saw Liam poke his head out of his own room. Neither of us spoke, but the feeling of urgency was palpable.

"Come in! Get him in!" people yelled.

"Hurry! Grab a chair! Grab *something*!"

"Wake the Madame."

"Quickly!

"Oh, dear God!"

I chased the voices down the stairs with my brother at my heels. We rounded the corner, stepping onto the lower landing, which opened over the foyer, and I stopped as if I'd hit an invisible wall.

No one spared a glance in our direction, but I lowered to my knees anyway, guiding Liam to do the same. Peering through the railing, I saw panicked servants crowded together in their nightclothes, bustling, trembling, the women gasping and turning away.

The only inert figure was a shape slouched over on a stool— a person with a man's height who wore a cloak so sodden with rain that it clung to his skin. I could see the rounded ridges of his spine through the thin material, and although he wheezed and tremored with every laboured breath, the crowd offered no aid. They hovered around him uncertainly—a mass of reluctant spectators to this stranger's peril—trying to decide how best to approach him as a puddle formed at his feet.

I watched in silence, Liam cowering behind me, holding onto the train of my quilt.

And then an anguished cry turned every head.

Mother stood at the bottom of the staircase, her arms raised in front of her face as if to shield herself from the figure. Celia dashed toward her, whispering and gently touching her shoulder, trying to make her turn, but Mother was inconsolable. Her hands shook as she pressed them over her eyes.

My whole body seemed to stiffen, the sight filling me with a peculiar mixture of interest and horror. I'd never seen Mother tremble so. I'd never heard the gasp of her sobs. I'd never even seen her touch her face without her handkerchief, but here, in her nightgown in the foyer, surrounded by people, she cried into her hands, uninhibited.

I looked back at the strange spectre of a man. Who was he that he could reduce my mother to such a state? Who could force her to abandon her severity? Was she merely overwhelmed by the poorness of his condition?

But the moment the questions entered my mind, I knew, and as if he felt my gaze upon him, slowly, deliberately, the man looked up. That face, gaunt as it was, stirred a sense of familiarity, and when our eyes met, I knew I was right.

I knew because I saw the same eyes staring back at me in the mirror every day.

Greenish irises ringed and flecked with gold, like summer leaves after the first touch of autumn's change.

These were the eyes he'd given me.

This man was my father.

LILY

Yawning, I clambered out from under my quilt, stumbling when I finally managed to wrestle myself free. I glanced at the other side of the bed where my brother still slept soundly, the duvet drawn up to his ears. He hadn't wanted to be alone after all that commotion, I remembered—after Celia saw us on the landing and ushered us back to our rooms.

I rubbed my eyes, and donning my housecoat, I started for the door.

I surprised Bennett when I entered the kitchen and realised how early I'd woken. He'd only just begun preparations for breakfast and insisted I still had plenty of time to sleep. But I deposited myself on a stool near the window, ignoring his little tut of protest.

"It was quite a party last night, young miss," he said, eyeing me from across the room. "The whole house was in an uproar."

I spoke through a yawn, not bothering to cover my mouth. "Indeed."

"You don't seem pleased at all by the news."

Shrugging, I replied as honestly as I could: "I don't know

what to do with the admittance of a stranger in my home."

He looked down at the dough he'd been kneading. "Many a stranger has visited the estate, Miss Lily, and your calm courteousness toward them has always surprised me."

I frowned. "Are you saying I'm not normally courteous?"

Chuckling, he flicked flour from his fingers in my direction. "Not to those of us with whom you're well-acquainted. But your manner among strangers garners their affection rather quickly. Perhaps that's how you should approach this encounter, too."

Rolling my eyes, I leaned back on the wall. "Except he's not a stranger, Bennett, not really."

He paused to wipe his brow on the back of his forearm. "Miss Lily, I beg your pardon if it's not my place, but I daresay this is an encounter you cannot avoid, nor should you. Go and talk to him; perhaps you'll learn something."

"You're just trying to get rid of me so you can get back to work."

He couldn't hide his sheepish grin. "As thrilling as I find your company, there is still much to do, especially with an extra mouth to feed." Then pursing his lips, he added, "And if I'm not mistaken, it appears I've fewer biscuits than I did yesterday. Might you know anything about that?"

I cleared my throat, adjusting the sash on my robe as I stood. "Well, I'm off then."

"Of course, you are."

I politely curtseyed at the door. "It's been a pleasure, good sir."

"Ha! Don't waste your good manners on me, Miss. I know you too well to fall for it."

I grinned and turned to leave. "I look forward to a lovely breakfast! And can we have sandwiches with our tea later? I'm bored of biscuits."

The sickroom was at the back of the house by Madame Renoir's little infirmary.

Slowing as I neared it, I peeked into the nurse's room and found her slumped over the table, snoring. Her head was cradled in her folded arms, and there were instruments and bandaging materials strewn around it. My eyes passed over the used and discarded things—the bloody rags and strips of gauze —but I didn't enter, afraid I might wake her, wondering how late into the night she'd been up caring for him.

I passed noiselessly to the next door but paused when I reached for the knob, stopped by the sound of muffled voices. I leaned in to listen, and as soon as I pressed my ear against the door, it opened. Leaping sideways, I flattened myself against the adjacent wall as Mother exited, though she saw me at once.

"Lilith!" She gasped, quickly securing the door behind her. She touched her chest. "You startled me. What're you doing awake at this hour?"

The usual stringency was absent from her voice, which disarmed me. I looked her over and cautiously observed, "You haven't slept."

"Your father is very ill ..." Her tone could almost pass as gentle.

I chose my words with care, unsure how to navigate the person that stood before me. "Madame Renoir is asleep," I said. "You should rest, too."

She inhaled sharply, opening her mouth to argue but deciding against it. The fatigue she felt was too evident. Dark circles had carved themselves under her eyes, and a sheen of sweat curled the shorter stands of hair around her forehead.

"Yes ... yes, you're quite right, darling." Absently, she reached toward me, her palm cold and clammy when it found my cheek. "Your father needs time, too," she said. "Don't burden him with company now. I'm sure Bennett will give you a treat if you stop by the kitchen. Come along."

I stood rigid as she peeled her hand from the side of my face, shuddering when they were finally separated. The gesture lacked any warmth or comfort. I wiped her sweat from my skin as she unfurled her sleeves, which had been rolled up to her elbows. Then I let her lead me back down the hall, sneaking glances over my shoulder at the door as it shrank behind us. We'd nearly reached the kitchen when I stopped her.

"Let me ask someone to help you up the stairs, Mother. I'm worried your weariness may hinder your balance." I figured the best way to respond to this odd mood of hers was with the same courtesy, even if I thought it too generous.

"How sweet of you, my dear."

It wasn't at all out of a desire to be agreeable, though her positive reaction pleased me. I wanted to see her ascend the stairs. I wanted assurance that she'd retired to her room so I could do the exact thing she'd told me not to.

I stood at the bottom of the stairwell and watched her go one step at a time, one hand on the railing, the other clutching Jane's, until they disappeared on the landing.

I didn't return to the kitchen. She couldn't know that I'd already been to see Bennett this morning, and if she inquired, he would honestly say that I had. Instead, I crept back toward the sickroom.

'*Don't burden him with company.*'

The trill of panic in her voice hung in my mind. The way she'd acted so kindly. The way she'd closed the door so quickly and ushered me away ... How grave was his condition? I had to, at the very least, look upon his face.

This time, I didn't waver. I marched right in, fearing that someone would discover me again if I lingered too long in the hall. Slipping inside, I pulled the door closed as swiftly and quietly as I could. Then, I looked up and was arrested in place.

Mother was right to shield me from this view. Whatever I'd been expecting to find, it wasn't this. I'd seen him already in the foyer, but I could hardly believe it was the same man.

I stumbled back into the door, my heart thrashing in my chest. I felt like someone had dropped a rock into my stomach.

Emaciated.

That was the word.

He'd withered away. There was no youthful glow, no flesh to round his face, nothing but skin stretched over bone, leaving sunken wells on either side of his mouth.

Who was this man? Surely Mother was mistaken. This was not Roderick Howell.

I shivered as I stepped nearer.

I should leave. I should walk away and pretend I'd never been here.

But I couldn't unsee the state he was in—the greying hair and curling brows, the scars and flaky patches of skin, the hands that belonged on a skeleton and not a living person.

Suddenly, I had a horrible yearning to touch him, to see if there was still some warmth—some life!—left in him. Without confirmation, this man was dead. He had to be. No one could survive like this. There was not even the movement of his chest with breath.

I stopped at the foot of his bed.

But then he spoke—a small, rasping voice like that of a child. "E-Elizabeth?"

I started, freezing in place because I'd expected him to be asleep or dead.

"Elizabeth?"

"Lily," I corrected softly.

His eyes snapped open as if he thought they would deceive

him. "Lily?" he asked, his gaze sweeping over me, frantic and blinking. "M-my daughter ..."

"Yes."

For but a moment, there was silence, the same two pairs of eyes staring at one another in quiet anticipation. Then, squeezing his shut, he drew his shrivelled arms up to cover his face and wept.

My breath held.

"Get out ..." he sobbed. And then again, with a wailing cry, "Get out!"

I flinched, but my feet wouldn't obey.

"Please! I love you, but please leave. Please," he begged, concealing his face with shaking arms. "Get out, my Lily ..."

I turned. I rushed to the door, but before I opened it, I risked one last glance. Beneath his wrist, I saw the tears dripping off his chin with every tremble of his jaw, and the sight held me back, a heaviness in my limbs seeming to sink my feet into the floor, rooting me to that spot.

I didn't miss him. I could hardly say I knew him. But every piece of my soul wanted to console the howling creature before me. How could anyone with a beating heart leave a man like this?

"Get out!" he screamed again.

Tears burned my eyes.

And then the door burst open behind me. I whipped around, at last finding a reason to tear my eyes away. Madame Renoir grabbed my arm and wrenched me from the room, leaving me shivering in the hall as she tried to soothe him.

"It's okay. It's okay," he cried over and over. "It's okay. Get out!"

LIAM

I found Lily perched in the arch of the garden building. She didn't seem to notice me as I approached, but when I deposited myself on the bench beside her, she automatically scooted over to give me more room.

Casually, I said, "I woke to shouting again. It sounded like a stampede going down the stairs." Swinging my legs, I peeked sideways at her. Quietly, I asked, "Are you all right?"

She swallowed, though her face remained expressionless.

"Lily?"

Heaving a sigh, she faced me at last, a gentle smile affixed to her lips. She patted me on the back. "Of course, Liam. I'm fine. Why wouldn't I be?"

I stopped my legs and furrowed my brow, unconvinced. "What was the fuss?"

"Oh, nothing much." She stood, stretching her arms above her head. "Mr. Howell just had a fit, that's all."

"Just call him Father ..." I glanced down at my hands, my voice falling. "Did—did you see him? Father, I mean."

Lily dropped her arms, the stillness returning to her face as she gazed outward. She inhaled a deep breath, held it for a few seconds, and exhaled just as slowly. "Is breakfast ready?"

"Huh?"

"That's why you came, right?"

"Well, yes, but—"

Rounding the bench, she started back toward the house. "Come on. Bennett's been preparing all morning; we shouldn't let it go cold."

It was my turn to sigh.

"You didn't answer my question, Lily …"

But she was already too far away to hear me.

LILY

I stood at the sickroom door for the third day in a row, this time late in the evening. The house was quiet. No one was awake to keep me from twisting the doorknob, but for the third time, I turned to walk away without entering.

What did I expect to gain from this encounter? I wondered as I retreated down the hall. Bennett said I shouldn't avoid it, but what was it I intended to do or say? I'd rehearsed this moment in my head a thousand times—what I would say to him should he ever return—but now, at the door, the script I'd memorised was lost.

But the door loomed behind me. I felt its pull as if it had grown, engulfing the walls and the ceiling, slowly creaking open to capture me.

I knew it wasn't real—that feeling, the growing door—but I still shuddered. I still stole a timid glance behind me at the perfectly normal corridor.

The door was still there where I'd left it, still shut like I'd left it.

It wouldn't reach out to me, nor would my father.

The door between us was still shut like he'd left it.

And it always would be ... unless I opened it.

Before I could convince myself otherwise, I flew back down the hall, ripped the door open, and entered, immediately greeted by both lamplight and a familiar voice.

"You finally decided to come in, did you?"

I raised my head to find him already staring back at me.

"I thought it must be you oscillating in the hall." He sighed. "Don't worry. I've found my head. I won't tell you to go away this time."

I pulled the door closed behind me, the calmness with which he spoke such a stark contrast to the writhing and shouting from before that I felt strangely, albeit cautiously, at ease.

"You can come closer if you'd like," he said, and when I hesitated, he chuckled as if he'd expected my reaction. "Is my appearance too frightening?" He lifted one hand, examining it. "I must look monstrous."

I didn't answer, though he was right. "Your voice is familiar," I offered instead.

"Ha! At least something about me is unchanged." Eyeing me, he said, "It's been a while, hasn't it? You've grown."

There was no remorse in his voice, not even a change in tone, as though his absence had been nothing more than a trivial happenstance.

I felt like my chest had been compressed under the weight of his indifference. I folded my arms, trying not to squirm in my discomfort, looking away so my glare didn't hit him directly when I responded.

"Yes, well, that does tend to happen." I couldn't mask the sarcasm. Bennett's suggestion of civility had never really been an option anyway.

He leaned his head back and smirked up at the ceiling. "You're cross with me."

"How ever did you work that out?"

Again, he laughed. "You speak so easily when you're upset. You're welcome to be cross if it allows us conversation."

"Don't expect pleasant conversation."

The smile spread on his face. "I should hope not, given the circumstances."

"Don't look so amused."

"Oh, but I am. You're not careful with me as the others have been. Of course, I expected nothing less."

I observed him—his grey skin and matted hair. The difference between the father in my memories and the person before me was jarring.

His eyes flicked down to my face before returning to the beams above him. "What's that look for?" he asked. "Are you trying to decipher why I left?"

I scoffed. "I'm trying to decipher why you bothered to come back."

He silenced, at last meeting my gaze. His smile faded until there was only the touch of it left on his lips. Then softly, he replied, "I wonder ... Come and sit, won't you? I won't bite."

"If I do, will you tell me?"

He considered, surveying the room. Finally, he said, "I'll tell you why I left."

I pursed my lips, contemplating, reluctant to agree, but my curiosity thirsted. I marched forward and sat at his feet, arranging my dress as I angled my body toward him. "Go on."

"Do you promise to keep it a secret?"

"I owe you no such promise," I replied calmly. "You only said I had to sit."

"You forget from whom you inherited your stubbornness. You may leave if you can't stay silent."

I was unconcerned. "You already said you wouldn't tell me

to go away. I'd tell you not to go back on your word, but we both know you're no stranger to that."

Stunned, he blinked at me.

"Like I said—" I sat up straighter, though my audacity surprised even me. "Don't expect civility."

With a dry laugh, he sank back into the pillow. "You will keep it to yourself though, won't you? I don't want the others to know."

His brows were drawn, but he seemed to be looking inward and not at me. He was ashamed of the response, I realised, and leaning forward to touch his hand, I said, "Okay. Between us. I promise." Although I didn't want to admit it, the prospect of bearing a secret offered a strange sense of closeness with him.

A smirk quirked his mouth. "You really do want to know, don't you?"

"Yes," I answered, perhaps too quickly.

His smile stiffened.

He opened his mouth and closed it, then opened it again, though no words came out. I waited, tensed. I would wait all night for the answer if I had to, but it came more easily than I thought it would—three words in a hushed voice: "I was bored."

I drew my hand back. "What?"

He turned away.

"What did you say?"

While my voice rose, his stayed soft. "You heard me, Lily. It's very simple."

"Y-you—" I stammered.

"I was bored. I was tired of sitting idle, tired of—of doing the same thing every day." Then, suddenly ardent, he threw his body forward and grasped my arm, forcing me to look at him.

I jumped. I pulled back, but his grip held. I didn't expect him to have so much strength.

"L-let go!" I demanded. The eyes that stared out of those sunken sockets were wild. His face was gaunt and grinning. "What're you—?"

He gave my arm a violent shake, and in the moment it took me to right myself again, he yanked me closer. I could smell his breath. I could feel it against the side of my face when he spoke in a quiet, urgent voice. "Just like you, Lily. I can see it. We're similar, you and I. That's why I'm telling you this. That's why I trust you with this."

"Let go!" Panicked, I threw my weight off the bed, and at last, his fingers broke apart and freed my arm before I crashed to the floor.

"Lily, wait! Are you okay? I didn't mean for—"

I leapt to my feet, bounded to the door, and slammed it behind me, my chest heaving. Then, I spun around and shouted through the closed door, "I'm nothing like you!"

My pulse raced as I ran down the hall, but I didn't pause for a breath until I reached the stairwell. Wheezing, I sat on the bottom step and leaned against the wall, sniffling and blinking.

It wasn't that I feared him. It wasn't the sudden burst of passion on his scarred face, nor was it his appearance at all. It was easier to see past it now that I'd spoken to him. In fact, he seemed far more pitiable than frightening.

I feared that he might be right about me.

No, that wasn't it.

He *was* right.

What I feared was that, had I stayed, he would've seen the truth on my face, and I didn't want him to know just how bored —how like him—I really was.

LILY

"Back again? Will you be storming off tonight, too?"

I stood in the doorway, scowling. I'd come with intention, but his haughty greeting made me question my return. Before I could talk myself out of it, I asked, "Where did you go?"

He narrowed his eyes, though it was offset by the amused smirk on his mouth. "You waste no time. Will you not wish me a good evening first?"

I blew air out my nostrils and with a half-hearted curtsy said, "Good evening, Mr. Howell. May I sit?"

The smile fell off his lips, but he gestured to the chair beside the bed. "Please."

I sat at his feet instead, ignoring his direction, and for a moment, the smirk reappeared.

"Where did you go?" I asked again, unwilling to abandon my goal.

He sighed. "You've never had a talent for subtlety."

"Don't talk like you know me."

"I did once."

Firmly, I said, "I'm different now."

He stared at me but didn't contend. Instead, he said, "I went anywhere my feet would take me—to places I still don't know the names of. Distant places. Strange places. This time, I got lost."

"Why did you go then?"

"I already told you." When I didn't respond, he rolled his eyes and continued, "Boredom. Monotony. The overwhelming feeling of being chained to a life you don't really want ... Whatever you want to call it, I suppose."

"That's it then? That's all the explanation you have for your absence?"

His gaze passed from me to the window. "It took me a long time to realise that I was alone, completely and truly."

"You left alone."

His voice was measured. "There's a difference between being alone and feeling alone, Lily. Surely, you understand that."

Squeezing my hands together, I nodded and let him continue.

"I'd no friends and no family. I left you all behind in search of—of something ... I don't know. Purpose, maybe? A renewed vigour for life?" The house creaked, and he flinched, pausing to look around before settling back into the cushions. He exhaled. "But I got swept up in the mess of it all, and I found myself missing home. Strange, isn't it?"

"Strange that you should miss your family for once in your life?"

He peered back at me tiredly. "Come on, Lily ..."

"Did you find it then? Your new vigour?"

Watching my face, he took a deep breath and released it before answering. "Yes, in a way, I think I did."

Though I expected his response, it still stung. I crossed my arms and faced away. "Well, that's just perfect for you, isn't it?"

The inflection of his voice remained the same. "Don't pretend you didn't get on fine without me. You did, Lily, and you'll be fine when I'm gone again."

I felt the force of his words as if he'd struck me. I leapt to my feet, backing away. "Don't do that!"

His expression softened, and he rubbed the back of his neck. But he didn't speak.

"We *were* fine."

"I know."

"We were fine without you! You can't come back only to leave again!"

"I missed you. I missed my family and my home."

"That—that's not fair."

There was no opposition on his face. "No, it's not." He shrugged gingerly, his expression tensing with the movement. "I know it isn't fair of me to come back like this and keep reiterating how much I missed you when it was my own choice to leave, but you get it, Lily. I know you do. You know what it's like to be bored by the tedium and to live without freedom. You know that feeling. That's why you left yesterday, isn't it?"

I could feel his eyes on me, but I refused to meet them. I knew my expression gave me away, but I couldn't get the words out to answer. I didn't want him to notice. I didn't want him— an outsider—to read me so easily and know my emotions so well.

Faintly, he said. "Lily, I'm—I'm sorry."

"Save it," I spit back.

"I am sorry. I know I could say it hundreds of times and still not deserve your forgiveness, and—and that's okay. It's okay if you don't forgive me."

"I *don't*, but ..." I wrapped my arms tightly around my waist. My eyes stung. I tried to swallow the lump in my throat to reply. "I want to know ... If you were going to be gone most of my life, then—" I gulped again. "—then why didn't you just leave in the beginning? Why did you keep coming back to spend time with us?" I felt a tear slip out and quickly brushed it away. "Those memories—they're …"

"They're what?"

I sniffled. "It wasn't fair of you to give us such fond memories only to leave again the moment we wanted to make more. How could you do that to us?"

"Lily, as a father, it—it's never my intention to make you cry."

"I'm not crying."

He sighed. "Sit down then. You're trembling."

"I'm not."

"Lily …"

At last, I obeyed, though I bowed my head so he couldn't see my expression.

"You may not understand, my Lily, but I had to get away before I suffocated. I was still so young when I became your father, and there're wide worlds out there that you've not seen. I craved more than this life, as reprehensible as that may seem to you."

"You chose this life!" I cried, whipping around. "You chose to have a family—to have me and Liam. Was that not enough?"

He stared me dead in the eye and asked, "Will that be enough for you?"

I silenced because there was no answer I could give him. He watched the defeat overtake my face, but he didn't gloat. He simply lowered his head.

"It never felt like a choice," he said. "It was a duty. A path that was laid before me, one I was groomed for my whole life."

In a quiet voice, I asked, "Are you saying you didn't want us?"

He didn't even take a moment out of courtesy. "No, I didn't, though I'm glad for it now. Does that bother you?"

I thought about it and realised it didn't, which surprised me. "Perhaps it should, but it's like you said. The same is expected of me. Even if I don't wish it, that's exactly the course my life is supposed to take."

Nodding, he licked his lips. "Lily, I ..." He paused a few seconds before deciding to continue. "I said before that you and I are similar. Would you like to know why?" I didn't respond, but he continued without my prompting. "I love your brother and your mother dearly, but you and I, we understand each other in a way they can't."

"How d'you know?"

"Because you don't want to be here. You've no desire to be in a room with me, and yet, here you are, still coming to the door every day since I returned even though you've every reason to ostracise and hate me. You don't keep coming back because you love and forgive me or because it's your responsibility. Those might contribute a little, but deep down, you know it's a different reason. And because we're alike, I think I know what that reason is."

"Then what is it?"

The smile that bent his mouth was grim. "You're longing to get out, too, and you want to know if it's worth it."

LIAM

Mother didn't join us for breakfast. She had business in the village, Celia said, but she left instruction for us to study with Miss Sawyer until she returned. We got up from the table, but the maid stopped us before we could leave the room.

"Ah! I beg your pardon, miss, but the master wishes to see you."

Lily frowned. "Mr. Howell?"

Celia nodded. "Yes, ma'am. He's asked me to fetch you to him after your meal."

I glanced at my sister, and sensing her reluctance, I said, "Mother wanted us to have a lesson with Miss Sawyer."

"Ah, yes, she told me this morning," said the maid, "but your father requested that Miss Lily visit him instead. He was very direct. I'm afraid I must insist."

LILY

"Do you keep many friends?"

I snapped into awareness. We'd been sitting in silence for nearly half an hour, and I'd begun to drowse. I hadn't expected him to speak at all, let alone ask such a straightforward question.

I raised a hand to my lips, stifling a yawn. Grudgingly, I replied, "No. I have Liam."

"Your nurse tells me he's quite the conversationalist. He appears rather fond of the townspeople's children, but she never mentioned you with them."

"I'm not a child; I don't need them."

"Everyone needs friends."

I rolled my eyes, leaning on the post at the end of the bed. "I haven't the time. Too many responsibilities."

"Which you are obviously neglecting while you sit around here with me." He nodded toward the window. "Go and play. Those children out there—they may surprise you."

"*Play*? My apologies, I don't believe I'm familiar with such a word."

He chuckled. "You are indeed a proper young lady. I suppose

it would be indecent for you to be playing in the dirt and running through the trees. Your mother must be proud of her accomplishments, though I daresay she hasn't been able to wrestle all the fun out of you just yet."

"She hasn't rid me of any of it; I've only gotten better at hiding it."

He grinned childishly, and even I relaxed. Our communication felt easy. I liked this playful banter, but I reminded myself to stay guarded. I didn't trust him yet.

"You like the garden though," he continued.

I quirked a brow.

"Mrs. Renoir."

"Madame," I corrected, glancing back toward the window, though the garden wasn't visible from it. "I do," I said. "It's quiet and pleasant, and there are always fresh snacks."

"Ah, yes! A healthy appetite is something I miss. I haven't the stomach for anything but broth lately, I'm afraid."

"You should try. You're looking thin."

You're looking dead.

"I wasn't particularly plump before."

"But this is different. I can see the tops of your shoulders." I stood, stepped toward him, and touched the bones that protruded from the wide collar of his night shirt.

As many days as I'd spent in this room with him, there had only been a few occasions where I'd felt confronted by his mortality—where I'd realised that the man sitting before me had been, or still was, very close to death.

I held my breath, and he dropped his shoulder out of my reach.

"Don't do that," he muttered, shuddering the same way one does stepping outside after the first frost of winter—the kind of chill you can't seem to shake. "I don't like for you to notice things like that ..."

I withdrew. "It's difficult not to."

He pulled the front of his shirt down so his shoulders were fully covered, but then I could see the dips around his collar bones. Even his sternum seemed to stick out, as if the skin were simply stretched over bone with no flesh at all to separate them.

"I look dreadful, Lily. It's embarrassing to be seen like this."

How pitiful his expression was. How uncomfortable he seemed in his own skin. I wanted to console him. I wanted to take his hand and assure him that he didn't have to feel ashamed, that this was only a passing phase, that his appearance now wasn't his fault, that he had all the time in the world to mend. He was home and safe and cared for and far away from whatever had left him with those wounds and those scars.

Sighing, I straightened his shirt, and although he squirmed awkwardly, he didn't resist.

"You're ill," I reminded him because it felt like he'd forgotten. "Everyone looks dreadful when they're ill. It's nothing to be ashamed of."

"No?"

"You just need time, and you have that. I've already seen improvement since you've been home. That first night, you looked positively ravaged."

This time, when he smiled, it moved his lips but didn't reach his eyes. "Yes ... I imagine I did."

I tried to ignore the scorn that stole the smile, wondering if I could bring it back with a little humour. "A haircut and a shave certainly helped."

His answering laugh was so clearly forced that even I had trouble pretending it was genuine. What had I said that made him suddenly seem so far away? I touched his face again to make him scold me—to make his expression match the disdainful look in his eyes—and again, he flinched, pushing his chin down to his chest.

"Stop it, Lily."

"This scar ..." I skimmed my finger along his jaw where a scar stretched from his ear to his chin. It was thin and lumpy, like a seam that had been hastily stitched together. "What's it from? You didn't have it before."

He shrugged my hand off. "It's from—from things."

I scoffed softly. "*Things.*"

Retreating, I turned back toward the window, folding my arms to show him that I wouldn't touch him again, and at last, he calmed.

He followed my gaze and said, "It's a pleasant day. Why don't you go outside?"

"It is a pleasant day. Why don't you?"

"I can hardly move from this bed."

I crossed to the window, unlatched it, and threw it open. Immediately, a breeze swept in, carrying the sounds of birds and rustling leaves.

"There." I leaned on the sill, peering out at the trees. "Now you can enjoy it, too."

"Shouldn't you be returning to your lessons?"

"You're the one who asked for me."

He looked down bashfully. "I just wanted to make sure you'd still talk to me. It gets lonely in this room ..."

"You'll be my teacher today, won't you? I'm interested in learning some history—your history. Next, you can tell me about all the places you've travelled. Surely, you've tales of these distant lands, even if you can't remember their names." When he didn't speak, I said, trying to press him for information, "The countryside is a lot different from London, isn't it? When the weather's fair, the sky is so clear and bright."

He nodded absently. "There's too much light and smoke in

the city.”

"Look, you can even see the moon.”

We both looked up at the pale arc that hung against a blue sky.

Softly, Father said, "They were distant places, Lily. Distant and so very different.”

"Different how?”

He held his breath for longer than I thought he should be able and then exhaled shakily. "Tomorrow, Lily. I'll tell you about it tomorrow …”

Perhaps it was the soft quake in his voice or the expression on his face that seemed more distant even than the places he refused to describe, but somehow, I knew that was a lie—an empty promise he didn't intend to keep.

A thought occurred to me, and I didn't hesitate. "You never answered before.”

His eyebrows pulled together, his confusion at my statement drawing him out of that dream state. "What?”

"Whether or not it was worth it to leave like you did.”

His eyes lingered on my face for a time, and then, shyly, he lowered his gaze. "You really want to know?”

"Yes,” I replied, sitting at his feet again. "I want to know.”

He wavered, wringing his hands. "I—I do love you, of course I do, but …” His voice trailed off.

I bowed my head and sighed. "That's not the only reason I'm here, you know. It's not only to know if it's worth it.” He didn't respond, but I hadn't really expected him to. I tried to gather my thoughts into clarity, but by the time they reached my lips, I had little control over them. There was no point trying to censor them for him anyway. "I don't entirely know why I'm here, to be honest. Perhaps I'm just forever clinging to that little bit of hope that you'll come round and stop doing it—stop hurting us. I keep hoping that maybe this time will be different, and you'll be better. Maybe if I sit here and talk to you and remind you who I am and that I love you, you'll choose to stay."

"Lily …"

"Maybe somehow my actions will make a difference, and you'll change."

He strained to sit up, leaning forward to touch my shoulder, inviting me to meet his eyes. "This isn't your fault, Lily. I never left because of something you or your brother or mother did."

I raised my head and stared back at him with a disbelieving smile, but I hoped he saw it, too—that my eyes weren't smiling.

"How can I know that?" I asked, shrugging his hand off. "How many times do you think I blamed myself? How many times do you think I said to myself, 'Maybe if I'd just asked him not to, he wouldn't have left. Maybe if I'd said I love you, I miss you, come back to us just one more time …' Maybe that one more time would've been enough." I shut my eyes, clearing the ache from my throat. "I-I don't know why I care so much—why, for some reason, I picked you to be the one to rule my heart over Mum, why your approval and—" I squeezed my hands together, glaring at the floor. "Why do I bloody care so much what you think? You may as well be a stranger to me now. I've barely talked to you in years. Why do I love you so much? Why am I still sitting here? It makes no sense at all."

I covered my eyes with one hand to hide the brimming tears. "Maybe I do," I said. "Maybe I do want to know if it was worth it because you're right. We are similar. I think we understand each other. I think there's always been that unspoken bond between us. I've always felt that way … When our eyes meet across the room, there's this immediate mutual understanding. No one else gets it."

Father's voice was low but detached—a quiet echo of my thoughts. "It's like we're sharing a secret without ever having to say a word."

I lowered my hand, defeated by the knowledge that he understood, that he felt the same, that he'd left regardless of this closeness we'd always silently shared.

"Well, that's why I'm here," I said, forcing the words out, though they were now coated with venom. "Because all this time, I've been holding onto the thought—the possibility—that *I* hold the secret. That *I* could make you better. That *I* could be the one to help you in some way ... I don't know why I believed it, but I love you because you're my father. And even if you're a sodding prick who couldn't find his way home because he was so lost, I still missed you."

He cupped my face in his calloused hands, thumbing away my tears, and although he didn't speak, his little gesture of consolation was like an antidote. The hostility I'd felt only moments before was soothed away. I'd never had my heart wrenched in so many directions at once.

"Don't leave," I whimpered, and his hands stopped moving. "Don't leave me behind again. We're the same, like you said. I want out, too, so ... if you must leave, take me with you."

I knew what his answer would be because I knew he was a liar. Any attempt at comfort was only for the moment and not for good. I knew what his answer would be, but I still felt brittle as glass as I waited for it.

His hold slackened, and slowly, he drew his hands back and hung his head.

I knew what his answer would be, but I still felt shattered when he spoke it aloud.

"I-I can't do that, Lily. I'm sorry."

Neither of us said another word. I stood quietly and left, and he didn't stop me.

LILY

I found Liam sitting in the garden, exactly where I predicted he'd be. I didn't call out to announce my arrival; I simply unlatched the gate and walked over to him. He hugged his knees to his chest, one hand combing through the new growth around him, but he looked up when I approached. He smiled, though I could tell it was forced, and I smirked with genuine humour, thinking that habit must be a family trait.

"Are you escaping, too?" he asked, his lips straightening out.

I gathered my dress and plopped down next to him. "Something like that," I answered, glancing around. "Seen any fairies today?"

My brother shot me a chastising look but shook his head anyway.

I tutted. "Disappointing."

Liam lowered his head, resting his chin on his knees.

"What're you escaping from?" I asked, surprised to see him in such an ill humour.

"Mother's been acting strange."

"She's always strange."

"No, she's different somehow." He flicked a leaf and

watched it bob up and down before continuing. "The way she talks about Father is different. The way she says things regarding him, it … it turns my stomach."

"What d'you mean?" Had she described his appearance to him? The malnourishment and scars would be frightening.

Liam's lips pressed into a hard line, and he spoke out of the corner of his mouth. "She talks about him like he's already dead."

My eyes widened. The observation disturbed me, but at the same time, I couldn't say it was unwarranted. Because I saw a dead man, too, when I looked at him.

"I don't think she ever really expected him to return, Lily. I-I think it may even—" Liam pinched his brows together. "—bother her that he did." Then all at once, his expression relaxed, and he sighed. "I dunno. It just feels strange …"

I touched his arm. Gently, I asked, "Have you gone to see him?" I already knew the answer.

Liam rubbed the back of his neck. "No," he said, but I barely heard the single word. As I watched him, his eyes seemed to glaze over and redden, but before he could cry—before the tremble of his jaw could release the sob it held back—I lifted my hand from his shoulder and tapped his cheek. He jumped, startled out of his trance, blinking obtusely until his eyes focused on me.

Aghast, he asked, "What was that for?"

"You were starting to disappear." I ruffled his hair. "I had to break the spell you were under, and that was the only way to do it."

Rolling his eyes, he said, "Lily, people don't just disappear. That's impossible, and there's no such thing as *real* spells. You know that."

I *harrumph*ed. "Liam," I replied. "People don't just find

hungry fairies in their gardens. That's impossible. There's no such thing as *real* fairies. You know that."

His face reddened.

"Sounds pretty ridiculous when you put it like that, doesn't it?" I challenged, and he glowered at me, blowing a loud breath out his nostrils, which flared like a pony's. I snorted at the thought of Liam clopping around on all fours and munching hay, but he laughed before I had the chance.

"What?" I startled, spinning around to see what was awry. "What're you laughing at?"

"Mum's going to kill you when she sees your dress!"

Playfully, I shoved him. "Not if she's already gutting you for what you've done to your sleeves. Just look at them." I pinched the loose cloth in my fingers and, examining it, made a face. "Filthy!"

"Yours is worse!" Liam stuck out his tongue and tried to push past me.

Lurching forward, I grabbed his waistcoat and yanked him back. "What d'you think you're doing?"

He shook himself free and took off. "What does it look like?" he shouted over his shoulder, grinning. "I'm beating you!"

"What? You are not!" I chased after him.

We wrestled our way to the garden gate, then raced up the path, weaving through the hedges up to the terrace.

This is good, I thought. *This is normal.*

But the sinking feeling in my stomach refused to retire, and when my heart started to pound, I couldn't tell if it was simply from the exertion of running or the awful sense of dread I felt the nearer we got to the house. Something here had changed the night Mr. Howell had returned, perhaps not for the better.

No, don't worry, I told myself. *It's okay.*

We slowed in front of the parlour door, and Liam whirled

around to smile at his victory, though I'd been too absorbed in my thoughts to put in a full effort.

"I win!"

I managed a smirk. "Yeah, yeah," I muttered, pinching his shoulder, shoving my other hand into the small of his back to guide him. "Let's go."

He nodded and slid the door open as I tried to quiet the frantic beating of my heart.

It's okay, I repeated silently to myself and tightened my grip on my brother's arm. *It's okay. I'm not alone.*

But the moment we were inside—the moment I let go of him—Liam vanished into the hall, abandoning me in the solitary confines of the parlour.

I was alone.

I felt alone.

LILY

"Why did you ask for me again? There's no point. If you're gonna leave, then just bloody leave. Don't ask me to sit here like nothing's happened because it's not okay to force your way back in. You must know that." Defiantly, I stuck my nose in the air and said, "You already broke my heart once. I'd be doing myself a disservice if I let you do it again." I did an about-face before his injured expression could shake my resolve, but it wasn't enough.

"Lily, wait."

I paused with my hand hovering over the doorknob. Somehow, I couldn't bring myself to turn it. I wanted him to fight for me to stay.

"My satchel is on the floor over there."

I peeked back at him, my brows pulling in. "What?"

"My satchel," he repeated, changing neither his expression nor the inflection of his voice. He pointed to the corner by the window.

Curious, I followed his direction, but I paused when I saw a little bottle on the windowsill. "What is this?" I asked, lifting it up to the light. The glass was tinted brown, but I could see powder inside.

The man sighed. "Ignore that."

"What is it?" The label had been scratched off.

He pursed his lips, and because I could tell he didn't want to answer, I stared at him expectantly until he did.

"A precaution," he offered at last.

"What does that mean?"

"It's not important."

"What's it for?"

"Leave it where it is, Lily."

I rolled my eyes, bending to retrieve the leather bag, holding it in front of me with two fingers.

He smiled at my expression. "It's a bit worn and dirty, isn't it? Not unlike me."

I scrunched my nose. "Well, at least *you've* had a wash."

Once again, I noticed how easily I still fell into conversation with him—how comfortable it was despite the obvious tension between us—but I let myself, ignoring the warnings that whispered in my mind.

I tossed back the flap, pulling the sack open to examine the contents, but there were none.

"It's empty."

"That's right. I won't be needing it anymore."

I stared back at him, and although I could guess the implications of his words, I didn't want to get my hopes up before he could confirm it. I waited.

"You've a strange sort of magic in you, y'know that?"

"Why did you ask for me again?" I wanted him to confirm it.

"I thought about what you said and about the tone of your voice when you said it. It seems you've quite a talent for being unforgettable. I've barely slept in days because that woeful little voice of yours won't leave me alone." He eyed me pointedly, if not sarcastically.

"I'm glad to hear it."

He laughed, his gaze lowering to his hands, but the smile on his lips seemed hesitant. "I made it home, Lily, after so long, and ... I-I think I can make it work. I could—" He swallowed. "—stay. I could be here for you and Liam, and then, perhaps, when I'm better, I could show you those new places. We could travel, all of us. Overseas or just to visit the city like we used to. You'd like that wouldn't you, Lily? Do you remember the city?" He was talking fast and excitedly, like a child passionately describing a new interest, though his eyes wouldn't meet mine. "We could go all over. To Paris, perhaps. It's been a long time since I've been, but I've connections there. It would be different, of course, but we could share that adventure, Lily. Would you like that?"

At last, he looked up again, and the dispirited look in his eyes didn't surprise me.

I tightened my hand around the bag's strap, wishing I could ignore how quickly his enthusiasm disappeared the moment he stopped talking. I knew he was trying to soothe me—to dispel the awkwardness and distrust that had wedged its way between us.

Because he's lonely, I thought. *He doesn't want me to hate him.*

"Get better soon then," I said. "We'll be waiting."

But I didn't say it as a happy response; I said it to challenge him because I suspected that he was lying again—simply saying the words he knew I wanted most to hear. And yet, in that moment, silently, naively, a little part of me believed them. For just a second, my heart fluttered eagerly, and the happiness I felt was pure and warm.

When I left the room, he was smiling, but I couldn't help

wondering what expression he wore after I'd closed the door, after he knew I couldn't see him, after he removed the mask that gave him that lifeless smile ...

I thought he must've looked dead.

LILY

I woke smiling and stretched over my bed, spreading my toes and fingers and twisting my back. When, at last, I exhaled a satisfied moan, I was fully awake. My eyes didn't burn and droop and blink with tiredness, I didn't flop over and bury my face in my pillows to block out the light and noise, and I didn't hesitate to throw off my quilts and jump out of the warmth they dutifully supplied. This morning was different. Today, I woke with a renewed vigour for life.

Stepping into my slippers, I pulled on my housecoat, peering out the window. The rising sun shone through the trees, the sky a mix of white and blue, and I could see the moon in the daytime again. It was nearly full now. I wondered if Father was looking at it, too.

I'd dreamt of travel and adventure, of distant places and Father's healthy face smiling at me. He'd been unwell for the last few days and had asked me not to visit him. I'd reluctantly obeyed. But today was different, and I couldn't seem to quell my determination to speak with him.

Somehow, I'd found myself believing his promise, and my mind gushed with questions about the places we would see.

How were the people like? And the food! Would I like it? What method of travel would we use? I'd been on a train but never a boat. I hoped it was a boat. I'd always wanted to go on a boat.

I combed my fingers through my hair as I hastened down the stairs. I paused on the landing and twirled round before descending the last flight, giddy and smiling, but when I reached the last step, I slowed.

It wasn't sudden, but I suddenly became aware of it. Like a flower wilts beneath the bitter frost of fall, gradually overtaken by the cold, my excitement was fettered. A familiar feeling swelled in me as I crossed the foyer—an unsettling feeling I realised had been building since that rainy night a stranger appeared in our home.

It was that same overwhelming feeling of dread, bringing with it a coldness that started in the pit of my stomach and seeped out into my limbs. My muscles tightened against it, and I shivered, though the hall was warm from the heat of the kitchen on the far end of the corridor.

Finally, I stopped outside the sickroom door—the very same door I'd been ready to burst through only a few minutes earlier—and I faltered. The house seemed eerily quiet.

Had I woken earlier than I'd thought again? The sun was up. Surely, Madame Renoir or the maids had risen with it. Bennett always woke before dawn to begin meal preparations. The house should've been bustling with the sounds of waking, but instead, it smothered me with silence.

Steeling my nerves, I breathed in and pushed the door open.

I didn't enter. I stood very still, peering inside.

The frost, at last, overcame me, my whole body devoid of internal heat, and I felt certain it would stop my heart. But it only beat harder, louder, dulling even the sound of my ragged breathing.

I studied the room and knew exactly what had happened,

though I didn't react the way I thought I would. I'd imagined my response before, of course, in those little moments when I saw how nearly dead he was, but it didn't play out the same. I simply stayed still and silent and cold. At once, numb.

Roderick Howell was a liar.

Some little part of my brain told me I should've expected this. At the very least, I should've registered it as a possibility, but even when I pictured my reaction, I don't think I ever truly believed it would happen.

The worst was over. He was getting better. He would recover soon. He'd said so himself. He'd told me what we'd do when he got better. We were going to travel and see new places together!

And yet ...

For a time, I wondered what the appropriate response was. Should I have been startled and surprised and sad and screaming? I wasn't certain I was capable of any emotion at all. Whatever scream might've been waiting to be released was like a knot in my throat. I simply remained where I was, anchored in the doorway by the sight of death and the fetid smell of vomit —by his body's last unsuccessful attempt to purge him of the poison.

And then, I thought: *Maybe this isn't real. Maybe I'm dreaming. Maybe he never actually returned at all, and I've just been imagining and rehearsing the conversations we'll have and the grievances I'll lay out for him if he ever comes back. Maybe none of this is real. None of it at all.*

But I was a liar, too.

My breath lodged itself in my chest, like my airway had been pinched between two fingers, and when, at last, the air burst through its constraint, the strength in my legs left with it. Immediately, I drew another breath. In and out, one after the other as my head dizzied. I gripped the doorframe. My stomach seemed to quiver, my muscles aching with the effort and the strictness with which I held myself.

Everyone else in the world was bereft of this knowledge. No one else could confirm the death of Roderick Howell, except me, and I thought maybe—maybe if I just stood there and didn't say a word and didn't cry or shout or react at all— I could keep it a secret. Maybe no one else would have to know.

I didn't want anyone else to know.

But some cruel god or spirit or devil was laughing at me. Some force had stirred my brother from his bed far earlier than the boy ever woke, and suddenly, he was there behind me, saying my name through a yawn. I hadn't even heard him approach.

My whole body seized up.

Look down, Lily. Don't look at him. Breathe. In and out. Don't look at him. Pretend you didn't hear. Step back and close the door.

But my shaking hand rattled the doorknob.

Breathe. Don't look at him. Don't cry. Hold it together, Lily.

It was that simple, right? If I closed the door and forced a smile and didn't cry, Liam wouldn't have to know, right?

But I couldn't go forever without speaking. I didn't know how long it'd been since he'd called to me, and I had yet to answer.

'Father's sleeping. Don't worry. Let's not burden him with company now.'

I was my father's daughter. I was a liar. It should be so easy to slide those words from my tongue, but I wasn't so practised as Mr. Howell was. And such a big lie would be quite a mouthful for someone who could hardly breathe, let alone choke past the lump in her throat to scream.

But the seconds ticked away as I contemplated.

Liam said my name again, louder, firmer, and when I still

couldn't manage an answer, he raised his voice, which I didn't expect.

"Lily!"

I looked up, but it was a grave error. The moment our eyes met, the secret came bursting out of me. My next breath fled my lips, my chest sank inward, and tears filled my eyes, and no matter how hard I gasped and coughed, trying to hold them in, I couldn't.

It was a secret that would be impossible to keep.

And Liam knew.

I wanted to scream. I wanted to curse myself for my silence.

Why couldn't I do it? Why only then did the numbness release me, thrusting me back into awareness, confused and shaky and tingling at the fingertips?

Seeing Liam was all it took. That innocent curiosity—the complete ignorance of tragedy—on my brother's face thawed my heart until it could again process the emotions I should feel.

What devilry was this?

I tried weakly to stop him from entering the room, but he saw, though his eyes didn't linger for more than a heartbeat. He swung around and crashed into me, smashing his face into my shoulder. I stared over his head, back into the room. I looked everywhere except at Mr. Howell, and it only took me a second to see it on the table: the empty bottle.

The *precaution*.

I could tell it was empty. The glow of the morning sun shone through the tinted glass.

'What is this? What's it for?'

I guess that's what.

But that was a secret I could keep—one I could spare my brother from. I placed a hand on the back of his head and held him there, shielding him, both of us rocking in time with his sobs. The sounds of his despair echoed in the corridor. Someone would hear soon; it was only a matter of time before we were discovered.

I stroked Liam's hair as he cried against my breast, waiting, gazing into the room of the man who'd given me a new dream and then dashed it away.

The fiery drive I'd felt upon waking flickered weakly and went out, but it was quickly replaced with a new feeling, something foreign to me.

And what a bitter feeling it was.

JASPER

I slipped through the trees with my hood pulled down over my forehead to cover my hair. I'd finally returned to Earth after a few weeks' absence, but for the fifth day in a row, Bridget reported that our target wasn't there. The young boy she'd revealed herself to seemed to have vanished, and since it was far easier for me to approach other humans than it was for her, I decided to have a look myself.

But when I arrived, wading through the thicket at the edge of the lawn, I had to quickly duck behind a little copse of trees, fearing, for a moment, that I'd been seen already. The house was bustling with people. It wasn't simply the occupants; there were men, women, carriages with horses, and a whole mess of foot attendants gathered on the lawn, ready to parade down the streets.

Someone here had passed to the world of the dead. I'd studied this part of Earth and its customs enough to recognise a funeral procession.

Confident that I hadn't yet been spotted, I crouched and crept closer, staying in the tree line, scanning every youthful face for the boy's, though there were few children. But people were gathering still, and I could see the shadows of figures flashing across the windows of the house.

It was a garish congregation.

Everyone wore black, including the horses. They had decorative blankets on their backs and plumes of tall black feathers on their heads. The poor things whinnied and stamped their feet in place, tossing their heads and trying to free themselves of the headdresses but unsuccessfully. The animals in this place couldn't speak against their mistreatment. They just struggled tiredly in their reigns, and the attendants ignored them.

The feathers were a staple in this ceremony's decoration, I noticed. They were on hats and fans, and they covered the top of one of the carriages—a long, flat thing I watched them load the coffin into for transportation. I frowned. They really weren't in good taste, the feathers, but at least everything matched. I wondered if they had some special property I hadn't learnt about.

The driver stirred the horses, and they obeyed, marching forward and taking the silly-looking carriage with them. As soon as it rolled out of the way, another replaced it, and when I turned to see whose carriage it was, without looking for him, I found the boy. But to my surprise, he wasn't alone.

He walked hand in hand with a young woman. She was older than him but far too young to be his mother or a governess, though the similarities in their faces implied a relation. His sister, I decided.

But as my eyes lingered on her, the boy, once again, seemed to vanish from my sight. Among this mass of darkly-clad people, she stood out, though not for the reasons one usually differs from a crowd. She was far from the most elegant woman there, nor was she the most handsome. Her steps didn't carry the light-footed gracefulness one expected of an accomplished young lady, and in fact, her features had a rather boyish look about them.

While every other woman in attendance cried in that giddy, practised way—dabbing their eyes with their little lace handkerchiefs—the young woman, alone, bore an expression of tired indifference. She peered ahead dispassionately as they walked, occasionally throwing a stern sideways glance at the showiness around them. Even the horses with their feather-plumed heads were met with her disdain.

I slunk through the trees, shadowing their movement.

That this girl was so dismissive in the face of death bothered me. The procession was clearly beginning at their home, so it must've been a close relative. But that expression on her face suggested otherwise, and because I couldn't make sense of it, I couldn't seem to look away.

I watched her curiously as she and her brother shuffled down the path until, finally, I was near enough to see their faces clearly. And I did see them but only for a second before a servant approached to draw the black veil down over the girl's face, darkening it and hiding her expression. Consolingly, the maid touched the young woman's arm, but the gesture was promptly shrugged off.

My heartbeat quickened as the two siblings disappeared inside the carriage, and the door was fastened behind them.

That glimpse had done nothing to ease my confusion; if anything, it added to it greatly. For a moment, I'd seen not simply indifference but a quiet, burning fury in the girl's eyes— a visible disgust for the individual who'd left this world and forced her to be a part of this ostentatious occasion.

The boy, of course, was customarily sad, but the girl ... She was angry.

How very peculiar, I thought, but also: *how perfect.*

Because the girl, although puzzling, wasn't the reason I'd

come. The boy was my target, and this disparity between him and his sister would aid me immensely. He would feel detached—alienated, even—from his family, especially this cold-hearted girl who did not seem capable of sharing his sadness. And that would make it so much easier to promise him an escape—respite in a faraway land, untouched by grief. Perhaps it was a cruel way to lure someone in, but I never claimed morality. This would surely guarantee my success, and yet ...

I watched the carriage leave, realising that I'd been standing in full view of the passing vessel, though it mattered little. My black cloak blended in, and everyone was too disconcerted to notice one more plain stranger among the crowd. I stared after the carriage until the remaining mourners came nearer to join the caravan. Then, I sank back into the trees and out of sight.

PART FOUR
THE MEETING

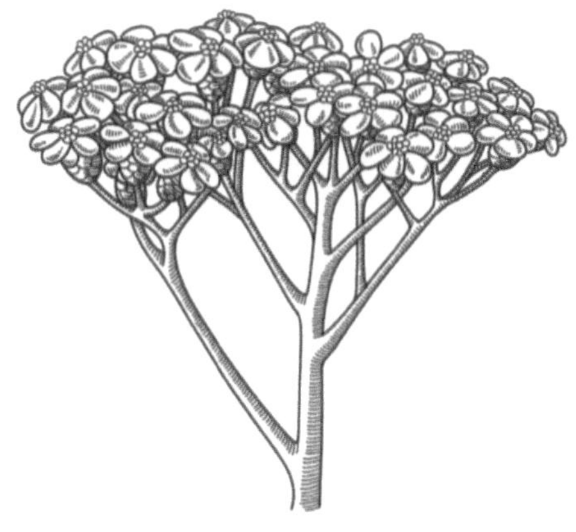

LILY

"Well, come on then," I said, arching an expectant brow at my brother. "Have you got it or not?"

Liam and I sat cross-legged between twin rows of tomato plants, the midday sun hot on our faces. His lips pinched tightly together, he rolled his eyes and opened his knapsack, procuring a salt cellar he'd thieved from the kitchen.

I grinned. "Good." It seemed he wasn't completely useless after all.

"I don't see why you made *me* get it," he huffed. "Bennett will be cross when he realises it's missing."

"*If* he realises, Liam," I corrected, scanning the rows on either side of us.

"He'll notice. You know he will."

I shrugged and picked a large bright red tomato. "This one's perfect," I said, smiling at my find. "Ripe but still firm. I think I've an eye for this sort of thing."

"Oh, good. Seems we've found your talent at last. You'll make an excellent gardener."

"Don't be snide, Liam; that's servants' work."

"Fine. Please accept my sincerest apologies," he said,

though the tonelessness of his voice didn't support his apparent sincerity. "I'm certain such an impressive talent will rocket you into high society and attract the perfect husband—one with a fondness for vegetables, of course."

I reached over and yanked the salt pot from his hand. "Is there a reason you're being particularly ornery today? Because it's quite a bother."

"Well," he replied, snatching the salt back before I could even get a pinch. "Maybe it's because someone made me steal something—" He gave the container a little shake. "—because she's too—"

"Oh, I didn't *make* you do it, and we only borrowed it. Obviously, we're giving it back. Why on Earth would I want to keep the salt?"

"You blackmailed me!"

"So?"

"So, it isn't fair."

"Life isn't fair, Liam. Best start getting used to it." I stole the pot back. "Y'know what else isn't fair? Your attitude toward me. I'd appreciate a little more civility."

"*I'm* uncivilised?"

"You're the one stealing things."

His mouth gaped open, but he sputtered and didn't argue. After a moment, he muttered, "Manipulating people is pretty uncivilised, too."

"Oh, Liam," I began sympathetically. "How do you think anyone who's anyone got there?" I raised my brows, inviting him to answer but not giving him the time. "By manipulating people." I shrugged. "Anyone with any sense or ambition does it."

"I'm plenty ambitious, and I don't—"

"Sucking up to Miss Sawyer is a form of manipulation."

"I don't—"

"Look, I take stuff from Bennett all the time. You don't. He won't be as cross if you're the one who returns it, we'll both get off with a minor scolding, and Bennett will have his spice. I manipulated our way into a win-win situation." Seasoning my tomato, I sank my teeth in. "Not to mention we get th' benefit of eatin' these delicious, salty tomatoes."

Liam's nose wrinkled. "Don't talk with your mouth full, Lily; it makes you look ugly. The suitors won't care that you can pick a perfect tomato if they see you like that."

I swallowed. "Didn't I tell you to stop being a prat?"

"I was being honest."

Narrowing my eyes into slits, I took another bite, talking as I chewed. "I don' think honesty suits you."

"Too bad it's the only way I know to be."

I tried but failed to hold in my laugh. A fleck of tomato flesh flew from my open mouth and hit my brother's cheek.

"Lily, you—you're so—what're you laughing at?"

Gulping down my last bite, I handed him a ripe tomato and the salt. He took them silently, waiting with a pinched expression for my reply.

"You know you just stole something, right? That's not very honest."

He spoke out of the corner of his mouth. "I thought you said we borrowed it."

"Borrowing without asking isn't honest either."

He abandoned his tomato to cover his face with one hand, dragging it slowly from his forehead to his chin. "You're awful ... Completely. Utterly. Awful."

Shrugging, I said, "Well, it's fine if you think that because I don't bother with opinions from dishonest people."

JASPER

My steps faltered, one foot crossing too far in front of the other. I threw my arms out, groping blindly for the tree. In one more stumbled step, it was within my reach, and I hugged it, straining for breath. Bridget flitted anxiously about my head. I swatted at her and muttered, "I'm fine … Just tired."

Patting the tree appreciatively, I lowered myself to the ground, flopping over to lean on the trunk. My face throbbed, my heartbeat pulsing at the centre of the wound, but already, the dizziness was beginning to subside.

Exhaling, I opened my eyes and peered up at Bridget, expecting to see concern on her little face, but she hovered above me, glowering. Before I could inquire, she shot down and jabbed at the cut on my mouth.

"Ow!" I hissed, jerking back as she swooped up into the air again. "What was that for?" Gingerly, I touched the swollen lump on my bottom lip and checked my fingers to see if the split had opened again. No blood. I glared at the tiny woman. "Okay, I'm not totally fine. Are you happy now? You don't have to reopen it to prove a point, for Spirits' sakes."

But even scolding her felt like a chore. My body ached. My eyes felt heavy. Before the fairy could do anything else, I shrank down and nestled myself between the roots of the tree, but she wouldn't let me sleep. She pulled my hair and poked my cheek and forehead.

"Go away. I'm so tired," I groaned, waving my hand aimlessly over my head. "We're here for a reason. Go check on the boy." But I could still feel the fluttering of her wings beside my face. "Go!" I snapped, and at last, she withdrew.

Carefully, I rolled onto my side, curling my legs up to my chest. Then, without my asking, the old oak tree fitted itself for my comfort. A tuft of moss blossomed at the base, softening the bark beneath my head, the roots rising from the ground and gently arching around my body. Sleepily, I flattened my palm against the earth, grateful for the Spirits' ever watchful eyes.

"Thank you," I whispered and drifted to sleep.

I closed one eye and peeked through the pickets, trying to look around the hedge creatures at the terrace. Madame Renoir had smoked her cigar until there was nearly nothing left and now sat slouched in a chair in a deep sleep, her head bowed forward with her chins piled on her bosom.

She was meant to be watching us, of course, but since Mr. Howell's passing, our mother had begun to require the nurse's nightly care and attention.

Initially, Liam's observation that Mother was unhappy about her husband's return had surprised me, but as the days wore on, I found myself agreeing with him.

She'd grown more reclusive, even neglecting to visit Mr. Howell at all during the week prior to his passing, but her act of devastation after had been quite thrilling. She'd put on an elaborate show at the funeral, but to someone that knew her, the emotion felt stiff. I imagined she'd practised and perfected it over the years so she could truly embody the tragic widow she'd always meant to portray.

There was no way of knowing if her reaction had been real or not, and really, it didn't matter. We'd barely seen her since the funeral. But without her looming presence keeping watch over our daily activities (and with our chaperone often indisposed), Liam and I were free to spend our time as we liked, with only the exception of our regular lessons with Miss Sawyer.

Sighing, I reached for the salt, wiggling my fingers, waiting for my brother to stop being inconsiderate and hand it to me.

"Excuse me." Liam didn't answer, and I glanced up to see his back turned. I raised my volume. "Excuse me, Liam."

Still nothing.

"Liam!"

"What?" He didn't even look.

"Salt please."

"Just a second …" He picked up the salt cellar, stretching his arm behind him to pass it to me, but before it reached my hand, he dropped it in alarm. It thudded on the ground, spilling a little white stream in the dirt.

"Oi, could you please pay attention to what you're—"

"Bridget!"

I internally groaned. No doubt one of his grubby little friends had arrived, though I couldn't quite recall him ever knowing one called—

I froze. "Who?"

Liam ignored me, grinning at the plants he held parted with both hands. "It's been an age! Where've you been?"

I scrambled over to him, shoving my way into the row, and when I saw the reason for his fervor, my breath caught in my throat. Floating above a stunted plant was a winged woman no bigger than the length of my hand. I stared, slack-jawed.

Grumbling, Liam jabbed his elbow into my ribs and said halfheartedly, "Bridget, this is my sister, Lily. You remember her from last time, don't you?"

The fairy nodded, peering from his face to mine and back again, flapping her wings to keep herself in the air.

"Wow," I muttered, leaning in.

"Is that really all you've got to say? Where're your manners, Lily?"

"Wow ..."

"There are loads of options. 'Nice to meet you' or 'it's a pleasure' or perhaps simply 'how d'you do?' Any of those would be appropriate."

I sat back on my heels, blinking as if waking from a dream, but there the fairy remained, gazing up at me with a docile expression on her tiny face.

"Honestly, I'm awe-struck. I can't believe you were telling the truth."

"Hey!" Liam swung around, trying to manoeuver himself so we were face to face. "I thought you said you believed me!"

"Oh." I waved him away; his uncommonly round head was blocking my view of the fairy. "Come on, Liam," I said, moving to see around him. "We both know I only said that so you wouldn't feel bad."

"But—"

With a huff I gave up trying to look past him and let him have my attention, dramatically dropping my shoulders. "Well, it made you feel better, didn't it?" Liam glared. "And I believe you now obviously, so it's fine, right?"

His brows lowered, creasing between them. Then he blew out a loud exhale and, finally, agreed. "I suppose so ..."

"See?" I smiled, slapping him reassuringly on the back. He pitched forward. "Everything's fine. Honestly, you should commend me for being such a good sister. Most wouldn't lie to your face just to spare your feelings."

Liam's eyes nearly rolled to the back of his head. "Oh, of course. Do forgive me. I forgot to ask the queen to knight you for such a selfless gesture."

My smile became a sneer. "A parade will do," I replied. "Oh, and make it peacock feathers this time, won't you? Those black ostrich ones were dreadful."

That slapped the sarcasm out of him.

"That's not funny, Lily ... You really are horrendous, you know that?" Naturally, I ignored him until he wrinkled his nose, pursed his lips, and chatted on to no one in particular. "If all girls are like you, then I never want to get married."

I shot him a cautionary look, but the fairy distracted me. She kept looking over her shoulder at the woods, her face pinched as though she were annoyed or concerned. It was difficult to tell with such small features, and of course, it was possible that fairies expressed their emotions differently than we did. How should I know?

"Well," Liam babbled on, "I suppose all girls can't be like that because Bridget's a girl, and she's very kind. And Sophie, that French girl who lives down the road is quite lovely, too." He paused to thoughtfully scratch his head. "Come to think of it," he muttered, "I haven't seen her in a while ... Oh, and there's—"

"Liam, are you talking to yourself?"

I couldn't have him thinking too far into his friend's absence. The fact that he hadn't seen her was a bad sign. I really hoped she hadn't gone off and died or something. That would be unfortunate for Liam as he'd have to find a new friend to replace her.

Sighing, I reached over to comfortingly pat his shoulder, though he didn't seem to understand why I offered my sympathy. He shrugged my hand off.

"I didn't think I was talking to myself, but you obviously weren't listening."

"It's nothing personal," I said, matter-of-factly. "It's just that, occasionally, I find you vastly uninteresting." I saw his face begin to redden and quickly guided his attention toward the fairy. "Especially when there are far more interesting things to pay attention to."

He frowned but didn't dispute.

Still, the tiny woman seemed uneasy, and Liam and I watched her, puzzled. She parted her hair in the back and pulled some over each shoulder, stroking it with anxious hands as she lowered herself to a tomato leaf. It bowed with her weight, dipping toward the ground, but she'd hardly stopped her wings before she leapt up again. Standing balanced on top of the stalk, she peered up at us with an alarmingly wide smile that nearly stretched from ear to ear.

I arched a brow, drawing back. Her sudden shift in temper seemed devious, but Liam moved closer, ignorant of the slyness I saw in her grin. In all the stories I'd read, fairies were not to be trusted.

Wings quivering, Bridget jumped up and caught the air, swooping toward my brother, tugging his sleeve and pointing behind her at the forest. Liam turned to me.

"I-I think she wants us to go with her."

She released him and nodded frantically, flying higher. I considered the idea, knowing she must have something mischievous in store for us, but it didn't take long for curiosity to win me over.

"All right," I said, abandoning my suspicion. "Let's go then."

Instantly, panic shook my brother's voice. "Huh? B-but—" he protested as I stood and dusted off my dress. He scratched his cheek.

I'd already resolved to follow her, so I couldn't back down now. When would we ever have a chance like this again?

"What's the harm?" I asked. "It can't be anything worse than a stray tomcat."

Besides, the more I thought about it, the more I realised it had been silly of me to have any hesitation at all. I mean, we couldn't just *not* follow a fairy when asked. It was a *fairy*. Did Liam not get that? Did he not realise we'd stumbled upon something that, by all accounts, shouldn't exist outside works of fiction? *It was a barking fairy*!

But he didn't get it.

"Well, w-what about Madame Renoir?"

I stole a backwards glance at the terrace. The old woman hadn't moved an inch. "She's dead asleep and will be for some time I imagine."

But still, he wavered. "What about our lessons?" he asked, as though our schooling was actually more important than finding a fairy (which it wasn't).

Already exhausted with him, I jadedly asked, "What about them, Liam?"

"They begin in half an hour!"

"So?"

"We can't just skip them."

Heaving a breath through my nose, I reached over his shoulder to pinch the base of his neck and steer his line of sight back to Bridget, who stood on a nearby fencepost with her arms crossed. Even she didn't have the patience for my brother's indecisiveness.

"Come on, Liam, where's your sense of adventure? You're being far too blasé about this. It's a fairy. A fai-ry. Do you understand what I'm saying?"

"Of course, I understand, but what if—"

"Honestly, whatever it is, it can't take long, right? And if we are late coming back, I'll take all the blame, okay? Promise."

His expression slackened, everything falling but his brows, which arched in surprise. "Really? You'll take the blame?"

I frowned. "Sarcasm isn't very becoming, Liam."

"I find it hard to believe you'd take the blame for anything."

I pushed his face back toward Bridget, leaning closer to

whisper in his ear. I'd found that people pay better attention to soft voices; it takes more effort, and they expect to hear things of importance, like intimate words and secrets.

"Liam," I said gravely, "I know you're curious, and I know you want to go. Stop letting all of Mum and Miss Sawyer's lectures about 'right and wrong' and 'knowing your priorities' cloud your judgement."

"I wouldn't really call it clouding …"

"Liam!"

"Fine! But I will not be getting in trouble on your account. Is that clear?"

Satisfied, I released my grip on his neck. "Honestly, when have I ever gotten you into trouble?"

Although my question had clearly been playfully asked, there wasn't even the hint of a smirk on his mouth when he replied, "Are you sure you want to ask me that?"

I pursed my lips. "Women don't like rudeness, Liam."

"Well, you're not a woman; you're my sister."

"Time's wasting."

Exiting the fence, I stole one last glance at our sleeping chaperone, hitched up my skirt, and together, Liam and I stepped into the forest and took off running after the fairy.

JASPER

I woke gasping, a sudden shout shocking me into awareness. I jerked and kicked my legs out.

"No!" I cried. "Get away!"

I leapt to my feet, floundering, the sudden movement disorienting me. My head swam. It felt heavy. My knees buckled, and I nearly fell. I reached for the tree with both hands, leaning my forehead against the rough bark.

Get ahold of yourself. Breathe.

Swallowing, I felt the ache in my swollen lip again and squeezed my eyes shut as if that might relieve some of the pain or dizziness. I waited for the attack to continue, but when I heard no movement and felt no blow, I realised that I hadn't been attacked at all but rather stumbled upon.

I gripped the tree, already embarrassed to think that someone had witnessed such an excessive reaction and even more so at the thought of turning to face them. Being awoken suddenly wouldn't frighten a normal person so much. But as I steadied my breathing and my mind gained more clarity, I knew exactly who it must be and relaxed.

It was those damned kids from the village. I could never

seem to get away from them unscathed. I'd barely spent any time in this part of the forest, and already, the local youths had managed to make a game of giving me grief. No doubt at least one of them had come to pester me, but I had no patience to spend on them today. I was too tired, too on edge, my face still throbbing and my body tender from whatever other damage I'd managed to acquire.

I made to turn, but my head felt too heavy for my neck to support. I leaned into the tree trunk again and groaned, more out of annoyance than pain.

"Spirits ..." I muttered. "How am I supposed to get any rest with a bunch of noisy arses tramping all over the place?"

I hadn't expected an answer at all, but the one I received fell even farther from my expectations. I didn't hear the innocent, teasing voices of children. In fact, it wasn't a voice I'd heard before at all, nor did it belong to a boy.

"Excuse me?" it said incredulously, and I flinched. I turned my head, peering over my shoulder to see the owner of that snappy alto, and in an instant, my heart was racing.

It was her.

It was the girl from the funeral—the angry girl who now directed that anger at me and stared daggers at my person from where she stood a few paces behind me.

I was arrested in place, my lungs filling in a gasp but not emptying.

I hadn't been wrong. She'd captivated me at the funeral, and she did still, though in a different way. Now that I saw her plainly in the full midday light, her burning eyes in contrast to the softness of her face struck me. I exhaled, blinking because I didn't know what to say. My cheeks grew hot, my palms starting to sweat. I lifted them from the tree and wiped them on my shirt, at last fully turning to face her. But the wild beating of my heart and the sudden warmth flushing through me wouldn't cease.

Something was wrong with me. The injury to my face had been worse than I thought. I was dying. Or maybe I was sick. I did feel a little queasy. A sudden flu? I'd been spending far too much time on Earth and had been afflicted with their plague from one of those damned kids.

Then again, I'd endured so many head injuries that I couldn't be sure if this girl truly was standing in front of me or if I was dreaming. I pressed the heels of my hands into my eyes, giving my head a little shake, but another shout brought me back to reality.

"Lily!" a voice cried, and her brother bounded out of the trees, hardly glancing at me as he rushed to her side. "Gosh, Lily, are you all right?" He touched her forehead as if she'd suddenly contracted a fever. She smacked his hand away.

Lowering my own hands, I observed them silently, pleased that I could, at last, put a name to the face of the angry girl. *Lily*, he'd called her. At first, I thought such a pretty name didn't suit her at all, but I couldn't think of one that would.

Lily it is then, I thought and committed it to memory.

Liam, whose name I knew already, gave Lily one more assessing glance, and then they both turned toward me. I saw exactly the same difference in personalities that I'd seen at the funeral. While he appeared timid, she stared at me with nothing short of disgust, her brow furrowed, her lips pursed, her eyes thinning as she studied me.

Perhaps she hadn't liked what I'd called them. Perhaps she hadn't realised that my words hadn't been meant for her.

And here I stood, gaping and flustered because I'd unknowingly called an attractive girl a noisy arse.

She really did have an appealing look about her, I thought.

It was a strange sort of attractiveness—her large eyes and smoothly angled face. Unconventional but unmistakable.

Then I swallowed and coughed, glancing between the two of them and wondering how long I'd been mindlessly staring at her. I cleared my throat, faced her brother, and wiped my palm on my shirt again before extending a hand. "I-I'm sorry, I must've—"

"Don't touch him!"

I stopped, slowly pulling my arm back. Lily glared at me. Whatever patience she had seemed to be waning and quickly. I narrowed my eyes a little, unsure what to do or say to appease her, but it was her brother's reaction that intrigued me. He slid an arm around one of hers and gave a gentle tug, trying to coax her back.

"Look," Lily said. "I don't know who you think you are, but wherever you're trying to get to, this isn't it."

I frowned. "Pardon?"

"This is our land. You're trespassing."

"Lily, please—"

"Trespassing?" I cast my eyes around the area. "We're in the woods." But turning my head was too much. I tried to ignore the turbulence, but I saw double. "Spirits ..." I covered my face with one hand and grabbed the tree with the other.

"Are you even listening to me?" the girl snarled, stamping her foot.

"Lily," I heard the boy whisper. "I-I think he's hurt."

"Yes, I can see that, Liam."

"If you can see it, then—"

"Ugh! Fine," she moaned, drowning out her brother's meek voice. I dropped my hand to see her coming toward me, but her two feet blurred into four. I shook my head to right the image. Too quickly. Pain burned, the pressure gathering at the front of my skull. I squeezed my eyes shut and heard the girl's footsteps cease.

The tone of her voice changed. "A-Are you okay?"

I clutched my stomach, feeling like I might be sick, though I tried to fight past the dizzying ache to answer her.

"I'm fine," I insisted firmly, and when she reached toward me, I impulsively smacked her hand away, not wanting her to come too close. "Don't." But then I stiffened, my eyes widening with the realisation of what I'd done. She was at least attempting to be courteous, and I'd rejected it without a moment's thought. "No, w-wait," I stammered. "I didn't mean—I'm sorry. I—"

The girl's face flushed deep red. "Excuse me? I'm trying to— even though you're—you're not at all where you're supposed to be, and even so, I was only—"

"No, please—" I felt the tightness and nausea surge through my stomach and nearly retched. "I have to go," I managed, spinning around, swallowing the sour taste in my mouth.

Lily recovered from her fluster. "Go? Go where? There isn't anywhere around for you to go."

"You—" I swallowed tightly again. "You just said I was trespassing, so I'll leave, okay. I didn't know."

"I'm not finished with you yet!" she snapped, then almost immediately, her voice hushed. "Besides," she added hesitantly, "you look like you need help."

"I don't," I shot back.

"But your lip, it's—you're bleeding."

I touched my face and looked down at the red on my fingers. "Shit ..." I muttered, wiping my chin and mouth on my sleeve.

"F-forgive us, sir," Liam said, tugging Lily's arm. "We'll be leaving. We're terribly sorry for bothering you. C'mon, let's go."

"Bothering him? I was trying to help!" Untangling herself from her brother's grip, Lily shooed him away and stuck her hands on her hips. "Fine, we'll leave, but before we do, you've something to say to us."

I raised a brow.

"Well?" she said.

"Sorry, but ... what was I saying?"

"You were about to apologise to us."

"Lily!"

I leaned on the tree, breathing heavily. "Was I?"

"Yes, for being rude."

"No, it's fine, sir," Liam insisted, but she shushed him.

"I—" I rubbed my temple. "I don't think I was."

She looked dead at me, flabbergasted.

Was that it?

Would a simple apology make her leave?

I wondered, and yet, I wasn't entirely sure I wanted her to. I had no explanation for this strange desire—maybe I simply wanted to observe the two of them more—but I thought I knew how to stop them going.

"I don't think I need to apologise."

All the muscles in her face sagged at once, apart from the ones that held her eyes in a glare; they tightened. "What?"

I almost smirked I was so amused by the exchange—by how her ire flared so easily. "You heard me," I replied.

This could be interesting.

"What?" she said again.

Fun, even.

I bit the inside of my cheek, trying to will away the dull pain in my head. Finally, something different was happening; I didn't want it spoiled by some silly injury.

"I was only sleeping. You're the one who came crashing through the woods without any mind to your surroundings. It's not my fault you weren't paying attention and got a fright. I've every right to be startled after being awoken in such a way."

"Well, I think it's rather rude to go around shouting at people without reason."

"There was a reason, and it was hardly a shout."

"Well, you—you may be in the woods, but it's still part of our estate."

I considered that for a moment, hearing the fluster trill its way back into her voice, then lowered my own voice and said, "Forgive me, I didn't realise I was trespassing. It's a hot afternoon, and I was tired. I thought I'd take a nap as I was passing through."

Instantly, she quieted. I'd surprised her. As easy as it was to get a rise out of her, disarming her instead was remarkably satisfying. I wanted to see what other emotions I could bring to her face.

"Y-you're sorry?"

"I am. I was just on my way through. I didn't know I was on anyone's land. Everything is so spread out here."

"Oh." She swallowed, her eyes dropping to the ground and her cheeks reddening. "Then," she said softly, "you are forgiven."

Embarrassment suited her, too.

"Thank you." I squatted down in front of the tree, my back against the trunk.

"But—" She recovered. "Not for calling us names! You're not forgiven for that, so don't misunderstand."

I peered up at her, and this time, I couldn't hide my smirk. "Well, you're not forgiven for waking me so rudely."

Her lip twisted up. "And why should I apologise if you won't?"

"I apologised for what I saw fit."

"Well, I never—"

"Lily, please. We need to go; we'll be late."

But something told me they wouldn't be leaving just yet.

Already, my flippant behaviour was luring her in, and my heartbeat quickened with nervous excitement as an idea crept into my mind.

My original intention had only been the boy, but what if—just this once—I tried for two instead of one?

The smile on my face grew.

Bridget had brought me something good, after all.

LIAM

I could see the veins in Lily's hands, her knuckles white from holding her fists so tightly, and I feared she might leap out and grab the poor boy around the neck.

He hadn't really meant to insult us, of course. I could tell that much from the surprise on his face when he'd turned around. I suspected he'd thought someone else had come gallivanting through the woods and disturbed him, perhaps someone familiar to him—someone who'd done it before. I was certain he would've explained and apologised had he been given the chance. It seemed like he'd been about to before Lily started shouting.

But I noticed something peculiar about the way the young man spoke to her. One minute, he'd seemed a bit harsh, then the next, calm, his voice and manner switching from sarcastic to placid with ease.

He was teasing her, poking and prodding to see how he could make her squirm. And already, he'd succeeded. She reacted in exactly the way he intended her to.

I couldn't help thinking that Lily deserved it, nor could I

help feeling oddly pleased that this stranger could read her so quickly and meet her attitude with equal might.

She threw her arms up. "Who sleeps in the woods anyhow?"

The boy sank back against the tree, resting his hands on his knees. He copied Lily's contemptuous snort.

"Who are you that you think you can stick your prissy little nose into other people's business?"

That did it. Her composure was lost.

Her jaw dropped, and she started to squeal, "How dare y—" before I managed to slap my hand over her mouth. I knew I'd get an earful about it later, but I had to intervene before she got really ugly. I'd just tell her I was trying to salvage her good reputation among men, and she might absolve me.

"I-I'm really very sorry," I said to the boy, fighting to keep Lily quiet. "Y'see, my sister and I were taking a walk, and we lost our way. She's just gotten a bit overexcited is all. She forgot her parasol, and I think the sun's affecting—" But I wasn't able to finish. Lily dug her nails into my fingers and pried my hand off her face.

"I am *not* overexcited! That little twat called me an arse!"

"Lily, please—" I tried, though I knew pleading was pointless.

She rounded on me. "Honestly, Liam, have you no pride? He insulted you, too! Are you gonna put up with that?"

I sucked in my lips, pressing them together to keep from yelling back at her. Her anger usually prevented any good brain function outside of the part that controlled her inflated emotions, so she paid no mind to my discomfort or embarrassment. But I didn't want to stoop to her level.

Drawing in a deep breath, I pushed out my chest and replied, "Yes, I am, and so are you. You've clearly unsettled him." But then Lily gave me that look—that penetrating stare that reduced my short-winded courage to fear—and as my lungs emptied and my chest deflated, I glanced sideways, lacing and unlacing my fingers. "I-I think you ..." My voice shrank, but I forced the words out. "I think you ought to apologise."

She looked at me like I'd thrown a handful of worms at her. "Me?"

Timidly, I nodded.

She opened her mouth, jabbing a finger at me, but the boy spoke first.

"Thank you, Liam. An apology would be most welcome."

When we heard my name, Lily and I both turned, surprised. He smiled, his brows arched in expectation.

"Don't speak to him with such familiarity! How rude!"

He addressed me without any reaction to Lily's rebuke. "Forgive me, but do you mind, sir? I fear I've made a mistake. We've not been properly introduced."

Even I was taken aback at his sudden politeness. I'd expected someone who would sleep outside to be more ... crude, perhaps? Uneducated? But the boy spoke eloquently when he wanted to, and I couldn't help wondering if he was making fun or if he truly belonged to a higher society than his appearance suggested.

"I-I don't mind," I replied, and Lily clicked her tongue.

The young man's eyes darted back to her face, watching her with that mild expression. "Sorry, did you have something to add?"

I squeezed my eyes shut, waiting for her to fire back, but I heard something else instead. As though everything around me was muffled the moment I closed my eyes, I heard ...

A laugh?

I blinked.

It didn't come from Lily, and I didn't think it was the boy. In fact, the noise had been so soft that I wasn't sure I'd heard it at all. It was a distant voice carried on the wind, like someone had shouted far away so that only the whisper of sounds remained. But somehow, I still felt certain I'd heard *something*.

I slid my gaze from the boy to my sister. Neither showed any sign that they'd heard, too, though they were so engrossed in each other—their eyes locked in a silent standoff—that I suspected they'd all but forgotten about me.

I closed my eyes again, straining to listen, and there it was!

An airy, almost coy giggle.

My eyes snapped back open in time to see Lily bending her lips around a word, but I shushed her before she could speak, waving my hands in a frantic gesture to quiet her. She gawked at me, but I ignored it, turning my head to try to discern from which direction the noise originated.

"Liam, did you just—?"

"Shh!" I hissed, but the sound was gone, replaced by my sister's annoyed moan.

"Liam, I swear—"

"Did you hear that?" I asked, spinning in a quick circle to see if I might catch it. "That noise?"

I wasn't sure why I felt so keen to discover its origin, only that I did. I didn't just want to know; I longed to know. I *needed* to know. But Lily didn't hear it, nor did she seem to understand that I required her to be silent for once in her life so I'd be able to hear it when it came again.

She rolled her eyes. "Liam, this is not the time!"

But the boy's expression darkened.

"What kind of noise?" he asked, knitting his brow.

I gulped. "I—I dunno really. Like a laugh maybe?"

"Ignore it," the boy said firmly before I'd even finished.

"What makes you think you've any right to tell him what to do?"

The boy lolled his head dramatically to the side to answer her. "Oh, sorry, that's your job, is it?"

I had to force a cough to stifle my laughter, and the boy shot me a sly little grin before Lily stole his attention with the beginning of what was sure to be a long rant about how inappropriate it was for him to speak to her that way.

But I didn't hear what was said because the noise rang out from somewhere to my right. It *was* a laugh.

Neither Lily nor the boy noticed when I stepped away, ducking under the oak's branches, carefully traipsing around its exposed roots toward the bushes beyond it. Then I paused, waiting for the laugh to direct me.

I could hear Lily and the boy bickering as the forest thickened around me, but I tried to shut out their voices. I knew I must be close. The noise grew steadily louder until I reached a small patch of shrubbery, and then, it softened to a doughy coo.

Finally! I thought, but the boy's insistence that I ignore the sound made me hesitate. For a few seconds, my curiosity fought the boy's warning in my head, but the urge was too strong to resist. And anyway, there couldn't be anything dangerous about laughter.

"Hello?" I said, stepping around the bush, leaning forward and craning my neck to look ahead. "Is someone there?"

Initially, I was met with silence, and then, a movement made me jump. My eyes darted around the area until, at last, I found the culprit.

I frowned.

It was only a child squatting down, half-hidden in the thicket. But even obscured, I could tell he was skinny and much too small to be in the woods alone. In fact, this child looked in even worse shape than the boy arguing with my sister. His spine stuck out sharply above his raggedy shirt, dirt or dried blood blotting his skin and clothes.

I considered returning to the meadow to fetch Lily, but I had the sinking feeling the child might run off if I left. And he seemed in desperate need of help.

"Hello," I said again, extending a hand, my fingertips brushing his bony shoulder. "Are you all right?"

"Are you all right?" that little voice echoed me.

"Sorry, are you—?" I began, and before I could finish, he repeated, "Sorry, are you—?" and giggled.

I drew my arm back, a twinge of fear coiling in the pit of my stomach, but it was irrational, wasn't it? I shouldn't worry over a kid's games. Lily used to copy me all the time to annoy me; it was only harmless fun.

Then the child turned around.

LILY

The boy and I both silenced when the scream cut through the air.

It was Liam.

He'd cried out my name.

I spun in a circle, but my brother was nowhere to be found. Frantically, I searched the boy's face, pleading for him to tell me he'd noticed something I hadn't.

Lifting a finger to his lips, he waited for me to nod my understanding. I clasped my hands over my mouth, petrified.

There was no time to waste! Liam was in trouble, but—

But something told me I should trust the young man.

He closed his eyes, breathing deeply through his nose as he sank deeper into his crouch. He flattened his palm against the ground, spreading his fingers and lightly scraping his nails in the dirt.

I chewed my lip, my heart thrashing as Liam howled in the distance.

Logically, I knew only seconds had passed, but it felt like eternity.

I had to do something.

This was urgent.

Liam was in danger.

Steeling my resolve, I lifted a foot, preparing to take a step in any direction, but the ground under my feet heaved, bucking me so suddenly and violently that I nearly fell. The grass moved and the trees quivered, their leaves dancing. Like a wave passed through the earth, the shudder pressed outward until I could no longer see its effect, and I thought that—though I couldn't be certain—that strange pulse had started where the boy crouched with his hand on the ground.

Stiffly, I held my arms out, trying to maintain my balance until the world stilled again, but when I turned to confront him, there was no time to ask. The boy sprang to his feet, stumbling a few clumsy steps before he righted himself and flew off beyond the oak tree.

I meant to follow. I should have. I would have, but my knees locked, suspending me in that first step.

My stomach dropped.

I was powerless.

Liam was in trouble, and I couldn't even bring myself to move.

I should've been paying attention. I should've been looking after my brother. I'd convinced him to go. I should've been watching him. He was only a kid ...

"Damn thing!" I heard the boy shout, and I stood at attention, clutching my chest. "Let go! Let—"

But his voice was drowned by a horrible wail.

It wasn't Liam. It wasn't the boy.

I took a slow step back, my clasped hands trembling in front of my face.

Something was wrong.

The boy came charging back into view, red-faced and puffing. But something else reached me before he did.

I yelped, pouncing backwards, but my shout drew the thing's attention. With a quick, jerking motion, the snarling creature trained its eyes on me, baring its teeth.

My knees felt weak.

It wasn't an animal; it couldn't be because it looked too human, and yet … It wasn't human either. It was shaped like a human, but …

I gulped.

It was small and bent like a child hunkered down, though I knew immediately that likening it to a child was wrong. Only the body was small. It was long-limbed and bony with skin that sagged in places where there might once have been flesh. And it was tall—or it would've been if it stood upright, but it didn't seem to possess the ability. It moved while crouched, thrusting its bent knees out with each step as though the backs of its thighs and calves had been stuck together, binding it in that awkward squat.

It grinned, opening its mouth wide, stretching out its fat lips and biting the air. It was almost as if—

"Oi!" the boy yelled from behind the oak tree. "Don't just stand there! Move!"

The creature growled as it flung a clawed hand at my legs, demanding my attention. Shrieking, I kicked my foot, knocking its arm aside, but my next breath froze in my lungs.

There was blood on its mouth.

Fresh. Red. Blood.

It could only mean one thing: Liam was injured. He was bleeding, and—

"Move!"

But I couldn't. My eyes were locked on the creature's mouth. It smiled at me, sweeping its tongue across its lips as if it knew how disconcerted I was by the blood etched into the cracks of them.

"Damn it all!" The boy trudged toward me, and drawing his leg back, he kicked the thing in the rear and sent it half-skidding across the clearing. I watched it clumsily push itself upright again, but I stood rooted to the spot.

Fairies, sure. I could deal with them. Maybe they had a reputation of being a little devious, but that thing …

And then it screamed.

The movement was so swift, it was no more than a streak of darkness across my vision. The boy lurched in front of me, shoving me behind him, shielding me with his body.

The creature was wheezing, its neck bent unnaturally in the jaws of a giant black cat. But it had no chance. Blood spit from the punctures in its throat with every strained breath, and its lips twitched around a cry it could no longer produce. With a horrible sound, the cat crushed the smaller creature's life between its teeth and spat it half-decapitated on the ground. Then it sank down, showing its bloody teeth, rolling its shoulders, preparing to pounce.

I felt the remains of my lunch press up my throat before I managed to swallow it down again.

But the boy in front of me stayed inexplicably stoic, his eyes bearing down on the creature intensely, and when, at last, the beast peered up from its prey, it stiffened. Even its flicking tail stopped mid-air. Its mouth opened as if in a gasp, and for just the sliver of a moment, it appeared discomfortingly human—its expression, its body language.

Slowly, it raised from its crouch, its unblinking eyes never leaving the boy's face, and although I didn't think it possible for an animal, it seemed to sneer at him. The boy tensed, and I waited, ready to rip him out of the way by his blouse if the beast attacked. But only a second later, the cat creature grabbed the mangled corpse in its mouth and darted into the trees, vanishing among the brush.

The boy staggered backward a step and released the breath he'd been holding, one hand finding his forehead.

"Spirits ..." he muttered, and when he turned toward me, I expected to find some comfort or relief on his face. But I was greeted, instead, with scorn. "You bloody idiot! Don't just stand there gawking! That's how you get hurt!"

"I-I ..." I stuttered, but I had no good explanation for my inaction.

He doubled over, resting his hands on his thighs. "You talk a big game, but Spirits save you, you're hopeless." Snatching my wrist, he dragged me after him into the trees. "C'mon."

My brother peered up in shy relief when he saw us coming.

"L-Liam," I breathed, relieved, myself, to see him in one piece.

"Are you all right?" the boy asked, and Liam nodded tightly. But the movement seemed so unnatural that I wasn't convinced. He must've been hurt somehow. There'd been blood on that thing's mouth. I'd seen it, and I'd heard Liam scream— not a startled shout, a shriek of pain. Fearful that he really *wasn't* okay, I dropped to my knees to examine him.

I clutched his shoulders, my hands shaking just as much, if not more, than his, my mind swimming with frightening possibilities. I had to remind myself that Liam was sitting in front of me in working order. It couldn't be anything like what I imagined.

"C'mon," the boy grunted from behind me. "Move it." He bent, looped his arm around my waist, and hauled me to my feet. I didn't even react because I was so surprised by how effortlessly he manhandled me. He knelt in the space he'd forced me to vacate.

"Let me see your arm," he ordered. "It bit you, didn't it?" I followed the boy's gaze to my brother's cradled arms. He lowered one to his lap but kept the other pressed into his belly.

"I-it ... Well ..." Liam mumbled. He looked up helplessly, glancing past the boy's head at me.

I didn't think we should fight the boy on the matter. The assuredness with which he spoke and his calm demeanour in the face of those creatures made me believe he could be trusted —or I hoped he could, at least. The only thing I knew for certain was that the situation would've played out very differently had the young man not been there.

"Liam, it's okay," I said as he drew nervously back, hiding his arm in the folds of his shirt. "Just let him."

The boy glanced back at me, seeming surprised by my assent, but he turned to Liam again without a word. Perhaps too flustered to resist my instruction, Liam surrendered. He sat up a little, and when the fabric of his shirt stretched out, I could see that it was already sodden with blood. I smothered a gasp as he peeled his arm from the sticky material, turning it over so the other boy could see the jagged wound on his wrist.

I stepped closer, my hands clasped over my mouth, watching, aghast.

Without even changing his expression, the boy grabbed my brother's arm below the elbow and lifted it closer for inspection. "That's a lot of blood," he murmured, and Liam squeezed his eyes shut, though his protesting whimpers were ignored. "It'll scar. Ruddy beast ..."

With Liam's arm still in his grasp, he cast around, twisting his body to look behind him. He nearly bumped into me when he turned, and huffing, he said, "Oi, could you not stand so close?"

"I'm trying to see."

"Yeah, well, so am I."

"What're you doing?"

Without answering, he stopped abruptly. "Ah!" He seemed to have found what he was looking for. "This flower," he said, reaching around me (and pulling my poor brother with him). He grabbed a plant at the base of its thick stem and ripped it up, roots and all. It looked like a weed—a tall stalk with feathery little leaves and a bundle of tiny white flowers at the top. Pinching Liam's hand between his elbow and his ribs, the boy picked off the flowers and leaves, discarded the stem, and tossed the bits he'd gathered into his mouth.

Dumbfounded, I watched his jaw move as he chewed, but before I could reiterate my question, he spat the mashed plant into his hand and pressed it onto the wound. Liam squeaked.

"What're you—?" I began again, grabbing the boy's shoulder, but he shook me off.

"Here," he said to Liam, taking my brother's free hand. "Hold it tight. This'll help."

My brother obeyed wordlessly.

The boy stood, untucking his blouse. He pulled it down tight with one hand and used the other to tear a strip off the hem.

"All right, move your hand," he instructed, and Liam did so. Then with more care than I thought he was capable of, the boy wound the cloth around my brother's wrist, trapping the tiny florets and gnawed leaves in the cut. He tucked the end under, pulled it through, and securely knotted it. "There we are." He wiped his hands on his trousers. "That'll do for now."

Liam stared at the makeshift bandage with wide eyes, and though a few stray tears had found their way onto his cheeks, no fresh ones formed. "Th-thank you, sir."

"Not *sir*." The red-haired boy chuckled, picking some dirt from under his nail. "My name is ..." He paused, licked his lips, and then, with the slightest smile, he said, "Jasper. It's Jasper Behrtram. Good to meet you."

JASPER

I wasn't sure why I said it. When it came to my quarry, I'd always introduced myself as Gabriel, though I hadn't been expecting to introduce myself to anyone today. I hardly looked the part of a dashing, otherworldly prince, especially with a busted lip.

The girl eyed me apprehensively but answered, "I'm Lily Howell, and my brother is Liam."

I nodded. "Howell, is it? Could it be you're the residents of that big house down the hill?"

The place where the funeral started, I thought.

"That's right."

"And you own this land as well?"

She didn't answer, staring so fiercely at my face that I started to feel anxious, but her scrutiny didn't last long. She nodded toward her brother. "What were the flowers for?"

"Oh," I glanced at the spot I'd pulled the plant up. Three more stalks still stood, so I pointed them out. "It's gearwe—er —yarrow. You can find it anywhere really, but it can help stop bleeding."

She considered my response, thoughtfully chewing her

bottom lip. Then, grabbing one of the yarrow stems, she plucked a bundle of the flowers and held them up to my face. I flinched back.

"What're you—?"

"You need some, too," she insisted.

"I-I'm fine."

"No, you're not. Your cut's reopened, and there's blood all down your chin."

I looked down at my chest, seeing the dots of red on my shirt, and sighing, I pulled it up to wipe my face. I held it there, speaking through the soiled fabric. "It's fine. Let me take care of your brother." Then averting my gaze, I muttered, "You don't need to worry about someone like me." She was too close not to hear, but she pretended she didn't.

"Liam's already been taken care of. Now, it's your turn."

I released my shirt. "I told you, I'm—"

"Look, you." She clicked her tongue, and before I could retreat, she slipped her hand over my shoulder, pinched my neck to hold me still, and pressed the flowers to my mouth. "For as well as you've just cared for him, you're awfully bad at taking care of yourself, aren't you?"

Heat rose in my cheeks when her fingertips brushed my lips. I turned my head, grabbing her hand to stop her from following my movement. I cleared my throat. "Thanks," I mumbled, "but I can do it." It wouldn't work as well if it wasn't chewed anyway.

As if only then realising what she'd done, she jerked her hand out of my grasp. I had to catch the little bunch of florets before it fell.

Bashfully, she apologised—a display I found surprisingly charming.

"It's fine," I replied, replacing the flowers on my lip to hide my smirk.

For a moment, she and I just stood there, awkwardly

stealing glances at each other, equally embarrassed by the strange intimacy of the exchange. When Liam cleared his throat, we both started, and secretly, I was glad for the interruption.

He eyed me curiously. I thought I saw him flash a smile, but it vanished too quickly to be sure.

"Are you okay?" I asked, trying to allay the awkwardness I felt.

Liam nodded.

"Mr. Behrtram," he began, and I had to remind myself that he was addressing *me*. Since Behrtram wasn't my real last name, it felt weird to hear myself called by it, but I responded without too much hesitation.

"Yes?"

"W-what was that—that creature?"

Lily, too, waited for an explanation, and immediately, a plan began to formulate in my mind. If I was going to get both, I needed to draw their interest. I needed them to ask questions— more questions.

"It was an erlking, of course," I replied as though the answer were obvious. As soon as their expressions reflected their confusion, I continued casually, "They'll try to eat you if you're not careful."

"E-eat?" Liam's voice shot up an octave.

"Yeah, but it's tricky cause that laugh of theirs is hard to ignore. It's odd, right? You feel so compelled by it for some reason; you can't help but follow it."

Liam nodded distractedly but didn't speak. Lily's eyes narrowed sceptically.

I lowered the yarrow from my lip, and on I went: "I was attacked by one when I was young, but my brother, Noah, got rid of it. He said I was lucky it wasn't a female; the males can't move around very well, so it's easier to get away." I furrowed my brow and scratched some dried blood off my chin. "They usually only go after smaller prey they can take down quickly. That one must've been awfully hungry."

Lily interjected, "That one doesn't matter! What about the other one?"

"Other one?" Liam eyes widened, dashing from his sister to me.

Unfortunately, I had no information on it either. I'd never seen anything like it, though it hadn't attacked when it very well could have. I shrugged, trying to maintain an air of indifference. "They're both gone now, so what does it matter?"

Lily sputtered, turning her head to peer back at the oak tree where the erlking's blood still slicked the grass and darkened the dirt. We couldn't see it from behind the brush, but just the thought sent a shudder through her body. She gulped, her voice dropping to whisper, "What horrible creatures ..."

I snorted, a little surprised by how easily she'd surrendered. "Well, they can't really help that, can they?" Then with a downward glance, I added softly, "Not all of us can be as lovely as you are." But when I peeked up again, she was watching me and frowning, like she wasn't sure whether I was flattering or insulting her. I'd meant it as a compliment, but I thought confirming it for her would be too embarrassing. She could take it however she liked.

Her cheeks grew rosy. "B-But, it seemed—I dunno— cognizant enough. Why would it do that?"

"It was ..." The ache in my head was starting to return. I could taste blood again, and groaning, I sucked my bottom lip in. Shutting my eyes, I inhaled through my nose.

"Mr. Behrtram?" Lily's voice sounded concerned.

I opened my eyes, resuming talking as if I hadn't paused at all. "It was just hungry. That's all there is to it. Like any other predator, it selects the weakest of the group, brings it down, and has its meal." I nodded toward Liam, who listened with bulging eyes. "Which would've been your brother had we not interfered ... Well, had *I* not interfered, I suppose; *you* were pretty much useless."

The girl curled in on herself a bit. "Yes, I'm fully aware how much you did and how little I did, okay? And seeing it snarling like that made its intentions very clear. I just want to know where on Earth that foul thing came from."

There it was at last: the opening I'd been waiting for! I nearly smiled, but I couldn't let my excitement show. I needed to bait them carefully.

"Well, it won't do to look on Earth. Obviously, it came from somewhere on Obscrys." Then I scratched my head because I wasn't actually entirely sure of their origins. "Or maybe Trigon," I thought aloud, then shrugging, concluded, "It came from Iraxhar anyway."

C'mon, take the bait.

"Pardon, from where?" Lily asked, and my heart beat faster.

Liam said, "We've studied geography, but I don't recall ever hearing about any of those places. They can't be nearby."

"Well, they are ... and they aren't at the same time."

Lily puckered her lips. "What's that supposed to mean?"

"Well ..." I tried to remember how I'd explained it before, but for some reason, as many times as I had, I kept coming up short. "The Gate is nearby, but the places themselves aren't exactly. They don't feel like they're far away, but they are."

They both stared back at me, confused. Then, suddenly, Liam's face brightened.

"Oh!" he squeaked, and Lily and I flinched, startled by his sudden intensity. A wide grin spread across his face as his eyes darted between us. "That's where Bridget came from, isn't it?"

"Bridget?" I felt a familiar smile building on my lips.

Liam started to speak, but Lily shook her head and sighed

deeply. "It's nothing," she mumbled, waving her hand as if wafting away a bad smell. She shot her brother a cautionary glance. "It's just some childish rubbish."

But to my delight, Liam didn't take the hint. "It's not rubbish! You saw her, too!"

"C'mon, Liam," Lily moaned. "You need to get that cut looked at, and I need to get back to where things actually make sense ..."

"But we can't—"

"Liam honestly, can we just—"

"Oi!" I snapped my fingers to get their attention. "Hang on. This Bridget you're talking about ... She wouldn't happen to be about 6 inches tall with black hair and blue eyes, would she? And wings, of course." I figured it couldn't hurt to confirm that I knew the fairy. If anything, it might add to the intrigue.

Liam nodded frantically. "That's her!"

I combed my fingers through my hair. "I thought so."

"D'you know her?"

"I do."

"Really? D'you know where she is? Lily and I were following her before Lily found you and got scared."

Lily quailed, whipping around to glare at her brother. "I wasn't afraid! Anyone would've been—" She pinched her lips. "—*surprised* to find a person in the woods! Lying on the ground like that, he could've been dead for all I knew."

"Oh, c'mon, I was helplessly sleeping, and you woke me up." I stared down my nose at her. "I don't believe I ever got an apology for that, by the way."

Liam gaped at his sister. "Lily!"

I could see her frustration—her unwillingness to yield illustrated plainly on her face—but with two pairs of eyes bearing down on her, I knew her resistance wouldn't last long. Finally, she blew out a loud breath and said, "All right. Fine. I apologise. Are you happy now?"

I chuckled because it was so clearly disingenuous. "For the moment, that will do." Then, with a suggestive flick of my brows, I added, "Perhaps you'll have another chance to apologise later."

She met my gaze more fiercely than before, sneering. "I wouldn't count on it."

"Well, it just so happens that I saw your fairy friend pass by here right before you started screaming your head off."

"Before you surprised me," Lily muttered. "And I thought you were *helplessly sleeping*."

"I was."

"Then how could you possibly have seen her, given that you were fast asleep?"

I shrugged, but she was right to ask. I hadn't seen Bridget, but I knew she'd led them to me. "Perhaps I was awoken by your stampeding feet just before you came upon me," I offered, though Lily didn't seem convinced. Liam, on the other hand, listened with great satisfaction.

"D'you know where she went?" he asked.

Yes, I thought. *Keep asking questions.*

"Sure, through the Gate, obviously. Where else would she go?"

"Gate?"

I nodded. "To Trigon. We came through it together only this morning."

"You're from there, too?"

I glanced over at Lily, holding her eyes until her face flushed.

"That's right," I said, but when I faced her brother again, he looked pale.

"Are you okay?" I asked, bending to inspect his arm again, which trembled slightly.

Absently, he nodded, though his tight expression said differently.

I addressed Lily in case Liam was too distracted by the pain. "He'll be all right, but you should take him to a clinic. A wound like that'll get infected fast if you don't clean it properly. Trust me."

"I know what to do," Lily snapped, grabbing her brother's shoulders and pulling him back.

I raised my hands in surrender. "Sorry?"

"Thank you," she said, though it didn't sound grateful at all, "for your help, but we'll be leaving now." She squeezed Liam's arm tighter. "C'mon, let's get you to Madame Renoir. She can fix you up and put a clean bandage on it." She emphasised the word *clean* with a pointed glance at my shirt.

"Lily, stop it!" her brother said, though she wasn't wrong. My shirt was speckled with dirt and blood, but ...

"What's wrong with you?" I asked because I wasn't sure how else to respond to her sudden terseness. She'd been trying to help me only a short while ago.

"Stop what? There's nothing wrong with me!"

"Why are you getting so angry?" I asked.

She looked away, her face reddening. "I'm not angry. I just want to go home and get away from *you*."

"Excuse me?" I tried to meet her gaze again, but she persistently kept her eyes away from my face. "A moment ago, you were trying to tend my wounds, so why're you acting cold now?"

She didn't answer, but the flush on her cheeks deepened.

I scoffed in disbelief. "I don't know what else you want from me. I've just saved your brother."

"Yes, and I've thanked you for that, but it doesn't excuse how rude you've been."

"You think that was rude of me? Your brother could've died. He's lucky he got away with his bloody hand!" My heartrate sped up. It was getting harder to breathe.

"Yes, yes, I understand. I've already shown my gratitude, but offences aren't simply one for one. You insulted us while trespassing."

"Are you still bringing that up? Is your pride worth more than your brother's life? What would you have done if I hadn't been here?"

I tried to ignore the growing pain in my head.

It's fine, Jasper. You're fine.

"Don't go misinterpreting however you like. I'm just stating that you've done wrong, and it was practically your obligation to—"

I cut her off with a dry laugh. "No, no, let me be clear. I've no obligation to you. I *accidentally* insulted you because I thought you were someone else, and I *accidentally* trespassed because I didn't know this was your family's land. So, I'm sorry for being ignorant, but I didn't help your brother out of obligation. I helped him because he needed help, and I happened to be here."

At last, she peeked up at me, though she kept glancing away, like she couldn't keep her eyes in one place. Some of the harshness smoothed out of her voice. "Thank you," she said. "I appreciate what you've done for my brother. I do, but I want to go home now."

"I'm not trying to stop you. I just want to know why you're suddenly acting so wicked toward me. What's wrong with simply saying goodbye?"

Now I was starting to wonder what was wrong with me. It shouldn't matter if this strange girl hated me or not. But I reminded myself that, if I intended to make her one of my victims, I'd have to get her to like me eventually.

"Well," she began, her voice soft but biting. "You said yourself that I shouldn't worry about someone like you, so I figured it wouldn't matter if I didn't waste any more compassion."

Before I could stop it, a laugh burst out of my mouth, and I stood there giggling like a child.

"What're you laughing at?" Lily demanded to know.

"You," I replied, grinning. "You really are most extraordinary, aren't you?"

She grimaced. "I'm not sure if I should take that as a compliment."

"Maybe ... or maybe not."

She glared, but she still couldn't seem to stare directly into my eyes. And then I realised something that both stunned and amused me.

Her face wasn't red from anger. She was frustrated with me, but it wasn't because I'd been rude. She was blushing. It was the same with all my victims—the ones who succumbed to my princely charm—but without my usual guise, I hadn't expected this kind of reaction at all. Yet, even as I was, this silly girl was inexplicably attracted to me, and more surprising still, I found that I was glad.

"C'mon, Liam," she barked, ushering the boy to his feet. "We're going. We don't need to stay in such *filth's* presence any longer."

I raised both brows. "It really is a complete turn with you, isn't it? Does it bother you that much?"

She ignored me, and with a swift, nose-in-the-air turn, she headed back in the direction she'd come. "Liam, come on. If you stay here with him, you might catch something."

This bloody girl ...

"Oi, can you just—" I began, but a sudden jolt of nausea

robbed my breath. I gasped, clutching my stomach. My vision blurred, and I threw my arm out to grab the tree. But it wasn't there. I swayed. "Shit ..." I covered my eyes with one hand, sinking to a crouch before I fell.

"M-Mr. Behrtram!"

Liam's hand pressed down on my back, and I heard Lily stop.

"Sorry," I muttered. "I'm fine." I lowered my hand, glancing up to find Lily frozen in place, watching me over her shoulder. "Don't worry," I said. The strain in my voice made it sound colder than I meant it. "This is perfectly normal for someone like me."

For just a moment, I saw the wide-eyed concern on her face, but as soon as our eyes met, she turned and hurried on her way.

"Lily!" Liam shouted after her. Then kneeling, he said to me, "I-I'm so sorry. Is there anything I can do? I don't know why she's being like this."

But I was laughing.

"Liam!" Lily called, but he didn't answer her. He stared at me, baffled by my amusement. I patted him on the back.

"You'd better go. She has quite the temper, doesn't she?"

"I'll say." He sighed. "Look, I'm really sorry, and—um—thank you for helping me, even though I'm a stranger. Not everyone would've done what you did, so ... thank you."

"I'm glad you're all right." Then, reaching into my pocket, I pulled out the yarrow sprig Lily had given me, twisted it, and held it up to my lip again. I smiled at him from behind it. "Tell your sister I said bye."

Lily shouted again: "Liam!"

I nodded in her direction, and without another word, the boy bowed his head to me and took off. I stared after them for a moment, waiting for my stomach to settle. Then hauling myself to my feet, I took a deep breath and began the slow journey homeward.

But while I walked, my mind was elsewhere.

Teasing her, flattering her, arguing with her—it didn't matter what I'd done. It didn't matter if she fancied or hated me. I was still smiling as I followed the path to the Gate because, no matter what, I knew that girl was going to remember me.

I twirled the yarrow in my fingers, and my smile broadened.

I certainly wouldn't forget her.

LILY

Why did I say that?

I didn't know why I'd said any of it. That boy ... he just made me so mad! Every time he looked at me with those golden eyes and that flashy smile, I couldn't help but quail with anger.

But then my steps slowed, and I paused because I knew that wasn't right. It wasn't that I was angry with him. He hadn't done anything to make me cross—not really. Somehow, I felt oddly uncomfortable in his presence. Not badly uncomfortable, just ... abnormal. It wasn't a feeling I'd ever experienced, and the unfamiliarity made me wary. When he looked at me so directly, my heart beat fast, and there was a fluttering in my stomach.

I felt so shy.

I didn't like it at all. I wanted those strange feelings to go away as quickly as possible, and the only way to do that was to get as far from that boy as I could.

Liam called my name, and I urged my feet forward, quickening my pace the closer he got. "Lily!"

I knew he already had a lecture in store for me, though it

was unnecessary. I wasn't proud of what I'd said, but it had served its purpose well.

"Lily, hey! Lily!"

I didn't answer, and Liam was panting when he finally caught up.

"That was … very rude," he puffed, trotting alongside me.

"So?"

"You really offended him …"

He waited, and I suspected he was expecting me to go into a long, heartfelt apology outlining my offences. But after a full minute of silence, he moaned. He threw out his good hand, caught my shoulder, and spun me around. I tripped to a stop, nearly toppling over.

"Ow!"

"Honestly, have you no manners?"

"Yes," I replied hotly, crossing my arms. "But I didn't see any reason to waste them on such a lowly little brat." This conversation wasn't going anywhere, and I didn't care to participate in it any longer than I had to. I started to walk away.

"Gosh, I mean really, Lily, just because someone doesn't have the same luxuries as you doesn't make them inferior. He's still a human being like you."

By my knowledge, that was precisely the meaning of inferior. Anyone could see that I was the superior one in a comparison between Mr. Behrtram and myself, but I only shrugged, knowing my brother would find some way to argue the fact.

"Calm down, Liam. They were just meaningless insults. I'm sure he'll manage."

"It wasn't only that! You walked away when he was hurt!"

"He said himself that we needn't worry."

"That doesn't matter! Even a blind person could see that he was in pain."

"That's not my problem."

He had to jog to catch up with me again. "Why are you acting like this toward him?"

"It's his own fault for being such an insufferable prat."

Liam scoffed. "Him? Lily, I think it's *you* who's being insufferable."

"Excuse me?" I skidded to a halt.

"You just kept at it!"

"He insulted us first!"

I thought the vein in my brother's forehead might burst, but I didn't care, especially since he seemed to find me so *insufferable*.

"You always have to have the last word, don't you?" When I turned again, he forced himself into my path, thrusting a finger toward the little clearing. "Go apologise."

It had been a while since I'd seen Liam so worked up; I'd forgotten how annoying it was.

Wrinkling my nose, I tossed my hair over my shoulder.

"Personally, I found everything I said back there to be quite amusing, and I don't think I did or said anything worth apologising for." Manoeuvering around him, I pressed on through the trees. "We'd better hurry though, Liam!" I called after me, a touch of sarcasm trilling into my voice. "Our lesson has probably started already!"

LIAM

"**O**h, mon Dieu! 'Ow did this 'appen?"

Madame Renoir seized my wrist, yanking me closer with more strength than I thought she had. I tensed as she shoved up my sleeve and examined the bloody bandage on my arm, but I was ready with the lie Lily and I had prepared.

"I-I tripped," I said, which was a lie. I sank down in a seat at the back of the room, afraid to meet her eyes, which were magnified by the thick lenses of her spectacles. "O-on the cracked stone. The steps. Yes, the steps," I continued. Also a lie.

"In the back?" Madame Renoir asked through pursed lips. "Les marches de la terrasse?"

"Um—" I began, fumbling my words, but thankfully, Lily jumped in and saved me.

"Yes, the terrace steps. Unless there's another set of steps that dip and nearly make you fall every time you walk on them."

"It is an old 'ouse." Her thin lips cracked a smile. "All steps dip 'ere, ma fille."

Lily puffed out her cheeks, rolled her eyes, and crossed her arms. "Would you just fix him please? We're in a bit of a hurry."

"Bah! You are gone when I wake, and I think you 'ave gone to the lesson. But 'ere you are, making problems for me!" Madame Renoir's smile deepened into a sneer. "And now, Regina will not be 'appy you are not where you should be."

Lily leaned in. "Yes, that's precisely why we're in a hurry."

"I wonder why you do not go now, Miss Lily. You 'ave tripped also?"

"Oh, I'm fine," Lily replied with a dismissive flick of her wrist. "I know how to keep my footing, thank you very much, but if I go alone, Miss Sawyer will skin me alive. I need a reason for being late, and she won't believe me without proof." She nodded exaggeratedly toward me, and my face fell.

She was an absolute ninny. She was going to pass the blame off on me. Again. I pinched my lips together, shooting her a stringent look, but she either didn't notice or ignored it. I didn't have the energy to fight for her attention. My arm throbbed, and I knew I'd need all my strength to endure whatever bizarre remedy our nurse had in store for me.

I resisted the urge to draw back when the old woman grabbed my wrist again, swinging my arm around and wrinkling her nose as she unwound the cloth and dropped the bandage in the bin. Then, peeling away the wad of blood-caked flowers, she lifted her face in surprise.

"Who knew to use the yarrow?"

My stomach dropped. Lily and I hadn't come up with an explanation for that. "Well—" I began shakily, but my sister spoke over me.

"That was me," she said, pushing out her chest. I knew we couldn't tell the truth, especially after we'd lied about the steps, but it still irked me that my sister could so easily take credit for something someone else had done.

Madame Renoir spent a glance on Lily, suspicion arching her thin brows for a moment, and then tsking, she relaxed her face and returned to me. Dabbing at the cut with a cotton ball, she squinted at the injury, blotting the fresh blood as she did.

"Oh, la vache," she said, puffing out her cheeks and letting the air seep through her teeth. "This will need 'elp. I will get the needle."

I hoped I'd misheard. I hoped that, in our nurse's accented voice, she'd meant to say that she'd seen a 'beetle' or that my cut was 'leetle' and not at all in need of sutures, but when I saw her rummaging in the top shelf of her cabinet, I knew my ears hadn't deceived me. She was going to get a needle.

"'Ere we are!" Madame Renoir preened, and I cringed down in my seat. She spread her finds on the table: a hooked needle, thread, forceps, and a small jar of cream.

I felt the colour drain from my face.

Scooping out a dollop of the ointment with her fingertips, she started toward me. "I make this myself. It is to 'elp make— er—numb."

Though the strange Mr. Berhtram's methods had been crude, the old woman was somehow more frightening. Adrenaline had helped ease my nerves in the forest, but that was all gone now. My arm began to quake against the tabletop. Lily noticed and laid her hand flat on top of mine, curling her fingers around my palm.

She addressed Madame Renoir. "You made it? Are you sure it's safe? Infections are dangerous, you know."

Our nurse abandoned her course toward me for a moment (I let out a sigh of relief) and swooped toward my sister. "Well now, 'ow about I tell your mum that you have skipped your lesson, hmm?"

I appreciated Lily stalling, but putting it off longer gave me more time to dread what was coming—more time for my heart rate to spike and my hands to sweat and the hair on the back of my neck to stand and prickle uncomfortably. I didn't want to wait anymore; I wanted it to be quick and over before I even knew what happened.

"Well, then I'll smash my fingers in the door and say it was you. It would give me a reason to be in your office as well as one for Mum to be cross with you."

Madame Renoir screwed up her wrinkled face, shying back a bit. "And I will say it was Regina. You 'ave probably already done something to warrant a punishing," she said, slathering the ointment over my wound with one quick movement. Lily held my arm still as I gasped and tried to jerk back, though it was more out of surprise than pain. The cream was unexpectedly cold.

I swallowed thickly, composing myself as my sister replied, "Yeah, but Miss Sawyer would never actually do anything; she's far too innocent."

"And you think *I* would?" Madame Renoir let out a throaty laugh, which turned almost immediately to a cough. When she got hold of herself, she worked the thread through the needle and clamped it in the forceps. "I would never *ever* do anything to 'urt either of you!"

I hadn't expected to find the lie in her words until she jabbed the needle into my arm. My whole body seized, my teeth clenching, my hand squeezing Lily's until she let out a yelp.

"Ow! Liam, that hurts!" she hissed, prying my hand off. I transferred my grip to the edge of the table, my knuckles turning white. But as soon as the initial sting disappeared, only a tingling sensation was left, followed by the promised numbness. I relaxed my body, releasing my grip on the table, which trembled a moment before stabilizing again.

"It is okay?" Madame Renoir asked, and exhaling, I nodded. "I know my business." She tapped the top of my hand with one finger. "If I say my medicine is good, it is better than you would get á l'hôpital."

I nodded again, feeling like I'd already used up too much energy to verbally answer, but I agreed with her. Whatever was in that ointment of hers had worked. I barely felt even a prick as the wound was drawn shut. I leaned my head back against the wall. Then, pulling the last knot tight, Madame Renoir clipped the string and smiled up at me.

"Now, tell me, children," she said, pushing her spectacles up her nose with one finger. "'Ow did this really 'appen, hmm?"

I swung my head forward and froze. Lily squeezed my arm, and I glanced sideways at her, knowing I'd already reacted too much to be convincing. Her eyes screamed at me to answer.

"I-I tripped," I choked out, fumbling to repeat the lie my sister had given me. "The courtyard—er—terrace—no—the step ..."

That was it. We were caught. I was a horrible liar. No one would believe me, not even a senile old woman. We were done for. We'd get in trouble, and I'd end up with the blame because my sister could lie through her teeth and throw everything on me.

My heart pounded as Madame Renoir eyed us one after the other, her wispy little brows raising. I bit my lip to keep my expression still.

"D'accord," she finally said, though she sounded doubtful. "I was just thinking that this looks very much like—uh—les dents." Her gaze flicked back to Lily. "You are not biting your brother, are you?"

Lily's chest sank as she released her breath. "Yes," she said, rolling her eyes, the sarcasm in her voice so thick that even the old woman couldn't mistake it for honesty. "I bit Liam."

At last, Madame Renoir retreated, gathering her instruments and returning them to her cupboard, though her puckered lips told me that she didn't entirely believe my sister's innocence. She walked back to us with a roll of dressing, and none of us spoke while she wound the *clean* bandage around my arm. Then, satisfied, she pushed a hand down on the table to lift herself out of her chair.

"All right," she said, her back cracking as she stood upright, "You are fixed."

I got up slowly, rolling my sleeve down over my bandaged wrist. "Thank you," I said.

Madame Renoir smiled and tiredly nodded, shooing me away. "Off to the lesson, children." She waggled her finger at my chest. "But change the shirt before you go."

Looking down at myself, I agreed. Lily took my other arm and led me to the door, but we stopped when Madame Renoir spoke again.

"Remember to be careful," the old woman warned, tapping a fingernail on the mole on her chin. "And be smart. People might get the idea that you are up to something."

I gulped, nodded, and hurried out the door, nearly dragging my sister behind me.

PART FIVE
REFLECTIONS

JASPER

I told myself over and over: *You shouldn't be doing this. You shouldn't be looking for her. You shouldn't want to look for her.* But I was, and I did. I paced in the trees just past her family's vegetable garden, my eyes sweeping across the terrace and the windows, watching for movement.

It's research, I insisted. I had to get to know these children better to learn how best to lure them in. They were together so often, it only made sense to catch them both.

I always had at least one target—something to work toward, someone to convince, some way to improve my act and my lies. For the last two years, my life had revolved around this task. Now would be a good time to increase the quota.

But that was only my way of avoiding the reality of the situation, though I was fully aware of it: my interest had shifted. Suddenly, I didn't care about the boy at all. He'd been my target for some time. Bridget had spent hours carefully baiting him. I *should* care, and yet ...

It was his sister that vexed me. I'd dreamt about her—that strange, angry girl. She'd stared at me with those passionate eyes, extended a hand, and then I woke and couldn't get her out of my head. Though it hadn't just been the dream or that encounter with her and her brother. From the first moment I'd seen her ungraceful march to join the funeral procession, she'd occupied my thoughts.

No, the boy didn't matter. Two years of dedication didn't matter. My task didn't matter. For some reason, the only desire I had was simply to see her again.

I'd witnessed her anger and apprehension, and I wanted more. She couldn't always be fiery. Those little flashes of embarrassment—the shyness, the blushing cheeks, the awkward glances—had tied a rope around my neck and led me straight back to her. I had to know: what disengaged her? What calmed her? What could possibly produce a gentle expression on this haughty girl's face?

Ah, yes, that's it, I thought. That's what I was interested in: the challenge of it.

After all this time, the difficulty had gone, my act perfected. It worked too easily. Every person succumbed every time. I charmed and lied and weaseled my way into their minds and their hearts. I stomped on their trust and spirited them away. It always worked exactly as I anticipated, and if I was being honest, winning so often made the game rather dull.

But thanks to Bridget's interference, these circumstances were already different. I wouldn't be able to play the charming prince from another world. I wasn't His Royal Highness Prince Gabriel Atwood of Egaldon, Gimlon. This time, I was Jasper Behrtram, a weary, mysterious explorer of other worlds, though both, in their own ways and times, were accurate. Personally, I preferred the latter version of myself, and it required far less acting.

I crouched down, instinctively hiding myself when I heard voices—laughter—and peering through the brush, I saw Liam sitting on the grass with two other smiling children. The girl leaned over in excitement or fear and with a shaking finger, poked a small frog that sat on Liam's palm. She squealed and jumped back when it leapt at her. The boys giggled, scrambling to catch it again, and I listened, all the while looking for her.

But Lily wasn't there.

Craning my neck, I surveyed the area, searching until, finally, I spotted her. I saw her face in a window, and yet again, I was stricken by the expression on her face. But this time, my heart sank.

I'd believed it entirely—that high and mighty performance she put on.

Slowly, I rose to my feet, forgetting any need for subtlety. I was so fixed on her person that someone could've walked up behind me, and I would hardly have noticed. But I had to get a better view of the face in the window because whatever else had been, this wasn't pretend.

The young woman that stared out of it wasn't cross. The emotion she wore now wasn't anger, fear, or annoyance. It was longing.

I felt my stomach constrict.

Every expression I'd seen on her face before dulled in comparison to the melancholy that held her now. Staring out of that window, she looked utterly defeated.

Suddenly, I felt a strange closeness to the young woman. She looked exactly how I felt—as if my own expression had been mirrored on that pretty face.

I should look away, I thought because I knew I shouldn't have seen. I felt shy, embarrassed with or, perhaps, for her. But I didn't turn or even avert my eyes. I watched her, silent, breathless as she disappeared from the window only to reappear a minute later at the French doors.

"Liam!" she shouted. "Get inside! Miss Sawyer called!"

The game was over as quickly as it had started. Without her knowledge, she'd just given me exactly what I needed to win.

This would be simple. Easy. I knew her weakness.

I wanted to smile and congratulate myself on my *research* efforts, but I couldn't seem to bring the curl to my lips. I felt like I was trespassing, like I'd witnessed an intimate moment she never intended anyone to see.

I didn't leave until she closed the door, passed the window, and vanished from sight.

LILY

"Lilith Iselda Howell, will you please pay attention to your lesson? Honestly, how can you expect to learn any history if you spend your every waking hour in a daydream?"

Tiredly, I raised my head and propped my chin up on my wrist. Our governess stood with a thick volume balanced open on her hip, her other arm affixed to her side in a sharp angle, and she was bristling.

Nothing out of the ordinary.

I yawned. "Hmm?"

Her eyes bore down on me expectantly. Generally, she preferred that I give a comprehensible response when she asked me a question, but I thought it was quite obvious that I was too tired to do so.

"Miss Howell!"

"Yes?" I managed—a vast effort on my behalf, though she didn't seem to appreciate it.

"Is there a reason you feel exempt from answering my question?"

I shrugged. "It sounded rhetorical to me; I didn't think you wanted an answer but rather a corrective action."

"Well, you've made no such corrective action."

"I did!" I insisted. "I'm looking up now, aren't I?"

Her lips pressed into a flat line, her glare intensifying because she knew I was right. Of course, the young woman would never admit defeat, so instead, she whirled around, seized a piece of chalk from a box on her desk, and hissed, "Pay attention!" Her next question came out sounding more like a demand than the innocent historical inquiry that it was. "Now, who deposed Edward II, and how did he eventually become the King of England?"

Liam was ready with the answer, as usual. His arm shot into the air. "That was his mother and her lover," he said, sitting straight up in his seat. He lowered his arm and folded his hands neatly on his desk. "Isabella of France and Roger Mortimer, that is, and King Edward gained power after leading a coup d'état against them."

When Miss Sawyer paused to exhale a calming breath, Liam's posture slackened, his eyes dropping to the open text in front of him to assure himself that he'd given the correct response. Our governess was usually quick with her praise, and her hesitance seemed to worry him. But even I knew his answer was accurate.

"Very good, William," she said at last, and his chest deflated in relief. "That is absolutely correct. Perhaps you should repeat the answer to your sister so it will at least have been heard by her ears and have some chance of sticking in her memory."

My brother, who always did what was asked of him, turned to the side and opened his mouth, but I cut him off with a loud groan before he could speak. He looked terribly offended, which pleased me.

"I'm quite aware of the answer, thank you very much. I just can't think of any situation in the future of my life in which I might need such useless information."

A curl sprang loose from our governess's tightly wound bun.

"The history of your country is not useless, Lilith!" She slapped a palm down on her desk, and out of the corner of my eye, I saw Liam flinch. "The past is equally as important as the present or the future; it's how we learn—from both our victories and our mistakes."

I quirked a brow. "If that's the case, then may I ask why you're still wearing that hideous dress? Obviously, the past didn't teach you very well because that was a mistake the first time you wore it."

"Lily!" Liam gaped at me, his eyes blinking rapidly, his mouth opening and closing, though only stuttered bits of words came out.

But he had to know I was right. It was a plain and shapeless old frock that had been dyed some colour that couldn't decide if it wanted to be brown or green, though it hardly mattered because neither hue was particularly flattering on her.

Miss Sawyer held one hand up to silence Liam, and although she said nothing, I could see her anger. Her teeth were gritted, her nostrils flared and her neck corded, but instead of screaming at me to *get out of her sight this instant* (which had been my intention and hope), she closed her eyes, swallowed thickly, and exhaled through her nose. When she looked at me again, she'd composed herself surprisingly well.

"I think, Lilith," she began softly, "that the surest way of punishing you will be to require your continued presence. Perhaps we can add a few chapters to our reading to ensure your familiarity with the subject." I sank down in my chair as she continued, "Your brother may leave as soon as the hour is spent if he chooses." Then smiling at Liam, she said, "I know he'll read in his own time."

My brother's cheeks flushed, and he straightened the papers on his desk as our governess returned to her seat. I rolled my eyes.

Liam didn't leave when the hour ended. He stayed where he was, hunched over his desk, squinting down at his text, his left hand scribbling notes on his parchment. Mother always encouraged him to write with his right hand like the rest of us, but Miss Sawyer was too preoccupied with reading herself to correct him.

But I couldn't focus. I stared at the words, and the small print seemed fuzzy. I tapped the tip of my quill on the desk, speckling the wood with black ink as I cast my eyes around the room. I'd read this section before, and I had no interest in reviewing it. Tiredly, I peered sideways at my brother.

Scribbling a note on the corner of my page, I tore it off and tossed it onto Liam's desk, watching the front of the room to make sure Miss Sawyer was still too engrossed in her book to notice. My brother pursed his lips, disappointed that I would disrupt his learning, but read it, nonetheless. With a resentful glance, he penned a quick reply, flicking the note in my general direction; I had to retrieve it from the floor behind me.

It read:

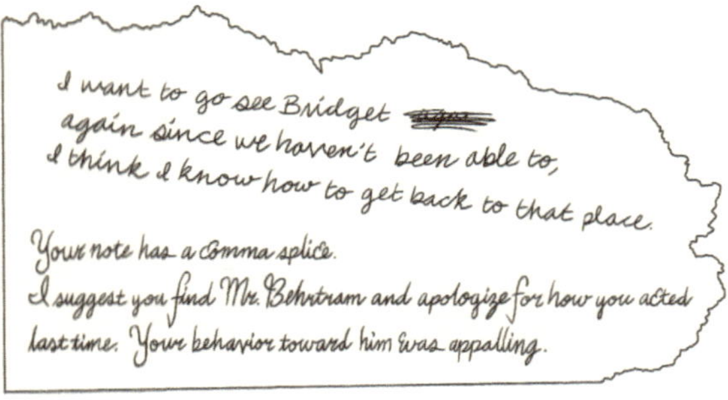

I stuck my tongue out at him.

"Lilith Howell, you put that tongue back in your mouth this instant!" Miss Sawyer shouted—a tone which seemed wildly inappropriate for a tutor—and drawing her arm back, she threw a piece of chalk at me.

***

"She actually threw chalk at me, Liam. Can you believe it? Honestly, there must be a law against that or something —governesses using cruel forms of punishment. Don't you think?" I heaved a sigh. "Why does everyone around here think we're up to no good?"

Liam snorted. "Well, I suppose it could be that we *are* usually up to no good." He paused, a crease appearing in the skin between his eyes. "Actually," he said, relaxing his puckered brow. "It's you who's up to no good. I just get dragged along as your slave and scapegoat ..."

I let my head fall back with a clipped laugh. "Oh, now that isn't true."

He stopped walking. "How d'you figure?"

"Well, you've never actually been my scapegoat cause you always rat me out first."

With an acrid look, Liam stuck his nose in the air and marched past me down the hall.

"Liam, where're you going? I thought you were coming with me."

He didn't answer.

"Liam?"

Nothing.

"Well, I thought it was funny!" I called after him, only to be ignored. "Fine!" I shouted. "If you're going to behave like that, I'm going to the garden, and you're not invited!"

He shrugged his shoulders as he walked.

"Liam!"

He didn't look back.

LILY

I trudged down the path to the garden, tugging at the collar of my dress until the top two buttons slipped out of their holes and gave me some room to breathe. I tore at the pins in my hair, flicking them at the ground one by one.

I shouldn't have to sit through lessons in my own house wearing dresses and pins. It was terribly unreasonable. What was the point in dressing up if we never left the house? I'd be far more comfortable sitting through those droning lectures in my nightgown with a pillow and blanket on hand. But that would never happen, not while Mum and Miss Sawyer had even a puff of air in their lungs. I was learning to be a proper young lady, and proper young ladies didn't wear their nightgowns out of their bedrooms.

What an awful business being a lady was.

Kicking off my shoes, I plopped down on the ground and pulled my stockings off, balling them up and shoving them into the toe of my boot. The grass felt nice on my bare feet, cold and a little damp from the previous night's rain. I leaned back on my arms, feeling the breeze, spreading my toes and trying to catch clover or blades of grass between them.

But then someone laughed at me.

I sat straight up, swinging my head to look back at the house, but there was no one in sight. Then I remembered: Liam had heard a laugh, too, right before he'd been attacked by that creature.

I scrambled to my feet, plucking my boots from the ground and peering cautiously around the fence. But there was nothing, and I didn't hear the noise again. Of course, logically, I knew the creature had been killed, but a part of me wasn't convinced that that encounter had actually occurred outside of my head.

I peeked over the fence into the garden, but there was nothing out of the ordinary. No fairies or erlkings, not even a perfectly ripe tomato.

I sighed. There was nothing to do in this bloody place without Liam to order around and keep me entertained.

Except ...

That wasn't entirely true, was it? In fact, there was a whole forest to explore just at the edge of the lawn. There was time yet until lunch; I could be a little adventurous. Perhaps I should've been more trepidatious, knowing there were creatures like that cat thing or the erlking out there, but based on what Mr. Behrtram had said, if I ignored its laugh, I'd be safe, right?

There weren't any discernible trails since Liam and I weren't allowed in the woods, but I was certain I could find my way. Glancing over my shoulder, I checked to see if anyone had followed me outside, and when I saw no figures or faces in the windows, I walked right to the edge of the lawn, hitched up my dress, and lifted my foot to take a step. But before my toes even touched the ground, a voice stopped me.

"You lost?"

I sprang backward, swiveling my head, and there, leaning against a tree with crossed arms, was Mr. Behrtram.

I tried to sound indifferent, but I could only manage a flustered, "E-excuse me?"

"I asked if you were lost."

Clearing my throat, I shook my head.

"Maybe you're looking for something?" He smirked. "Or someone, perhaps?"

"No," I muttered, finally finding my voice. "I was … taking a walk."

I hadn't wanted to see him again. No. Of course not. Not at all.

"Just a leisurely stroll through the woods in bare feet?" His eyes swept my figure from my hair to my toes, though they paused on my exposed legs. Immediately, I released my dress so it fell below my knees again.

I tried to ignore the heat rising in my cheeks. "What d'you want? Why're you here?"

He observed me calmly and smiled. "Giving you another chance to apologise."

My face turned sour. "I already did."

He shrugged. "Yeah, I know you did."

"So, what d'you want then?" I asked, then hesitantly added, "I see your lip's healed."

Surprise arched his brows. "Were you worried about me?"

"Hardly," I shot back, and then, again, my voice shrank. "Though you were in quite a state. You do look better now."

"Wounds heal."

"Right …" I stared back at him until I couldn't anymore. His gaze was too direct. "What did you come here for?"

"Does it matter? Maybe I came to say hello."

I scoffed. "As if we're friends."

"True, you could hardly even call us acquaintances, though I feel like there might be something between us, don't you?"

"Like what?" I asked.

"Who knows?" He leaned toward me and cheekily wiggled his eyebrows. "Do you want to find out?"

I swallowed, my eyes widening at the implications. "Th-that's inappropriate."

His calm demeanor broke with a burst of laughter. "Is that what you're thinking? I didn't mean anything indecent by it, though it seems your mind might be elsewhere."

Somehow, he remained completely unperturbed, and that infuriated me. I blew out a loud breath, making sure my annoyance was audible. "Y'know, this is a waste of my time. I'm going home." Setting my jaw, I crossed my arms and waited for his objection.

But he didn't object. In fact, he didn't say anything at all, and when I finally peeked up at him, he wasn't even looking at me. I readied myself to stomp angrily away, but before I could take the first step, the boy drew me back again.

"Is that your house then?" he asked, his expression surprisingly mild.

I frowned. There was obviously something wrong with this boy. "Yes."

"Isn't it sort of ... too big?"

"Yes, it's rather large," I said as shortly as possible. I waited for him to react in some way, but he stayed uncommonly stoic.

"Curious ..."

"What is?" I asked, shoving myself into his line of sight, but being nearly a head taller, it wasn't hard for him to overlook me.

He stared at the structure, his brow furrowed. The softness of his voice caught me off guard, though not nearly as much as his question.

"Do you ever feel lonely in such a big house?"

I blinked at him. It should've been an easy answer—a swift, '*No, not at all*'—because I was very aware of my privilege. I had my brother and mother, and we had maids, a housekeeper, a cook, a governess, a nurse ... There was plenty of life in our house to drive away any feelings of isolation.

And yet ...

I delayed answering because I was perplexed. Perhaps I wasn't so surprised by the question as I was by the sincerity with which he'd asked it—like he already *knew* it was lonely, despite the number of occupants.

But how could he know?

He didn't know what it was like to live in such a grand old house with so many rooms that one could get a little lost wandering around at night. He couldn't know what it was like to sit in a room as people came and went all day without ever uttering a word. He couldn't know how it felt to sit at a piano, staring at the keys and trying to convince oneself to play because the silence from those high ceilings was suffocating. But of course, the echo of even a single note could be just as unsettling if there wasn't an audience to enjoy the melody. He had no idea at all that I sometimes sat by the window, alone, watching Liam playing with his silly friends, nor could he know that sometimes—on very rare occasions—I longed to be out there, laughing with them ...

But I couldn't do that because I wasn't a child. I was a proper young lady who was far too busy for friends, and I certainly couldn't acquaint myself with those poor children because they died so often. There was no time in my schedule to mourn them, and of course, no suitors would want me if the only colour I ever wore was black.

So instead of replying, '*Yes, I do get lonely. I'm lonely all the time. I miss my father and my mother. There's too much space and too few people to talk to and—*'

Instead of replying that loneliness was like a curse in that big, awful house, I bowed my head and quietly said, "No, it doesn't get lonely at all."

When he didn't respond, I looked up and found him staring straight at me. I quickly averted my eyes to keep him from seeing the truth in them, and he snorted, clearly amused by my reaction.

"Yeah, all right. Whatever you say, miss." Then, he leaned closer to whisper beside my ear. "Don't worry, I'll keep your secret."

I didn't move, stricken by this reduced proximity. My stomach gurgled.

Chuckling, he shifted his weight to his back foot again. "You don't have to look so bloody scared. I'm not gonna bite you."

I released my breath shakily, surprised by how timid I suddenly felt. "How should I know what you're gonna do? You're unpredictable enough as it is."

He bent and angled his head to meet my gaze. "I could say the same to you."

I shied away. "I'm not ... unpredictable."

Then, unexpectedly, he agreed. "Yeah, maybe you're right."

I felt restless; I clasped my hands to keep from wringing them. "Did you come here just to harass me?"

"No, I came to find Bridget."

"Bridget? Is she nearby?"

Mr. Behrtram shot me a playful glance, and I recoiled.

"What's that look for?"

He grinned. "I thought fairies were just *childish rubbish* to you."

Flushing, I looked away and muttered, "Yes, well ..."

But he didn't tease me about it further. He simply shrugged. "I dunno. I thought she might've come this way, but I can't possibly keep tabs on her all the time."

"Oh." I fiddled with the lace on my sleeve, unsure what to say next. There were a great many things I'd been curious about since our first meeting, but I also didn't want him to know that I'd been thinking about him. I cleared my throat, hoping I sounded believably casual when I spoke. "This Iraxhar place you talked about ..." His eyes flicked up to meet mine. "It seems rather magical."

He considered. "Yes, I suppose it is in its own way."

"So, are there people who can do it then? Magic, I mean."

He cocked his head, shaggy red hair falling in front of his eyes. "Some. Though it's uncommon to find a creature with such talents."

"Humans, too?"

He eyed me curiously. "Some," he said again.

"Like you?"

His lips pressed into a flat line, but he didn't deny my allegation.

"That's how you made the ground move like you did before, isn't it? To find Liam, I mean."

His shoulders hunched. "I guess," he mumbled, his voice pitched low as if he didn't want me to hear him.

"So, you *can* do it?" I asked, disregarding his reluctance. I wanted an actual confirmation.

"I—" he began haltingly. It took him a moment to decide how to answer. "I don't know that I would call it *magic* exactly, but—well, I suppose that's what it might look like to an outsider."

Somehow, it pleased me to see him so uneasy. "But you can do it, whatever you call it?" I pressed, and he sighed.

"Yes, I can do things that you would consider *magical*."

I looked him over, assessing. He wasn't like Liam; it wasn't obvious whether he was lying or not. I felt certain I'd seen something happen that day, but ...

"You're lying," I said to provoke him. Maybe he would try to prove or disprove it.

But he just shrugged and yawned, speaking through it to say, "Okay."

"Okay?"

"Think what you like."

"You don't mind being called a liar?"

"Sometimes I lie," he said honestly. "And sometimes you do, too, I'm sure," which was a declaration I couldn't dispute.

With such a simple statement, he'd somehow made me feel like the awkward one again. "Yes, well, I suppose everyone does at some time or another." I tapped my foot in the grass. "That still doesn't mean I believe you."

"I'm not asking you to. Like I said, you can think whatever you like."

I pursed my lips. "Y'know, you—you're just so—"

"So what?" he asked, his eyes daring me to answer.

"Well ..." I turned my face up, sticking my nose in the air. "That's none of your business, now is it?"

He clicked his tongue. "If it's something about me, I think I've a right to know."

But I wouldn't indulge him. I peered to the side, dodging his gaze.

At last, he gave up, but instead of yielding to my demands and showing me proof of his magic, he turned away.

"Well, if you won't tell me, I'm leaving," he said loftily. "I've better things to do with my time. Besides, I was looking for Bridget, and here, there's only you."

With a brisk nod over his shoulder, he started into the forest.

"Wait!" I called, stepping after him. The twigs and acorns under my bare feet stopped me before I'd made it very far, but I threw my arm out and managed to catch his shirt.

He waited, letting his head loll lazily to one side to look at me. "What?"

"I—Well ..." I hadn't actually expected him to stop, so I was lost for words.

Unimpressed, he asked, "Is that all?" and began to walk again without waiting for an answer.

"Wait!" I called. "Come back! Where're you going?"

His back to me, he shouted, "None of your business!" and a minute later, he disappeared fully into the trees.

Even after he was gone, I stared into the forest, my heart pounding. My face felt warm, and I touched my cheeks, wondering if they'd reddened—if he'd noticed it. I blew the hair out of my eyes and stalked back to the garden. Snatching my boots, I scowled all the way back to the door.

The appearance of my brother when I turned the corner only added to my agitation. He stopped in his tracks the moment he saw me, opening his mouth like he wanted to say something. I ignored him, trying to sidestep without an interaction, but he stole my hand.

"Listen, Lily," he began. "I—I'm sorry about earlier." He bowed his head. "I mean, I'm sorry for being so—well, I guess I just ..."

He was dreadful at articulating anything.

I ripped my hand out of his grasp. "Just piss off!" I growled, shoving past him to climb the stairs. He didn't follow, and when I reached the next landing, I paused, glancing over the railing at the bottom of the staircase. Liam still stood where I'd left him. Shaking my head, I continued down the hall.

I stared through the glass, absently scanning the tree line for that mop of red hair. It was hard not to look for him. In fact, every time I passed a window, I looked. I'd bumped into Celia yesterday and made her drop the linens because I'd been too preoccupied with my search.

I couldn't get him out of my head, and it was positively vexing.

I wanted to see him again, if only to discern what it was about him that was so—

I didn't even have the word for it.

I leaned over the back of the sofa, one arm set up to hold my chin. The view out the window blurred as my eyes turned inward, thoughts wrestling around in my head.

I wanted to see him again, but what was it? The way he talked or the way he stood? The way he looked? I pressed two fingers to my temple. And then I knew.

He was detached. Anonymous. Removed from anything else going on in the world. He had no rules. He was on his own, but—

Yes, that's what it was. He had no one to answer to. He

didn't care what he said or how people perceived him. He didn't have a care in the world.

But that hadn't made me flush and stutter and act a mess.

I frowned and sat upright, sliding my stockinged feet off the cushion to the floor.

Was I ... attracted to him? Was that part of it?

I bit my lip, trying to picture his face. There was something pleasant about it, I admitted to myself. He wasn't particularly handsome in a traditional sense, but he held himself with confidence. He was unlike any of the boys I'd ever been forced to meet, but perhaps that made him more appealing to me. His hair was shaggy, unkempt, and his jaw was strong, his features well-spaced and well-angled, even if his nose was a tad crooked. And there were freckles splattered across all of it, even his lips.

Silently, I lifted a hand to touch my own lips.

How silly of me to notice, I thought, but for some reason, I had. I'd fixated on them when he was talking. I thought they were cute. Then, immediately, I hushed myself, covering my mouth with both hands. I hadn't said it aloud, of course, and I was alone in the parlour. But even thinking such a thing was terribly embarrassing.

But then I leaned back into the cushions and found myself smiling.

He *was* handsome. How could I have stopped looking at him? The more I thought, the more I noticed just how amiable that face was—those features, those freckles, that hair, those eyes ...

I inhaled slowly through my nose, my stomach aflutter.

His eyes were a different matter entirely. They stirred something in me, though I couldn't discern whether it was in a good way or not. There was an intensity in them that, at first, I couldn't place, but now, I realised it reminded me of staring at the sun. I wanted to look directly, but the severity made me shy away. His stare never wavered, like he'd seen everything and, therefore, couldn't possibly fear anything.

I laughed at myself. Here I was daydreaming about someone I barely knew, and yet, I couldn't seem to stop. Because it wasn't his appearance alone that drew me in. It was all of him. It was the way he carried himself.

He was, in a single word, free.

And that was the most elusive and attractive thing of all to me.

JASPER

I planted myself beside the garden, leaning on the fence and stretching out my legs. Then I clasped my hands behind my head and closed my eyes, settling in. Both siblings seemed fond of their garden, but it was Lily who stared out the window at it day after day. I'd watched her, studied her schedule. She'd see me sitting here eventually and, at the very least, order me to leave.

But I wouldn't be going anywhere, not after discovering her weakness. She was a lonesome thing that yearned for companionship, and I could cure her solitude. I could be her friend, if only until I convinced her to go to Gimlon with me ... Or perhaps I simply wanted an excuse to spend more time with her. It didn't matter either way; the result would be the same.

I reclined on the grass for a long while, drowsing as the Auric Sun began to smear shadows across the earth around me, when suddenly—

"What d'you think you're doing?"

She was late.

Timidly, I opened my eyes, wondering how long she'd watched me from the window before deciding to come outside.

I lifted my gaze until it found Lily's face, and already, my palms felt clammy. She loomed over me with her hands on her hips, draped in a dark mourning dress with white lace and gloves. Her hair had been pinned up close to her skull, a few mutinous curls falling around her chin.

"Well?" she asked.

We weren't well enough acquainted for me to say, but this person seemed foreign somehow. Someone else had bound and dressed her in this neat arrangement, and if not for her haughty attitude, I might've assumed she was another person altogether—a relative of the girl I'd met.

Coughing out my exhale, I cleared my throat.

"W-what does it look like I'm doing?" I asked in reply, though it didn't come out quite like I'd intended. It ought to have been uttered with feigned annoyance, but it rasped out breathily instead. I swallowed and closed my eyes again, willing my heartbeat to slow, hoping I might recover some composure if I couldn't see her. But just knowing she was there made me feel weak. My hands nearly trembled behind my head. "I'm taking a nap," I added in the steadiest voice I could manage.

She kicked the side of my boot, forcing me to look at her again.

"I can bloody well see that," she snapped, "but why're you taking your nap *here*?"

At last, I could see Lily beneath the guise. Her face puckered, distorting the pretty image enough to loosen my tension.

"This grass is quite comfortable; it's very well-tended."

"Honestly, can't you just—"

"You were the one who invited me," I said before she could finish.

"I did what?"

Sitting up, I ran a hand through my hair, trying to give the impression of casual confidence. I knew how to play this game.

"You told me to come back," I replied with a shrug. "So, I did."

Defiantly, she crossed her arms. "And what if I told you to leave? Would you?"

Gaining my feet, I patted off my trousers. "Certainly," I said and turned to walk away.

"Wait a second!" She flew after me but paused when I did. She wrung her hands, her eyes flicking to the ground as she muttered, "I-I wasn't actually telling you to leave ..." Her cheeks reddened, but I could only see a little of it on her downturned face.

Closing the distance between us, I reached for her chin and lifted her head with two fingers. I leaned even closer, lowering my voice, dipping forward to meet her eyes directly. "Then what are you telling me?" I asked.

Startled, she flinched back. "I—" she began weakly, then as if to reset the moment, she cleared her throat, rolled her shoulders back, and drew herself up. Pushing out her chest and placing her hands lightly on her hips again, she said, "I had one more question for you."

I chuckled, knowing she wouldn't let herself be so easily seduced, though her momentary fluster amused me. "Ask away."

But she hesitated.

Arching an eyebrow, I began to turn slowly toward the forest again. "If you don't actually have a question ..."

"What if I asked you to stay?"

The question fled her mouth in a jumble, swift and desperate. I froze mid-turn, my own words stopping in my throat. I peered behind me, expecting to be met with cynicism or laughter, but her expression was as earnest and nervous as I felt.

My voice came in no more than a whisper, and the words weren't at all the ones I intended to speak.

"I wouldn't move from this spot."

SINS & SMILES

LIAM

"Haven't you some coursework to do?" I asked, eyeing Lily from the doorway. She sat at her vanity, pinning her hair up and obviously having trouble doing so.

She jabbed a pin into place and winced before answering. "Haven't *you*?" She stuck a few pins between her lips to hold them as she slid another into her hair.

I shook my head. "Already finished."

She rolled her eyes and mumbled, "Of course."

I leaned on the doorframe. "What're you doing?"

She glanced up at the reflection of my face in the mirror. "What does it look like I'm doing?" she asked, careful not to let the pins fall out of her mouth as she spoke. They bobbed up and down with each word.

"Well—" I smirked. "It looks like you're trying to make a bird's nest on top of your head, but you could also be doing a rather poor job of putting your hair up. I can't really be sure which." I'd never seen her attempt styling her hair on her own; Celia usually did it, and it was often to Lily's displeasure.

"Ugh!" She dropped the strand of hair she'd been holding. It fell in front of her face as she tore the pins out of her mouth and slapped them down on the tabletop. "If you're not going to be useful or encouraging, Liam, go away."

"Why d'you need your hair done? We haven't any plans today."

"Maybe I want it up."

"Going somewhere?"

She twisted the loose strand of hair around her finger before tacking it in place. "I don't see how that's any of your business."

"Where're you going?"

Dropping her head back, she let out a heavy exhale. "It doesn't matter, Liam. Maybe I just want my hair out of my face for once." She extended her hand with the pins poking out toward me. "Look, if you're gonna stay, can you at least make yourself useful and help me put these bloody things in? They're infuriating."

Lazily, I moved closer, taking the pins and positioning myself behind her. Strand after strand, I fixed her hair in place. When I'd finished, she examined my efforts in the mirror, turning her head this way and that, and satisfied, she said, "Good enough," and scooted her chair back.

Was a simple 'thank you' too much to ask?

With one last spin in front of the mirror, Lily grabbed her boots and strode through the doorway, leaving me standing in her bedroom. I shook my head and followed her.

"Where're you going?" I asked again as we went down the stairs.

"Who says I'm going anywhere, Liam?"

"Well, the boots in your hand for one, not to mention the speed walk toward the door."

Halfway across the foyer, she came to an abrupt halt. "What?"

Lily pointed a finger back toward the staircase. "Shoo!"

"Excuse me?"

"Go away. Stop following me."

"Lily, you can't shoo me from my own house."

She flicked her hand at my chest. "Well, I can shoo you away from me, at least. Now *shoo*."

I crossed my arms, standing my ground until she swung around and marched down the hall, glancing over her shoulder every few steps to make sure I didn't follow. I waited for her to disappear around the corner before chasing after her. By the time I made it to the parlour, she'd already crossed the terrace. I barely caught sight of her before she disappeared behind a hedge.

Curious, I went to the kitchen, smiling shyly at Bennett as I shoved a stool up to a tall window. He quirked a brow at me, then shrugged and returned to what he was doing. I braced myself against the wall, curling my fingers over the windowsill and stretching up on my toes atop the stool. Outside, I could see the fenced garden, and on the lawn beside it was my sister.

She plopped down on the grass on her bottom to pull her boots on, taking no notice that her dress slid up above her knees as she did, her stocking-less legs uncommonly white. I frowned. Honestly, did she even know the definition of modesty?

But then, as she pulled her laces tight, her attention was stolen. Staring in the direction of the forest, she hurriedly covered her legs and jumped to her feet, straightening her dress. My face fell.

What had she noticed?

But following her line of sight, I saw exactly what—or rather, whom—she'd noticed, though I failed to understand her enthusiasm.

Mr. Behrtram waited at the edge of the lawn, slouched against a tree with his arms crossed, his face bearing a crooked smile. Lily ran up to greet him and after a few words were exchanged, she followed him into the woods, peeking back at the house before they both were swallowed by the forest.

What just—?

"Huh," I said aloud, stumped. I lowered onto flat feet and stood on the stool for a moment, trying to process what I'd witnessed.

"Good show out there, young Master Howell?"

I glanced at Bennett, who didn't look up from peeling a potato.

"Just Lily," I said, carefully climbing down off the stool.

"Not here to lift the salt for her again, are you?"

My face flushed. "I-I—"

He laughed. "Don't worry yourself, sir. She actually brought it back for once. It reappeared sometime in the night."

"That's a first," I mumbled, and he chuckled again.

"You tell her I'm still waiting for my paring knife, though. Heaven knows what she's gone and done with that. You'd think we had fairies, the way things go missing in this place."

I nodded. His mention of fairies made me feel strangely anxious, but he'd said it jokingly, not knowingly. There was no reason to fret.

Bennett was already preoccupied with his potatoes again and didn't acknowledge my departure. Pausing just outside the kitchen door, I scratched my head.

What on Earth was Lily up to?

Sighing, I continued down the hall, confused but unable to seek out answers just yet. I had coursework to finish.

JASPER

"You—you actually came."

"Of course, I did. You asked me to." I leaned against the closest tree, trying to give as calm and collected an air as possible, but my heart had begun racing long before I'd arrived.

"I ..." she began meekly. "I want to talk to you, but ... not here."

Behind her, the house loomed, its many windows glinting in the daylight.

"Shall we take a walk?" I suggested.

She followed my gaze over her shoulder and nodded.

"Where to then?"

"Anywhere."

"Anywhere?" I smiled. "All right, *anywhere* it is." I offered her my arm.

Absently, she pulled my sleeve back to examine the bruising on the back of my hand and wrist. I tensed, surprised that she'd even noticed, but she didn't ask how I'd come by such a misfortune. She simply adjusted her hold on me so she wouldn't disturb it and asked, "Mr. Behrtram, was it?"

I still wasn't used to my new moniker, and although I was often spoken to formally, for some reason, it sounded silly coming out of her mouth after she'd been so rude when we'd first met. "You don't have to call me that. Jasper is fine. Shall I call you Miss Howell?"

She peered sideways at me and smirked. "Just Lily please, if we're already being informal, that is."

Her coy glance made my mind wander for just a moment, and when I realised it, I almost stopped dead. I felt my face heating up and looked at my feet, clearing my throat. "You don't seem as guarded as you were the other day."

She nudged me with her elbow. Her sudden playfulness and the ease with which she spoke both surprised and delighted me, which felt dangerous, but her unexpected reply broke my tension almost immediately. "You don't seem as scary."

I snorted. "Was I scary?"

"Perhaps intimidating is a more accurate descriptor," she said. Then falling into my step, she asked, "So where do you live? Is it nearby?"

"No, far away," I replied, and she paused, confused. I added, "I told you I was from somewhere else."

"Why're you here then?"

I gave her arm a little tug. "C'mon, you can still see your house."

A panicked look flashed across her face, and she charged forward a few steps, dragging me with her. "Well, c'mon then."

I laughed, remembering the first time I'd seen her walking with her brother at the funeral—how ungraceful she'd been then, too. "You really did mean *anywhere*, didn't you? Haven't you ever left your house before?"

"Of course, I have, but I've never done something as tawdry as this."

"Tawdry?" I touched my chest in feigned shock. "Just what're you planning on doing to me?"

She stopped in her tracks, her face at first blanching and then reddening. "N-nothing like that! I only meant going for an unchaperoned walk in the woods with a stranger! That's all. It just … seems a bit … inelegant, doesn't it?"

"I'm only teasing," I said. "We've met a few times now; at least upgrade me to an acquaintance."

She frowned at my smile.

"Why did you ask me to come back, Lily?"

The redness in her cheeks appeared to deepen when I said her name, which pleased me.

"I dunno," she muttered, her pace slowing. "I suppose it's because I couldn't stop thinking about you after we met."

It was my turn to gape and blush. "You—you're rather forward, aren't you?"

She seemed only then to realise what she'd said and clammed up again. "No! I-I mean—well …"

I turned and started walking again for an excuse not to face her, fighting to keep my composure, though, in truth, her confession had me feeling rather giddy. Silently, I asked the wind to pick up and cool the warmth in my face, and kindly, it obliged.

Lily caught up to me, her head bowed and her fingers furiously twisting the ribbons at her waist. "I mean, here you are telling me about fairies and other worlds. How can I not be intrigued? And—and you're out here on your own, far from home … It's just rather admirable, I think."

I looked at her, puzzled.

"I've never been very far from home," she added, "and lately, home seems far away even when I'm there."

The corner of my mouth turned up in a sombre smile. I knew the feeling. "So," I said, "you want to run away?"

"Well, no, not run away, just ..." She let out a breathy chuckle and scratched her head. "Why am I even telling you this?"

"Because it's easier to talk to a stranger who doesn't know or care enough about you to judge you."

Her feet stopped moving again, so I turned to smile at her.

"I thought we'd upgraded you already," she mumbled.

"Even an acquaintance can't know you that well." Then I asked again, "Why d'you want to get away?"

From the way she chewed the inside of her cheek, I knew she hadn't really thought about it, but she answered as best she could. "I suppose I just want to see something new, that's all. A change of scenery perhaps." Then her voice shrank, and in it, there was a touch of spite. "Who knows ... maybe I'll find a renewed vigour for life."

I didn't inquire about the acidity in that comment. It wasn't meant for me, and even if she spoke openly now, I could tell that I'd be overstepping my bounds if I asked who the intended recipient was.

Instead, I said, "Well, I can help you change the scenery, at least. What sort of trees do you like best?"

She considered for a moment—another inquiry she hadn't been prepared for—and replied, "I like oaks, but why?"

That same smile crept onto my lips. "Let's go then."

LIAM

I sat back in my chair, releasing my breath in a contented sigh as I stared down at my mathematics exam. Every answer was neatly marked, each individually checked for correctness. Miss Sawyer would be pleased. Only one side left.

With another big exhale, I dipped my quill in ink and flipped the page, leaning my face closer so I would be sure to read every question thoroughly. But just as the nib touched the parchment, Lily threw her arm in the air and announced, "Finished! Can I go now?"

I ogled her. She sat half out of her chair, stretched over her desk with her test crumpled in one fist.

"Pardon?" Miss Sawyer said from the front, peering over her lenses at my sister.

"I'm done," Lily repeated, waving the wrinkled page in the air. "Can I go?"

"You're done?" Our tutor arched a quizzical brow.

"Yes, I'm barking done! Now can I please leave? You're cutting into my free time."

"Why're you so eager?" I asked.

She flashed me a scathing look. "There's no talking during tests, Liam."

But Miss Sawyer was curious, too. "Why *are* you so eager to go, Lilith?"

With a low whine, Lily sank back into her seat, her body flopping down on her desk. "Does it even matter? I've got places to be and things to do, all right?"

Sceptical, our governess stood and made her way to my sister's spot, taking the paper. She smoothed the parchment against her chest before examining it.

"Everything's right," Lily said. "I checked it already."

Nodding, Miss Sawyer considered the test a moment longer before peering up at Lily again. "All correct," she agreed, both eyebrows now raised in surprise. "You may go."

"Finally." Lily flew out of her seat, her books already tucked under her arm. Without another word, she strode through the room, deposited the books on the shelf, and disappeared through the door. Miss Sawyer and I stared after her for a few seconds before I returned to my exam and she to her seat at the front of the room.

When I'd finished (all correct), I carried my paper to her desk.

"Well done," she said upon inspection, and I smiled.

"Thank you, ma'am."

"William," she said as I put my things away. "What's the matter with your sister?"

Lifting my shoulders, I said, "I've no idea at all."

But that was a lie. I knew—or rather, suspected—the reason for her haste: she was going to see Mr. Behrtram again. She'd been so keen before that it was the only logical explanation. Still, it perplexed me, especially considering her previous behaviour toward the boy.

But strangely, I thought I could understand it from the

young man's end. I'd seen the way he looked at her—that mix of curiosity and delight. He hadn't really seemed all that bothered by her burst of anger. He'd even been smiling when I left him that day.

But Lily …

What did Mr. Behrtram have to offer that could possibly motivate her to *do what she was told* for the chance to see him again?

The answer came to me as soon as I'd asked the question in my head, and it was far simpler than I'd originally expected: Lily wanted companionship. For some inexplicable reason, she'd chosen him to be her friend. It seemed odd after all my sister's impolite speeches about those less fortunate, but then I smiled, reminding myself that friendship doesn't care about appearance or wealth; it happens regardless.

"William?"

"Huh?" I looked up to find Miss Sawyer's eyes on me. "Oh, forgive me, I got lost in my thoughts for a moment." I stacked my books and returned them to the shelf.

She allowed a gentle smile. "Well, go on then. I'm sure you'll want to figure out why your sister is so impatient."

I turned to leave, though I knew there was no discovery to be made. Lily and Mr. Behrtram would already be wandering in the woods, and it would be impossible to catch up to them now. There was no point trying.

"Oh, and William, do tell me if you find out, won't you? I must know what on Earth has succeeded in inspiring her."

Nodding, I said, "Lily pays attention; she just doesn't do the work."

Miss Sawyer grimaced. "I know your sister is very bright—bright but unmotivated—but if she has found a reason to pay attention to her studies for once, I'd be interested to know what it is. Goodness knows I've tried to no avail."

With a quiet laugh, I completed my walk to the door. "Of course. If I know, you'll know."

"Thank you, William. You've always been such an honest young man."

Lily didn't return until Miss Sawyer and I were already ten minutes into the afternoon lessons, but still pleased about her willingness to complete her exam this morning, our tutor barely reprimanded her. Not that a scolding would've done much to dampen Lily's spirits. She was still grinning when she slipped into her chair and began the evening's assignments, though she refused to say a word of explanation.

I sighed, dipping my quill in ink.

JASPER

I smiled to myself as I moseyed through the trees. I couldn't seem to get that stupid grin off my face, and I kept peering over my shoulder as if I might find Lily still trailing behind me, complaining that my strides were too long for her to keep up. She'd gone home, of course. I'd left her at the edge of the lawn.

I wouldn't see her tomorrow. It would be the first time in nearly a week that we wouldn't meet. There was a family outing to attend, she'd said, so instead, I wished that today had been extended, that the hours passed between us could've lasted just a bit—

But that thought stopped me in my tracks.

I'd only spoken to this bloody girl a handful of times; I shouldn't be so enthusiastic. This was just business, after all. It was part of my plan. I had to take her to Gimlon like all the rest, by order of the queen.

I shook my head as if to clear it and struck the smile from my lips.

Well, I tried to.

But I thought about her, replayed the day's conversations in my head, and felt that keen little smile creep back onto my face. What did it matter if I smiled anyway? There was no one here to see me, and it was a long journey home.

LILY

"Have you any family?" I asked, staring up at Jasper. He lounged on the lowest branch of the oak, his back against the trunk. He had one leg on the bough, bent so his knee stuck up in the air, the other dangling off the side.

A leaf floated down from above him, set loose by the wind, though it was still bright green. When it got close enough to my head, I moved under it and blew, lifting it a few inches higher before letting it spiral toward the ground again. Jasper watched it disappear in the grass before answering, picking up another that had settled on his chest.

"On Trigon, I do," he said, twirling the leaf in his fingers by the stem. "They live in the royal city of Egaldon in Gimlon."

I rolled my eyes. "Still on about this *other world* business? We're close enough acquaintances now. You can tell me the truth."

But Jasper was unaffected. "Still don't believe me I see." With a long exhale, he sat up, shifted his body, and dropped his right leg so they both hung over the side of the branch. "Can't really expect you to, I suppose. You are from Earth."

"And what's that supposed to mean?"

"You're from Earth," he said again with a shrug. "It shouldn't offend you. People here are just a bit ... disconnected."

I uncrossed my arms, raising my hands in surrender, though I wasn't willing to let the subject rest. "But *why*? You said there are other places, and clearly, we're connected somehow—by your gates or whatever. So why doesn't anyone here know about it?"

Without a word of warning, Jasper dropped out of the tree, landing on steady legs barely a foot from where I stood. My hands flew up to my mouth, stifling a gasp, but his expression remained mild.

"Iraxhar," he said. "That's the name, and you aren't really supposed to know." Then examining my face, he added, "Sorry, did I scare you?"

I cleared my throat. "Not at all," I mumbled, lowering my hands, though my heartbeat still raced.

He sneered. "No, of course not. You're Lily Howell. Nothing in the world could possibly frighten you." Nudging my shoulder, he slipped his hand around my wrist, one finger probing for my pulse. I jerked my arm away but too late. Jasper laughed.

"Shut it."

"Must've been a good scare if you're still that flustered."

"Why not?"

Jasper's forehead creased. "What?"

"Why is Earth disconnected?"

"Oh, changing the subject, are we?" he teased but indulged me. "It's been a long time since anyone from Iraxhar came here and even longer since there was any regular travel or trade."

"But *why*?"

He turned so I couldn't see his face. "The Departure, they called it—when Anim Zenith drew the veil between our worlds. Well, diplomatically, I suppose it made the most sense at the time." He scratched his neck. "Now, the Gates are the only way Earth is connected to the other worlds, and they're mostly forgotten thanks to the Anim. What's the point in trying to preserve or recreate something that isn't viable?"

He started walking, his shoulders rolling forward, and I followed. The topic seemed to make him a tad uncomfortable, but I still didn't want to dismiss it yet. "Well, that doesn't seem very fair. No matter how long it's been, we *are* still connected, and that's a special thing, don't you think?" I caught his sleeve, encouraging him to look at me.

"Special how?" he asked.

"Well," I began, rubbing the fabric between my fingers. It was worn but soft. "You and I wouldn't have met without that connection, right?"

Jasper's eyes widened, and immediately, he looked down, though I could see his cheeks redden. His skin was so fair that any change in his complexion was extravagant. I smiled to myself, strangely pleased that I'd managed to make the boy blush.

"I-I'm sure it sounds great to have your world included in all of this, but reality isn't so grand. Iraxhar isn't all fairies and elves, you know."

"Elves?"

He glowered at my excitement. "Look, Earth's been separated for a very long time—centuries." He stretched his arms above his head. "I doubt Iraxhar will ever really be complete again. Earth's massive. It's too populated now, and every country has a different king or queen." He dropped his arms. "And not one of them is willing to surrender any power to be a part of something bigger. It just won't happen. They all fear the new and unknown. If the existence of the other worlds was discovered, they'd think us a threat."

I considered his words and found myself agreeing with him. "Iraxhar doesn't have a king then?"

"I didn't say that. There's the king on Trigon and other rulers on each world, but they coexist … for the most part."

"They're good rulers then?"

Judiciously, Jasper replied, "I suppose it depends which ruler and who you ask."

"Gimlon is your home, right? That's what you called it. What about the ruler there?"

He watched me, quiet for a moment, his smile straightening out. "You ask a lot of questions, don't you?"

"I'm trying to learn. Tell me about your king."

Jasper hesitated again, seeming to contemplate his response. Finally, he licked his lips and said, "King Gilmer is a levelheaded man, generally respected and always just, though almost to a fault, I'm afraid."

"And what about his queen?"

At that, he fell silent entirely, his eyes tightening. The corners of his mouth twitched as though he couldn't decide whether to smile or frown. His voice was soft when, at last, he spoke again.

"Come now, Lily, if I told you everything straight away, there'd be no mystery or intrigue to keep you coming back." He winked, and although a smile accompanied it, I got the impression that he wasn't smiling internally. But that was his business, I decided, and I didn't press him further.

Instead, I crossed my arms and blew a noisy breath out my nostrils in an attempt to lighten the mood. "You can be rather maddening, you know that?"

To my relief, the effect was almost instantaneous. Jasper's shoulders relaxed. "Yeah, well, you can be rather annoying with your barrage of questions, so which of us is worse?"

I sighed in jest. "A sin is a sin, I suppose."

But when I faced Jasper again, I was greeted with disdain. He spoke out of the corner of his mouth. "That's something I just don't understand ..."

"What?"

"That religion and God nonsense."

My face fell. "Who says it's nonsense?"

Jasper thrust a thumb at his chest. "I do."

"It's not."

"Says a girl who can have a fairy right in front of her face and still not believe in other worlds. Your logic is clearly skewed."

My frown deepened. "That's entirely different."

"Is it?" He quirked a brow. "People choose to believe what they want and ignore the rest. That's why every person on Earth has a different religion, mind you a lot of it seems to be varying interpretations of the same thing." He shrugged. "But no two people will think or interpret in the same way. It's like one person decided something, then others just liked it and attached themselves to the idea until they generated a following. Except times ten."

"Well, how else could it get started? Everything starts with an idea."

"Right, but that's all it is—an idea. How can you dive in and blindly believe something like that and then totally reject an alternate possibility even when there's tangible evidence sitting right in front of you? It makes no sense."

"You're really cut up about this, aren't you?"

"Well, why aren't you?"

I folded my arms, closing in on myself a bit. Honestly, I wasn't sure I'd ever paid enough attention in church services to be able to effectively argue the subject, though disbelievers weren't uncommon. "It's not blind belief. My family have always been well-acquainted with the Lord."

"Well-acquainted, huh?" He leaned in, his voice and posture imposing. "They meet up and have tea then? Have nice little chats from time to time? And what about you? D'you join them?"

I pursed my lips. "Do you have a point to make, or did you just want to piss on my family's entire belief system?"

Jasper dropped his shoulders, groaning. "I just don't get it. Why d'you need someone or something to tell you how to live your life? Aren't there already enough people doing that without the addition of some presumed higher power? Why can't you just live freely?"

"We do—quite comfortably, I might add—because we know there's someone who'll love and forgive us regardless of our sins."

But the scowl didn't leave Jasper's face. "I can't believe that."

"What?"

"He'll love and forgive you? He tracks every bad thing you've done—every mistake you've ever made—and holds them over your head like a ransom, threatening Hell and promising salvation but only if you accept him. I refuse to believe in a god that frightens and guilt trips his way into a following."

I raised both brows, speechless.

He stared hard at my bewildered face and then, sighing, bowed his head. "There are many bad things in these worlds, Lily—dark moments that only ghosts can see. If your god could see them, too, and was truly merciful, I like to think he wouldn't let them happen." He swallowed, his voice shrinking. "But they still happen. People still hurt—living, tangible, *real* people."

I didn't know what to say, so I replied as best I could, though I was only parroting something I'd heard. "Light wouldn't seem bright without darkness. Good things wouldn't feel good if there were no bad things to compare them to."

Exhaling, Jasper said. "If that reasoning satisfies you, then fine. But I'll still choose not to believe in a god that promises love while constantly allowing suffering."

I gulped. "It's—it's about the balance of good and evil. There always has to be a balance ... I think."

"Yeah, well, I don't get it. And anyway, why does it matter if an incomprehensible being forgives you? Your sins will always leave a mark—on a place, on a person, on you. The consequences won't just disappear by believing an invisible god forgives you. Shouldn't you focus on earning the forgiveness of those you've wronged instead?"

I huffed; his insistent rejection was beginning to get on my nerves. "Not everyone is willing to forgive."

"Then live with the guilt and learn from it," he said, as though it were really that simple.

"Not everyone wants to live with guilt ..."

He smirked and flicked his brows at me. "Then maybe you shouldn't do wrong to people in the first place."

I puffed out my cheeks and released the air in a loud exhale. "It's not always easy to avoid. I'm certain you've wronged plenty of people in your lifetime."

Jasper snorted and nodded slowly, thoughtfully. "Sure, loads." He looked back at me, that coy half smile still on his lips. "But I'm not asking for anyone's forgiveness, am I?"

Swallowing, I shied away. "I think we should just agree to disagree on this one."

Jasper grinned. "Got you thinking, didn't I?"

His confidence boosted my annoyance. "My beliefs are what they are," I replied stiffly. "I'm a product of my world—of my experiences, my environment, and my teachings. It's what I believe to be true because, my whole life, it's been taught and spoken of as truth. Can't you just accept that?"

Jasper observed me silently, the hardness on his face

dissolving. It made me nervous when he did that—just stared. I never knew how to respond to it. It felt a little intense, but when he spoke, his voice had softened along with his expression.

"Yeah," he said. "I can accept it ... A product of your world, huh? I like that. It's true, isn't it? We're all molded into who we are by what happens to and around us, by the people who come and go and the things they teach us, by the errors we make along the way ..." Turning his back to me, he peered up through the treetops. "But you could take it more literally, too. When we die, our bodies decay and blend perfectly with the soil; it's like we're made of the same ingredients. So perhaps we are just a product of our worlds—figuratively and literally."

"That's not exactly where I was going with that ..."

He laughed. "I know, but it makes you think, doesn't it? I rather like the idea of being a part of the worlds—the trees, the oceans, the mountains, the sky ... I'd rather exist as one tiny part of that than spend my life trying to live up to the expectations of the unknown."

I stared at his back, unsure how to answer him or if he wanted an answer. Even though he addressed me, he almost seemed like he was talking to himself, reciting a self-affirming soliloquy. I decided not to interject.

"There are so many unanswered questions that come with your god, so much mystery and secrecy and ... blindness to cruelty. I can't accept that, not without knowing *why*. But my questions can never be answered because you can't show me definite, tangible proof that your god or your heaven exists."

"Well, that doesn't mean they don't," I mumbled, folding my arms again. "It's called having faith." Jasper acted like he didn't hear me, taking a few steps out of the shadows and into the sunlight.

"But this place," he continued, "these worlds, this grass,

this tree, this air—every one of my senses tells me it exists. I know if I search long enough, any confusion I have about these things will be cleared. I'll find my answers; they're waiting for me somewhere ..." His arms outstretched, he turned in a slow circle, his head dropping back to look upward again. I could see the glow of the sun on his cheeks—the warmth. There was a smile on his lips as he drew a long breath in through his nose. "This place," he said. "It exists." His feet stopped, and slowly, he lowered his arms. Then he waited, and in that voiceless moment, I felt as if I could hear everything all at once: the wind in the leaves, the birdsongs, the flutter of wings, the distant babble of the creek we'd passed by earlier in the afternoon ...

He let his head fall to the side and winked. "And you can't tell me it doesn't."

He was right; I couldn't because it existed for me, too. And perhaps I was being overzealous, but watching him smile at the sky, I thought: so did he.

PART SEVEN
SECRETS

JASPER

"Get back here!"

My foot slid out from under me when I lunged after the thief, one knee thudding against the earth as my hands flew out to catch myself. I winced, arms braced on either side of my leg, and for a moment, I struggled for breath, watching the moisture from the ground slowly darken the cloth of my trousers.

"Dammit, Jeryth!" My boot squeaked against the wet grass as I righted myself and took off through the meadow. I swung my arms, trying to drive myself into a sprint, but my efforts were wasted. Dress clothes were impossible to run in. My arms couldn't go back far enough, and when I forced it, the cloth stretched so tight across my chest that the buttons threatened to pop off. Then again, this ensemble had been fashioned for formal occasions, not midnight pursuits of thieving jarvies.

Winded, I staggered to a halt, bending to rest my hands on my thighs. I clutched my side as I straightened up again, panting, sweeping my gaze across the meadow, but nothing stirred. I squinted, hoping for some small whisper in the grass—anything!—but the night was still. I'd lost him. I'd been bested by a rodent, and I was convinced these damned clothes were to blame with their tassels and buttons and tight-fitted collar. Groaning, I pulled my trouser legs up to squat down, propping my elbows on my knees to take one last look around, but I knew he was long gone. And so was my coin purse.

I emptied my lungs in a defeated sigh, unfastening my houppelande, fighting with the baggy sleeves. "Shit …"

If I could see better, perhaps I could've traced him, but there were only patches of pale white light pressing through or the curve of a moon as the clouds moved over them—certainly not enough to allow a proper hunt. All around me, the sky was soaked in shades of grey with no wind to sweep it away, which, mixed with the humidity in the air, held the promise of more rain.

I stood to twist and stretch and opened my eyes as wide as I could in an attempt to wake myself up some before I turned eastward. But then I looked west, then down at my feet, trying to coax myself to take a step in one direction or the other.

Instead, I stayed where I was.

I didn't want to go home. What I wanted was to immediately return to Earth, but I'd already put miles between myself and the Gate. Not Earth, I decided, but I still had options. The meadow was equidistant between the castle in Egaldon to the east and Quade's clinic just outside the village of Erisilon to the west. I enjoyed the doctor's company. He always had extra beds and never asked too many questions.

West was clearly the better choice.

But still, I wavered. It'd been weeks since I'd been home; I knew I should make some manner of appearance, if only to assure them I was still alive. I'd just completed my objective yet again—passed the girl off to the guards shortly after we'd gone through the Gate. She should already have arrived at the castle for the queen's inspection. At the very least, my continued success would put Lady Lenore in a more manageable mood.

I turned and headed for home, but I barely made it a few yards before a raindrop slipped down the back of my neck. I grimaced, pinching my shoulder blades together as it slid down my spine.

I peered upward as a slow groan of thunder shuddered in the clouds.

"Don't cry," I whispered to the sky, but why would a Spirit listen to me?

NOAH

I stopped beside Gabriel's suite, nodding at Soren, who stood a little straighter but not at attention. "Is my brother in, by chance, Mr. Behrtram?"

The guard lifted his head, glancing at either end of the hall before answering. When he saw no listeners, he said, "I'm afraid 'e ain't returned yet, your highness."

I pinched my lips together, attempting to conceal my frustration—it was already the fourth time I'd come this week—but the man was observant and chuckled at my efforts.

"I wouldn't worry yourself too much, sir." His smirk relaxed into a gentle half-smile that looked out of place on his marked face. Even his voice softened. "I worry less when 'e's gone away. Got a good 'ead on 'is shoulders, that one."

I furrowed my brow at what he'd said, but I saw a servant coming down the corridor and didn't inquire, afraid our conversation might be overheard and reiterated. As far as anyone in the castle was concerned, Gabriel was home in bed, and I didn't want to give anybody reason to suspect otherwise.

Responding to my silence, Soren snapped to attention, and I pretended to inspect and correct the strictness of his posture.

The servant stopped to bow and then hurried on around the corner and out of sight. When she was gone, Soren relaxed against the wall, but I waited another minute before speaking again.

"How long has he been gone this time?" I asked the guard.

"A full 18 days." Soren's face screwed up, and despite what he'd said before, I knew he worried for Gabriel.

But observing the man—with his dark, severe eyes and the scars left over from some violence that warped one half of his face—it crossed my mind that he'd likely been given this particular job years ago in an effort to frighten Gabriel into obedience. But even as a child, my brother had been unintimidated.

I wasn't aware of the nature of their initial acquaintance, but the relationship between the two had long since been established. I didn't think there was another person in all the worlds that Soren cared for more, though by my observation, I thought Penna was a close second.

"Sir?"

I sighed. "Did he tell you how long he'd be gone or where he was going? It's usually only a week or so, isn't it?"

"The longest it's been in some time, but 'e said 'e may be gone a few weeks. I expect 'e'll turn up any day now. As for where 'e's gone ..." He cracked a smile. "I'm sorry, sir, but I'm under strict orders from 'is highness not to say outside a case of emergency."

"You know I outrank my brother."

His eyes thinned, but the smirk didn't leave his lips. "And you know where my loyalty lies." Then, in a slightly haughty tone, he added, "Sir."

I pursed my lips. "You spend far too much time with Gabriel, Mr. Behrtram. His behaviours are starting to rub off on you."

"I think quite highly of the young master. I'll take that as a compliment."

I snorted. "I assure you, I didn't mean it as one." I heard another set of approaching footsteps and decided our conversation had ended. I bowed my head to the man, extending a hand. He shook it and smiled, copying my bow.

"Always a pleasure, sir."

"Tell me when Gabriel returns, won't you? If only to ease my nerves."

"I will, your highness." Then, shyly: "Give Penna my best when you see 'er next."

I glanced down the corridor and saw her familiar form striding our way. I tossed my head in her direction. "Give it to her yourself."

As the housekeeper approached, I turned to greet her. She curtseyed as best she could, though her arms were full. In one hand, she carried a short stool, and in the other, she held a tankard of mead with a plate of meat and potatoes balanced on her forearm.

"Good evening, sirs," she said, and turning to Soren, she offered him the stool. "Care for a chair?"

He took it, bowing and stuttering about her kindness.

"Oh hush," she scolded playfully. "Can't let you just stand here until the young prince decides to return; you'll be standing till your death. Now, go on, sit and have a bite. You must be hungry."

He took the meal graciously, and I turned to leave. It was long past nightfall. But I recalled what Soren had said before and spoke over my shoulder to him. "Mr. Behrtram."

Grudgingly, he pulled his eyes from Penna's smiling face. "Yessir?"

"Earlier, you said you worried more for Gabriel when he's home than when he's away. May I ask why that is?"

For but a moment, the shadow of pure rage contorted the guard's face. The look was so severe that I flinched, but it fled as quickly as it had come, replaced by a soft melancholy.

Exhaling, Soren lowered his gaze and said gently, "Another time, sir." His eyes then flicked sideways, and I understood that he would not answer in front of Penna.

Curious.

I nodded. "All right," I agreed, though not without reluctance. "Another time."

"I'll not betray the young prince's trust, but I will tell you when 'e arrives. You 'ave my word, your highness."

The conversation, I could see, was over. The guard would say no more, and although I could've ordered his submission, I didn't press him. I bid the two goodnight and returned to my chambers, feeling a little relieved and at the same time, a little more unsettled.

JASPER

I paused in my trek homeward to stare up at the dark, clouded sky, squinting and blinking in the dewy air.

Something horrible must have happened, or worse, something was still yet to come. Lady Animaero couldn't seem to stop crying, and the thought that she could be so terribly sad injured me.

"What is it, Aery?" I whispered to the night air. "Why're you so sad?"

I held my breath, waiting and listening as attentively as I could, but the only reply I received was a raindrop to my cheek. Blowing out a big puff of air, I hung my head and walked on, though I couldn't help my disappointment.

Animaero was the first Spirit I'd ever spoken to, and after all the years since, I liked to think she could consider me her friend —a trusted ally, at least. We spoke often. I would never have described her as shy, but lately, the distance between us seemed, inexplicably, to have grown. Gee, Igni, and Mara were friendly, too, though not nearly as eager to grant me their time as Aery was. Now, it seemed, all four of them had withdrawn.

I stopped again, pondering.

There was a place I could go to speak with them. I'd been there before plenty, though only ever for a few minutes at a time. I'd never felt particularly unwelcome (sometimes I found my way there without meaning to), but with their sudden reserve, I thought it might feel like an intrusion.

I didn't want to impose on them; I just wanted to understand. I wanted to help them if it was in my power, but I couldn't heal what I couldn't understand. And it hardly seemed like four inconceivably powerful Spirits had any reason to entrust a lowly human with their troubles and their secrets.

I would never know how to stop the rain from falling.

I laughed grimly to myself. In their eyes, that's all I was: a flighty, untrustworthy being that would create and destroy until it bore an heir to its destruction or died. That's what a human was to them, and silently, guiltily, I resented them for it. I hated that they would lump me in with all other humans as if I weren't special, as if I couldn't see and hear and speak to them. No one else could. I'd never encountered another person in that void-like place where they existed. It was only me.

I stamped my feet. "Damn it, Aery!" I shouted at the sky, throwing my arms down at my sides. "Why are you so—?"

A rumble of thunder surged through the night, effectively drowning out my voice. I raised my arms above my head, preparing myself for a repercussion, but her wrath came in no more than a steady drizzle of rain. Sighing, I dropped my arms again, slumped my shoulders, and let my head fall back in exhaustion. I stood in one place with closed eyes as the rainfall thickened, peppering my face with water.

"Sorry," I mumbled through tight lips, and another loud crack of thunder opened my eyes in time to see a flash of lightning. It lit the whole sky for a haunting second, silhouetting the trees that circled me in an ominous display.

"Okay! I get it!" I hollered. "It's your business! I accept my defeat and eventual doom because I'm a flighty, untrustworthy human, all right?" Then, relaxing my face, I continued, my voice disappearing into the torrent. But Aery would hear me; she could always hear me. "Please don't forget that—" I bowed my head, the last words barely making a sound as they crossed my lips. "Well, I'm here if you need me, and I'll do what I can."

The rain only fell harder.

SETH

The morning dew collected on the faces of the dead, little beads of moisture perched delicately on eyelashes and brows. I angled my foot to step in the space between a man's arm and his side as a low haze of mist and smoke drifted slowly across the field. The air was thick with the spirits of the fallen, their bodies splayed across the meadow and in the trees, empty husks of beings that had had lives and loves and futures before the Flaxen Sun set not even a day past.

Everything was so fresh.

The stench of decay hadn't yet settled over the land. Instead, it felt muggy, as if the moisture leaving the bodies had fled into the air above them. Every breath I drew was hot in my throat. Every step touched gore.

It was the silence that made it feel real—as if this moment and I were suspended in time. It was the unnatural humidity. The sky wasn't crying; it was sweating, seeping, oozing.

Some sacrifices were always necessary. That was what we believed. One gruesome night would be the toll for our salvation, our freedom, our happiness. A few hours and a few thousand strangers in exchange for peace. It genuinely seemed a worthy trade, but to think our efforts had culminated in this ...

I'd talked about it, thought about it, dreamt about it, planned it for years, but reality was far crueler than I could ever have imagined. When I agreed to the coup, I was thinking about freedom. I was thinking about my brothers and our people.

But not this.

This was my city, raided and pillaged.

This was my home, painted with blood.

These were my dead, strewn and piled.

This was my army, reduced to a lesson and a memory.

I hadn't even fought alongside them. This new stain in our history would forever bear my name, and I didn't even know how many had lasted until Flaxsol's rise.

But when the others joined—when I heard Liam gag and cough behind me, when Lily gasped at the horror that spilled at her feet— that's when I knew I'd truly made a mistake.

This was not peace.

How easy it had been to imagine it from afar. How noble to claim that some casualties are required for the sake of the greater good. How simple it seemed to imagine it, to plan it, to execute it ...

I turned to face my companions, and for just a moment—a quiet, awful, guilty moment—I envied Noah. He who could close his eyes to this, who did not have to deal with the aftermath ... I envied him the moment I met Gabriel's gaze.

If I could've vanished, I would have. Because he didn't speak. He didn't cry. He looked at me with such a hollow expression that I felt a wrench of pain in my stomach. He looked at me with just a touch of disbelief, not at the battlefield littered with bodies but at me.

I had betrayed him. I had betrayed the image he'd had of me. I had betrayed the person I'd always been.

He looked at me as if he'd never imagined his brother capable of such savagery, as if his opinion had changed, as if he could not fathom what wretched sort of person would condone this.

He looked at me as if I were a stranger.

And maybe I was.

Maybe I'd strayed too far from our path. Maybe our good intentions were misplaced and selfish and heartless. Maybe I was every bit the monster people said I was.

What other sort of creature could strive and spend tireless hours building an army for this purpose and this outcome?

And we had done it, in part, for him.

For him, for ourselves, for Haven, for Soren—for every person we held dear.

We'd planned it with the best of intentions.

We'd planned it for love and vengeance.

And I could see in my brother's eyes that he would never forgive me.

Thankfully, I didn't have to sit under his scrutiny for longer than a minute.

The man at my feet let out a gargled laugh, spitting blood on my trouser leg, wheezing in levity. I startled, ripping my eyes from my brother's face to sweep the field as the dead sat up, raising their hands. One by one, they began to clap.

This part wasn't real. I knew it wasn't real. This wasn't the future; this was just my mind and my guilt and regret personifying itself in my dream.

But how real it felt. How loud this cacophony of applause and laughter was. How thin the veil of blood that scattered in the air each time a soldier opened their mouth. There were so many that the bloody mist never dissipated; it hung mercilessly in the air, the whole world around me tinged in red as if I were on Obscrys, not Trigon.

And then the noise dulled—dulled, not stopped—as though I were hearing them from afar, as if a great blanket had smothered them and stifled the sounds.

All except a single steady clap.

Slow.

Deliberate.

And when I turned, Gabriel stared back at me, his arms outstretched, his hands meeting in that measured beat.

The world around me quieted, the sounds of the dead silenced. But Gabriel's applause slowed and intensified, every clap rattling the earth beneath my feet, echoing, moisture exploding from his clasped hands each time his palms met—the moisture from the bodies in the air.

I could see it. I could feel it. I could hear the screams and wails of sorrow as the last proof of their warmth and life was snuffed between my brother's hands.

I shut my eyes because I couldn't stand it, but the noise grew.

I opened them, and—

I was alone. My brother was gone. There were no bodies. I stood in the meadow on a dark, clear night, a breeze flirting with the tall grass around me.

I turned in a circle.

The steady beat continued, though it was no longer a clap; it was a bird tapping on a nearby tree.

But that couldn't be right. There were no birds here, not in the meadow, not on the battlefield. It was something else, something in the past. A knock on the door, only not on wood, on glass. There was someone at my window.

I slipped slowly out of my nightmare and opened my eyes. There was my ceiling in my room and the soft rap on my window. Immediately, I recognised it as my brother's.

I took my time, trying to wipe away the dream, to rid my

countenance of its horror. Remove the fright, the guilt, the pain, just as I did every morning—erased the night's desolation to greet the day.

Those feelings were for the me that existed somewhere in the future—the wretched man I was sure to become. Today, I was just me, just Seth, just a prince and a brother. Someone gentle and easy and caring.

There were tears in my eyes, and because I knew Gabriel could see me through the sliver in the curtains, I rubbed them and faked a yawn to give reason for the watery redness. He knocked again, thinking I hadn't yet noticed him. I smoothed my tousled hair as I stood, but my legs shook, and I sat back down on the bed, surprised by the lethargy I felt. I'd seen it so many times; I should be used to it by now. But I would pretend I was only tired.

It was easy to pretend; I was good at it.

Yawning naturally now, I crossed the room, threw the curtains back and recoiled when we came face to face. I hadn't expected him to be so close.

"Let me in."

I sighed, dragging a hand down my face as I reached for the latch with the other. But I paused, puzzled by his appearance. It took me a moment to notice because he'd removed the decorative houppelande and unfastened his collar.

"Why formal attire?"

He shrugged. "Felt like it."

"You hate dress clothes. And you're covered in mud and grass."

"Yeah, and I'm soaked. And it's freezing, so let me in." He ducked his head under the eave, holding his cape and boots in a bundle at his chest.

Gabriel was up to something. He always was, though

usually not so blatantly. Unfortunately, my ability had never quite been able to pick up on his intentions, and he never let Noah close enough to try. And, of course, getting information from the subject himself was nearly impossible.

It had always struck me as odd; I dreamt about a great deal many things involving those close to me but rarely Gabriel. He was only ever a figure in the background or a spectre when the dream turned sour and untrue.

"Where've you been?" I asked, unlocking and pushing the window open.

"Earth," he replied to my surprise, but he stiffened for a second after as though he'd answered without meaning to.

I didn't press it, moving on so he could relax from his blunder. "You're not coming in here like that."

"What?"

"Look at you. Step back." I didn't want him here, not after the dream. All I could see was that look he'd given me—the disgust and disappointment.

"What?"

"Take a step back," I said. I wanted him to look away. I wanted to distract him. I wanted him to close his eyes to the grief I fought to keep from my face. I reached for the first thing I could find that contained water—a vase of fresh flowers a maid had placed on my bureau earlier that evening—and flung it at him before he could protest.

His arms flew up to shield himself from the attack, but the water was quicker. He squeezed his eyes shut, sputtering and cursing as tulips crashed against his body.

"What was that for?"

"You're filthy, and a chamber pot would've been too cruel."

He grabbed a handful of the flowers and hurled them back at me. Bulbs broke off when they hit the glass, exploding in a shower of water and petals. Automatically, I dodged out of the way, but when I did, he charged into the room, wiping his bare feet on the rug.

I frowned down at the woven carpet, watching him pull the window shut behind him.

"Was that necessary?" I muttered, but he ignored me, stripping off his sodden clothes, and dropping them with a wet slap on the floor. I sighed. "You're a real prick sometimes."

"Can I have some clothes?"

"Get your own; you're too tall for mine."

Gabriel flopped down on my bed, toweling his hair off with my duvet. "Just a shirt'll do."

Rolling my eyes, I bent to pick up his sopping jerkin in two fingers. Water dripped onto the stone, and I let it fall again, wiping my hand on my trousers. There was no point arguing. I crossed the space to my bureau and withdrew a blouse I rarely wore.

"Black tulips, huh?"

"What?"

He nodded toward the window where the flowers were still scattered across the balcony.

I froze with my mouth open, suddenly realising my error. I swallowed and cleared my throat, searching for an excuse.

"A gift from a well-wisher," I muttered offhandedly, closing the drawer.

Gabriel smirked. "Are they from Milehna?"

For just a moment, I held my breath, shocked that he'd guessed correctly. But then, I remembered I'd already sown that seed. I pinched my face in a show of disgust, tossing the shirt at him. "How'd you guess?"

He caught it effortlessly. "Isn't it usually the guy who gives the girl flowers?"

"Allegedly." I kept my answers short, trying to easily pass over the lie, but he seemed to enjoy my discomfort.

He tapped a finger on his chin. "Defies expectations. I like that in a girl."

I groaned, annoyed that he kept pressing the matter, though my unwillingness did seem to help the deception. Milehna was far from having any romantic feelings toward me, but if it gave us a reason to be seen together, it was fine for my brother to believe it.

"By all means, take her affections upon yourself. I've no use for them, and they are very much a bother."

"Why d'you keep the flowers then?"

I answered with a roll of my eyes, and his cheeky grin broadened.

"How sweet," he mused. "They suit you. Are they your favourite kind?"

"No."

Chuckling, he patted himself dry.

I wondered if he realised how careless he was being, if he realised how many of his scars I could see. He seemed to notice my eyes sweep across his chest and pulled the shirt over his head, hiding himself.

"Why dress clothes?" I asked again, nudging his wet boot with my foot. The stone around the rug shone under the growing puddle.

He ran a hand through his hair, slicking it back, trying to give off an air of indifference, though I could tell I'd made him uncomfortable. "Does it matter what I wear?"

"It's a simple enough question. Satisfy my curiosity." He must've known I'd loop back, and I knew he had no intention of explaining himself. It was just a ploy on my part to get him to leave faster because that image from my nightmare refused to be vanquished.

But he was surprisingly reluctant. He sank back into the mattress, snuggling into the blanket. "If there is a reason, you'll figure it out eventually. Why take all the investigatory fun out of it?"

I tried a different question. "Why were you on Earth?"

He shrugged.

But something else occurred to me, and I knitted my brow. "How d'you even know where the Gate is? Its location was hidden years ago." He lifted his shoulders again, but before he could drop them, I warned, "Spirits save you, Gabriel, if you answer with another shrug, I'll drag you to Noah's room and tell him you want his advice on women."

He sat up and shrugged as exaggeratedly as he could. "You wouldn't."

I narrowed my eyes. "I assure you, I would."

"You won't," he said as he let himself fall back onto the bed again.

"You might appreciate it. You're at that age, after all." If threatening wouldn't move him, maybe teasing would.

But still, he was unresponsive, folding his arms behind his head. "I do fine on my own, thanks."

I managed a smirk to go with my jest, though he wasn't looking at me. "Are you telling me you already have experience with the ladies?"

He snorted. "Well, certainly more than you."

Even I had to laugh. "Noah still has more than both of us combined," I mused, relaxing into our banter.

"Yeah, I heard plenty of rumours when I was younger, but he seems to have tamed the beast in recent years ... Or maybe he's just lost his touch. Now, why would I want advice from someone like that?"

An amused grin crept onto my face. *"Tamed the beast."* I

shook my head, snickering. "How uncouth. But y'know, he is rather fond of you. He'd enjoy feeling useful."

"No thanks," my brother said.

But even in the face of mirth, I couldn't shake that discomforting feeling. I let the playful cadence trickle out of my voice. "So, shall I send for his highness? Or did you want to answer me?"

His face fell, his eyes tightening as he stared up at the ceiling. "You seem irritable tonight."

I kicked his wet clothes again, making sure he could hear the squelch. "Can't imagine why."

Don't notice.

But Gabriel was nothing else if not observant. He propped himself up on his elbows to look at me. "No, I don't think that's it."

Don't notice. Don't ask.

"Actually," he continued, "I've got a question for you."

Immediately, I tensed. "Gabriel ..." I murmured, warning him not to continue, but he pretended not to take the hint.

Tossing his legs over the edge of the bed, he sat up and leaned closer, sneering up at me. "What were you dreaming about?"

I jerked back, my stomach hardening against the force of the question. How dare he ask. He knew not to ask. He *knew*—

The sarcasm dripped from his voice. He knew exactly what he was doing to me. "Well? Are you gonna answer my question, or—?"

I swept toward him, my voice a hiss. "You know very well that it's none of your business. The future isn't something to be carelessly talked about, Gabriel."

"Well, maybe what I was doing on Earth is none of your business, Seth. How's that for an answer?" Shoving me back, he crossed to the window, dramatically ripping his houppelande up off the floor. "You're as nosy as Noah these days—or worse."

"Gabriel—" I protested as he gathered the rest of his clothes and stalked toward the exit.

"What?" he growled, spinning in the doorway, flinging his arm out. The baggy sleeve of his jacket slapped the wall, spitting rainwater. "Both of you are constantly in my face about where I am, what I'm doing, and who I'm with, and y'know, it's really getting old. So, if it's not too much trouble, you can both just piss off and stay out of my business, all right?"

"Gabriel!"

His voice lowered, cold and barbed. "You've got your business; I've got mine. Let's leave it at that." He stormed out of the room, trailing wet footprints behind him.

I flinched when I heard the outer door slam and pressed a hand to my forehead, sighing. Gabriel was never any good at masking his emotions, but I couldn't concern myself with that now.

I'd been a fool to discard the flowers so carelessly. I hadn't even thought about it! I threw open the window and ducked out onto the balcony, glancing back inside to assure myself that the door was closed. I moved quickly, sifting through the flurry of cast-off petals and stems, panic urging me until I found what I searched for. Coiled and fastened around a stem just below the bulb was a thin strip of parchment—an update from my informant.

I exhaled in relief, clutching the flower to my chest.

It hadn't been lost.

Gabriel hadn't noticed or suspected anything.

The secret was safe.

Shoving my hair out of my face, I climbed back inside and closed the window, drawing the curtains and scanning the room again before unfurling the little note.

Milehna had hidden and transported it well.

I read the message by candlelight, squinting to decipher the thin, cramped handwriting:

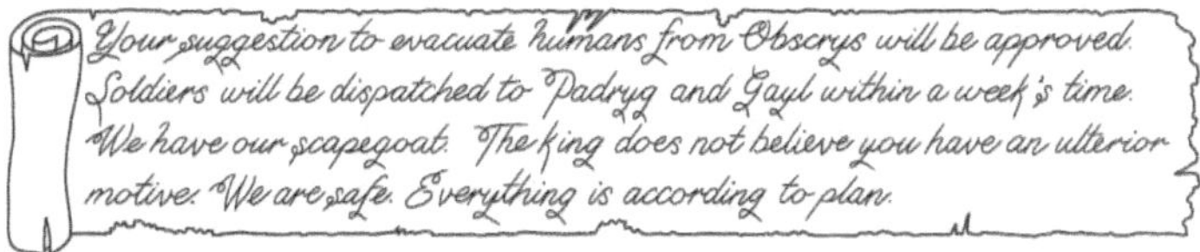

I inhaled and exhaled slowly, reread the note twice more, and then, smiling, dipped the edge of the parchment in the candle's flame and watched it turn to ash in my fingers.

JASPER

I slammed my door, but I'd already reacted too much. I knew I had. I knew I'd given Seth even more reason to suspect I was doing something I shouldn't.

Shouting, I balled my jacket and hurled it at the wall as hard as I could, but the impact was dissatisfying. Perhaps it had been foolish of me to expect it to produce a noise loud enough to express my annoyance, but I couldn't help it. I was bristling, though I didn't really know what I was mad at.

Seth hadn't overstepped his bounds. His questions were understandably asked. Of course, he wondered why I was dressed formally. I did hate dress clothes; it wasn't a secret.

C'mon, be honest with yourself, Jasper. You know what's bothering you.

I groaned into my hands.

I *did* know.

I wasn't mad at Seth; I was mad at myself. I was mad because it should've been Lily and Liam that I'd passed off to the guards. It was supposed to be them—that was the plan—but it wasn't. It was a girl called Blaire from the neighbouring village instead.

I was stalling. I was maintaining my 'friendship' with Lily longer than was necessary, and why?

Because I thought she was charming?

Because she was interesting enough to be entertaining?

Because I wasn't ready to be rid of her yet?

Dragging my hands down my face, I sighed exhaustedly, and the answer whispered in my head: *Because Lily never asked for anything in return besides my company. Because I felt strangely at ease in her presence. Because she was gentle and attentive.*

She seemed to possess all the qualities I'd been craving. She seemed to know what I was thinking. She seemed to—

I stared blankly across the common room. No matter what, a problem remained: Lily was my target, and that couldn't change. I'd bought myself more time by delivering today's victim, but eventually, I'd have to bring Lily and Liam as well.

The thought left a bad taste in my mouth. *All* of it left a bad taste in my mouth, but Mother had made it clear: it wasn't my place to challenge her.

Do as you're told, and all will be well.

There would always be days that I questioned this mission of mine, though I'd found myself toying with the idea of abandoning it more often since I'd met Lily. But it was only a silly thought—a daydream.

Being with Lily was new. Our interactions stirred feelings I'd never felt before, and I liked it. But the thought of any future with her was just a fantasy to entertain.

This was only a fleeting moment, one of many I was sure to experience in the course of my life—a time I might look back on someday with fondness or remorse or both. That was what my life was built of: moments and people. Some I yearned for long after they'd passed, some I simply forced myself to endure. But they were all ephemeral. Nothing could last.

There is comfort in predictability and fear in change. If I did anything but let these moments and these people fade away, I would lose my comfortable place by my mother's side—the only link I had to something permanent. And I didn't want that, despite the repercussions I may have to bear.

Moments always passed. People always left.

But the blood I shared with her would always be the same. She would always be a piece of my life, and she was predictable. Every interaction could be anticipated. Every mistake—every *sin*—had a consequence. If I did wrong, I'd be punished. If I excelled, I'd be rewarded. It was simple, really. Cause and effect.

Seth and Noah would say she was dangerous, and that was true.

They would say she was base and vengeful and selfishly taking advantage of my love for her, and they would be right about that, too.

I'd known for some time what sort of devil she was; I simply chose to ignore it.

I wasn't sure it could even be called manipulation anymore because I was getting something out of it, too. We were the user and the used, two equally selfish people supplying what the other sought in some way or another. Mother took what she wanted from me in the form of missions or favours, and in small gestures—a gentle smile, welcoming arms, praise, affection—and promised permanency, I got what I wanted, too. It seemed a fair enough exchange.

Maybe to others, my incentives were trifling. Maybe they were things that, as her child, I should have been provided with anyway. Maybe that was true. Maybe she was a cold woman who wasn't particularly affectionate or motherly, even to her own children.

Regardless, I still wanted those things from her.

I wasn't exactly the lovable sort, and if she could bring herself to care for someone like me and give me an anchor to chain myself to, I was willing to do whatever she asked to draw that affection out of her.

A thought occurred to me then, and humourlessly, I laughed.

I hated the idea of Lily's god because it reminded me of my relationship with my mother. But she wasn't a god. She was just a person, like me, like all the other flighty, untrustworthy humans that occupied our worlds. And a human could be ruthless. A god, I thought, should be held to a higher standard.

I felt a breeze suddenly, though there were no windows in my room, and on it, a whispery chuckle. I looked up and around, surprised to hear Animaero's voice cutting through the quiet.

"What's so funny?" I asked aloud.

We are not gods, the wind said bitterly.

"What's that supposed to mean?"

She laughed again—a deep, cold sound—but said nothing else.

Heaving a big breath, I climbed the stairs to my bedchambers to change clothes. Then, gathering some bedding, I lit a candlestick and started for the door.

When I stepped out into the corridor, a voice greeted me.

"Off again already, young prince?"

Soren sat on a short stool a few paces to the right of my door, his back leaned against the wall and his legs stretched out in front of him. He'd been there the whole time, I realised, as always. I felt a little embarrassed that I hadn't noticed him before when I barged into my room in anger, but he didn't mention it.

He peered up at me from under his heavy brow, the sconce above him casting a shadow over his face. "Y'know, sir," he said. "You went into your brother's room over a fortnight ago and ain't come out 'til today." He eyed my damp hair. "Been outside lately?"

I grinned. "Just out on the balcony, of course."

Soren grunted. "Of course."

"And how would you know if I haven't come out of Seth's room? You're only supposed to be on duty at night."

"Don't mean I ain't been sittin' 'ere for days on end waitin' for the likes of you."

My face fell. "Soren, you've got to eat."

"Penna made sure I was fed, Spirits bless 'er. She even brought me a pint." He winked, and I rolled my eyes.

"Haven't you anything better to do?" I asked, but in truth, the knowledge that there was always someone waiting for me brought a smile to my lips.

His eyes found mine for but a moment before lowering to the floor. "Ain't got no one but you, young prince," he replied honestly, and the faint melancholy in his voice nearly leeched all the buoyancy from mine.

My next words were softer, more concerned than light-hearted. "Tell me you got some sleep, at least."

Soren answered with a dismissive huff. "Lookin' after you stopped bein' a duty a long time ago, young prince. Any sleep I get ain't restful 'til I know you're safe."

I stared down at his tired face—at the bags under his eyes and the worry-deepened creases in his forehead. He wasn't elderly by any means, but I sometimes wondered if my frivolity aged him more quickly than the passing of time alone would.

"C'mon," I said, nodding at my suite door. "Sleep in here tonight. I won't be sneaking off on your watch again, not for a few days at least."

Snorting, he shook his head. "D'you know what the queen would do if she came down 'ere and found my post empty?"

"Soren ..."

"Gut me an' skin me alive, she would, an' I don't fancy the sound of that." Then he smiled, but it wasn't a joyful one; it was more an attempt to release some tension—an upturning of the lip so his expression wasn't as grim as his words, though one side still sagged, permanently pulled downward by his scar.

"As if she ever comes to the east wing ..."

His lips parted to contradict me because he was well aware that she did, but instead, he said, "You've still got a few years of troublemaking left in you, young prince, and I plan to see you through all of 'em."

"It's one night, Soren. You need sleep, or you'll age yourself to death long before I'm done causing trouble."

He chuckled—a soft, breathy sound, more like a wheeze than a laugh—but he wouldn't be convinced; the man was as stubborn as I was. "It's you that bloody ages me ... And it's that witch that keeps me up at night." He cleared his throat. "Pardon, I meant *queen.*"

I felt my stomach tighten at the ice in that word.

"People can have more than one title," I muttered.

"Puts fear into the 'earts of men. Sounds like either."

I nodded slowly, mechanically, a little annoyed by the shift in mood. "She is something, all right ..."

"Ain't seen ol' Gilliam since she got angry with 'im, and that was four months ago."

I opened my mouth but decided not to speak. I knew his assumption was correct. Gilliam was dead. I'd overheard Seth and Noah discussing it, but it wasn't common knowledge, though everyone knew the queen had a bite if you crossed her path—one people didn't recover from.

But I couldn't bring myself to confirm his suspicions.

"I'll ask around," I said instead. "See what station he's been moved to." Carefully, I extracted a blanket from my bundle of bedding and tossed it over the guard. "Rest easy, Soren."

He smiled more softly this time and drew the quilt up over his shoulders.

"Off to the library again tonight?" he asked.

"That's where they should post you."

"Just don' let 'er catch you, young prince, or it'll be a lashing for us both."

I began to walk away, but after a few paces, I paused. "Will you join me? After the night passes, I mean." I looked back at him, smirking. "Reading to someone keeps me out of trouble."

This time, the smile enveloped his whole face.

***

The library was quiet except for the sound of the rain.

I deposited my candle on the windowsill in the far corner of the room, dropping my bedding in a heap on the floor below it before turning to choose my reading material —something to fall asleep to and something Soren would enjoy hearing when I woke.

There were shelves from floor to ceiling, sliding ladders propped up against them for access to the higher books. Climbing a few feet up the closest one, I pulled a copy of *Luvhena: A Portrait of the Elves of Olde* from the shelf and returned to my corner. The elves had always fascinated me, and although I'd read *Luvhena* more than once already, I still delighted in it. Soren liked it, too, though I questioned whether he actually did or if he simply said so because it was one of my favourites.

Propping my back against the wall beneath the window, I wrapped the blanket around me and set the book on my knees, using a mixture of moon and candlelight to see. I skipped to the seventh chapter—the one about the elves' respect for the natural world and their connection to the Spirits. It talked about earth, water, fire, air, and the corresponding Spirit beings, and as I finished a passage about Animaero, I fell asleep listening to the rain against the window, thinking that someone's sadness shouldn't sound so beautiful.

HANDLE WITH CARE

NOAH

"My lord, it's nearly noon. Will you get up?"

I lay still, pretending, for a moment, that I didn't hear, but Haven would know. I inhaled a slow breath through my nose and rolled over onto my back. Exhaling, I peered across the room at her shadowy figure.

"I suppose I can't stay in bed all day, can I? There are plans to be made, people to oversee, meetings to attend. What a noble life."

"Are you feeling ill, my lord? Shall I fetch Dr. Byrne?"

"You'd go all the way to Erisilon? There's a physician here at the castle."

"If you were actually feeling poorly, you'd prefer Quade, wouldn't you?" She bowed her head. "Besides, travelling isn't so difficult for me …"

I watched her, wondering if she'd added that afterthought to remind me that she was different from me—that she was dead, while I was alive. She was always keen to remind me … as if I could forget.

"My health is fine," I replied dully. "But Haven, did you ever have those days where you just didn't want to get up or do anything? When there's simply no reason to?"

"Yes. I think everyone does from time to time, but I got up anyway. It was a necessity because I had to work if I wanted to eat, and I had to eat if I wanted to survive." I could hear in her voice that she didn't have the patience for my laments, but I persisted.

"I don't have to do either of those things. I am a most fortunate man. In fact, if I genuinely wanted, I could stay here in this bed until my death ... so why shouldn't I?" Then even more softly, I said, partly to rile her more and partly in earnest, "Haven, give me a reason."

The room was quiet for a minute before she sighed and said, "Your brother returned."

"Gabriel?"

"Perhaps you'll want to greet him?"

"Yes, perhaps ..." I muttered as I rubbed my eyes, and when I lowered my hands, the ghostly woman had vanished. Huffing, I threw the blankets back. "That is a good reason."

LIAM

I stared daggers at Lily from across the table. I wasn't angry with her; I just wanted her to snap out of her daze and notice me. One word would've sufficed. I'd even take an eyeroll or an annoyed huff—any sort of acknowledgment to prove I wasn't sitting at this ridiculously large table alone.

The dining hall felt bigger still with only the two of us. Mother hadn't had a meal with us in weeks, and Madame Renoir and Miss Sawyer were too preoccupied with her care to join us.

Every tiny scrape of my silverware echoed off the high ceiling, and even the noise of my eating seemed intensified. I grew self-conscious and slurped my soup more slowly, peeking up at my sister again to see if she noticed, but in her fanciful daze, she remained. She had one elbow on the table, resting her chin in her hand as she gazed upward, pensive but smiling.

The door pushed open, and Celia entered with the next course from Bennett. She tutted at Lily's untouched bowl, but my sister didn't so much as flinch she was so absorbed in her thoughts. The woman replaced my bowl with a plate, half-rolled her eyes at Lily, and winked at me before disappearing through the door again. Lily transferred her chin from one hand to the other.

Groaning, I grabbed my dinner fork, shoved my vegetables to one side, and scratched it across my plate. The grating squeal of it ripped Lily from her daydream at once; she nearly fell off her chair. Flustered, she swiveled her head around. Then, at last, she looked at me.

"Oh, good evening," I said and set my fork carefully in its assigned spot. "I hardly even realised you were there."

JASPER

Lily puffed out her cheeks, releasing the air in a big huff. Distractedly, she picked at the grass, twisting and pulling it while I watched, grimacing.

"What's wrong?" I asked, reaching over her lap to grab her hand. Animgeo wouldn't appreciate Lily killing her grass, but the girl just resumed the exercise with her other hand. Frowning, I grabbed that one, too. "Well, don't take it out on the grass."

Her head lolled to one side. "Why not?"

I turned her hands over without answering. Her fingertips were stained a faint shade of green.

"Jasper?" she said, but my eyes were fixed on her hands—so small and slender. I slid my fingers between hers, joining them.

"Because it's alive," I replied absently, watching my own hand envelop hers, marveling at how well they seemed to fit together, though I supposed most hands would. I'd never held anyone's hand like this before.

But then I felt her stare and tensed, realising how forward that might've been. Was this normal? Or was it more intimate than our acquaintance allowed? I knew my knowledge of proper etiquette with this sort of thing was skewed. I'd been plenty cheeky with my other victims, but it was different with Lily. It didn't feel obligatory; I simply wanted to satisfy this strange desire I had to touch her.

Then again, my image of our relationship might be different than hers.

For a moment, I dreaded her reaction. But when she didn't pull away, I let my eyes travel cautiously from her hands, up her arms, and finally to her face. The only difference in her demeanour was the addition of a rosy blush on her cheeks.

"It's only grass," she muttered, lifting one shoulder to try to hide her face. I pinched my lips to keep from smiling. It was a rare treat to see her be so shy.

"No, it's not. It's life."

"It's *grass*."

"Yes, it is, but that doesn't mean it isn't alive." I released her hands, shoving them back toward her. "Look, its blood is on your fingertips."

She observed them with a tired, contemplative look. Then she dropped her arms and wiped her fingers on her dress.

"Forgive me," she mumbled, "for a second, I thought you were trying to make me feel better ..."

Chuckling, I took her hands again, confident now that she wouldn't object, and she didn't.

"You haven't told me what's wrong, so how am I supposed to know how to comfort you or if you even want to be comforted? Besides, Animgeo wouldn't like you picking her grass. Even something small takes effort to grow."

Lily arched a brow. "Animgeo?"

I nodded. "The earth Spirit."

"Oh." Her brows pinched together in confusion or curiosity. "Well, how d'you know there's a spirit?"

"She's—" I tried to think of a good way to explain it. "—one of my ... mentors."

Her lips flattened into a hard line. "Your mentor? Like you speak to her? A spirit?"

I could hear the disbelief in her voice, but I ignored it to answer, "All the time. Well, not Gee as much as Aery."

"Gee and Aery?"

"Animgeo and Animaero, the air Spirit."

"Oh."

Releasing her hands, I leaned back on my arms. "You can believe me or not, but they're always around."

"Where?"

"The ground, the ocean, the sky—they're everywhere."

"Oh," she mumbled and folded her arms over her chest.

She did seem off today. Usually, she'd argue the believability of the subject with me, but the obedience she displayed in its stead was new. And bizarre. I scooted closer and nudged her in the side with my elbow.

"C'mon, Lily," I said. "What's bothering you?"

"It's nothing."

"You're alarmingly quiet today. It must be something."

At last, I saw a change in emotion on her face as she chided me for teasing her.

"Come on," I pressed.

She sighed exasperatedly but, to my surprise, answered rather quickly. "Why do people die so often?"

I knitted my brows, not expecting the question. "People live, and then they die. That's just how it goes."

"What about people who die before it's their proper time?"

"I don't think anyone knows their proper time, Lily," I said, then snorting, added softly, "unless they plan on doing it themselves, that is."

She flinched in alarm.

"S-sorry!" I squeezed my hands together. "I didn't mean to offend. It's not funny, it's just—it's easier to talk about heavy topics when you add a little humour, I suppose ..."

I saw her swallow, watched her face relax, and then, finally, she nodded. "I-I was just surprised to hear you say that. I—" She wavered. "I was thinking the same thing."

I froze as her gaze flickered up to my face and then back down. Before I knew what I was even saying, I asked, "You think about it, too?"

She glanced up again, her eyes thinning, but she left the subject there. Turning away, she said, "Y'know, Liam is friends with these children from town who aren't so well off. Sometimes they disappear."

"Die, you mean?"

She nodded. "They're there one day and gone the next, and he shrugs it off like they never existed outside of his memories in the first place. He just— he acts like it's normal and pretends he's okay, but I know he isn't. It's happened here and there over the years, but lately, there've been more."

"A sickness or something?" I offered.

"Two have gone in the last few months, and they were some of the more fortunate ones."

I licked my lips. It felt like we were edging toward uncomfortably familiar territory. "Sometimes people die, Lily. It's just the way of things."

"I know, but I wish it wasn't, at least not for kids. I mean, Liam was so fond of Sophie, and Maple seemed nice enough. I never actually met her, but she was always smiling when I saw her. It seems so unfair."

My chest tightened, my discomfort immediately validated.

I knew those names.

Sophie Dubois and Maple Burdock had both been my victims. I'd targeted Liam because of his acquaintance with them; I'd seen them all together long before I met him and Lily.

I exhaled slowly, quietly, glancing at Lily to make sure she hadn't noticed me tense, but she was preoccupied with pulling the grass again. When I reached over to stop her, she groaned.

"Sorry, sorry. I know, the grass is alive and all that."

"It is," I said, leaning on her, thankful for the distraction.

She smirked, and not only did she lean back, she rested her head on my shoulder. I held my breath, suddenly very aware of my every noise and movement. I'd thought just holding her hand had been overly intimate.

"Y'know," she said lightly. "I think I'd like to see where you're from." Her eyes closed, a faint smile on her face, and after a moment of silence, I couldn't tell if she was awake or asleep.

This is it then, isn't it? I thought bitterly. *The mark of the end.*

I should be smiling, too, right? I'd been successful yet again. At long last, Lily wanted to go with me. She wanted to see Iraxhar—and quite willingly!

That had always been the plan, right? To befriend her. To convince her that she could trust me. To take her to Trigon when she desired to go. It wouldn't be a struggle at all. In her eyes, it would be the adventure she'd always craved.

My plan had worked perfectly.

But then, Lily lifted one hand to gently stroke my forearm, dancing her fingers across my skin. I felt like my heart might leap from my chest with only that soft touch.

My breath shuddered as it left my lips.

What was I going to do?

Try to rationalise it, I thought. *You only anticipated one in the first place, so why does it matter if it's Lily or Liam? Just take her to the castle like all the others. Take her, and then everything can go back to the way things were.*

Moments pass. People leave.

Except ...

I peered down at the girl's peaceful face and pulled my lips in.

Except, I didn't want things to go back to the way they were before.

This—seeing Lily nearly every day, walking in the woods with her, sitting, talking—had long since begun to feel like the new norm. So then ... what if it was? What would I do? How would I navigate it? How long could it last?

I drew in another slow breath, careful not to disturb Lily.

No, I thought.

I couldn't do it, could I? It simply wasn't possible. This routine could only last so long. It'd had an expiration date from the start.

This was just a moment of weakness.

And moments always pass.

I sighed and set the side of my face on top of her head.

Wouldn't it be grand if I could though? If there was a way to keep Lily because that's what I really wanted, wasn't it? It seemed about time I admitted it: I wanted to keep Lily in my life. I liked her more than an acquaintance and even more than a friend.

But how could I do it?

Switch my focus back to Liam and take him to the castle instead?

The thought made my insides feel cold.

No. That would hurt Lily, and I couldn't do that. I couldn't hurt her; I couldn't bear it.

I snorted, lifted one hand, and covered my face with it.

Oh, Jasper, you messed up.

You really messed up.

No, I told myself, *no, you've succeeded. Your plan is working perfectly. This is the exact outcome you wanted. You wanted her to say those words. You should be bloody grinning at how perfectly successful you've been.*

So why couldn't I bring the smile to my lips? Why did I suddenly feel so hideously scared? Scared of what? Of losing her? Of losing ... this?

This.

This was the problem. This attachment. This infatuation I had with her that I couldn't seem to let go of. Would I be able to part with her? If I took her to the castle, could I pass her off to the guards and surrender her to the unknown?

My stomach twisted.

I'd made a mistake, and I knew the solution.

I should bow out—quietly disappear from Lily's life like the children she talked about. She might be sad at first, shed a few tears for her absent friend, but then, I would become nothing more than a memory. And when you're the only one keeping them, the only one reminding yourself of them, when the only other person who shared those moments with you is gone ... those memories will eventually disappear, too.

It was a terrible thought. A terrible reality.

I didn't want that at all, but what other choice did I have if I couldn't see Lily as my victim? Tell Lenore? How would my mother react if I said I couldn't go through with it this time— that I'd chosen this girl over following direct orders? The possibilities made me shiver.

The queen had a bite, they said—one people didn't recover from.

Would *I* recover? Would her majesty have mercy on her lovesick son? It injured me to think it though I knew the answer: She most certainly would not.

Yawning, Lily lifted her head, rubbing her eyes. I tucked my chin to see her better as she drew her knees up to her chest. But the calm was gone from her face, replaced by a creased brow and downturned lips.

"Lily?"

"I just keep thinking about it."

"About what?"

Her voice was meek. She leaned back to face me properly. "You won't die on me, will you, Jasper?"

I blinked back at her, my heart thumping. I felt a twinge of guilt, but I tried to lighten the weight of her question—tried to avoid answering when it felt like a falsehood—by asking playfully, "Would you be sad if I died?"

She grinned, a welcome response to my levity. "Oh, I'd be gutted."

I laughed myself, though I looked away so she couldn't see the lack of humour in my eyes. "Oh really?"

"Of course," she said, driving her shoulder into my arm. "Who else would I talk to when I tire of being around Liam all day?"

"Well, it's nice to know I'm just a replacement for your brother."

"You're an escape from my brother," she corrected.

I rolled my eyes and ruffled her hair, which she'd worn down today.

Don't look at my face. Don't notice.

"Hey!" She cringed away, trying to straighten out the mess, but as she did, the smile on her face began to fade and her movements grew sluggish. Her hand found mine and held it. "Jasper?"

"Yes?" I brushed a stray lock of hair off her forehead, smoothing it against the side of her head.

Although the hint of a smile was still on her lips, I could tell that she struggled to keep it. "I-I don't want to be left here all alone again." Then, in a voice so soft I didn't know if she'd meant it to be heard at all: "I can't stand feeling lonely."

It was the whisper that did it.

It was that shy, quiet voice that seemed almost embarrassed to have admitted those words aloud. I felt a pain somewhere deep, something that ached more than anything physical could. It reminded me that, in this matter, Lily and I were the same, and perhaps it was that very loneliness that brought us back to each other day after day.

Why else would I adhere myself so tightly to my mother's promise of permanency?

I knew that feeling. I knew how wretched and hollow it felt to be lonely. I didn't want Lily to feel it, too.

What was I supposed to do?

Don't, Jasper. You're already too invested. Don't make this harder for yourself than it needs to be. Just a quick pat on the back ought to do it. That's comforting enough.

I released her hand, wiping my sweaty palm on my thigh. "I'm here, aren't I?" I asked softly, slipping my arm behind her and stretching it over her shoulders.

"You are here," she said and closed her eyes again, reaching for my other hand, and although her voice was now composed, her grip was surprisingly firm. "Will you always be?"

I glanced down at our hands, suddenly stricken with a mixture of urgency and desire. I pulled her closer, and to my amazement, Lily didn't object. She responded with equal fervor, and in a flurry of clumsy limbs, we wrapped our arms around each other, pressing our bodies together so tightly that I couldn't tell if the heartbeat I heard was hers or my own. When we'd found a comfortable embrace, Lily exhaled softly beside my ear, and I wondered if, perhaps, she'd had the same desire. I wondered, too, what words I could say to satisfy her anxiety, but they didn't take much thinking. I simply said what I felt.

"If you're here," I whispered back, my voice quaking, "then so am I, Lily."

She stiffened at first, and I feared I'd said something too brazen. But then she relaxed into me. I felt her tension ease, but I still held her tight, clutching the back of her dress, clinging to her so desperately that I felt a little foolish. And yet ... I couldn't bring myself to let go. Her hands on my back were soothing, her breath on my neck was warm, and the weight of her body against mine flooded me with an odd sense of relief, which wasn't the emotion I'd expected to feel.

I feared it might be awkward, like the closeness and tightness of our embrace would make me feel scared or trapped, but it didn't. I wasn't uneasy. I didn't have to stop myself from cringing away. I felt ... comforted.

For a long while, we sat together in tranquil silence, and Lily never asked me why my hands were shaking. Even when I led her home, no words were exchanged, though we walked hand in hand until we reached the edge of the forest. There we lingered, both reluctant to separate, but I knew I couldn't keep her too long.

As I watched her disappear into the house, I held my breath, trying to find a way to describe the strange new emotions our embrace had inspired, and when I exhaled, I knew.

I felt like I could *breathe*.

I felt like I'd been understood without even a word of explanation, and over and over, I replayed the moment in my head. It was embarrassing to recall, but I didn't scold myself for my impulsivity. I was glad.

It wasn't the first time my heart had cried out so loudly and so longingly. But it was the first time I'd felt that somehow, incomprehensibly, someone else could hear it.

ACTS OF DEFIANCE

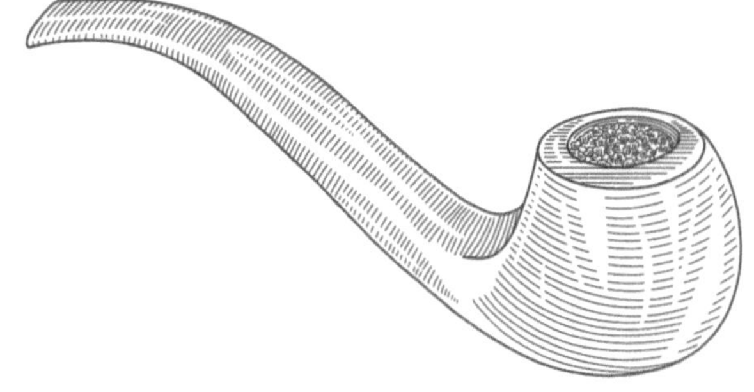

LIAM

I rounded the corner and stopped short at the door, surprised to find Lily in the sitting room after lunch. By this time, she'd usually be off with Mr. Behrtram somewhere.

She glanced up from the book that lay open on her lap. "Hi," she said dully and looked back down.

"Hi," I replied, watching her face as I took the seat opposite her. I could tell she wasn't really reading. Her eyes didn't move across the page but seemed glazed over like she was more absorbed in her thoughts than the story. "How is it?" I asked, partly to tease her.

Puzzled, she peered up again. "How is what?"

I nodded at her lap. "The book."

"Oh." She frowned and blinked as though she'd only just realised the novel was there herself. "Oh, it's not keeping my attention, I'm afraid. I can't really say if it's good or bad."

I smiled to myself because I knew who occupied her thoughts. Mr. Behrtram must've been unable to meet her today, and she was sulking. "Something on your mind?"

She stared at me for a few seconds in silence before shutting the book and briskly standing. "No, nothing in particular." She strode through the door, her cheeks rosy, but a moment later, she poked her head back in and said, "I'm gonna call for some tea. Would you like some?"

I pressed my lips together to suppress my smirk and shook my head, waiting for her to vanish into the hall before releasing the little giggle I'd been holding back.

JASPER

The king's voice boomed in the throne room. "Praise be! Long has it been since all my sons gathered before me. Come!"

Noah, Seth, and I approached, placed our hands over our hearts, and bowed stiffly in unison. We'd been instructed to don our finest clothes, and even my brothers seemed uncomfortable in their carefully-pressed garb. It was the usual custom when appearing before the king, of course, though to me, it had always seemed superfluous. Then again, I supposed there was something to be said about showing one's respect even when aware that the recipient cannot see it.

The weight of Father's voice pressed down on me. "Young Gabriel seems to find it difficult to remain stationary and troubles my guard with an endless pursuit."

I shrank where I stood. My brothers regarded me critically, and as if he knew what their shared reaction would be and could see it himself, our father laughed. But even his mirth couldn't soothe the disquieting feeling in me.

This was a rarity—all of us in one place—and the possible motivations behind the king's invitation had me on edge. But that wasn't the only reason for my discomfort. Our mother was also present, and although I could feel her gaze, I didn't dare look up to meet it.

"Fret not, my son," the king said with another big belly laugh. "Your brothers, too, were young and tameless once, though perhaps not so untamed as you. It is no secret you've an adventurous soul, but alas! You've been summoned today to hear a most auspicious announcement. I have decided upon an arrangement that I pray will suit you all amiably, especially you, Gabriel, whose innermost desires I cannot begin to fathom."

I snorted and muttered, "If you only knew." Seth smacked my arm, but Father's chuckles filled the space again. He, at least, was fond of humour.

Before the king continued, I stole a glance at my brothers, assuming they already knew the purpose of this gathering. They *always* knew, and despite our differences, my brothers and I usually shared the same opinions on matters of importance. The emotions on their faces would tell me how I, too, should feel about this new *arrangement*.

But the emotions I sought weren't there. Seth stared forward, stone-faced, and Noah watched him with an expression like a spurned child. Then, noticing me, my eldest brother met my eyes with far more alarm than comfort. Immediately, I realised that he didn't know what this was about either. Seth hadn't told him.

The iciness in my gut grew.

Had he not foreseen this meeting? If even they didn't know, I had the sinking feeling we were in for something shocking.

But Father didn't continue right away. He let the echoes of his laughter dissipate, let his words settle in our minds, perhaps allowing us time to prepare for what was to come. But I couldn't bear such a prolonged silence.

I cleared my throat and addressed the king. "Permission to speak, your majesty?"

"I welcome it," he replied smoothly.

"What permits us this great honour, sir? What is this proposal you speak of? And in such small company ..." I'd never listened to an announcement from the king without his advisors and captains present, if not all Egaldon, but here, there were only the five of us. What secret had he to tell that the doors were shut and the only ears meant to hear were ours?

"You have not the patience of your brothers," Father said heartily. "Gabriel, a new future is upon you, my son. Thus far, you have refused all I have offered, but I shall lay a new path at your feet."

Tentatively, I asked, "And if I should refuse this as well?"

"This—though I suspect you may initially scorn—you may not dismiss. My authority is absolute. This is not mere predilection on my part, my son; this is your future."

I narrowed my eyes, studying the king's still face, trying to decipher his expression. It was unchanging, always calm and reserved, even in distress, his lips bearing that constant half-smile. Perhaps because his eyes could not betray him, it was impossible to know what emotion he truly felt.

My insides twisted. The longer Lenore's eyes bore down on me—and the longer I avoided them—the more the walls seemed to close in around me. I wanted this assembly to be over. I wanted to flee before I was forced to confront her. "Let's hear it then."

But this time, my father was not amused.

"You forget your manners," he said, and although the inflection of his voice hadn't changed, the words felt firm, their echo imposing. "I am not the answerer of commands; I am the giver of them."

Immediately, I bowed my head. "Y-yes, your majesty. Please accept my apology. I only desire to hear your word."

"As you should. Now, I address you all, my sons." King Gilmer raised both arms, stretching them wide, and even with his burly frame, there was a certain elegance about the movement. "This is the future of us all. For thousands of years, our Iraxhar has been ruled by one. Even Earth once was governed from this very throne but no longer. Time has been unforgiving since the days of the Departure. Just as Earth parted from our bonds so many years ago, I fear for the unity of the remaining three. Changes are upon us." He lowered his arms and rested them on either side of his seat. "Our worlds grow more divided and mistrustful of one another. Rule is less simple than it was in the time of the last Anim, and self-proclaimed leaders have begun to surface and threaten the sanctity of the monarchy."

My stomach hardened.

I turned toward my brothers, ignoring subtlety because the king's words insinuated one of my greatest fears. Noah's jaw was clenched, his eyes trained hard on the floor, while Seth simply watched Father speak, his face utterly void of expression. I waited, leaning in, hanging onto every word that passed through the king's lips.

"We must match these times. We must do all that is in our power to unite once again."

In one swift motion, Noah jerked his head up, drawing all eyes. "What're you saying?" he asked, and I gaped, astonished to hear him speak out of turn.

It was expected of me, but Noah wasn't the prodigal son; he was the crown prince. He was the picture of a perfect pupil. He accepted every new task with grace and appreciation. Never in my life had I heard him speak with such impudence in the presence of the king or queen, and yet, there he stood, wide-eyed, his lips parting as though he couldn't believe what he'd just heard.

Were his suspicions the same as mine?

King Gilmer, too, was confounded by the voice that spoke. "Has your opinion suddenly grown more important than my own, my eldest? Is your objection so great that you would bestow your word so curtly?"

Noah didn't heed the warning in Father's voice. "Then you confirm it. You're splitting the rule? Leave Earth to its own devices and divide the remaining three worlds among your sons. That is your plan?"

I drew in a sharp breath, my eyes darting from Noah to the king.

Our father licked his lips. At last, in a low voice, he replied simply, "Yes."

Even our mother, who sat beside him like a silent spectre, blanched in surprise, but my voice flew out quickest.

"You're joking!" I cried. "Please tell me you're joking."

The king's voice hardened. "I am not."

"You can't do that!"

"Do not patronise me, Gabriel," he spat, breaking his mask for the tick of a second, but it was enough to silence me. "Do not speak as if my word has no authority over you. I am the king; you are a prince. I am the father; you are my son. Your life is in my charge. Whose voice do you think should be heard the loudest?"

I bit my tongue when Lenore's eyes slid back to my face, and automatically, I lowered my head in submission. My outburst had crossed the line; already, I knew the consequences would be grave.

Noah laughed dryly, quietly. "This is real, is it?"

Then, all at once, I sank into silence, into darkness, into—

I snapped back, returned to my body where it stood before

the king and queen in the deserted throne room. My throat grew tight. I swallowed. I flicked my eyes from one person to the next, wondering how long it had been and if anyone had noticed the momentary absence of my soul. It seemed only seconds had passed, but it was only a few seconds more before it happened again.

I felt myself drifting and fought against the pull of the Void, this time aware and ready to contend. But my efforts had little sway over theirs. I heard the whispery voices of the Spirits, inviting me to join them in their domain, tempting me with a reprieve from the turbulence I felt, and then—

Seth reached behind me and gripped my shoulder. I started, blinking, my heart racing, but the sensation disappeared. Aery's voice ceased.

I nodded slightly to assure Seth I was okay, certain my brother would see the gesture, but I kept my eyes fixed on the floor. He released me with a movement that was slow and natural, and I could only hope the exchange went unnoticed.

Seth addressed Father. "Permission, my lord, to state my objection," he said softly, and hearing his second son's voice, the king relaxed, leaning back in his seat.

"Your objection is noted but must be dismissed, my son. This decision is final."

"The way we were raised and taught ..." Noah uttered. "Each prepared to wear the crown if need be ..." He didn't have to raise his voice to be heard; even his whisper echoed in the near-empty chamber.

"After your mother blessed me with a third son, it felt appropriate to consider such a possibility. Gabriel is nearly of age, and I am growing older still."

Noah didn't respond.

Seth said, "Forgive us, your majesty, for speaking out of turn. We mean you no disrespect. You have told us something quite unexpected, and we find ourselves emotional in our surprise. Let us be silent to hear the remainder of your word. I desire to know which world will be in my care."

I gulped. I felt shaky. When at last, I dared to look up, I couldn't hear Gilmer's voice, though I knew he was answering Seth. But I peered ahead to meet our mother's gaze, and all noise around me dulled like I'd been submerged in water. Her hands gripped the arms of her chair so tightly that her fingers looked constricted. Her face reddened. The cords in her neck were taut.

She watched me—only me—and her eyes burned.

NOAH

My forehead *thunk*-ed on the door, my chest heaving, my breath fleeing my lips in a mixture of fear and relief. "Spirits ..." I flipped over, letting my body sag against the aged wood. My weight shoved it closed the last few inches until it latched. Every bit of me trembled with anxious laughter. "Look," I said, holding my hands up for Seth to see. "I'm shaking."

Seth nodded, though only his widened eyes exposed his distress.

Before either of us spoke again, he swept the perimeter, peeking into every room to assure we were alone before returning to the common area.

He covered his eyes, at last lowering his guard. "Oh shit." His throat contracted with a thick swallow as he dragged both hands down his face. "I thought—when he started talking about self-proclaimed leaders—I thought he was talking about us. I thought he knew about the coup. Shit, I thought he knew."

"So did I. I panicked. You, on the other hand," I said, jabbing a finger at him, "are a damn good actor, Seth."

"I—I wasn't expecting that."

"No, nor was I." I dropped my head back against the door. "Spirits, I think I just lost a few years of my life. D'you feel like that, too?"

Seth cast me a cold look, ignoring the question. He strode farther into the room, flopped into a chair, and rubbed his face again, groaning. "If he'd known about our plans—if he suspected us—I'm certain he would've confronted us the same way."

"In a locked room with only family present?"

"There could've been others in the room; we've no way of knowing. There could've been guards hiding somewhere in the dark or ..." His voice shrank. "I feel like we've just escaped utter chaos."

"The thought that we were anywhere near chaos is only in our minds, though. We're safe. The plan is safe. Everything is going perfectly."

Seth's hands seemed to fall out of the air. "Perfectly? What part of this says perfection to you?"

I pushed off the door, shrugging. "On the contrary, I don't think our reactions did us any harm. They were well within reason for the arrangement he presented. You saw how Gabriel reacted."

"Gabriel overreacts to everything, but ... I agree. I think your reaction was most surprising, but you can chalk it up to being the selfish crown prince wanting to rule on his own. Dividing the rule takes power away from you."

"Ha! I suppose that's a believable excuse if it comes down to it."

Seth didn't laugh with me. "Seriously, Noah ..."

"Come now, this is far from the worst-case scenario. In fact, I think we should be able to use it to our advantage."

He arched an incredulous brow. "How?"

"Well," I began, crossing my arms as I ambled toward him, "I always expected this for me—we all did—but ..."

Before I could gather my thoughts into words, a tiny, whispery voice stole through the air: 'Who knows if you'll be around long enough for that.'

I glared past Seth at the ghost who'd spoken, warning him to silence himself, but my threat had little weight. The young boy snickered and flashed his tongue at me. But my brother didn't follow my distracted gaze; his eyes stayed on my face, patient. I suspected he already knew the source of the disturbance.

I cleared my throat, trying to ignore the apparition. He could never truly be silenced, though. He was my oldest companion—a little poltergeist of a boy that had followed me around all these years. But as attached to me as he was, he would never allow another living person to see him.

"Alwyn?" Seth guessed.

The boy in the corner behind him grinned.

"Shove off, will you? We can talk later."

Alwyn scoffed. 'Why would I want to talk to you, Noah? You're no fun anymore. You've let yourself get so old.'

"Go, Alwyn!" I snapped, and at last, the sniggering ghost vanished. I moaned, pressing a thumb to my temple. "What a headache ..."

But Seth didn't ask what Alwyn had said. Instead, he urged me back to our conversation.

I gave my head a little shake, trying to resume where I'd left off. "Well, I—I assumed I'd rule from Trigon one day, but having you in charge of Obscrys ... Honestly, I think that's a stroke of luck."

He opened his mouth to contend but closed it in silence. Then softly, he said, "No, you're right. It is rather a good match, isn't it? Or it will be."

"We needed to get you there anyway; now it won't have to be a secret."

Nodding along with my words, he lifted a hand and pinched his chin, falling deep into some thought he wasn't quite ready to share. Then, exhaling, he raised his head again. "And Gabriel?"

"A visit to his new kingdom will get him off Trigon when we need him to be."

"It won't happen."

"No?"

"Gabriel, the leader of the elves? He respects them too much to force his leadership on them. There's no way he'd go to Azlinehn without an invitation, despite Father's decision."

"Then we'll get him an invitation. You can ask Lady Carys. We just need him off Trigon when the day comes. I won't risk him getting caught up in this; we must be sure he's somewhere safe."

I watched Seth's jaw tighten as if he had more to say, but he settled on, "You're a master of damage control." He sighed, letting his head fall back, his gaze washing slowly over the ceiling. "An auspicious announcement indeed."

"Gilmer is blind, but he's not ignorant. We need to be even more cautious when sharing information. His network is dangerous."

Seth's eyes thinned, and he stared upward for a moment longer before whispering, "Lenore is more dangerous still."

I bit my lip, secretly glad he'd brought her up so I wouldn't have to. I wrung my hands. "Did you notice how she looked at him—at Gabriel?"

Absently, Seth nodded. "I'll contact Carys as soon as I get a chance."

"The sooner we get him out of here, the better."

"The promised day is still a long way off; we have time."

I swallowed, my eyes drawn back to the corner of the room where my little poltergeist had reappeared. "We must be prepared for anything. Waging war is a terrible business. These things don't mend themselves as prettily as we would like, nor do they follow the timelines we set." I heard my voice drift off as if it had been stolen from me. I had to concentrate just to push out the last words I'd meant to say, and the taste of them was bitter. "History has taught us that at least."

For just a moment, the ghost boy changed. His phantom visage flickered back to the day he departed. His little body wrapped in plates and chainmail that didn't fit, wearing gauntlets and sollerets that made his hands and feet appear comically large on his slight frame. His head tipped backwards so he could see in a helm that was far too large, exposing a neck that was barely strong enough to bear the steel. A neck that opened in a bloody split as if it had a mouth of its own. As if it had words to say. As if death had given it another voice to warn me against my mission.

But I did what I did every day with every other ghostly stranger that crossed my path, begging for the attention of the one living person who could see and speak to them.

I closed my eyes and pretended I couldn't.

JASPER

I heard footsteps on the gravel, the noise strengthening as the man neared me. "Spirits, kid, what're you doing sleeping on the back stoop?"

I lifted my head from my arms, blinking, rubbing my eyes. "You weren't home," I said through a yawn.

"As if you don't know how to pick a lock." He stepped around me to climb the stairs, his jacket tucked under one arm and his surgeon's bag hanging from the other, which he nearly dropped while rummaging in his pocket for the key. When he got the door open, he gestured with a nod for me to follow.

I unfolded my arms under me to push myself up, but one buckled. I bit my cheek, taking a sharp breath through my nose and lowered again. The adrenaline had worn off, I realised, the pain radiating from somewhere beneath the skin. Only my static position had prevented me from feeling the full effect of my injuries until now.

"Late night house call?" I asked when Quade reappeared in the doorway, having deposited his belongings. He didn't seem to notice the strain in my voice.

"People die at the most inopportune of times." He scratched

the stubble on his chin. "Are you gonna get up or should I leave you here all day, too?"

I lifted my shoulders in a half-hearted shrug, and even that made me wince. "I'm feeling a bit peaky," I said. "I think I'll need help."

The teasing smile dropped off his face. "I guess I should've known ... What've you gone and done this time?" He descended the steps and sat beside me, frowning.

"Miscalculated," I replied, leaning my head back to look at him. "Ended up at the bottom of a staircase."

"*Peaky*, he says."

I smacked his knee. "Just help me, would you?"

I raised my arm, stretching it over his shoulders, and he heaved me up. When we made it inside, he set me on a chair just inside.

"I'll prepare a cot. I'm too tired to try to drag you upstairs."

He busied himself as I scanned the room. It'd only been a month since I'd been, but it was drastically changed. Rows of drying herbs hung from the ceiling, tins and jars and mortars stacked on the shelves and littering the tables, of which there were four, along with three cots and a mess of instruments and glassware.

"This place is turning into an apothecary," I observed.

"I like having things on hand instead of sending out for them."

"You could get an assistant for that."

He shook out a dusty sheet and spread it over the cot, coughing and turning away to say, "I do a better job than the apothecaries in town anyway. An assistant would mess everything up."

"Always modest."

"Always honest."

I laughed. "You'd have a selection. I'm sure there're plenty of people who'd want to ..."

"What?"

"... share your space in hopes of absorbing some of your wisdom, maybe?" I offered. Quade snorted, and I was glad to have amused him. I wanted the mood to be light. "I'd say learn, but I know you wouldn't be bothered to teach."

"Well, as it turns out, I hate people, especially in my space."

"You spend a lot of time saving lives for someone who hates everyone."

He ignored my statement and said, "Come on, let's have a look at you."

"Have you looked at yourself lately? I'd prescribe a bit more sleep." He was a sallow-faced man with a heavy brow and even heavier dark circles beneath his eyes. The scruff along his jaw hid it some, but I could still see how his cheeks dipped in. "And more food, too," I added. "You're looking thinner than last I saw you."

He crossed the room. "Tell people to stop dying, and maybe I'll get more of both." He helped me to the cot, dragging the chair behind us, then sat himself in front of me. "What hurts?"

"Everything."

He rolled his eyes. "What hurts the most?"

I held out my arm. "Wrist. Left side. And my back."

"Take off your shirt," he ordered as he bundled his hair and tied it messily at the nape of his neck.

I started to, but I found trouble. Quade grew impatient and stood to pull it off over my head. Immediately, he dropped back into his seat, his hands tightly clutching the garment. I looked away, embarrassed. I didn't even know what the damage was; I'd been too scared to check.

I watched his grip slacken, watched my shirt slide from his fingers to the floor.

"Oh, Gabriel ..."

I drew up an apologetic smile. "Not good, eh?"

He didn't answer, though his lips tightened. Without a word, he carefully lifted my wrist and examined it. Despite the size of his hands and his rugged demeanour, his touch was light and soft, his fingers moving across my skin with delicate finesse.

"Just a sprain from the looks of it. I'll splint and wrap it, but don't be careless and make it worse."

I nodded. "I tried to catch myself, but it went wrong." Then, shyly, I peeked up at him. "If it's okay with you, could I stay and rest tonight?" For some reason, I felt nervous asking, though his response to the same question had always been agreeable in the past.

His hands stilled. "You don't want me to fetch you a ride home?"

"I just came from home."

His face hardened, and his frown deepened. Then, gently, he continued to wind a strip of dressing around my arm. "I suppose you don't want me to tell your brothers what I've seen or where you are either."

"I told Soren I was coming here."

"They'll worry."

"They worry regardless, usually over nothing."

"This isn't *nothing*, Gabriel ..."

"Well, they'll worry anyway, so why add to it?"

Securing the bandage, Quade leaned back in his chair and fixed his eyes on me. "Look, it's not my business what you do, but you've been awfully reckless lately. I don't want to be drawing the sheet over your head next time."

I spoke out of the corner of my mouth. "I'd rather you do it than anyone else."

"Gabriel ..."

"It's a compliment. You're my favourite physician. It'd be an honour to have you declare me dead and prepare me for burial."

His lip curled up in contempt. "You and your brothers are all so pleasantly apathetic when it comes to death." Pushing down on his knees, he stood, joints crackling, and crossed the room. He dug through a cupboard and returned with a round tin of ointment.

"I could say the same to you. Aren't you rather desensitised yourself? Death is part of your daily life in this trade."

"Lift your arms."

I rolled my eyes but obeyed. He smeared the thick salve over the bruising on my ribs, and I tensed, clutching my elbows with either hand, pressing my face into my folded arms. I held the tension as he wrapped me with another bandage, biting my lip and trying to focus on anything else.

Quade's voice was soft, private. "Seth and Noah talk about death enough as it is. I don't need it from you, too." Then he said, "You can lower your arms now."

I blinked to refocus my eyes, gingerly touching my side and flinching again. "Well, what difference does it make? We'll all surrender to it eventually. The sooner the better, I say."

"Stop that. The ointment will help with the pain. Now, lie down and sleep, you imp."

I didn't argue. I lowered myself onto the cot, groaning as I readjusted, trying to find a position that I could bear until the salve started working. Quade waited and then opened a blanket over me. He walked to the window and drew the curtains, darkening the room.

My eyes grew heavy almost immediately, but then I remembered something, gave my head a shake, and called out, "Quade!"

He paused at the bottom of the stairs.

"I brought back some tobacco from Earth. You mentioned

last time that you were running low." I yawned. "My cloak's probably still out by the steps, but the pouch is with it."

I couldn't see his face in the dim light, but I could hear the smile in his voice when he responded. "Thanks, kid. Get some rest."

He extinguished the lantern and left the room.

JASPER

I woke to a sweet smell, and when I rolled over, I found myself staring into a steaming mug, the hot air moistening my skin. I blinked, tipping my head back until I could see Quade's face towering above me.

"Drink this," he said.

Stiffly, I sat up, bending over my knees to stretch and crack my back, though my bruised ribs ached in protest. Then I took the beverage in my good hand.

I cleared my throat, but my voice rasped. "What is it?" Sniffing first, I sipped it.

"Tea with some medicine and honey."

I nodded. "Thanks."

Quade poured himself a cup from a teapot and settled into the chair in front of me, propping his legs up beside me on the cot. "How'd you sleep?"

I swallowed another gulp, the liquid warming my throat all the way down into my stomach. "Well, actually. Probably the best sleep I've had in a month."

"You certainly slept a while. The rest of the day and through the night."

My face fell. "It's morning again?" I grabbed the curtain and yanked it up, releasing it again the instant I was blinded by Flaxen Sunlight. "Damn ... Lost a whole day."

Quade stared disapprovingly at the hand I'd used, but he didn't need to scold me. The sharp pain I now felt was punishment enough.

He asked, "How d'you feel?"

Sheepishly, I lowered my bandaged arm, raising the mug to my lips with the other. "Oh, I feel awful but not as awful as I did yesterday."

"Was it Lenore?"

I coughed and nearly dropped the cup, but when I lifted my head, Quade wasn't looking at me. He faced the wall, dispassionately sipping his tea. I didn't even open my mouth because I didn't know what to say, but he spoke before I could.

"You don't have to answer. Like I said before, it's your business."

The voice I managed was quiet. "Then why did you ask?"

Quade took a drink, held it in his mouth for a moment in silent contemplation, and then swallowed, delaying his response long enough to make me squirm in my seat. "Because you cried out in your sleep."

I watched his throat contract as he took another swig.

I asked, fearing the answer, "What did I say?"

Quade exhaled through his nose, placing his cup on the table beside him. "Only two words: 'Mum' and 'no.' You sleep very uneasily, by the way; I'm surprised you feel rested at all."

My eyes found the floor.

He wiped a hand down his face, pausing at his mouth to yawn against it. "It's always her, isn't it?"

I wasn't prepared to answer—to be confronted at all. All this time, I believed that we'd silently agreed to never acknowledge it. I struggled for words, but he stopped me.

"Don't answer. If you want it to stay a secret, don't answer. I don't need something to report to your brothers. If you don't say anything, then I won't feel obligated to tell them when they ask about you."

I closed my mouth and nodded, but I could feel Quade's eyes on me. I passed the empty mug back and forth in my hands.

Then we can both go on pretending you don't already know.

"Noah suspects something," he said, "and if Noah does, then Seth does, too. They've long expressed their concern about the amount of time you spend with her, but lately ..."

I inhaled. "I try my best to avoid the topic with them. I'll try harder."

Quade tutted.

Sighing, I glanced down at my splinted wrist and wiggled my fingers. "I'm sorry to burden you. I'll leave soon. I just needed some sleep somewhere safe."

He leaned over, reaching across the table for his pipe. A touch of acidity bled into his voice. "I suppose home isn't very safe for you, is it?"

"It's dismaying how observant you are," I replied flatly, watching him pack tobacco.

"It's not a difficult leap. I ask if you want to go home, but you say you've just come from home with these injuries." For a moment, his hands stopped moving, and he seemed to be holding his breath. When he exhaled, his voice lowered. "And it's not as though this is the first time I'm seeing you under these circumstances."

I forced a chuckle, trying to lighten the mood, to chase away the darkness that seemed to overtake his face. "You're right. I wonder, how many times does this make?"

"How many times you've *miscalculated*?"

"It wasn't bad this time, really." But I couldn't even finish the sentence before guiltily curling in on myself. How laughable it was to try to pretend when he'd already seen my injuries, though I still didn't want to admit their severity. "This time, it was just a small ... misstep."

Quade grunted. "I don't doubt that it was. It seems you were amply punished for your *misstep*." He eyed me. "But again, none of my business. I'm but a lowly surgeon, and you're just a young and reckless boy in need of medical attention." He fingered the pipe but didn't light it.

"Look at that, we complete each other. Face it, I'm great for business."

"Young and reckless and apparently unable to grasp just how far you're pushing it."

"Well, that's why I show up injured and exhausted, so my favourite physician can fix me and send me on my merry way again."

"And because you can't sleep at home without one eye open."

He refused to respond to my attempted humour, and I felt the smile on my face disintegrating.

He continued, narrowed eyes fixed on my face: "So instead, you come here where you feel protected and safe, knowing that no one will appear to drag you out of bed and throw you down the stairs." He flicked his brows, though his expression remained severe. "But what do I know?"

I gulped and dropped my gaze. "Right," I muttered. "What do you know?" I could feel my fingers beginning to shake, so carefully, I put the mug on the table. I cleared my throat to distract him from it. "I should get on to Earth."

He stopped me when I started to push the blankets off my legs. "Why?"

"I've a friend there I'd like to visit."

"You spend a lot of time there?"

"Lately," I said, then quietly added, "It's one of the few places my mother won't go."

He observed me, scratched the back of his head, and sighed. "You always have a safe place here, Gabriel. You know that, right?"

I fingered the edge of the quilts, noticing now that there were two. He'd put another one on me while I slept. I smiled at them—at this little act of care. "Why d'you think I'm here?"

"Good." He patted my shoulder. "Don't leave yet. Stay and rest a few days. Doctor's orders. I'll get you more tea." Before I could speak even a word of protest, he stood, grabbing my cup on his way.

I watched him fill both mugs, abandoning my resistance because I knew I wasn't in any shape to decline his offer. "Did you already send a message to my brothers?"

He pretended not to hear. Silently, he measured a white powder, which, together with a spoonful of honey, he stirred into my cup.

Rolling my eyes, I teased, "You just wanna see Seth."

Quade shoved my drink at me. "I don't play favourites."

"Sure you don't." I smiled, inhaling the sweet aroma as the steam warmed my face. "Seems we're both more transparent than we realise."

He picked up the pipe again, busying himself, and I stared into my cup, the liquid still rocking gently within, the powder that hadn't yet dissolved swirling around the bottom.

"Thanks, Quade. I mean it. You're a good friend."

He lifted the pouch of tobacco. "So are you."

I snorted. "A good assistant maybe. They're just dried leaves."

"They are. Just leaves that I casually mentioned I was running low on—not even to you—a month ago, and you overheard and took it upon yourself to collect them for me from another world." He grinned, and I peered down into my cup again, strangely embarrassed.

"It's not like it was difficult," I mumbled.

"You're a good person, Gabriel. You can't convince me otherwise." He held up the pipe. "I'm gonna smoke. Drink that, and when I'm back, we'll have breakfast."

I watched him step through the doorway.

For a second, I forced the smile on my lips to stay.

Maybe I could pretend his words hadn't stung me—that the earnestness with which he'd said them hadn't made me feel like an imposter.

Maybe I could wear this mask a little longer.

"A good person, huh?" I sighed. "What do you know, Quade?"

PART TEN
EXPECTATIONS

LIAM

We passed the window, and Lily nearly tripped to a stop. It had become a habit of hers to peer out at the garden after our morning lesson. I suspected she searched for Mr. Behrtram. It had been more than a week since he'd come to collect her, but I could see on her face that he'd appeared again at last.

I paused myself and asked, "Something wrong?"

She swung around, shaking her head, but any attempt to keep the excitement from her face was useless. No amount of darkness could overwhelm the light that bloomed in the girl's soft green eyes.

"Everything's fine," she said unconvincingly as she hurried past me. "I'll be late for lunch. Don't wait up!"

I giggled, returning to the window. There he sat beside the white fence, hugging his knees, his forehead resting on top of them: the gallant Mr. Behrtram. He lifted his head when Lily approached, and as I watched the smile build on his lips, I felt the one on mine slacken.

It wasn't that I was unhappy; his expression simply took me

by surprise. I didn't know how to react because it held a senti-
ment I'd never seen so plainly. Maybe it was the way the sun
shone on his face or the sleepy daze in his eyes, but staring up
at her, he seemed so much at ease. And it was more than that
even. He was in awe of her, his smile growing the longer his
eyes lingered on her face—as though some beautiful, ethereal
being stood before him instead of my unruly sister.

She ushered him up off the ground, and although I couldn't
hear the words they exchanged, I could see his chest hiccough
with laughter. The moment he'd gained his feet, she threw
herself forward into his arms.

My eyes widened.

I hadn't expected such a bold gesture, though I knew how
badly she'd missed him while he'd been away; she hadn't tried
very hard to hide it. He, too, appeared momentarily caught off
guard, but then he held her back, his arms looping around her
waist, his face disappearing in the hair that fell around her
neck.

For a single minute, the world around them seemed to fall
away. I wasn't sure even a leaf moved in the breeze—as if the
sky itself held its breath. There were only the two of them
standing there on the grass beside the garden, embracing, their
figures swathed in the light of the midday sun.

I watched them, holding my own breath so it wouldn't fog
the window.

Mr. Behrtram was the first to pull away. He gently, albeit a
little reluctantly, extricated himself from her grasp, though he
held onto one of her hands. Then he nodded toward the woods,
and together, they disappeared into the trees.

I exhaled at last and let the scene blur behind the clouded
glass, but I stared after them for a while. The image of their
sunlit silhouettes was still fresh in my mind—the picture of

something so naively intimate that I decided right then to pretend I'd never seen it, even though I knew I wouldn't forget it for a long time.

LILY

Jasper and I lounged in the shade of the oak tree for the third day this week, and although I hadn't realised it, he pointed out that I'd been sighing since we'd arrived. He asked, "Are you all right?"

"I'm fine, it's just—" I forced a chuckle. "I—I dunno. I dunno what's wrong with me."

Jasper rolled his eyes. "Of course you do. It's okay if you don't wanna tell me, but you don't have to pretend you're fine when you're clearly not."

I focused on the freckles on his lips because I didn't want to meet his gaze.

You're sad, Lily. You're grieving. He's your friend; you can tell him that.

Instead, I glanced down at my hands. "Just having a bit of a day, that's all."

"Did something happen?"

I swallowed.

My father is dead. He killed himself.

"I-I just—" I cleared my throat, trying not to steer too far from the truth. "I just miss my father today. He was supposed to stay for a while this time, but he left without telling us."

He left forever.

Jasper studied me, and then, as if he'd read my thoughts, he asked, "Did he die?"

I froze.

It was different hearing someone else say it.

My heartbeat raced. I opened my mouth. Closed it. Then the rejection of his question left my lips before I knew it. "No, no," I said, waving the inquiry away. "He left, like I said. I'm just feeling a tad resentful that he didn't tell me he was leaving." I surprised myself with how easily the lie left my lips and how believable my voice sounded despite the hiccough. "He left on business; he does that—travels a lot."

Why are you lying to him, Lily?

Hesitantly, Jasper smiled. "A traveler, huh? D'you wish you could go with him?"

"Very much. I've always wanted to. Adventure, meet new people ... He was—*is* good at that. Liam, too."

You're rambling, Lily. Calm down.

But Jasper didn't seem to think much of it, or at least, he pretended not to. He asked, "Good at what?"

"At meeting new people. I'm not so good at it."

"Why d'you say that?"

"My father, he could strike up a conversation with anyone. He just—he starts talking and makes friends anywhere he goes. Me, I can't do that."

"Well, you met me."

I shoved his arm. "That's not the same."

"You approached me first."

"You put yourself in my way," I countered.

"Maybe." He looked away shyly, and a question came to mind that I hadn't considered before.

"Jasper," I said, "did you want me to find you? In the garden, I mean. Did you want it to be me and not someone else?"

He stared down at his hands, then lifted one to anxiously tug his earlobe. "Yes," he admitted. "I did. I wanted to know you. I didn't feel like our first meeting really counted for much, y'know?"

His confession made my heart flutter. "No, you're right." I scratched my neck, suddenly feeling bashful. "I-I really am sorry, by the way, for being so rude to you at first. You were injured even, and I—"

"We were both a little abrasive."

"No, it was me. I should've realised. I told you, I don't know how to meet people. You were different, and I panicked." I exhaled heavily, turning toward him. "Forgive me?"

Jasper answered with a crooked smirk. "Only if you forgive me, too."

I had the sudden urge to touch him—to confirm the closeness and understanding I felt. We'd embraced each other before, so I didn't think he'd oppose the idea. But when I placed my hand lightly on his arm, he winced. I jerked back and sat upright.

"Sorry, I didn't—a-are you okay?"

He peered down at his wrist, looking startled himself.

"Yes, yeah, I'm fine. Sorry." He gave it a little shake to show how *fine* it was, but I saw his jaw tighten with the effort. "I fell the other day and tried to catch myself. Must've bruised it or something."

"Do you want me to get a bandage or—"

"No, no." He chuckled, but it didn't sound genuine. "It'll be fine, honest. I can handle this much. I'm durable."

I wasn't convinced. The way he pulled back ... It must have really hurt, but I could tell he hadn't wanted me to notice. He'd already pulled his sleeve down over his hand as if to hide it.

I bit my lip, trying to resist, but I couldn't help asking, "Are you sure? It could be a sprain. How did you fall?"

He lifted his shoulders in a half-hearted shrug, avoiding my gaze. "I injure myself all the time. You really don't have to worry about me. I'm clumsy."

I turned away, and although I believed my worry valid, I accepted his weak explanation. It was clear I'd already exhausted the subject, and his face told me he was far more uncomfortable than I was. I tried to dispel it a bit. "As if I'd worry. Don't go getting cocky."

Jasper took my cue and responded with a changed expression. He seemed relieved. "Y'know, my father always jokes about my clumsiness. He's blind and is still more sure-footed than I am."

I raised my head, shocked to hear him talk about his family without any prompting. "Your father is blind?"

He nodded. "Since birth."

"What's he like, your father?" I asked quickly, not wanting to waste the opportunity to learn more about him. "I'm trying to imagine how your parents must be, and I just can't."

At first a little surprised by my interest, Jasper smiled, his expression mellowing. "He's stern but fond of humour when he's in the mood for it. To be honest, though, I don't know him very well."

I arched a brow.

He explained, "I never spent much time with my parents. They were always busy."

"What about your mother?" I couldn't help my curiosity. We'd spent so much time together, and I still knew so little about him.

He swallowed, glancing down at his arm again, absently rubbing it with the other hand. "She's ..." His voice trailed off. I assumed his injury distracted him, though I didn't want to draw attention back to it.

"She's what?"

He cleared his throat. "She's fine. The way we grew up—my brothers and I—we lived separately from them mostly, so they've always just been these distant figures. We did a lot of caring for ourselves." Timidly, he curled in on himself. "I guess that's why I am the way I am."

I scooted a little closer, saying matter-of-factly, "Well, I like the way that you are."

He didn't look up, but I could see the curve of a smile on his lips. Gently, he placed his hand on top of mine, and when he answered, his voice was soft. "Yeah, I like the way you are, too, Lily."

LIAM

Lily wasn't eating again, though she was far more present than before, frowning and shoving her cabbage back and forth across her plate. Then, with a backwards glance at the door, she set the fork down, squared her shoulders, and trained her eyes on me. A little daunted by her sudden acknowledgement, I sat up straighter to listen.

"Liam," she began slowly, perhaps deciding whether to continue. She paused a moment before asking, "Can I talk to you about something?"

I folded my hands on my lap and nodded to show that she had my full attention. "What is it?"

"It's about—" She stared down at her plate, squirming in her seat. "It's about that boy we met some time ago. The one we met in the woods …"

"Mr. Behrtram, you mean?"

"Yes," she said without looking up, though a little smile appeared on her lips.

"What about him?"

She hesitated.

She had to know that I'd seen her. She *had* to, but I wouldn't admit it first. I wanted to make her say it.

If I was being honest, although we disagreed often, I missed her company. The house was lonely without her presence. I had friends, of course, and saw them on occasion, but it wasn't the same. They didn't understand me and my feelings like my sister did. They weren't experiencing the same kind of grief that Lily and I were, and when I felt sad and solitary as a result, it was her sympathy I craved, not theirs. Despite her being a spoiled brat more often than not, she had always been there, and her recent absence had me feeling rather bleak. In a way, I felt that I deserved an explanation regarding her desertion.

I would wait for her to say it out loud and admit it, not only to me but to herself as well.

"Lily, what about him?" I pressed.

She licked her lips. "Well, I—I know you know already."

I nodded.

"I know you've seen us together over the last few months."

"It seems you've found a friend at last," I said, but it came out snider than I meant it.

Her face fell. She tsk-ed and turned away, muttering, "What's the point of talking to you anyway?"

"Oh, c'mon, Lily. Don't act hurt. You tease me about my friends all the time." She eyed me, but the scowl didn't leave. "I don't think there's anything wrong with Mr. Behrtram. I mean, he saved me from that creature." I smiled, hoping she could see my sincerity. "In fact, I think it's lovely—the two of you becoming friends."

She looked up, taken aback, and with flushed cheeks, she lowered her head again. "Well, I-I know you know, so ... I wanted to ask you: do the kids you talk to—the ones who live on the streets—are they always ... beat up?"

I leaned back in my seat. "What?" It wasn't at all the sort of question I'd expected.

"Do they often have injuries?"

I thought about it, confused by the inquiry. "Some of the time, I suppose. Nothing much to fret about, just scraped knees and bruised shins. Stuff like that."

"You remember Jasper when we met him …" she began, and I noticed that she called him Jasper instead of Mr. Behrtram. They must've grown close, I thought, though I should've expected at least this amount of affection between them, all things considered. She continued, "When we met him, he was sort of disoriented, and he had that cut on his lip."

"Yeah, so? We asked him about it, and he said it was fine."

"But, you see, it wasn't only then. Every other time I see him, he's got some injury, and I don't want to ask because I don't know that it's my business. But it's—it's worrisome, don't you think? Or is that normal?" She scratched her head. "I don't think there's anything I could do even if I wanted to, but it's always something."

I found it rather alarming as well, but it wasn't hard to find some logic for it. "Well, when the erlking attacked me, he charged right in. He didn't even think about it. Maybe he's simply the kind of person who would throw himself headfirst into any situation. He did seem that way to me." I shrugged. "Maybe he's just reckless."

Lily considered that for a moment, then agreed, though she sounded doubtful. "Yeah, maybe." She picked up her fork, poked at her food, and set it back down again with a sigh. "I suppose it just worries me a little."

I feigned surprise. "Lily Howell is worried about someone?" Dramatically, I threw a hand up to my lips. "Unfathomable."

She chuckled softly. "You said yourself that he's my friend. Isn't that what you're supposed to do with friends?"

I could barely keep the smile off my face. "Yes, that's right."

She grabbed her bread and took a big bite.

I watched her quietly, feeling a little pang of jealousy toward Mr. Behrtram because I had to share her attention with him. Brash as she was, she was gentle with those she allowed in her care, and because I knew the weight of her presence, I was certain the young man felt equally affected.

Lily peered up to find me staring. "What?"

"Nothing," I said, still smiling, and she rolled her eyes.

LILY

I sat as close as I could be without touching him, though I couldn't help wanting to. The warmth of his embrace and of his hand holding mine seemed to resonate, and although those moments hadn't happened often, I felt my skin light up every time I saw him, as if it, too, remembered the feeling—as if it also yearned for that contact again. I knew Jasper wouldn't mind, but the thought of initiating was mortifying.

Curious and wanting to make conversation, I asked, "Why're you here?"

Jasper lifted his gaze, puzzled by either the question or my need to interrupt the silence with such a random inquiry. "Here in the forest with you?"

I shook my head. "Here on Earth."

He shrugged. "I come for lots of reasons." Pressing his fists into the ground, he lifted and scooted his body around. "Today," he said when he faced me, "I came to see you."

With a dry laugh, I muttered, "Quite the charmer, aren't you?"

"That wasn't charm, Lily." He winked. "It was honesty."

Wiping his knuckles on his trousers, he stole my hand from my lap and raised it to his lips. I felt the warmth of his breath as he whispered, "I can show you charm if you'd like," and he kissed the top of my hand.

I tensed, trying to find my voice to reprimand him, but I was left stifled. For a breath of time, I forgot where I was. I forgot everything except that Jasper was here with me, wherever here was. Then, sucking in a sharp, sobering breath, I pulled back. His ability to fluster me with such a simple gesture was maddening, though I'd wished for such a thing only minutes before. Perhaps that's what made it so disconcerting. It was as if he'd seen my thoughts.

The back of my hand burned.

He grinned, clearly aware of the effect he had. "Much more charming, don't you think?"

"D-don't do that ..." I mumbled, wiping my hand on my dress.

He watched me, his smile bending into a frown. "Why not?"

"It's—" I began, but I couldn't seem to find the right word. It was nice and pleasant and romantic, but those wouldn't do. "—improper," I decided with a resolute nod.

Jasper snorted. "I only kissed your hand, Lily; I didn't ask for it. Where I'm from, that's considered polite and gentlemanly. It's the same here, isn't it?"

"Well, it's ..." My face reddened, and the impish grin crept back onto his lips.

"Admit it, you're flattered."

"Shut it."

He inclined his body toward me. "Make me."

"Y'know, according to my mother, being alone with a boy at my age is improper."

"And yet, here you are."

Huffing, I dropped my shoulders. "Here I am."

Jasper observed me quietly for a moment, licked his lips, then took my hand again.

"Y'know," he said. "There is a gesture where I come from that's a bit more intimate, one that would be rather *improper* of me to do, as you say."

He turned my hand over and gently unfurled my fingers, lightly tracing the lines of my palm.

I forced a chuckle because the mood had shifted so suddenly that I didn't know how else to respond to it. "Sh-shouldn't you only be doing something so intimate with someone you—"

But ignoring me, he leaned over and softly kissed my upturned palm, letting his lips linger there for a few seconds. My curled fingertips grazed his cheek, and when he opened his eyes, I felt the flutter of his eyelashes against my skin. Coyly, he peered up at me as he released his grip, but I didn't pull away this time. For a moment, we were both completely still, gazing into each other's eyes in shared embarrassment.

But I was bound by that expression, those eyes, and that kiss, and although he'd only flipped my hand over, somehow that gesture felt far more passionate than if he'd kissed me on the mouth.

And then Jasper turned away, patted my shoulder, and got to his feet.

"G-going somewhere?" I asked, breathless.

He dusted off his trousers and offered his hand, though he avoided my eyes. "We are."

I took it without hesitation and let him pull me up. "Where're we going?"

"For a walk. We're getting lazy just sitting around talking all the time." Realising that he still held my hand, he freed me. "Sorry," he mumbled a bit awkwardly. It seemed suddenly to dawn on him just how daring an act that kiss had been. He started into the trees, sweeping an arm to beckon me.

I smirked as I ran up beside him, falling into his leisurely stride. It was my turn to be bold. I slipped my arm around his, leaning into him as we walked. His face flushed almost instantly, though he didn't try to hide it.

"Aren't you being a little improper, Lily?" he asked.

I snaked my hand down his arm to intertwine our fingers. "And who's here to stop me?"

Jasper grinned. "Not me."

LILY

I crept up to the house and quietly pushed the French doors open. Before I went inside, I peeked behind me at Jasper, only to find him still watching from the forest's edge. Then he waved, turned, and vanished under the trees.

I closed the door, leaning against it. My heart beat fast as I lifted my hands, one of which was still warm and a little sweaty from holding Jasper's for so long. Gently, I touched the spot on my palm where he'd kissed it and smiled.

I could hardly wait to see him again. If I could've returned and caught up with him just then, I thought I would've kissed him.

And then I thought, *why shouldn't I?*

I peered back through the glass, touching the door handle, wondering if there was a chance he was still there just out of sight, stricken by the same desire. But I'd barely tightened my grip before the world around me shattered, and it only took four little words to bring it crashing down on me.

"Do you enjoy it?"

I froze with my hand still on the handle, the smile immediately dashed from my lips. Gulping, I looked over my shoulder at my mother.

She stood tall, her hands clasped at her waist. The dark crepe of her mourning gown was crisp and her face, held high, was expressionless, her voice bearing no ire. But her eyes burned.

I turned slowly to face her.

"Enjoy it?" I asked.

Feign ignorance, Lily. Don't condemn yourself before you know exactly what she saw.

Which was it? Me outside when I should be in? Smiling when I should be sombre and mourning? With Jasper when propriety said I shouldn't be alone with a boy at my age—and one so far beneath our class at that?

I waited for her answer, carefully composing my face as I prayed that all she'd noticed was that I'd willfully neglected to put on a corset this morning.

"Do you enjoy disgracing your family?" she said at last, but I still didn't know how to answer. Her question gave nothing away. To her, any of the things I'd done could be considered disgraceful; she was very liberal with the word.

My face and voice void of expression, I said quietly, "No, Mother."

"Then why," she began pointedly, "do you so often make a game of it?"

Still nothing. Still no way to gauge what she knew—no way to answer her. I bowed my head but didn't speak.

"Have you nothing to say for your indiscretion, Lilith? Have you no apology to give for your scandalous behaviour?"

"Forgive me, Mother," I replied, my words slow and compliant, "but I am unaware what indiscretion you speak of."

She lurched toward me, her hand flying up. I stumbled back into the door, squeezing my eyes shut, waiting for the hot sting on my cheek, but it didn't come. When I risked a glance, Mother's hand still hovered in the air beside me, her face tight, her eyes glaring. I was nearly as tall as her, but she seemed to loom over me with that presence.

She spoke through gritted teeth. "I won't have my only daughter eloping with some mongrel from the streets. You were bred for better."

My heart sank.

My jaw trembled.

"J-just a friend," I choked out, unable to raise my volume higher than a whisper.

Her hand moved closer to my face. I flinched.

"He's only a friend, Mother," I assured her, reaching behind me to grip the doorknob. "A-an acquaintance, that's all. I promise."

For a moment, she didn't move or speak. I couldn't even feel her breath, though her face was only inches from my own. Then slowly, her fingers curled down into a fist, and she let her arm fall back to her side. She raised her head higher.

"Not anymore," she said and swung around to walk away.

My fingers slid off the door handle.

Not anymore?

"No," I said aloud, and the clack of Mother's boots stopped. My hands flew up to cover my mouth but too late. She swept toward me, closing the distance between us faster than I thought she could, grabbing my arm, wrenching me forward.

"Do you know the sacrifices I've made for this family?" she seethed. "*Do you?* I've fought more than you know to uphold the honour of this house."

I bit my tongue, but it wasn't enough to keep the words in. "By not telling anyone that Mr. Howell killed himself? That's so honourab—"

This time, when her hand raised, it met its mark. My face

was thrust to the side, my eyes wide and my skin burning, her grip on my arm keeping me in place so I felt the full force of it. I blinked the tears from my eyes, fighting not to release the cry of pain I held in my throat.

She leaned in, positioning her lips beside my ear, and her voice was like ice. "I've devoted my life to bringing you up as accomplished and marriageable as you could possibly be, and I won't see my efforts wasted."

I couldn't keep the whimper from my voice. My pride be damned. I would beg if I had to—anything to preserve my relationship with Jasper. "Please," I whispered. "Please, I beg you, don't ask me to—"

But before I could finish, she threw me back, releasing my arm. I yelped when I hit the door, my hands groping my side where the handle met me.

"It seems his visits have become more regular. You expect him around noon, correct?"

I didn't answer.

"Noon it is," she said. "Tomorrow, you will make it very clear that he is unwelcome here."

I sank to the floor, listening to the clack of her heels until the sounds of my sobs drowned out everything else.

JASPER

Lily paced beside the garden, gazing up at the sky, checking the time by Aurisol's position. Then she bowed her head, stepping side to side impatiently. She hadn't yet noticed me under the cover of the trees, but the way she waited, anticipating my arrival, made my stomach flutter.

My heartbeat quickened when, as if she could feel my gaze, she looked up. The moment our eyes met, a soft, hesitant smile graced her lips. Eagerly, I walked toward her. But as I shortened the distance between us, I watched her smile falter and then disappear altogether.

I slowed, stopping when I reached the lawn.

Something was different today. Something was wrong.

She stared back at me from her spot beside the garden fence, both of us rooted in place. I watched her expression wither into an echo of the one I'd seen in the window some months ago—that tired, lonely, dejected look that twisted my insides.

She almost—

I furrowed my brow as she lowered her head.

She almost looked like she wished she hadn't seen me.

That was it.

She didn't want to see me.

Her face downcast, she anxiously wrung her hands. Then, with her eyes still trained on the ground, she moved slowly in my direction.

What was she doing?

If she didn't want to see me today, she should've just stayed inside. Why had she come out and waited? Did she feel obligated to meet me? Had she grown tired of our little game—bored because I'd yet to take her to this other world I talked about so often? Had something happened to her or her brother?

Possibilities raced through my head, and when she stopped a few paces from me, I reached for her hand, impatient to discover the reason for her reserve. But the moment my fingertips brushed her skin, she cried, "Don't!"

What did she just ...?

"Lily?" I whispered to no response. "Lily, what's the matter? Are you all right?"

Still, she said nothing, though she swallowed tightly.

Something wasn't right. The way she stood with her shoulders rolled forward and her chest collapsed inward wasn't right. Her silent restraint wasn't right.

Urgently, I closed the gap between us, desperate to see her face. Before she could react, I seized her shoulders, forcing her to meet me face to face. Immediately, panic flashed in her eyes, and she jerked away, stumbling backward out of my grip.

"Don't touch me!"

Every muscle in my body tensed.

Such a direct rejection was far from anything I expected or imagined. I wasn't sure I could move if I'd tried. There was nothing I could do but stand there and await an explanation, but she didn't offer one.

Who was this? Surely not my Lily. Surely not the girl who'd

thrown herself into my arms in this very spot only a short time ago.

I struggled to bring voice to my thoughts. "Lily, please tell me what's going on. A-are you—? If this is a joke, it's not funny."

"You need to leave now, and don't come back." The words left her lips swiftly and hit me like a blow to the chest.

What had she just …?

Then with a little more resolve, she said again, forcing me to acknowledge exactly what she meant, "Leave."

My response was equally demanding, flying from my lips less than a second after she'd spoken. "Why?"

Finally, she raised her head, pausing with her mouth half-open. For a moment, her firm expression faltered, and her jaw shuddered around whatever excuse she tried to gather. But all she managed was a stuttered, "B-because."

"Because why?" I pressed, advancing toward her.

I knew it was wrong of me. I knew I shouldn't corner her like this. I knew I looked threatening, and the fence was behind her. She had nowhere to run. But the wave of anger that surged through me drove my feet forward.

What was with this fragile resolve of hers? How half-hearted. How unconvincing.

I urged her backward until she hit the fence.

But then I saw the whisper of fear in her eyes. I saw them dart left, then right, then back at me, trying to decide which way to run. I stopped, and when the fear was replaced with relief, my heart sank.

This was wrong of me. It was shameful and unfeeling.

I offered her my hand again, this time extending it in apology.

But she smacked it away.

"Stop it!"

My breath hitched, and I retreated, stepping a few paces backward.

What was going on?

Something was terribly wrong.

Did I do something? Had I hurt her? Injured her in some way I wasn't aware of?

"Lily, I don't understand—"

"Please, just go away!" she shouted, charging forward and shoving me hard in the chest. Her voice quivered and shrank. "You said that if I asked you to leave, you would, so please ..."

The space around me darkened.

The Void pulled on my mind.

I felt myself slip out of reality—and maybe I did disappear for a moment—but I forced myself back, fighting against the fierce desire to flee into that blank mind state. The Spirits obliged, though not without reluctance, and I was thrust back into awareness to find Lily's eyes wide with confusion and worry.

How long had I been gone? Seconds? Minutes? I could never accurately assess the passing of time in that state.

I shuddered, unsure what to do next, though I could tell she wanted to ask what sort of glitch in my presence had occurred —if something really had happened or if it was only her imagination. She began to wring her hands again, but she made no attempt to understand. She seemed to have decided to pretend it hadn't happened, which I was fine with. I had no explanation for it either.

But the price of even that momentary lapse was dizzying. I blinked my eyes and cleared my throat, pushing past it. "So—so that's it then?"

She bit her lip.

My anger flared again at her reticence. "That's it? That's all? You're really gonna—"

"Jasper," she said, softly this time, pleading. "Please just go."

The tone of her voice defused me, but I clenched my jaw, resisting. I didn't want to give up this fight so easily. I didn't want this to end.

'... *and don't come back.*'

"O-only if that's what you really, *really* want, Lily," I said because I couldn't believe it. I couldn't believe that I'd done something awful enough to illicit such an abrupt goodbye.

But I must have.

I must have been horrible to her.

I must have hurt her.

I must have done *something*!

But that wasn't the case, was it? This was something else entirely. I wasn't the only one upset by this. I could see in her eyes and hear in her quaking voice that she, too, was distraught, though I couldn't speak to ask why. I could only plead in my head.

Please, Lily, don't ask me to leave. Don't act like you want me gone. Please. We're friends, aren't we? Maybe better than friends. You and I, we're—

A realisation struck me then. I'd been so absorbed by our conversation that I hadn't addressed the discomforting feeling that now seemed to envelop my whole being: we were being watched.

Warily, I pulled my eyes from Lily's face and peered past her at the house, my eyes moving over the doors and windows until, at last, I saw her: the ghost—the pale woman who stood in that second-floor window dressed in black, ever watchful. I'd seen her before, or rather, caught glimpses before she disappeared, but this time, she stayed. And although I'd never asked, I knew she must be Lily's mother.

That was it then.

It wasn't Lily.

Lily wasn't telling me to leave; her mother was.

My mind flooded with thoughts, plans, imaginings of me taking Lily's hand and running away with her into the woods. Would she go if I did? I dropped my eyes from the window, searching her face for any sign that she might.

Let's go, Lily. Now. Let's run.

But those weren't the words that came out.

"Lily," I pleaded as gently as I could. "Please ..."

Her eyes glistening, she threw out her arms to push me back again. "Just go away, Jasper! I—I don't want to—to see you anymore, so just leave already!"

She spun and took off toward the terrace. I bumbled after her with flailing arms, grabbing for her hand, her skirt—any part of her to make her stop again. But my reaction was too slow, and Lily didn't look back. I watched her disappear, helpless, and when I glanced back at the second-floor window, the ghost had vanished, too.

I wanted to chase after her. I wanted to charge up to the house and rip the door open. I wanted to scold and scream at her: *don't let someone else dictate who you can and can't be friends with! Don't let your mother—*

But even if Lily had turned back—even if I'd burst through the door and forced her to listen to me—I'd never be able to say it. The only reason I'd come to Earth was because my mother had told me to. The only reason I'd *befriended* those other children and taken them to the castle, the only reason I'd befriended Lily ...

I stepped backward, my heart thrashing in my ribcage, but I kept walking, quickening my pace until the manicured grass changed to weeds under my feet. Then I fled into the trees. I ran until I couldn't breathe, until I was farther into the woods than

I'd ever gone with Lily, until I didn't recognise my surroundings anymore.

I was panting when I finally paused to nurse the stitch in my side.

I didn't know what to do.

It shouldn't be that much of a surprise.

Rationally, I knew that. I knew that Lily's mother had good intentions, and I knew how it must've looked—her only daughter running off every day with some raggedy boy. Of course, she would want me gone! It made perfect sense. It was justified, and yet …

I inhaled again, still winded by my sprint, but I couldn't stay still. I had to move. I had to keep going, but my next thought stopped me in my tracks—a thought which had been building in my mind and only now came to light: *what if I never saw Lily again?*

My chest tightened, and I clutched my shirt over my heart, suddenly feeling lightheaded. I gulped in another breath, lowering myself to my knees. My eyes moistened. My fingers shook.

Why did the thought of never seeing her again affect me so much?

She was the one who told me to leave. I should be livid. She brutally rejected me, and it didn't matter whether it had been at her mother's request or not. Why couldn't she have just stayed inside? Why couldn't she have ignored me or told me to pretend? It would've been far less cruel.

I crawled to the nearest tree and sat against it, drawing my knees up to my chest.

I wasn't wanted here anymore.

Sniffling, I covered my face with my hands, squeezing my eyes shut, tighter and tighter until I could see blotches of white against my eyelids. I tried to breathe slowly, evenly, fighting to ease the ache in my chest and throat. But each inhale trembled. Each exhale wheezed. I wrapped my arms over my stomach as I dropped my forehead to my knees. My eyes felt hot, and my nose ran; I wiped it on my sleeve.

Damn it! Stop it, Jasper.

You shouldn't feel this way.

You shouldn't feel like you've been abandoned; you haven't been.

Lily wasn't really your friend. She was your victim, remember? She was nothing to you—another child for the dungeons, another captive to please the queen. That's all she was, right? Nothing else.

But I didn't believe it myself. I couldn't. I pressed my lips together to hold in the sob that bottled in my throat, only a soft whimper escaping. I clasped my hands over my head.

As much as I didn't want to admit it, Lily was my friend, whether I'd expected her to be or not, whether I'd only been pretending at first or not ...

No, I was never really pretending with her. She didn't get His Royal Highness Prince Gabriel; she got Jasper. She didn't get smoothly spoken lies; she got me.

But she wasn't supposed to be my friend! She wasn't supposed to hurt me. That was my job. *I* was supposed to hurt *her*. I was supposed to entice her into coming to Iraxhar with me. That was my job! It wasn't to make friends. A prince doesn't have friends. He has parents, siblings, servants, guards, allies, enemies ... all of which must be treated as friends but never trusted. No one could be trusted. Eyes were always watching, ears always listening. There was no freedom. We were brought up as liars and manipulators. Acquaintances were all I could have because they were easier to discard should the need arise. Betrayal was so common that I couldn't afford to let my guard down.

That's who I am.

That's who my parents, teachers, and siblings created.

I can't be trusted.

Lily's right to throw me away.

I wiped my eyes.

Lily was only an acquaintance, right? She was a part of my plan, but this time, the plan fell through. That's what I was feeling. It wasn't pain over losing someone. It was simply disappointment because my expectations hadn't been met. It was disappointment that I'd wasted time instead of fulfilling my orders.

Wasted time.

That was a lie.

None of the time I'd spent with Lily had felt wasted.

This wasn't disappointment. That was a lie, too.

This was heartbreak.

That was the truth, and it felt bitter.

PART ELEVEN
BREATHING UNDERWATER

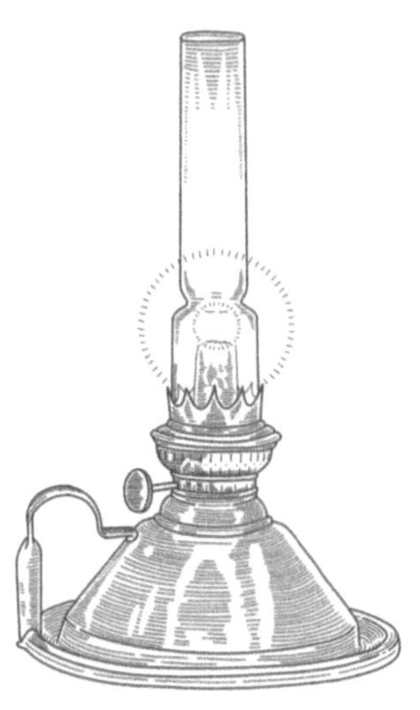

LIAM

I chased her up the stairs and down the hall. "Lily, wait!"

She shoved through the door, and at last, she slowed, stopping in the middle of her room, though she kept her back to me. Her chest heaved. One hand shrouded her eyes. "G-go away."

Panting, I let the door fall shut behind me. I couldn't remember the last time I'd seen her so hysterical, and the novelty of it both unnerved and intrigued me. Even Father's death hadn't produced such an emotive response from her.

I approached and placed a cautious hand on her shoulder. "Lily, talk to me," I whispered, but she didn't reply. "Lily, c'mon, you must've known this was gonna—"

"This is your fault!" she cried, whirling around, and I leapt back before her swinging arm could hit me. She jabbed her finger at my chest. "*You* told Mother, didn't you? *Didn't you?*"

"No." I shook my head. "I didn't—"

"Don't lie to me, Liam." She wiped her nose on the back of her hand. "It's always you. Always. I always get in trouble because of you, you little rat!"

"Lily, how could I? Have you had an audience with her

recently?" Her eyes thinned, and I knew she already planned to disregard any argument I could assemble. "I didn't tell her anything!"

"Don't lie!"

"I didn't tell her!"

"Then who did, Liam?" she asked but didn't let me answer. Her mind was already made up. In her eyes, I was already guilty. "Because of you, I had to say goodbye to my only friend! I'm alone, and it—it's your fault!"

"I didn't tell her."

"Then tell me who did!" she demanded, and when I didn't respond, she grabbed my shirt collar and yanked me closer. "Tell me who did! I need to know so—"

I threw my arms up between us, breaking her grip, shoving her back. "You did, you bloody idiot! It was you!"

"What?" The shift in her expression was immediate.

I regretted my aggression, but there was no other way to silence her. I had to explain properly, or she wouldn't understand. "It was you. It was the way you acted before you ran out the door to meet him, the way you dressed and finished your assignments so lessons ended faster. I noticed straight away, so how could they not?"

"No, you're wrong! I didn't—"

I spoke over her. "Mother may ignore us, but she still talks to Miss Sawyer and Madame Renoir." Biting my lip, I stepped slowly toward her, lightly placing my hand on her arm again. "How could they not notice? You weren't discreet, Lily ..."

"No!" she snapped, smacking my hand away. "No, because that—that would make it my fault, and it—" Her bottom lip puckered. "—it can't be my fault. I didn't want to make him go away ..." The volume of her voice shrank until it was hardly audible. "I-I don't want to be alone again."

"Am I invisible?"

She faced away from me. "Just go away ..."

"Lily, you're not alone now, and I'm not going to leave you like this. I'm here."

"It's not the same," she mumbled.

"What isn't?"

"It's not the same when you say it!" Sniffling, she wiped her eyes and crossed her arms. Her voice lowered, though the hostility in it rose. "Why don't you just go, Liam? Go play with your friends. I know you want to. Shove it in my face some more that you can make them so easily, and I can't."

"Lily, that's not fair. When have I—"

"Just go away! You didn't seem to care before, so why are you bothering now? I was just as lonely before we met Jasper, so just—"

"As if you'd ever accept any kind of help from me! You played your little high-and-mighty act so often, how could I have done anything? How could I even know how lonely you were if you never let me see it?"

"Jasper saw it without me saying anything ..."

"Well, I'm not him, am I?" I felt a lump growing in my throat, that familiar twinge of jealousy brewing in me. I knew she'd grown fonder of Mr. Behrtram's company than mine lately, but comparing us like that was heartless. Sarcasm bit into my voice. "I'm sorry if I didn't pick up on it when you were so damn careful about hiding it! I'm the worst, aren't I? How bloody awful of me not to notice something you were going out of your way to keep a secret!"

Lily didn't answer. She stood unnaturally still with her back to me, her shoulders hunched forward.

Exhaling, I tried to reign my emotions in. "Look, Lily, I'm sorry if you felt alone around me, but I'm here for you now. Right now. I'm your brother and your friend, and I—I want to be here for you. Let me."

Her responding voice was soft but sharp as a knife. "If you were really my friend, you would've noticed before." She glanced tiredly over her shoulder, eyes red and teary. "But you didn't, so just go away. Leave me alone."

I bit my lip to stop it from trembling. I cleared my throat, trying to speak over the ache that grew in it, trying to answer with equally as much venom. "Fine, I give up. Mope. Cry. I don't care, but don't look for comfort from me."

JASPER

The guards at the outer wall shuffled and gasped when I appeared in front of the gate, and with a shout signaling my arrival, the scene devolved into frenzy. Men rushed this way and that, abandoning their usual reserve for chaos, like rats fleeing a sinking ship. I heard the command to lower the drawbridge and then the clatter of armour as the order was executed.

I watched, unimpressed. Usually, their flustered haste would have amused me, but today, I found it irritating and incompetent. If I could sneak out under their watchful eyes, who else could sneak in?

I ignored their nervous welcomes, crossed the bridge in silence, and waited to be admitted. They bowed as I passed, and a man ran to my side when I entered the grounds.

"May we offer you a cart, your highness?" His voice cracked as he took in the state of me, and clearing his throat, he added, "You must be weary from your travels."

Shaking my head, I waved the man away. He bowed and retreated, almost immediately replaced by another servant carrying a tray that offered an assortment of beverages. I quickened my pace, but he trotted alongside me, walking as fast and as carefully as he could without spilling them.

"Would you care for a refreshment, my lord? You must be parched in this heat."

Again, I dismissed the eager servant, but before he left, I said, "You would do well to inform the others that the next person to interrupt me on my way to the castle will be reported to my mother for harassment." Any mention of invoking even the queen's *presence* was enough to put a subject in his or her place.

The man's eyes widened, and then he bowed over his tray and hurried back to disclose my threat. The remainder of my walk passed uninterrupted.

I spurred right of the main entrance, heading for the armory, where there would be less of a welcome and which was nearer to my suite. But when I arrived, I wasn't met with the solitude I'd hoped for. A crowd of soldiers clogged the entrance, filtering in and out, and when I approached the doorway, I came to an abrupt halt. My brothers stood with the blacksmith only a few feet away, their heads huddled together in muted conversation.

I stepped backward, silently pleading that I might go unnoticed and disappear into the crowd, but men were already staring. I shrank where I stood, feeling the weight of their gawking eyes. Even with so haggard an appearance, anonymity didn't exist for me inside the castle grounds.

When the blacksmith recognised me, he pointed, and immediately, my brothers' attentions were redirected. My throat tightened.

Seth's brow furrowed when our eyes met. "Gabriel?"

Noah turned and recoiled like he'd been struck. "Well," he said, pursing his lips, "don't you look a lovely shade of horrible.

Do you try to look like a war-ravaged refugee, or does it just happen naturally?"

I exhaled but didn't answer. Seth smacked Noah's arm to scold him, but I wasn't particularly bothered by his comment because it had been my intention to look as ignoble as possible. On Earth, the faces of the poor were as anonymous as the bodies in a mass grave.

"Oh, forgive me." Noah rolled his eyes. "I meant to ask if you enjoyed leaving all your responsibilities to others while you were off playing in the dirt?"

"Noah," Seth hissed, and our brother held his hands up in sarcastic surrender. Seth faced me. "Are you all right, Gabriel? You seem distraught."

I gazed back at them, but I couldn't bring myself to speak. I wouldn't explain myself regardless but especially not with so many spectators, all of whom were sure to be listening even if they didn't appear to be. I didn't want to deal with them. I didn't want to deal with anyone. I wanted to sleep until I could forget everything—Lily and Liam, their mother, my orders, Father's arrangement ...

By the time I'd finished the list in my head, my heart pounded, and my feet were frantic. I turned to walk away, fighting not to break into a sprint, trying to void the emotion I knew showed on my face.

I'd made it 50 yards when I heard my brothers' footsteps coming up behind me, and knowing I couldn't shake them without a confrontation, I spun around.

"What?" I growled.

They stopped in front of me, but when neither spoke, I turned again. Seth's hand on my shoulder kept me where I was.

"Gabriel," he said gently, "What's wrong?"

I shrugged him off. "Nothing. I'm tired."

"Well, that's obvious," Noah muttered, and Seth shushed him.

"But what's wrong?" Seth pressed.

I sucked my lips in, inhaling deeply and exhaling through my nose before answering. "Remember what we talked about last time? When I said that *my* business was none of *your* business?" I surprised myself with how spiritless my voice sounded. Not cold. Not threatening. Timid.

I watched them exchange a glance. When they worried about me, they always looked at each other—a sort of mutual confirmation that the worry was valid. I'd seen it time and time again.

Maybe this time it was.

Maybe every time it was.

"Don't worry about it," I mumbled, floating my gaze away from their faces.

But then Noah scoffed and asked, "Do you think we can't see when something's wrong with you?"

My head snapped up. They didn't know. They couldn't. I'd never let them, but for some reason, I felt resentful that they'd never noticed on their own—or worse, noticed and done nothing.

"Can you?" I snarled back, and the stringency of my voice silenced him.

His jaw set, he stared at me with slit eyes. Then quickly, quietly, before I even realised what he was doing, he threw his arm toward me and touched my cheek. I jerked, stumbling backwards out of his range before any of my memories could flash from my mind to his—before he could steal an explanation from my head.

My shout fled my mouth before I could stop it. "Don't fucking touch me, Noah! When I say it's none of your business, I mean it's none of your business!"

My heart raced. My lungs burned. I wanted to run, but I couldn't purge the horrible pang in my chest. Tears stung my eyes, and I faced away from my brothers to wipe them. Then I strode on without so much as a glance over my shoulder.

They didn't follow.

I barely noticed Soren as I pushed through the door of my suite, not bothering to close it behind me. I went straight to my room and collapsed on my bed, digging my fingers in the blankets, pulling them to me, burying my face in them.

I heard a gentle knock and didn't answer, but I listened to the quiet shuffle of Soren's feet as he entered. He said nothing as he untied and pulled off my boots, nor did he speak when he took my night clothes from the armoire, rolled me over, and pulled my shirt off to help me into them. He didn't speak when he arranged my pillows, drew my quilts up to my chin, and tucked me in ... or when he touched my face with a cold hand, shoved my hair back, and placed a light, whiskery kiss on my forehead. His lips lingered there for a moment. I could feel the lump of the scar on his bottom lip and relaxed against it—felt the odd comfort of his calloused hand and chapped lips. I almost protested when he withdrew.

Then he said, "Rest easy, young prince. I'll be right outside."

I should've spoken then. I should've thanked him. But instead, I fell asleep.

JASPER

"Good morning, Gabriel."

I startled into awareness, blinking, struggling to see her through bleary eyes.

No other voice could rouse me so quickly, but my immediate recognition was not a comfort. No other voice could flood my body with a fear that painted my skin in gooseflesh, every hair raised as if bracing for an attack.

I rubbed my arms to soothe the prickly feeling, managing to produce a quiet, "Good morning," my voice still rough with sleep.

Haltingly, my eyes travelled up her silhouetted figure, and I waited for them to adjust enough to see her face properly. She'd lit all the lamps in my room and herself sat in the glow of one of them—the one nearest my bedside.

When she said nothing else, I felt sweat begin to bead on my chest and back. I asked, "What is it? Have I done wrong?"

My heartbeat quickened as possibilities ran through my head. I clutched the blanket to dry my clammy hands. The last time she'd appeared in my bedroom unannounced, I'd ended up at Quade's. I'd have to be better prepared this time. More alert. More obedient. Perhaps I could—

But my wishful thinking was folly. I knew this visit wouldn't end peacefully. They never did anymore.

It used to only be sometimes.

It used to only hurt my soul.

But physical pain was really not so bad. It was manageable. Those wounds always healed. A few days or weeks, and there would be only scars. And eventually those would fade, too. It was only a matter of endurance—of patience and fortitude.

It was the fear she had embedded in my bones and my skin that truly tormented. It walked with me every day, wrapped itself around every step I took. It was a fear that could wake me and make me sweat. It was something that once had been a passing feeling but now elicited a physical response. That's how I knew it had penetrated my very being, anchored itself to the pieces that made me who I was so I could never forget it—never forget her.

And yet, the face that observed me now was tranquil, though if I didn't know her, I'd have described it as hollow or perhaps simply expressionless.

"No, no," she replied gently. "Nothing is wrong. I just wanted to check in. How is everything going with your secret mission?" She put an emphasis on the word *secret* and smiled thinly. It was a tactic she used often—talking to me like I was a child. I often found myself speaking to my victims the same way. It was effective; she swayed me as easily as I swayed them.

I chose my words carefully. "The mission is successful thus far."

She nodded, sitting with such a strict posture that it seemed unnatural. "This is the second time you've returned empty-handed."

My stomach tightened at the twinge of disappointment in

her voice, but I refused to let any distress show on my face. "Forgive the delay, Mother. I'm working on two this time."

Her lips pursed slightly. "You would do well to follow your orders exactly. It says little for your efficiency to bring multiple candidates if it still takes the same amount of time it would to collect them individually."

"Understood, ma'am," I said and bowed my head.

She lifted a hand, swept a strand of hair out of her face, and smiled again, but it was her practised smile—the one she wore when she felt obligated to seem kind or interested. "You've also been gone longer than usual this time. Your father was beginning to worry. I told him you were fine; boys love adventure, after all."

I licked my lips.

'*Your father was beginning to worry,*' she'd said. Not her, only Father. I waited to see if she had anything to add—'*I was nearly ill with worry myself!*' perhaps—but she didn't.

I asked softly, "Do you worry about me, too, when I'm gone?"

Her answering silence was unwanted but expected, and I sat just as quietly, studying her face, which seemed softer in the lamplight—her eyes more pronounced, her cheeks splashed with more warmth and colour. I stared, probing for any sort of reply, but her eyes moved around the room instead of meeting mine, stopping on random items for closer inspection but not staying too long. She almost seemed confused, like she didn't understand the question or didn't know how to respond to it.

"Your majesty," I prompted, letting myself believe for a sliver of a second that maybe she hadn't heard. Maybe she wasn't listening. Queens always have a lot on their minds— orders to give, tasks to complete. They were awash with things to worry about; her youngest son's whereabouts were hardly pertinent. He was gone so often and always returned in working order, so why fret?

Although I already knew what her response would be, I still felt my heart sink when she finally replied with forced cheerfulness, "Oh goodness no, of course not!"

She leaned forward, sliding to the edge of her seat to reach for my cheek. I resisted the urge to pull away. Her hands always felt cold as death, but it wasn't comforting like that of Soren's weathered fingers. It wasn't from years of hard labour and poor circulation. In fact, they might not have really been cold at all. It might've just been the coldness I'd assigned to it because her touch always made me shudder—another reflex she'd instilled in my body.

She sat back again. "I know I don't have to worry about you, Gabriel. You're—" She paused as though searching for the right word, deciding with, "—sturdy."

I scoffed at the word without thinking, then froze when her voice ceased, unsure how to explain myself. I waited for her hand to fly up and reprimand me for such a crude reaction, but it stayed on her lap.

"I-I apologise, Mother. I meant no disrespect. I—"

Her eyes tightened, her voice pitched low when she said, "Explain."

"F-forgive me."

Her volume leapt to a shout. "Explain!"

I could hear the panic trilling into my voice. "I merely had a-a moment of weakness, your majesty. It has passed. It won't happen again."

She pondered my answer and asked, "What has brought about this feeling of weakness? You must confront it in order to correct it."

"It was nothing. I—"

"Oh, Gabriel." She'd slipped back into that cooing voice.

"You must address this. It's so important to learn from your flaws and weaknesses. I simply want to assist you in being the best you can be, don't you see? Don't you want to make your mother proud?"

I inhaled, considering a lie but deciding to be honest. "F-for a moment, I wanted to hear that you worried for me, too."

"Anything else?"

By the tone of her voice, I expected her to roll her eyes. I expected her question to be accompanied by a huff or a sigh. I was surprised it wasn't because her expression reflected the sarcastic dismissal so well.

Suddenly, I felt foolish.

In that expression, I could see that she didn't believe such a silly reason deserved even to be stated. I may as well have been joking, though I was certain she knew I'd answered sincerely. But in the face of rejection, I had to say something else, something more convincing, something worth her time. To continue asking her to worry about her *sturdy* son would be absurd.

But I had so many reasons and questions stored away in my head that there was barely a lag between my two statements. "I wanted some reassurance, that's all."

"Reassurance?"

Reassurance that you care.

But I nearly scoffed again at the thought of articulating my true sentiments. Instead, I answered, "Reassurance that my mission was just and that I would be rewarded for my efforts."

"What reason have you to care if it's just?"

"I want to understand why you requested this of me. The victims—they're children. How can they have any use to you?"

The sarcasm fled her voice. She stared down her nose at me. "I don't believe their use to me is any of your concern. My orders are absolute. Don't compromise your usefulness by humanizing the candidates."

But they are human. They have names and feelings.

Lily's face formed in my mind, and I lowered my head, afraid my feelings for the girl would show. But she couldn't know about Lily; in the queen's eyes, I was simply another subject bowing his head in submission.

"Yes, you're right," I said. "I apologise, Mother. It's not my place to question you."

But I did. Confusion and anxiety followed me as closely as fear did, and even motionless in bed, my heart pounded. No one else would give—no one else *had*—the answers. Mother was the only one.

So, I asked.

Because today, I already felt defeated.

Today, I thought I could stomach whatever punishments she had in store.

Today, I simply didn't care what the outcome would be.

"Why do I have to do this?"

Then, I felt like my heart had finally sunk beyond retrieval because as soon as I heard the words roll off my tongue, I knew I'd done wrong. I shouldn't have asked. I should've suppressed the impulse because I wasn't defiant and uncaring; that was only a front, and already, it had shattered.

Mother's eyes widened. I rushed into my apology. "I'm sorry, Mum—ma'am—I didn't mean—"

But her placid expression didn't change, which unsettled me more than if she'd started screaming. She gripped my shoulders to calm me.

"Oh no, dear," she whispered, and once I'd closed my mouth, she lifted her hands to cradle my face. "It's okay, Gabriel. It's okay."

I gulped, forever jaded by that soft, motherly voice. I tried to relax. I tried not to tense my entire body.

"Don't be afraid," she said as she slid her hands from my

cheeks down over my jaw and onto my neck, the pressure of her fingertips increasing with the movement. She leaned closer. "Everything's fine."

But it wasn't fine.

I wasn't fine.

I was afraid.

She should've been mad.

There was comfort in predictability and fear in change. This sweetness was different—this softness and affection in response to my error. This was a person I couldn't anticipate.

But then—

Her fingernails pierced my skin, and she flew out of her seat, her grip tightening. She threw her weight at me, and with no time to react, I was thrust backwards, my next inhale choking me as my head hit the bedpost. I gasped, but her thumbs pressed into my throat before I could get a full breath. I grabbed her wrists.

"Why do you *have* to do this, Gabriel?" Her voice was quiet, but it spared no civility. There was only acid where there had been gentility mere moments before. "You don't *have* to do anything, do you? *Do you?*"

Tears welled in my eyes as I tried to shake my head. Her hands closed tighter around my neck, preventing me.

Push her off, Jasper. Shove her back. You're stronger than her.

But my fingers trembled around her bony wrists, and I couldn't bring myself to do it.

There was comfort in predictability. There was relief that she had reacted the way I'd expected her to. And anyway, this was a fair punishment, wasn't it? I'd brought this on myself. I shouldn't have asked. I *knew* I shouldn't have asked. She had to correct my behaviour, right? It had been my choice to help in the first place. She wasn't making me do anything, right? Nothing at all. She wasn't—

Mum, please. It hurts.

"You know I wouldn't *make* you do anything, right?"

I strained to nod, and at last, she seemed satisfied. Her grip slackened. I sucked in a deep breath, coughing it out as her hands reversed their course, moving from my neck back to my cheeks. I melted into the pillow, and again, she looked at me with that warm expression as if those last few seconds hadn't happened at all, as if I wasn't wheezing and trying to sink deeper into my bedding to get away from her, as if I hadn't yet asked such a silly question.

With no effort at all, her voice shifted from that sharp hiss to her velvety coo. "But Gabriel," she said. "My sweet Gabriel, you'd never dream of disappointing your mother, would you?" She slid her thumbs over my cheekbones.

I stared back at her.

This was wrong.

She was wrong to do this to me.

She was wrong to ask me that.

But I simply shook my head because she was right, too. I really *didn't* want to disappoint her, and for my obedience, I was granted that smile—the smile that said she had gotten what she wanted, the one that everyone gets when a plan goes exactly the way it was imagined ...

I blinked back tears.

I didn't want that smile from her. I didn't want to see how pleased she was with herself and with my submission. I didn't want her to praise my resilience as if there was a victory in enduring.

Look how strong you are, how sturdy, how durable. Look how much you can handle.

She kissed the air above my forehead, her lips not quite reaching my skin. She stood to leave but stopped in the doorway. Her back to me, she said, her voice returned to its usual strict, unyielding tone, "Assure your father that you're well, and then get back to work. I haven't the patience for people who waste my time."

I was glad she hadn't turned because the tears were already on my face, and I didn't want her to see how much it injured me to love her. But I couldn't stop loving her, could I? Deep in my memories, there was a beautiful woman who smiled and laughed, who sometimes gazed into my eyes with such love that it seemed mournful ... I was haunted by her. I wanted her back. She was locked away in the body of this woman in front of me, and I wanted her back!

But that was the problem, wasn't it? She wasn't coming back. No matter what I did for her, nothing changed. She didn't trust me. She wasn't the sad, tortured damsel in need of a healing hand. She wasn't waiting for me to mend the festering wounds of her heart.

Why had I believed that she was?

The smiles and laughter I remembered weren't for me. They weren't happy; I was just young and couldn't yet tell that they were forced.

But I needed to justify her cruelty. I needed to believe that enduring so much pain and hate would amount to something positive. I needed an image to cling to.

How dolefully I'd painted her in my mind.

Somehow, in that moment, staring at her back through bleary eyes with her icy voice ringing in my ears, I knew the mother born from my memories was lost.

She hadn't ever existed in the first place.

Her words seemed to echo in the space between us: *'Get back to work ...'*

Get back to what? Stealing the lives of children? I'd gone into the dungeon and looked in the cells. Of all the victims I'd charmed, only a few remained. I was responsible for those deaths. Every single one. Because they couldn't be alive somewhere, could they? That was wishful thinking. I was responsible for their absence—those gentle, unknowing children whose only fault had been that they were far too trusting.

But I was a good actor, and my lies left my lips as easily as truth. And when it counted, what I said was true. They saw another world and new creatures and *magic.* I played the part so well, it would've been hard not to trust me. It would've been hard to see through my lies.

I'd been taught by the best, after all.

Of course, the scenario with Lily had strayed from my original plan, but it had only taken a little more time. She'd wanted to see another world. If I were sneaky enough to avoid Lily's mother, she would still greet me the same way, wouldn't she? In fact, she might like the adventure of sneaking around, that silly girl. I could *get back to work* rather easily if I just put forth the extra effort. I could go back and ask her to leave with me.

Come on, Lily, let's go.

I could. It would be easy.

From the doorway, Mother's voice said, "I expect a response."

It would be so easy to simply say *yes* and return everything to normal, but every ounce of my being repelled the thought. Every cell in my body screamed, "No!" and the word escaped my lips before I knew it.

"Excuse me?"

"I-I'm sorry—"

"No?" I heard the incredulousness in her voice.

But the word had already been spoken, and as much as I tried to twist my lips into the right shape and just say *yes,* I couldn't because I couldn't hurt Lily. Even if she had pushed me away. Even if she could only live in my memories.

Mother's heels scraped on the stone as she faced me.

I breathed heavily. I gasped and sniffled. My throat hurt. My eyes burned. My whole body screamed out against her, prickling uncomfortably all over, like I might be sick, like every place she'd touched me was alight. I ached. I wanted out of my skin. And I just ...

It wasn't a surge of energy I felt. It wasn't a sudden motivation to be better or a desire to be rid of her. It wasn't empowerment.

I was just so tired.

With that simple *no*, ten years of exhaustion wracked my body in a single moment. Ten years of lying to myself and pretending nothing was wrong, pretending I was helping her, pretending I hadn't lost myself somewhere along the way ... Ten years of hiding at Quade's clinic and having wounds bandaged. So many visits, so many nightmares, so many times sitting alone and crying and—

And I was just so fucking tired.

For so long, I'd felt like I was drowning, slowly suffocating beneath the vast blanket of her influence, and I'd exhausted myself fighting for the surface. Then, without realising how little oxygen I had left, I'd used it up. There was no struggle in me anymore. There was no air. I'd already sank to the bottom. It wouldn't matter. Nothing mattered.

I just wanted to open my mouth, take a deep breath, and sleep.

What was I even fighting? The orders she'd given? The violence she did on me? The guilt I felt for committing her crimes?

It doesn't matter, I thought. *Who cares what you do or say anymore?*

I knew what I wanted to do, and I knew what I wanted to say.

With whatever power was left in me, I would make her abandon that fucking smile.

I squared my shoulders, set my jaw, and stared right back at her. I said, nearly breathless, "I can't do this anymore." Then, with a little more conviction, a little more finality: "I won't."

JASPER

The corridor was empty. How was it empty? Hadn't anyone heard the screams?

It didn't matter. I had to flee.

She screamed still; I could hear her muffled voice through the open door, but I paused, both in horror and simply because I couldn't seem to catch my breath.

How muffled it was ...

I considered closing the door just to see—to hear the screams vanish, to let them seep into the stone of the walls and the floors but no farther.

How many times had my voice been confined to this room, sealed inside for no ears but hers or my own?

I shut my eyes, holding my throat, gulping in as much air as I could fill my lungs with, but the more I took in, the harder it became to breathe. I stumbled back until I collided with the wall.

Still, she screamed. Bellows and curses. But there was something else, too. There was another noise slowly building beneath her voice.

I dragged myself along the wall, away from the door, into

the shadows, flattening myself, folding into the darkness as a stampede of feet tore down the hall. I slivered my eyes and held my breath as, one by one, armoured guards flew into my suite. I heard the clattering and shouting from within as the hallway emptied.

Go, go, go. Jasper, run. Get out of here.

But my legs wouldn't move.

I opened my eyes, and the stone around me swam. I nearly heaved, clamping a hand over my mouth. Shakily, I lowered it and spat.

Go. Run. Now.

My head lolled, and the walls smeared before my eyes. I blinked, and they seemed to blink back. My heartbeat throbbed in my head. I peered in the other direction, the floor and walls and windows moving across my vision in slow motion.

What was I doing? Where was I going?

Anywhere. Just run.

Run where? And how?

It doesn't matter! Run!

I urged my feet forward in lurching steps, farther down the corridor, farther from my chambers and the wailing woman within. This solitude couldn't last. I had to act quickly. I had to hide.

Wheezing, I flung myself at the nearest door, fumbling for the handle. I muscled it open and tripped inside, but I couldn't leave it that way. I had to close it. The door had to be sealed. I had to hide. They'd find me if the door was open.

I threw all my weight at it until it drove shut with a soft groan, but that was all I could do. I couldn't let go of it. I'd fall over.

I inhaled through my mouth, but the air stung my throat. I choked, I coughed, and everything in my stomach came bubbling up. I braced myself against the door and retched, ejecting it. My body shook. I heaved again, my knees buckling.

Carefully, I turned my body and slumped against the wall. I pooled all the moisture in my mouth and spat, trying to expel the sour taste of vomit from my mouth, but it wasn't enough. I shook, gagging and panting and wishing I could catch my breath, but there didn't seem to be enough air. I squeezed my eyes shut, clutching my throat, and—

Darkness stretched out around me as the world fell slowly away, and for a second, I felt weightless. For a second, I could breathe.

But then a jolt brought me back.

I opened my eyes, and Noah stood in front of me as if he'd materialised out of thin air, his hands on my shoulders, shaking me. His lips moved frantically. He was talking, but I couldn't hear him over the pounding and ringing in my head.

Noah, you're mumbling. Speak up. I can't hear you.

His grip tightened, and in an instant, I was lucid again. As if all my awareness amassed in those spots, the weight of his hands felt immeasurably heavy because they weren't gloved as they often were. He wasn't touching my skin, but still, his bare hands were on me. It wouldn't be difficult for him to just shift his hold another inch or two, but I couldn't let him. I couldn't let him touch me. If he used his ability, I'd be found out.

"No!" I cried. My throat burned, strangling the word, but the shout was enough to disarm him. He released me, and throwing my hands up between us, I shoved him back. "Don't." I folded over my legs on the floor.

Noah put his hands behind him, his eyes like saucers. His face blurred. I put my head between my knees until the tightness in my chest ebbed enough for me to draw a full breath.

But that little gratification was short-lived.

Slowly, carefully, I sat up. My head felt too heavy to support on its own, so I let it fall back against the wall.

The regret was instantaneous.

The fire in my neck intensified, ignited by that small movement. I touched it and immediately pulled back.

Warm. Wet. Viscous.

I looked at the blood on my fingers. My stomach churned, and the resulting convulsion shot pain through my head.

Noah lowered slowly to his knees in front of me, still in his night clothes. His mouth hung open, like he wanted to speak but couldn't find the words. He glanced down at my hands, then at his own, at my sick on the floor, at my neck and the blood.

We stared at each other in choked silence until a clamouring outside the door made us both jump. He leapt up to bolt the lock. I watched his chest expand with three big breaths before he returned to the space in front of me.

"What's happened?" he asked, his voice barely loud enough to hear. He raised a hand to touch me but resisted, drawing it back.

I shook my head, and gritting his teeth, he stretched behind me, pulling a rag off the basin. He balled it in his fist, crouched, and reached toward me again, but I shrank away.

"Let me help you," he said. "Please. Please let me help you. Tell me what's going on." His arm trembled in the air. I watched the slow rise of moisture in his eyes until a tear slipped down his cheek, and I was so stricken by this rare show of emotion that I obeyed, leaning forward so he could press the rag over the wound on the back of my neck. I felt the pressure, and then I felt it slacken.

His voice cracked. "Y-your neck," he said. "Your neck is—"

Immediately, I threw my hands up to cover the bruising. I grabbed the rag and shoved his arms away.

"Gabriel, what the—"

"Jas—" I strained. "—per."

Don't call me that. That's not my name. That's what she calls me.

"What?"

"My ... name ..."

"Gabriel, this isn't the time to—"

"Jasper!" I shouted, and pain clinched my chest. I pitched forward, coughing.

"Okay, okay," he said at once, holding his hands up, palms facing out. "I'm sorry. It's Jasper. I got it. Jasper." He swallowed thickly. "Please just—just let me help you. You're bleeding, you're ill, and y-your neck! You look like someone tried to—" But he didn't finish. The realisation passed over his face, his gaze lowering from my eyes to my throat. "Oh shit ..."

For a moment, I held my breath, stifled by my brother's silence.

Did I want him to know? Should I let him see? Or would the aftermath on the other side of that locked door be enough even without my explanation?

I faced away, dragging my free hand across both cheeks. I tried to push myself up, that quaking arm holding the wall, but before I could get even one leg out from under me, Noah seized my wrist. With the force of his grip, I was subdued, shackled to that spot with him, and the scene played between us, my brother's magic conjuring it from my mind.

I closed my eyes, but it was on the back of my eyelids. I shook the images away, but the memory reformed immediately as Noah squeezed my arm. I couldn't escape it. Didn't he understand that I didn't want to relive it? I didn't want to see the hatred in her eyes or watch her fly toward me, her cold hands battling for my neck again, forcing me back, shaking me, smashing my head against the bedpost until my vision blurred. Her curses screamed out around me, and over and over, between the moments of vertigo, I saw that look in her eyes—that feral, ardent, hateful look. I gasped, nausea knotting my stomach as she bore down on me.

She wanted to kill me. I saw it plainly on her face. No other punishment would do. I panicked. I grabbed her wrists. I clawed at her hands. My head throbbed. My body ached. I was shivering and panting and fighting for air.

And then Soren appeared, ripping her away, throwing her against the wall with all his might. I saw his frantic eyes, his feverish face, his lips that shaped into words I couldn't seem to hear.

I closed my eyes.

I startled awake again at his shout.

Then, suddenly, the silence around me broke, and I heard him repeating a single word as he tried to lock his arms around her writhing, shrieking body. His voice boomed louder than anything else: '*Run!*'

For a moment, I lurched back into the present, and a wrenching sob escaped my lips.

Stop it, Noah. Please.

I don't want to see it again. I don't want to see myself flee. I don't want to see myself leave him there with her!

Tearing my arm out of Noah's grip, I collapsed against the wall, and the scene vanished. Instead of her or Soren, I stared at my brother's bewildered face.

He knew.

He saw.

My next exhale fled my lips in unexpected relief, and somewhere deep within me, despite the pain and nausea and fear, I felt ... glad. I could've laughed at how light I felt the second the shared image disappeared.

It wasn't a secret anymore.

If he disapproved of the tasks she'd given me, it didn't

matter because I was done now. I wouldn't do it anymore. I wouldn't. I couldn't ...

I breathed out again, blinking, marveling at this sudden and strange reprieve.

Noah couldn't be cross with me over that, right? And now—I jerked my head up, ignoring the surge of pain—he knew that Soren was in trouble.

Go find him!

Please, Noah. Go help Soren. I'm fine now. I can breathe again, so go find him!

But I couldn't speak, and Noah stared back without seeing me, his mouth agape, his brow knitted. Silently, he pulled me to him, wrapping me in his arms, cradling me. One hand gently held the back of my head, his chin resting on top of it, and in an instant, I melted into his embrace. Any urgency fled my mind as I was swathed in warmth. Any subtlety or strength I'd been trying to hold onto dissolved and left me sniffling and whimpering against his chest.

This was a new kind of relief. This was another breath of oxygen. This was a hand reaching beneath the water's surface and lifting me to safety. This was a blanket wrapped around me as I emerged from that cold, dark, suffocating ocean.

I clung to him.

"I-I'm sorry," I breathed, and although I didn't know what I apologised for, I couldn't stop saying it. "I'm—" I hiccoughed. "—so s-sorry. I'm sorry."

"Shh, it's okay," he whispered. "It's okay. You're okay."

"I—" I spoke haltingly, gasping between words. "I said something ... I shouldn't have."

"No, you did nothing wrong."

"It's my fault. I'm sorry. It was me. I said something I shouldn't have. Don't blame her."

He stiffened. Carefully, he grasped my shoulders and

pushed me back, holding me at arm's length. "What did you say?"

I wiped my sleeve under my nose. "Don't blame her. It was me. I did wrong. She had to punish me. I—"

The expression on his face stopped the words before I could speak them, it was so horrified.

I drew back. "N-Noah?"

It was my fault, wasn't it? I shouldn't have told her no. I knew how she would react. I knew. She wouldn't have had to punish me if I hadn't—

He slowly shook his head, his expression unchanging.

But if I'd just been obedient and done what I was told and agreed with her, it wouldn't have been so bad. It's always that way. It's always me saying or doing something I know I shouldn't that makes her like that. It's always a fault of mine.

I just wanted her to stop giving me that smile.

I just wanted her to stop lying to me.

I just ...

But the thought made me shudder. "I-it's my fault ... isn't it?"

Noah blinked at me. "No," he whispered. Then, louder: "No, this isn't ..." His voice trailed off. He pressed a hand over his mouth.

"I-I—" I stammered. "I just couldn't do it. I couldn't. Lily doesn't deserve—I'm sorry." I didn't know what else to say. I covered my eyes, my hands slick with sweat and blood and tears. "I'm sorry. I won't do it anymore. I promise, I won't. I just wanted her to—to love me ..."

There was a moment then where all the noise seemed to vanish, where even the room seemed to be holding its breath. Then, with a light squeeze on my shoulder, Noah released me and swiftly gained his feet. He turned the bolt, grabbing the door handle. His voice was lower and firmer than I'd ever heard it. "Stay here. Lock the door."

I peered up at him through my fingers. "W-what're you doing?"

"She can't get away with this."

"But—"

"Do you understand what she just tried to do? She could've killed you! She—" He dragged his hands down his face. "I saw all of it! I saw her, and—and ..." Exasperated, he whipped around again, grabbed the door, and wrenched it open, but I flung my arm out to catch his sleeve before he disappeared.

"Wait!" I cried. "Just—just wait, Noah ... Please ... I-I'm all right. Soren stopped her. I'm fine. S-so please just—" But then my eyes drifted past him into the empty hall. The tremor that hit me was sudden and violent. I crossed my arms, gripped my shoulders, folded over to try to combat it. "Shit ... S-Soren. Noah, we have to go—we have t-to—"

With all the strength left in my arms, I grasped my brother's hand and hauled myself to my feet, but almost instantly, I recoiled, feeling like I'd been struck. I teetered, hanging on Noah's sleeve as I swayed and tried desperately to keep my balance. I dropped the bloody rag on the floor.

"Soren, he—he needs help! I left him ..." My voice shook. My vision blurred. I extended an arm, probing for the door handle, but my fingers couldn't find it. My heart felt as though it had frozen in my chest, though I could feel its beat in every limb. I could hear it throbbing in my ears. "P-please. I left him there! I left him with her! I—"

I fell forward, plunging into darkness. A voice called out to me. A quiet, airy voice. A whispery song seemed to envelop me. I felt light as the air itself. And then—

Noah shook me conscious again. My eyelids fluttered open and closed.

"Hold on! Stay with me," he said. "I have to call for help. I—"

"Help," I whispered. "S-Soren. Yes. Please, help." I gasped. "H-he n-n-needs ..." My chest tightened around each breath, like the air had suddenly grown thick. "Noah," I said, releasing his arm to clutch my throat. My heartbeat pulsed under my skin.

"Gabriel!"

Noah caught me as my knees buckled. I leaned into him. I couldn't breathe. His fingernails dug into my skin he clenched my arms so tightly, and he shouted behind him into the empty room. "Haven! Haven, I need you! Get Quade! Go get Quade! Please!"

I tried to meet his gaze, but my eyes were dark. I squinted. I blinked. The light reappeared, and—

Noah was crying.

My breath hitched. The shadow of his hand slipped in and out of view as he erased the tears from my cheeks and brushed my hair off my forehead, but he was clumsy and frantic. He smashed the soiled rag against the back of my neck again, and when he touched my face, his hands were bloody.

My throat tightened. The pain in my chest strengthened.

And Noah was crying.

My eyelids were heavy. They wanted so badly to close, but I fought them. It seemed such a rare, odd thing to witness. Twice tonight I'd seen him cry and not once before. Was he crying for me?

But the harder I tried to focus, the softer the lines of his face became.

I felt dizzy.

I saw his face. I stared until it blurred from my brother to the vague smudge of a stranger standing too far for features, until there was only a haze of colour with a human shape and shadows where there should have been a face.

I heard the last whisper of his voice like a distant cry—a sound without discernable words or structure.

And then the world went black.

THE AFTERMATH

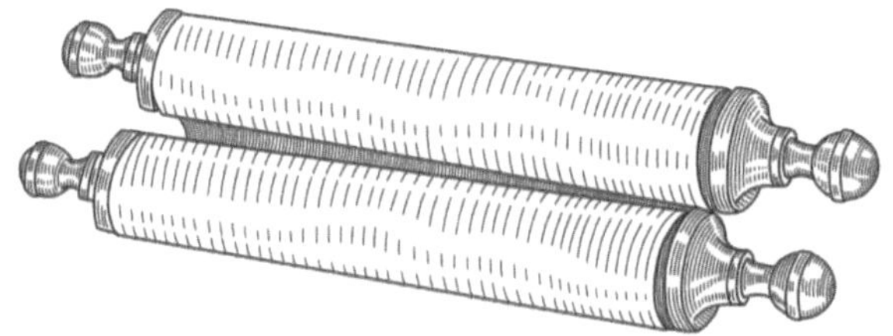

NOAH

I hovered in the doorway and stared blankly into the room. Gabriel turned over in his sleep, a tiny whimper escaping his lips, but he didn't wake. Zephyr perked her ear at the noise. There was little space in the room, but the gryphon hadn't left his side. She lifted her head, glanced tiredly at me, and then returned to her curled spot on the floor beside the bed.

I leaned into the doorframe, silent, though my mind was not idle. Inhaling, I closed my eyes, drawing a memory to the forefront of my thoughts and replaying it. It was a short scene from some months prior—a seemingly insignificant moment that I'd allowed to pass by me without much thought ... and which I now regretted disregarding.

I slumped over my desk, writing until my quill was dry and the letters tapered off into grey smudges and then merely scratches on the parchment. I'd been awake through the night, and the tiredness had been building behind my eyes for hours. My head felt heavy. It drooped forward. My eyes shut. But with a startled breath, I shook myself awake, dipped the quill, and retraced over the incomplete letters.

Behind me, the door creaked open, and expecting a servant with my tea, I didn't look up. But it was my brother's voice that greeted me. I saw his figure in my peripherals a few paces away, but whatever disagreement Gabriel wanted to have so early in the morning could wait. I had to finish my letter.

His voice was weak. "Noah," it said.

Dragging my quill across the paper, I asked, "What is it?" I hadn't seen him in at least a week, so I assumed he must've recently returned from one of his lollygagging tours of the surrounding villages.

He didn't answer.

I sighed. "Gabriel, did you need something? I'm busy."

But again, the boy was noiseless, his presence lingering behind me like a ghost, and for a moment, I wondered if I'd been mistaken—if it wasn't my brother at all. Sometimes the differences between the living and the dead were indiscernible to me. And then, with a horrifying thought, I spun around.

I exhaled, my fears mitigated.

It was, indeed, my brother, and he was very much alive. But when I examined him more closely, I grimaced. "Is that—what happened to your lip? It's bleeding."

He stood very still, slouching and looking as tired as I felt. Curling his bottom lip in, he licked the blood off it and swallowed tightly.

"Gabriel?"

He flinched as if suddenly awoken. His eyes darted to my face and away again in less than a second, then he coughed into his fist to clear his throat. "It's nothing. Never mind."

I narrowed my eyes. "Spirits, you're always bloody injuring yourself. What did you need me for? Penna is awake if you need a bandage or ice."

He licked his lip again, winced.

"Nothing," he repeated, lowering his head. "It's nothing. Don't worry about it." Without another word, he left the room, and sighing again, I picked up my quill and returned to my letter.

<hr>

I blinked myself back into the present, my view of Jasper now obscured by Haven's shadowy being, and automatically, I refocused my eyes to look at instead of through her. I sucked in a staggering breath.

"Haven," I whispered. The corner of her mouth turned up slightly in acknowledgement before her lips flattened into a hard line again.

"My lord, you need not linger here," she said gently. "Lord Byrne has never failed you as a physician, nor will he fail Gabriel. With patience and rest, your brother will mend."

Her voice was a tonic—the sound, not the words—that soothed my rampant heart, and gazing at her face, I nodded. But I wanted more from her. More comfort, more assurance, more sweetness.

How deeply I desired, in such moments, to simply rest my head upon her shoulder, to press my face against her neck, to take her hand. Simple pleasures as they may seem, they were luxuries she and I had always been denied.

It didn't help to be reminded.

I turned, strode down the short hall into Seth's bed chamber, and collapsed into a chair beside Quade. I dragged my hands down my face, a shaky exhale wrestling its way through my fingers.

I peered across the room at Seth, who stood in front of the window with his arms folded and his back to us. Next to me, Quade sat hunched over with his elbows propped up on his thighs and his clasped hands pressed against his mouth. He didn't look at me or even acknowledge my presence in the adjacent space. He just stared straight ahead with glassy eyes. None of us spoke, nor did I think we could find the words to say, though I knew we shared a guilty conscience. The tension in the air was palpable.

Haven appeared again, soundless though I could feel her there—a shift in the air, a subtle brush of coldness in an otherwise balmy room. When my gaze found its way to her, my heart seemed to shrink in my chest because she wasn't alone. I tipped my head back and pressed my palms against my eyes. From the hall beside Haven, I heard a little voice—Alwyn's innocent, childish tone—and in it, the truth I didn't want to admit aloud: 'He tried to tell you, you silly man. He wanted to tell you.'

I groaned, bending forward over my knees.

'He tried to tell you.'

JASPER

When I came to, I didn't know where I was. Flaxen Sunlight shone through the crack between the curtains, cutting the semi-darkness. Sunrise or sunset, I couldn't tell, but if there was a window, I knew I couldn't be in my own room.

I blinked, but I could only seem to open one eye. I tried to lift my head, but it throbbed. I had to turn my whole upper body to peer to either side, and slowly, the obscure forms surrounding me sharpened into actual people. Seth sat in a chair to my left and Noah to my right. Both stood and bent over me when I stirred, though neither spoke.

Noah reached toward me but stopped himself and nodded to Seth, who touched my forehead to check my temperature. His palm was comfortably cool against my skin. I leaned into it, drowsing. My eyes closed, but I opened them again when my brother withdrew his hand. In its place, Quade's face appeared above me, and I furrowed my brow. Why was he here? He hated the castle.

Oh, right.

I was hurt.

It must be bad if he came all this way.

I felt embarrassed for inconveniencing him. I rolled over, ignoring the soreness and burying my face in the down pillow, which felt uncommonly warm in contrast to Seth's hand.

"Where's Soren?" I asked, but my voice was hoarse. The words came out too muffled to be understood. Stiffly, I turned onto my side and asked again, a little louder, "Where's Soren?"

My question was met first with silence, and then, hesitant, Seth replied softly, "I'll ask around and find out what station he's been transferred to."

But I knew I'd never see Soren again.

LIAM

I paced in the hall outside Lily's door. I'd come to collect her for our lesson with Miss Sawyer because she'd never been one to watch the time. I knew the tick of the clock in her room was imposing enough to remind her—I suspected it'd been placed there with that intention—but still, she couldn't seem to do anything punctually. I wondered if she purposely ignored the noise or if it had simply become such a constant that she didn't notice it anymore.

It didn't matter. Either way, she'd be late.

With a great breath, I lifted a fist to knock but paused with my hand in the air, and when I exhaled, my courage deflated as quickly as my lungs did.

This had gone on too long already. Despite what Lily had said in anger, it was clear that what she needed most now was comfort. I really shouldn't have been so harsh with her. I knew how much she cared for Mr. Behrtram and how heartbroken she must feel. Of course, I knew! I'd watched their silly little courtship begin the day we met him in the woods. I'd seen Lily grow more excited and bashful and candid by the day. It seemed a strange thing to feel since she'd spent much of the last few months neglecting me, but I liked the Lily that liked Mr. Behrtram.

I'd already resolved to apologise, but still, I wavered. She'd rejected my attempts before. She'd said she wanted to be left alone and that she—

Then I heard a quiet whimper from inside the room.

I lowered my hand, stooped closer, and pressed my ear against the door to listen.

A hiccough, a sharp inhale, a sniffle ... Lily was crying.

I reached for the knob. I almost grabbed it and flung the door open, but I stopped myself. As quickly and quietly as I could, I turned and slunk away down the hall.

"Miss Sawyer," I said as I found my chair. "Lily won't be joining us today."

She turned from the blackboard to face me, peering over her spectacles. I couldn't help but notice that she wore the green dress Lily hated, and looking at it now, I could see that my sister had been right. It was incredibly unflattering.

"Oh?" She clicked her tongue.

I straightened my book. "Yes," I said, lowering my eyes. "She isn't feeling well again."

Our governess considered for a moment, her expression mild. She glanced down at herself, fingered the cloth of her dress, and then sighing, she tutted and said, "So she is ... Well, let's just get started."

And then I realised: she'd worn the dress hoping Lily would be here to comment and complain. She'd worn the dress to try to cheer Lily up.

JASPER

It was dark when I woke again, but a lit chamberstick had been left on one of the chairs. I swept the room with my eyes, observing the few furnishings before my gaze floated up to the ceiling. For a few seconds, I lay still, watching the shadows from the candle's flame twist in a dizzying array on the beams above me. I shut my eyes and exhaled slowly through my nose. I swallowed and winced. My head hurt.

It was a small space, but I recognised the room. It was little more than a closet tucked away at the back of Seth's bedroom that was used to house and hide Artemys and Flynn when they came to visit. There was barely space for the bed, two chairs, and the dusty old looking glass that hung on the wall, but it had always served its purpose.

I breathed a relieved sigh. In here, for the moment, I was safe. But how long had I been here? How many days had passed while I slept? My body felt stiff. I wanted to fall back into silence and darkness and—

A sudden desire opened my eyes.

Shakily, I sat up, gripping the edge of the mattress. I exhaled through my teeth as I freed my legs and swung them over the side of the bed. I teetered when I stood and immediately dropped back down, my head swimming.

"Shit ..."

When the stone under my bare feet stopped moving, I tried again, standing and stumbling over to the mirror. I held the wall on either side of it, steadying myself on one hand before wiping away a strip of dust with the other.

My reflection made me cringe. I pressed my chin to my chest, lifting my shoulders to my ears, shrinking down so I could see less of myself.

But avoiding it wouldn't change anything.

I shut my eyes, drew a big breath, and then shyly, I forced myself to look again.

The mirror was unforgiving. Staring back at me was a pale-faced man, bags under bloodshot eyes, moisture from all the tears I'd cried in my sleep clumping my lashes together. One of my eyes had been blackened, dark bruising in a crescent moon from my brow to my cheekbone, and it was swollen half-shut. A bandage sat above my ears, looping all the way around, and I suspected the source of my headache was covered by it.

Gingerly, I touched my head, following the gauze to the base of my neck where my hair was crusty and stuck to my skin with dried blood. I picked at it, my fingers probing under the bandage, following the scab until it pulled on the skin and made me wince. I twisted my body to try and see it in the mirror, but my eyes stopped on my neck.

Purplish bruises circled it, thinner in some places and wider in others, thumb prints on my throat where she pressed down. I leaned closer to my reflection. There were little claw marks, too, stretching from my chin to my collar bone. I'd scratched myself trying to pry her hands off.

I rested my forehead on the glass.

Look at what I've done to myself, I thought.

No, I corrected. *Look at what she did to me.*

The face in the mirror wasn't mine. I hated him—the tired boy that gazed out at me. But I needed to see. I needed to assess the damage. I needed to see how long I'd have to sit with these wounds until they were healed and gone, and I could pretend that night never happened.

Except ...

It had happened. This time, even after they disappeared, the wounds would still be there. Soren would still be gone, and—

Thumbing the tears from my eyes, I steadied my hands on the wall and lifted my head.

I looked like I'd been in a fight.

But that wasn't what it was.

It wasn't a fight; it was an attack.

But it wasn't that bad. My skin bruised easily; it exaggerated the injuries. They always looked worse on my skin. It wasn't really as bad as it looked, right?

I pushed myself away from the wall, staggered backwards, and deposited myself on the bed again. I relaxed into the mattress and lay there, laughing at myself.

It *was* that bad.

The pain was bad.

I held my neck, every little chuckle rasping its way out. My throat stung with every contraction, burned with every swallow, and even I couldn't tell if the noises that escaped were really laughter or stifled sobs.

Drawing my arms up, I covered my face, but as my eyes darkened, the only thing I could conjure in my mind was Lily's face. I wanted to see her, nothing else—just to sit beside her in a quiet place somewhere no one could find us.

I wondered what the nature of my feelings for the girl were. Was it a romantic attachment, or was I simply clinging to her because she'd given me her time and undivided attention—

because so far away from this place, she felt like a refuge? I'd never thought of romance as a possibility for myself, and yet ...

Somehow, the inaudible cries of my heart had been heard by her, my uncommunicated desires met. Somehow, this felt strange and new and frightening and wonderful all at once.

Maybe I didn't have to give a name to these emotions. Categorizing them wouldn't change the fact that I wanted to be near her, whether that was as a friend or something else. It wouldn't change the fact that she, alone, put my heart at ease with only her presence—that in the desert of my life, I'd made her an oasis.

I stared up at the ceiling with its little light show, breathing as deeply as my body would allow, inhaling the musky scent of the room that went largely unused. It only took a moment to settle my resolve.

I sat up again.

There was only one choice to be made, but in reality, it didn't matter. I would go to Earth, to Obscrys, to Azlinehn— anywhere but here.

With one last deep breath, I stood, determined to leave this place behind me ... perhaps for good.

<hr>

I slipped through hidden passageways, ducking behind tapestries and into dark nooks that hid walkways. I knew them well; I could navigate them without a light. The path to the kitchen was narrow, but I'd memorised how many careful side-steps it took to reach the right corridor. I silently counted them, but my head wasn't in a state for numbers. Soon, my steps became awkward shuffles, and although I could see little in the darkness already, the floor and the walls seemed to sway. I held the cold stone, leaning back and sliding across the wall. Then I had to stop. I squeezed my eyes shut.

I'd been in pain before, hadn't I? This wasn't bad. I'd endured it before.

You'll be fine, Jasper. You're always fine. Despite your best efforts, you've survived this long, so what would be the point in giving up now?

The pain will pass. It always passes. Just keep walking.

At last, the floor felt familiar again, and when my probing hands found an opening, I crouched and gently lifted the tapestry to see an empty corridor. Lowering to the floor, I pushed myself through, the tasseled bottom of the drapery brushing my head.

The unoccupied hallway told me it was still early enough for me to go undiscovered, regardless of my slow pace. Holding the wall, I rounded the corner to the pantry, slipping inside without trouble, but halfway to the cellar, I heard a noise.

In less than a second, my mind flipped from easy caution to complete panic. My heartbeat surged into a frenzy. I dropped to my hands and knees and scrambled behind the nearest table, pushing myself back, wedging my body into the corner between an empty keg and a sack of flour.

Breathe.

You're okay.

Breathe.

I tried to merge into the space, collapsing my limbs any way I could to fit, clasping my hands over my mouth and inhaling through my fingers.

Any confidence I had in my ability to escape vanished in an instant. Any other day, I could've kept my wits and snuck away before anyone could even turn the corner, but today, if I moved another inch too quickly, I'd be sick.

I shrank down, peeking through the pantry shelves at the

entrance, waiting with bated breath. But the feet that appeared moved with an uneven gait. My heart beat faster, out of relief instead of fear because the movement was familiar.

It was the housekeeper, Penna, who'd been Noah's nursemaid when he was a child. She paused in the doorway, her hands on her hips and her head bowed. She turned in a slow circle, and then she wiped her eyes.

My breath hitched, and for a few seconds, I held it bottled in my chest, reminded of Lily's desolate face in the window back on Earth, before I'd spent much time with her, before I'd—

Before I had time to duck or turn away, the woman crossed the room, rounded the table, and stopped dead when she found me staring back at her.

I froze, frightened though I was in no danger. I knew I looked a mess, crouched in the corner, dishevelled, bleary-eyed, and trembling. I lowered my face, embarrassed to think that someone else saw the same face I'd seen in the mirror, but she was only startled for a moment. She set one hand on the table and sighed like she'd expected to find me somewhere, hidden and afraid like a wounded animal.

But then the door opened behind her.

Without a moment's hesitation, she spun around and stepped to the side, placing herself in front of me, shielding me from view. I hid my face in my hands as she spoke to the visitor.

I recognised the other voice: the kitchen boy. The cook had asked for something. Penna answered calmly, her voice not betraying that anything was out of the ordinary.

"You need more eggs? I came for something from the cellar, too. Shall I fetch them for you? Go on back to the kitchen. I'll bring them. Don't you fret."

He took little persuading. He thanked her sincerely because he didn't like the cold of the cellar, and his knees ached from climbing the stairs so often.

My breath rushed out in a gasp when the door finally shut behind him. Penna turned again, unaffected, quietly observing me.

"Oh, young prince ..." she whispered. "Why're you here? You shouldn't be out of bed at all."

I didn't answer, but she didn't wait for one.

"Come on. Come here. Can you stand?" She slipped the shawl from her shoulders and wrapped it around me as she scooped me up off the floor. "To the cellar, your highness, before Grip sends him back."

I watched her eyes sweep over my face when I'd gained my feet—the black eye, the bloody bandage. They paused on my neck, her breath catching as if someone had grabbed her throat just then, too, and for a moment, the woman was stilled.

I didn't know her well enough to act bold, but I couldn't think of anything else to do. I stole her hand and held it, squeezed it, pumped some life back into her sombre face because Noah trusted her, because she hadn't exposed me, because Soren had always spoken so fondly of her warmth and her smiles. And he was right—always. Her hand was as warm as a sleepy afternoon passed under Flaxen Sunlight.

Her eyes flicked up to meet mine, widened by surprise, her brows pulling together. I felt the slight tug of her hand as if she wanted to withdraw it, though she didn't right away. She squeezed back, tight enough to make my fingers tingle. Then exhaling, she shook her hand free and urged me in front of her to the cellar door.

She propped it open as I started downward, lighting a candle before descending herself, and when the door slapped shut behind her, it was only the two of us in the cold dimness, struggling down the steps. But as soon as we reached the bottom, she stowed her light on a nearby crate and swung around to face me. I jerked back, but she grabbed my shoulders, shaking me, forcing me to meet her gaze, which was suddenly manic.

"Did you go in your bed chambers?"

I blinked.

"Your suite, prince! Did you go in your suite?"

Her shout echoed, and bewildered, I shook my head.

"No?"

"No," I mouthed, shaking my head again.

Her breath burst out of her in one huge, cloudy exhale that seemed to simultaneously relieve and exhaust her. Abruptly, she released me, clutching her chest and straining for breath. "I-I am sorry, sir, to place a hand on you. I just—I had to make sure ..."

It was then that I realised what concerned her so deeply— what I might have seen had I gone into my bedroom. The strength left my legs. My back hit the wall, my breath steaming. I didn't want to imagine it, but horrible possibilities flooded my head.

My whole body felt tight with the effort of keeping my stomach from rebelling. I pressed my knees together, my arms wrapped firmly around me, my toes curling in the boots I'd taken from Seth's cupboard. But I couldn't remember when I'd eaten last. It was only bile that rose in my throat, and I swallowed it back down, coughing.

"I'm sorry," Penna said again, covering her mouth, and in the candlelight, I saw the shine of tears in her eyes. "I'm so sorry ..."

I breathed out slowly, shakily, watching the air leave my lips in a soft white cloud.

Then she turned to the shelves, rummaging through the stock and piling her arms with various items. She dropped them atop the crate before stealing her shawl back from around me. I looked at her, confused, as she wrapped vegetables and fruit in the scarf and tied it up.

"Here," she said, holding it out for me with shivering arms. I took it silently. "You're leaving again, aren't you, sir?"

Mechanically, I nodded, surprised that she'd guessed my intentions.

"Quickly then, before the rest of the staff are up. But let me go first to make sure the way is clear." Without another word, she took her eggs and her light and bustled up the stairs.

JASPER

I killed him. I killed Soren. I killed him, and Penna loved him. I was a murderer. I killed him. I killed her. I broke her heart. I ruined it. I ruined everything. And she …

Penna helped me. Why did she help me? How painful was it to give me kindness when she knew what I'd done—when she knew that Soren's blood was on my hands?

It was me.

It was my fault he was gone.

I sped up, clutching the wrapped goods to my chest under my jacket. But my hands were shaking. I felt sick. I let the bundle fall from my grasp and stumbled over it as I pushed my pace from a jog to a sprint.

I'd memorised the guards' watch schedules. I knew when they weren't looking. I knew, at all times, where their eyes were and where they weren't. And as soon as I'd exited the passage through the outer wall unseen, I knew where I was going.

The Flaxen Sun would rise soon, and I felt a sudden need to watch it, to see one last sunrise—one last beautiful moment stretched out before my eyes.

The cliffside wasn't far, though the spike of adrenaline that had fueled my sprint seemed to vanish the moment I slowed, reintroducing my body to the pain and dizziness. I swayed. I shivered. I lowered myself to my seat on the rocky ledge.

I wasn't ready to jump just yet. I wanted to see Flaxsol rise first. I wanted to determine which spot was best to fall from and which angle and whether I should go forwards or backwards and whether I should take a running leap. There was a lot to consider. Did I want to aim for the rocks below, or let the rough water trap me against the cliffside until it bore me down into its depths? I was too weak to struggle long, though there might be easier ways than drowning.

I turned my arm over and examined the little blue welts on my wrist. How would those veins look if they were severed? What colour would my blood be and how steady would it flow? How long would it take? I wondered if my fingers would constrict or if they'd gently unfurl when my body was too bloodless to function.

But then I realised someone would have to find me eventually. How much would that upset their day? How long after would they see the boy who slit his wrists in their nightmares? What if it was a child?

... What if it was Penna?

She, alone, had seen me leave. She'd seen the state I was in, and she was such a busybody, always worrying about everyone. She might come after me and find my lifeless body with my little curled fingers and bloody wrists.

I squeezed my hand into a fist, tightening it until my fingernails made crescent imprints in my palm, and then I watched them slowly fade. I closed my hand again and turned it over to see how ugly it looked, curled and splotchy and red. I imagined how the stiffness of death would preserve the pain I felt when the life finally left me.

What would Penna think, knowing that I'd given up despite

her aid—that, in my last moments, I was alone and in terrible pain? How would Noah feel? Or Seth or Zephyr or Quade? How long after would that image and that knowledge haunt them?

No, drowning made more sense. If nothing else, it could seem like an accident. It might even be peaceful. Instead of jumping, I could simply swim out until my muscles couldn't take it any longer—until I was bereft of strength and the weight of my immobile body sank beneath the surface. The bubbles of my last breath wouldn't even be visible among the waves.

'Poor thing. What a tragedy!'

'What an awful twist of fate for him to go this way so young!'

I scoffed at the thought, and for a while, I stared out at the dark water, listening to it crash over the rocks and itself.

I felt strangely calm as my heartbeat slowed. Then I peered behind me at the castle in the distance, the turrets and battlement just barely visible above the tree line. The guards could see the ocean and any seaborn attack but not the cliffs.

I'd checked before, just in case.

I didn't know how else to vanquish this fear. Not only the fear of what she could do to me but the fear of being forever within her reach, of never being able to run far enough, of being drawn in again by her sweet-sounding lies.

I didn't trust her.

I didn't trust myself.

I didn't want to hurt anymore, and I couldn't think of another way to dig this fear out of my bones, to purge the poison she'd injected in my veins and cut away the guilt. They'd been there so long. My insides had grown around and accepted these foreign entities without realising how devastating the incorporation could be.

They were a part of me now.

I couldn't escape. I couldn't run from them. I was trapped.

She'd turned me into a weapon against myself.

And I—

I just wanted her to love me.

That's all anyone wants, isn't it? To love and be loved. I'm not special. But if even nature can't bring out those feelings in someone—if a person who is biologically programmed to love you can't—then you must be fucking rotten. If even the one responsible for your creation can't bring themself to love you, then why do you even exist?

Why do I exist?

How could anyone else in the worlds love me if not even my mother does?

I didn't even know what it looked like anymore—love.

The contrast between the people I read about and what I experienced at home was so vast that I assumed the familial relationships in my books were pure fiction, nothing more than make believe … until I left the castle for the first time and saw real people with real lives and real love.

And it was the same.

The stories were right. Embellished sometimes, perhaps, but they were right. And all I could think was, *if this is love, then what is this feeling she's given me?*

Because those can't be the same. They can't.

There would be a great deal fewer people in these worlds if *this* was love—what it felt like.

Because no one would want to live with this feeling.

No one would want to feel so worthless and solitary.

And all I could fucking think was, *I must be unlovable. There must be something wrong with me. She must've used up all her love on everyone else—on my father and brothers and our kingdom.*

I'm the leftover. I'm the one that doesn't matter. I'm worthless and useless. I'm incapable of being the first person in someone's heart. I will never be so important.

How lonely.

I wished I could just cease to exist—vanish out of sight, out of mind, out of memory, like I'd never existed at all. Wash away with the waves and disappear. There was nothing left anymore anyway—nothing except this skin bag walking around with no purpose but to die.

Feed the fish, nourish the soil, let the roots of plants soak up whatever life is left in me. That's all I'm good for now.

And yet ...

Somehow, I was stalled, anchored to my place on this cliff overlooking the sea.

Because there was this tiny piece of my mind that kept replaying a fantasy I'd long nurtured of a love beyond that of my family—of a future with someone who truly did believe that I was important enough to make a part of their life unconditionally.

But Lenore ruined that, too.

She created a world in which love and violence were conjoined. I could not have one without the other, and my poor little heart didn't know how to separate them. Soft touches, then rough ones. Greedy hands and empty words. Promises she never intended to keep.

It was frightening and strange and *wrong*, but surely, you wouldn't touch the body of another person like that if you didn't love them. And that was the cost of being loved, wasn't it? Letting someone touch you—letting them hurt you—if that's what it took.

She always seemed different then, like it wasn't really her at all. The way she looked at me was different. I memorised it— that carnal expression. I feared it. She would stare into my eyes until I changed in her mind, until I was no longer her son but some other young man to lust after. She would forget that our blood was the same. Or maybe she did realise it and just didn't care. Maybe she thought she had some claim over my body because it had once been a part of her.

And what else could I do?

I was worthless, and she was so kind to love me because no one else could. If I just surrendered ...

'If you let me do this, I'll love you. I'll trust you. Show me that you love me. You want to make me happy, right? Prove it.'

I believed her. I did, but ... how wrong it felt. How unloved and uncomfortable and undesired I felt. How could she want something so passionless?

'What? You can't? What's wrong with you? I thought you said you loved me. Why are you being like this? Stop crying. That didn't hurt. I'm trying to help you. Didn't you say you wanted to make me happy?'

I wonder ... how many times did she have to convince or negotiate with me? It might've been every time.

What could I do but submit?

If I gave in and stopped trying to fight back, eventually she would go away. The attacks were shorter. So I stopped saying no. I stopped resisting. I let everything happen. I endured anything she had for me. I sat and bit my lips raw trying not to cry out because I didn't want her to know that she was hurting me. Because I loved her and didn't want to hurt her with that knowledge.

And soon, it would end. That feral look would leave her eyes, and she would go about her day as if nothing out of the ordinary had happened at all. But I think I knew it wasn't ordinary. Or, at least, *I* wasn't ordinary. Because I was a boy, and I was supposed to be strong and resilient. I was supposed to be *sturdy*. I was supposed to like things like sex and violence, not cower from even the slightest touch.

When did she stop trying? When did she start to find my

unwillingness a burden? When did those moments transition from desire to hatred to pain?

I have not the words to describe it—how disgusting I felt, how dirty, how I wished I could peel away my own skin, tear it off just to have a body that woman had never touched. Maybe I could wash my skin in the water below, scrub it clean, and put it back on. Maybe then it wouldn't feel like it was crawling.

I could do it. I already had an opening.

Carefully, I drew my hands up to my neck, reaching back and shoving my fingertips under the bandage to touch the sutures. I inhaled, picking away dried blood so I could hook my nail under the tiny knot, and before I could hesitate, I ripped it out, immediately recoiling from the pain. I clenched my teeth and pinched another stitch, tearing it from my skin. A stream of fire tore up the back of my skull, and the fresh blood felt hot as I dug my fingers into the wound. I tried to peel it open, but I couldn't get the right grip with wet fingers. The flesh kept slipping and my skin kept burning and my hands were shaking so badly that I couldn't seem to find the wound anymore.

I threw my arms down and screamed, not in pain but something else. There was something raw and wretched inside of me, and I wanted to expel it. I wanted to rid myself of whatever poison had made me believe that Lenore had ever loved me. I clawed my scalp, gagging, breathless. I wanted to roll forward and tumble off the cliff into the sea so I could drown the part of me that had succumbed to her empty promises. But my legs felt like lead. My arms didn't have the strength to push my body over the edge.

Then I laughed—a rough, gurgling sound that hurt my throat.

Look how weak you've made me. I can't even kill myself properly.

Somehow, suddenly, it was funny. All of it—my submission and my pain and my fantasies and my ugly, trembling little fingers all covered with blood. I held them out in front of me, turning them over, and then I pressed them to my face, gasping and laughing.

What was wrong with me?

What was I doing? Why was I here? Why couldn't I have just thrown myself over without hesitation?

She ruined it—something as important as touch. How does one survive without touch, without love? She stole that and left me with only this fantasy of true love I created from excerpts of novels and dreams. A fantasy of intimacy, of connection and affection and kindness and shy giggles and soft kisses on the palm of your hand. A fingertip gently brushing over your lips. Something deep and grasping and desperate—a person to melt together with instead of endure. Something sweet and simple and intoxicating—a person who rests their head on your shoulder and nuzzles closer, satisfied with only your presence. A person who whispers, '*I love you,*' simply because they feel it, and in the moment that it sweetly leaves their lips, your world is dissolved. For a breath of time, everything is just right.

And then …

Silence. A quietness shared between two people, the only noise the gentle thrum of their heartbeat and the soft sigh of their breathing as they drift to sleep beside you.

I craved it.

'I'm thinking of you, I'm dreaming of you, I'm cherishing you.'

'I love you.'

I craved that more than anything.

I wasn't laughing anymore; I was crying, rocking, holding my face in my hands. My chest felt like it might break open with the force of the wracking sobs, and I wished that it would.

Let it all pour out at once, instead of in these painful bursts that keep fighting their way up my throat.

I cried because my body ached.

I cried because my heart hurt.

I cried because I'd never realised what a deep feeling of aloneness exists.

I cried because it was so fucking lonely to love her.

Why couldn't I have noticed it sooner? I was miserable. I was exhausted. I was hopeless and dreaming and—

I was wishing that Lily had never come into my life.

I wished it desperately. I wished she'd never made me feel like a normal person. I wished she'd never made my fantasies feel real. I wished she'd never held me and made me feel safe. But most of all ...

I wished that I could see her.

Because even if it was only for a heartbeat of time, her smile would clear my mind. And if she held my hands, I could resist the urge to scratch Lenore's caresses out of my skin. And if she fell asleep beside me with her head on my chest, I think we could be the only two people in existence, and I still wouldn't feel alone.

Every moment with her, my heart rejoiced, *This is how it's supposed to be. This is how it should feel.* But even when it seemed right—when it seemed perfect—it was still wrong.

Lily left.

She made me feel loved and then vanished. She teased me with normality. She happily gifted me the friendship I'd intended to manipulate her with and then withdrew it.

The moment passed, like they always did.

But the feelings didn't. They were stronger even than before; only now, they were accompanied by emptiness, as if a hollow had carved itself in my chest, as if I'd lost something. It was another strike, another blow to remind me that my fictional love didn't exist, and if it did, then I was incapable of receiving it.

But I felt it, let it pour freely from the hole in my chest, bled until I was reduced to this empty shell teetering on the cliffside.

These weren't the same feelings I had for Lenore. These were romantic, and nothing about those dreaded unions had been. They were fleeting moments I shut my eyes to, pretended I was somewhere else with someone else, cursed my body for responding if it did and cursed it when it didn't because then the pain would be afflicted physically, too.

How heavily had this been weighing on me? How long had I been sitting with these feelings, not knowing how to confront them?

It was Lily who'd lifted the veil and exposed it.

It was the betrayal that she could never have known would be so devastating.

It was Lily who'd revealed to me just how broken my heart really was, how desperately I wanted someone to wrap me in an embrace, to hold these crumbling pieces together, even for a moment.

It was Lily who'd made me realise that permanency didn't have to mean chains. It was a choice and a desire to stay.

I wanted that moment to last.

I wanted Lily to stay.

Nothing in my life had ever felt so right, so why was it still wrong? Why was I still alone? It felt so *right*. Where had I erred? What had I done to ruin it?

There was no love. There was no security.

They didn't exist, not for me.

And Lily's abandonment felt like the proof.

I sat back, let my arms fall to my sides, and drew in a slow, ragged breath.

I didn't know what to do. I didn't know how to fix this.

I didn't even know who I was anymore.

Where did Gabriel end and Jasper begin? When stripped of

all the parts of me that were built or changed or twisted because of Lenore, what was left? How much of me was made of poison? How much of my true self had actually been there beside Lily under the oak tree?

When the only way to receive affection is to make yourself small, to break your bones and curl your body until you fit into the little shape they want you to be in, you just … make yourself fit. You sacrifice your whole existence, and you press through your days uncomfortably until the discomfort starts to feel normal and you lose sight of the person you wanted to be.

I really did this to myself.

I really let this happen to me.

I really let it go this far.

'It's such a tragic, fragile sound …'

I didn't start at the voice. I'd noticed my companion's presence some time ago. Tiredly, I glanced sideways at the ghost and then returned my gaze to the glittering water as the Flaxen Sun's rays stretched slowly toward the sky.

"What is?" I asked hoarsely.

Alwyn's smile was soft, meek, his eyes downcast. 'The voice of someone who wants to die.'

"I haven't been talking."

'Why are you sitting on this cliff then?'

"Enjoying the scenery."

For a moment, the ghost was quiet. Then, he said, 'You've never told Noah you can see me, huh?'

Gingerly, I shook my head.

'I wonder why.'

I didn't answer, and he didn't pry. Alwyn and I sat silently, staring out to sea as Flaxol crested the horizon, spilling light across the water and the mountains, highlighting the world around us until it rose enough to reach the cliffside. The Flaxen Sunlight was bright and felt warm on my face.

I took an aching breath. Exhaled.

"Every time I think about dying, my first instinct is to drown. Somehow, it seems like it would be peaceful."

'Noah says the same thing ... But I dunno if that's true.'

"Did you call him yet?"

'If I say no, will you jump?'

I snorted. "It wouldn't matter. You couldn't stop me if I did."

Alwyn didn't laugh. 'What an awful thing to say.'

Wiping my bloody fingers on my trousers, I heaved myself up on unsteady legs and started back in the direction I'd come. "Don't follow me," I said.

He didn't, but his words remained with me long after the ghost boy disappeared: 'Y'know, I've seen thousands of sunrises and sunsets. They never stop being beautiful, but they do lose a certain quality when you die. They no longer seem so hopeful. They're just colours and light and warmth that can't reach you anymore. It's a shame.'

SETH

I leaned against the wall, staring vacantly ahead when Noah turned the corner. I closed my eyes and listened to his footsteps slow as he approached, and then, at last, they stopped. I heard the scrape of his waistcoat on the wall as he propped himself up beside me, but I didn't speak.

"You look tired, Brother. Have you been having nightmares, too?" he asked—a grave question, though his tone remained casual. I nodded, and he sighed. "I've barely slept this week, and now I'm off on a suicide mission."

Tsking, I muttered, "I'd hardly call orders to rally troops a suicide mission."

"It will be if I kill myself while on said mission. Building an army for that witch, I'm bloody tempted to."

I opened one eye, peeking sideways at him. "Don't joke about that."

He dismissed my reproof, ignorant of my glance. "Though I think I can manipulate it to our advantage. We wouldn't want it interfering with our plans." Then tipping his head back, he exhaled heavily and asked. "D'you have orders, too?"

I reached into my pocket and produced a roll of parchment, offering it to him. "Padryg on Obscrys."

Noah took the scroll, unfurled, and read it. Immediately, the levity left his voice. "Well, there's your suicide mission ..." He handed it back. "Do us a favour and meet with a connection there. She's a fine ally, and she should be able to get an update for us, too."

"An ally?"

He nodded. "I have it on good authority that we can trust her. A young woman by the name of Rune Agrata."

I knew the name, but I held my tongue, contemplating a moment before speaking. "You're ... certain this person is an ally?"

He shrugged. "She wants the same thing we do."

"She's part of the Shyva Clan."

Noah turned to me, surprised that I knew. "Is that a problem? You sound disappointed."

I picked at my cuticle for an excuse not to look at him. "Not at all. I intended to meet with their leader after I arrived in Padryg anyway, so she shouldn't be hard to find. Did she approach you?"

"That's right."

"I wonder what she could have to gain ..."

Noah drew a slow breath, his eyes flicking from one end of the hall to the other. I heard the quiet tut of his tongue unsticking from the roof of his mouth as he considered what to say. "She told me she's witnessed atrocities happening within the castle walls, though she refused to recount them. She said we could use her any way we liked—that she would do anything to aid us—if it meant the queen's removal."

I swallowed. "You don't think ..."

"We already have a rapport with the Shyva."

"We do?" My dealings with them had only happened in

dreams thus far. But there was something else that unsettled me. "It sounds as if this Miss Agrata has spent some time here."

"How else could she have witnessed anything in the castle?"

"Are you saying she was a spy?"

Noah nodded again.

"For us or them?"

"Do not underestimate the power of a common enemy."

He offered no further explanation. Instead, he groaned, sliding down the wall to sit at my feet. His voice lowered, and hesitantly, he asked, "Have you seen Ga—" He stopped himself. "—Jasper? I mean Jasper ..."

As prepared as I was for this topic, I still felt a strain in my chest. I shook my head. "He was gone when I woke up."

"D'you think he went to Earth?"

I furrowed my brow and, at last, opened both eyes and faced him. "You think he'd go there before Quade's?"

"Quade's here."

"Still ..."

Noah rested his elbows on his knees, his eyes trained on the floor. "I—" He cleared his throat. "I keep replaying the memories he shared with me. I keep watching them over and over again. That's why I can't sleep. I keep watching her." His voice shrank, though the acidity in it rose. "I wanted to kill her, Seth. I pictured it. I wanted to squeeze the bloody life out of her. I haven't seen her since because I'm afraid of what I might do or say." His hands balled into fists.

"Noah, not here ..." I hissed, my eyes darting to assure we were alone in the corridor. My own feelings weren't dissimilar, but those words in the wrong ears would be very troublesome. I tried to steer him in a different direction. "Why d'you think he would go to Earth? Jasper, I mean. He has bolt holes here."

Slowly, I watched his white-knuckled hands relax, and he dropped his head back again, eyes closed, breathing in and out.

Finally, he said, "There were other memories, too. He was so shaken that he didn't separate them. Everything he was thinking about just flooded in, and in many of them, there's a girl. When I'm reliving those memories, it's only at that point that I can finally sleep. As soon as the nightmare is over and Lenore is gone, I see this girl's face, and—" He paused, his eyes narrowing. I touched his arm, encouraging him to continue. "It's strange, but suddenly, I feel more at ease than I ever have. That's what Jasper feels with her: peaceful." Noah looked up at me. "I think he's in love with her." A faint smile brushed his lips. "He's on Earth. He must be. That's where she is."

"Lily," I said, a face forming in my mind—a handsome countenance with large eyes and yellow hair. Noah looked at me in alarm.

"H-how did you—?" Then, nodding his understanding, he said, "You've seen her then."

Another image flashed in my mind, a reminder of the first time I'd seen her in my dreams. The physical effects of the memory were instantaneous—the cold sweat and distant throb of pain that seeped from somewhere at the core of my being. My brother observed me quietly until I sat beside him.

"Yes," I said. "There's a dream she always comes up in."

"Is it the one where I die?"

I jerked my head to the side. "I've never seen you die," I snapped, but I answered too quickly and too harshly to be believed.

My brother snorted, staring down at his hands. There was a quiet ache in his voice. "You've seen everyone die ..."

I squeezed my eyes shut, inhaling through my nose. "Shut up. Stop talking about it."

Noah rubbed my arm. Then in the dullest whisper: "I see everyone dead."

I tensed. I knew he was trying to comfort me, which seemed

a strange thing, but it was also a gentle reminder that I wasn't the only one eternally suffering the deaths of others.

Noah sighed, his hand falling off my arm and coming to rest in his lap. "Can I ask a different question then?"

I pinched the bridge of my nose. "What is it?"

"I know you're not comfortable revealing the future, but ..." He bowed his head, snaking his arms in around his waist, wrapping them firmly about himself as if it were the only way to hold himself together. Even his voice seemed more fragile than before. "Is he—is Jasper gonna get over this?"

I lowered my hand, watching him as he continued.

"It's haunting him already, Seth. You didn't see him when he ran into my chambers ... You haven't watched his memories and felt the terror he felt. He feared for his life the very moment he woke and saw her. I-I've never felt such fear."

I couldn't speak; I had not the words to say.

Noah raised his hands to cover his face, his glassy eyes staring forward through his fingers. "Seth, you didn't hear him cry and try to tell me it was his own fault. You didn't hear him try to make excuses for her. While she was hurting him, he was agreeing with her. He wasn't fighting back because he believed the punishment just. He was terrified and exhausted and—and he thought about just letting her do it! It was as if he just ... He just didn't want to deal with it anymore." He turned suddenly, his hands braced around his face. "Look at what she's done to him! How could we not see it happening?"

I had to remind myself to breathe. "I don't know," I whispered.

"He crosses us so easily and stands up to us, and yet ... How deeply—how long has she been polluting his mind to make him think this way—to make him submit so easily to her? He almost gave up!"

"I don't know," I said again, my throat tightening around

the words.

"This—there's no way this is the first time. I-I never imagined I'd find a better reason to overthrow her than I already had. I knew what great violence she was capable of, but ..." He hid his eyes behind a hand. "Now I can't help wondering if the atrocities Miss Agrata wouldn't speak of were related to what happened to Jasper—if she saw something else that bitch did to him, maybe even something worse."

Even I was unaware of Noah's true motivation behind our rebellion. I, myself, had reasons I wouldn't disclose, so I never asked. I just assumed his reasons were like mine—something so awful that he couldn't bring himself to say it aloud. I only knew that I supported his objective, and I agreed with him now. This could only add fuel to flames already kindled. And this new ally, Rune, was the same—reluctant to reveal what she'd witnessed. Perhaps that was why Noah believed we could trust her.

"You did see," I said softly. "You noticed something happening, but Jasper refused any help. He hid it so well, and even then, you guessed."

"Sure, but a guess is just a guess. I lost some sleep over the thought maybe, but I never imagined that—that I could possibly be right. They were just suspicions, that's all. I thought that's all they were. No mother would do that to her child, right?"

I didn't answer. I saw a soft shimmer in the air as Haven appeared noiselessly beside him. The ethereal woman placed the shadow of her hand on my brother's shoulder, and as if he could feel her presence there, he laid his own hand on top of— or rather, through—hers. He shut his eyes for a few slow breaths, and when he reopened them, he turned to me with such a defeated expression that I nearly gasped at the sight of it. I nearly cried.

But he wouldn't speak if he had to console me. I blinked back my tears and let him continue.

"I need to know that we haven't lost him to her. I need to know that he'll heal from this—that the memories of what she's done won't follow him forever." Noah stared at me, wide-eyed and pleading, gripping his own shoulder as though squeezing Haven's hand. "I—I can't stop thinking about how many times that kid must've cried himself to sleep all alone in that fucking room ..."

I had to swallow the lump in my throat to respond. "I'm sorry," I breathed. "I don't know. I wish I did."

I really wish I did.

He faced forward again, his throat contracting with a thick swallow. His jaw clenched and unclenched. "Seth, we must stop her. I don't know how else to help him, and when the time comes—" His voice lowered until it was barely audible. "—I'll kill her myself."

"My lord," Haven whispered, "Please don't say such things."

He swung his head toward her. "Why not? After what she's done to—" but he stopped himself and looked away from the ghost.

"I don't know what to do, Noah," I said. "For us or Jasper. I don't know how we're gonna end this. I think we may be in over our heads."

Noah's voice was surprisingly composed. "Stick to the plan. Contact our ally on Obscrys. We'll get an update on our army, and after that, we'll make our move."

Cautiously, I nodded.

"In the meantime, I'll do my best to sabotage Lenore's army from the inside out." He pulled the coiled parchment with his orders from his waistcoat pocket and waved it about. Then, wiping his eyes, he hoisted himself to his feet and offered a hand to me. "You could come with me to the coast beyond

Vrodon. Then, we could go to Padryg together." He pulled me to my feet. "It'd be a longer journey than going directly to the Gate, but it'd be safer. Obscrys is a dangerous place to be a human these days, especially on your own."

Slyly, I peeked up at him. "Well, I guess it's a good thing I won't be human for very much longer."

Noah quieted, his eyes widening and his brow lowering. He opened his mouth, wrestling with the words he couldn't seem to say. I'd caught him off guard.

"What I mean to say," I began, "is thank you for your kind offer, but unfortunately, I must decline it. I've been given an order directly from the queen herself, after all." I lifted my scroll and poked his chest with it. "I wouldn't dare disobey ... that, and I've a date with a strigoi woman that I really shouldn't miss." I smirked, but my brother didn't acknowledge my attempted humour.

"Is it that time already?"

I glanced down the corridor, observing the stripes of shadow on the floor between the windows. "It's been a long time coming. Eventually, all the things I've seen must come to pass. If anything, I'd say it's rather good timing."

"You're prepared then?"

"To become a monster?" I shrugged. "As prepared as I can be, I suppose. I am rather keen to meet this woman, though. It seems she has quite a role to play yet ..."

I watched Noah's chest rise and fall with a heavy breath. "All right. Send word when it's all over. I'll meet you in Erisilon at Quade's. We'll regroup and discuss our next step then."

"Deal."

He stared at me for a moment, then huffing, said, "C'mere."

I opened my arms and embraced him, and when we broke apart, he held me at arm's length.

"I'll see you soon then."

I nodded, unable to match the gaiety he'd tried to kindle with that smiling embrace.

Noticing, he slapped my arm. "C'mon now, you'll always be my brother and my confidante." Reaching behind my neck, he knocked our foreheads together. "Always. No matter what changes. Remember that, Seth."

Again, I nodded, this time managing a quiet smile to go with it.

Noah released me, satisfied. "By the way, have you ever come across a being called Ixchel?"

"Ixchel? I—" I paused. "Yes, I know the name. Carys mentioned it to me before."

"What did she say?"

"That I should trust her should we ever meet."

Thoughtfully, Noah nodded. "Good."

"You've met her?"

"Recently, yes. Her and her companion. I believed them trustworthy, too."

I frowned, daunted by the idea of yet another possible ally. Large numbers were harder to conceal, harder to keep silent. Then again, no great wars were ever won alone.

I asked, "What did she say?"

For a moment, my brother fell silent, scratching his chin. "She told me we needed to keep Jasper close. Not informed ... but close."

I quirked a brow, not entirely understanding. I wasn't sure what to say or what questions to ask because I wasn't certain Noah had any answers to provide. Finally, I settled with: "You are a curious man with a curious number of friends."

"Increase thy friends to decrease thine enemies." He winked. "I'll send someone to collect Jasper, make sure he's safe. And don't worry; no matter how many new friends I make, no one could ever take your place."

Snorting, I muttered, "I wasn't worried."

"Good. You shouldn't be. Who else would bother listening to me plot and cry in an empty corridor? I need you."

"Who indeed?" Sighing, I added, "I couldn't get rid of you if I tried, could I?" just to wedge a little more distance between us and the dark clouds that had begun to grow around us—this storm we were intent on stirring.

But that was the problem, wasn't it? No matter how carefully—how desperately—you tried to control a storm's conditions, it would always be unpredictable. We simply avoided thinking about what devastation one little variance could cause —how untamable a force we may be releasing upon our worlds.

We simply pretended we didn't realise what fools we were, hiding our burgeoning terror with humour that could never quite cut through the awkwardness.

And exactly as I knew he would, Noah laughed. "That's the spirit!" If I hadn't known him my entire life, I would've believed it genuine. He started down the hall, Haven's phantomlike figure following closely behind him. Then, pausing, he twisted his body to look at me. "This isn't a suicide mission I'm going on, right?"

I felt a knot in my stomach again, slowly shaking my head.

His awkward smile broadened as he swung around again and exclaimed, "Excellent! I'm still invincible!"

After Noah had already begun his silly, theatrical walk down the hall, my eyes met Haven's, but the exchange lasted only a second before she vanished, fading into stone and shadow.

Exhaling, I leaned against the wall, dropped my head back, and closed my eyes. "See you soon, Brother ..."

Noah

I tossed my waistcoat on the floor as I walked in, rolling up my sleeves. I leaned over the basin, closed my eyes, and splashed my cheeks with water. Then, I sank down farther and submerged my face, wondering, for a tired moment, what it might be like to open my mouth and inhale then, but I ignored the impulse. When I couldn't hold my breath anymore, I jerked my face up out of the water, gasping and sputtering.

Slowly, I opened my eyes again, watching the droplets fall from my nose and chin back into the bowl, every tiny splash distorting my reflected image. I waited until the water settled and the excess had left my face before I stood upright again.

"You shouldn't sneak up on people, y'know," I said without looking behind me. I grabbed a rag and smothered my face with it.

Quade answered from the chaise beside the fireplace. "I'd hardly call it sneaking; you saw me the moment you walked in." Then he paused, his eyes drifting to the drapery on the wall above the basin. He stared at it pointedly for a moment, frowned, and added, "I see you still keep all the mirrors covered in here."

"Did you need something?" I turned toward him, drying my neck. "I thought you'd be with Seth."

He gripped the armrest, tapping a finger on it a few times. "I've something to show you," he said, ignoring my little quip.

My movements slowed as I set the towel down, taking the time to run a hand through my hair before answering. "And what's that?" I asked, though I already knew.

He uncrossed his legs, leaning forward like he might stand, though he didn't. He steepled his hands, perhaps contemplating how he wanted to say it. "How exactly does it work?"

I arched a brow in inquiry.

"Your ability," he clarified and asked again, "How does it work?"

I licked my lips, hesitant. "Just picture it in your mind, and I'll be able to draw out the memory when I touch you."

"*Memory*," he said, scoffing, though his voice shrank. "Come now, you know there isn't just one, Noah ..."

"How many are there?" I feared the answer.

He wrung his hands, clearly anxious. I knew it must've taken some careful thought to approach me like this, but I could see the determination in his eyes. Gently, he said, "I want you to see how many times I treated him without telling you over the last—" He swallowed. "—the last ten years."

"Ten years?"

Quade looked down.

"You're not—please tell me you're not serious."

"He was a child the first time I treated a bruise on his cheek, back when I was an apprentice here at the castle. He told me he got into a tousle with one of his friends ... I've never seen the act; I've only ever been a witness to the aftermath, though the injuries weren't usually so obvious." He rubbed the back of his neck. "He always smiled, laughed it off, gave me some vaguely believable excuse, and I accepted it."

I opened my mouth to shout because I felt a horrible flood of anger crash through me, but I resisted. Quade was not at fault for this. Gritting my teeth, I said, "He is cunning, is he not?" because my little brother smiled at me while lying, too.

"I wish he wasn't her child. I wish none of you were ..."

I stepped closer with the desire to console him, but I didn't dare touch him yet. I hovered just out of reach, trying to work out what to say, but he spoke again before I had the chance.

"Do you understand what I'm trying to tell you, Noah?"

Yes, I know. Of course, I know.

"I wish I didn't," I whispered.

"I'm in."

I inhaled sharply, setting my jaw. "You shouldn't be."

"I'm not the one who needs protection."

"You will if you get involved in this."

"I'm already involved. How long have we been friends, Noah? Do you think I wasn't involved then when you first presented the idea of an uprising?" He shook his head. "Why tell me at all if you didn't want—"

"We'll need you after to—"

He threw his head back with a clipped laugh. "For what? To clean up the mess? To drag the bodies of the only family I've got off the battlefield?"

I bit my lip, turning away.

"Do you think this shit doesn't keep me up at night?"

"Quade, listen ..."

He pinched the bridge of his nose, clearing the knot from his throat. "Look, we both know."

I felt as if a hand had been thrust upward into my gut. "What?"

"Seth may think his mask is emotionless. He may think he's good at hiding things from us, but he isn't. He's let on what he's seen. We both know that—"

I slammed my fist down on the table beside me, the cap on my anger finally bursting, my voice rising to a shout as water sloshed out of the basin. "What? What do we fucking know?" Tears stung my eyes because I knew the answer. I knew what he would say; I just didn't want to hear it aloud.

How dare he bring that up now? How could he—?

He didn't heed the warning in my ire. A tremor shook his jaw, his voice low but direct. "We both know you're not gonna survive this battle ..."

I pressed a fist against my mouth, slumping back against the wall.

"I can't keep doing this, Noah ... I can't just be the one who cleans up at the end. I can't just sit back and wait. If there's anything I can do, I want to help you."

When I didn't respond, he bowed his head. "I regret never saying anything about Gabriel. I-I'm not blameless. I saw the trend over the years; it only ever escalated, and I did nothing. I patched him up and let him give me his fake little laughs and lies." He paused to take a slow, calming breath, but I could still hear the small break in his voice. "Forgive me. I thought—when Haven came to get me the other night, I thought we'd be losing him, too, and I couldn't live with myself if my lack of action—"

"Don't!" I snapped before he could finish. "Please don't ... Lenore is to blame. She's the only one to blame."

Quade's mouth moved around silent words until, at last, he hung his head and said, "You know that's not true. Do you not feel guilty, too?"

I didn't answer because to deny it would be wrong, and I knew he saw that on my face.

"I can't let myself sit idly by again."

"Gabriel didn't die, Quade."

"But you will!" he cried. "If I didn't do something to try to stop it, I—"

"It won't change ..."

"What?"

I wiped my eyes, raising my volume. "Nothing Seth sees ever changes."

"You believe that, and you still want to move forward?"

I froze. Slowly, I closed my mouth, turning my body so I faced him head-on. He needed to see how truly firm my resolve was. "Yes."

Suddenly, Quade slid forward out of his seat, his knees hitting the floor. "What do we have to lose by trying then?" His lower lip trembled as he sat back on his heels. "You three," he whispered. "You're all I have. And there is nowhere in these worlds that I would not follow you."

I exhaled shakily, understanding but unsure how to respond. There were no words. I could only meet him with action.

"You have always been on our side, haven't you?" Before I could think to hesitate, I crossed the room and held my hand out to him. "I warn you, we're a selfish lot."

"You think I don't already know that?" His lip curved up in just the hint of a smile as he stared at my extended hand. "So, does that make us the good guys or the bad guys?"

I smirked. "Everyone's a villain to someone, so who knows?" His eyes flicked up to mine. "But what's one more ghost to either of us?"

"I just have to picture them, right? The memories."

I nodded. He took my hand and closed his eyes.

PART THIRTEEN
A MOTHER'S LOVE

JASPER

A warm breeze pressed through me, though the night air was cool—a subtle indication before Animaero's voice sighed in my head.

Why do you flee, child?

I inhaled slowly. "Flee … That is what I'm doing, isn't it? Fleeing."

Why do you do this?

I coughed, wrestling with the ache in my throat. My voice was still scratchy, though I didn't really need to produce any sound for the Spirits to hear me. It was simply a habit to speak aloud.

"What d'you want, Aery? You've barely spoken to me in months."

You've barely spoken to us, she countered.

"Why're you here now then?"

Is our timing inappropriate? Why are you here?

I swallowed. Winced. "She won't come here."

She fears this place, and so it remains free of her presence.

Staring out into the growing dark, I nodded, though the

pain in my neck intensified with even that slight movement. The wound hadn't fully closed again since I'd reopened it.

"That means it's safe," I muttered through clenched teeth.

Yes.

"But is anywhere really safe for me, Aery?"

A gust rustled my hair. *The only danger to you here is yourself.*

Immediately, I dropped my gaze, though there was no face to look away from. I shouldn't be surprised, but I still felt embarrassed to think she'd seen yet another weak, dark moment in my life. They saw everything, knew everything. They just usually had the decency not to bring it up.

"I'm—" I curled in on myself. "I'm not thinking about that anymore," I whispered, then quickly added, "Not now," to make it less of a lie.

You are in pain.

"I'm ... okay."

You would speak a lie so openly to those who have seen the blackest recesses of your mind?

I drew the collar of my jacket up to hide my face, but I didn't change my answer.

We know you.

"I just need to rest."

Have you no sense of urgency?

"It'll heal. They always heal ..."

You sound so assured.

Snorting, I muttered, "I've some experience in being injured."

This injury is unlikely to heal on its own.

"Quade stitched it up."

You have ... She paused ... *lost two of your sutures.*

I chuckled, realising that she was attempting to be delicate. "*Lost,* she says." As if they hadn't watched my violent wailing on the cliff. "Don't worry; it'll close." I shut my eyes, feeling drowsy, but Aery's voice rang insistently in my head.

You mustn't sleep now, child. Sit up. You're losing blood.

"I can't sit up. I'm losing blood."

For a few seconds, there was silence, and then the Spirit's gentle voice stole through the air—an arrow aimed directly at me. *It is still death by her hand if the wound she inflicted takes you now.*

"Shall I find another cliff then?" I snapped, but my ire was short-lived. I was only angry because she'd said what I didn't want to hear. Shyly, I lowered my face to my knees and wrapped my arms over my head. "It was just a passing thought ..." I mumbled.

But it was a male voice that responded. "Tilt your head downward; I must see the wound."

I hadn't heard him approach, but recognition took only a moment. I peeked up through my hair, at once stricken by his brilliance. The fiery mane of feathers, the colours glaringly bright in the darkness, the incandescent glow against the yellowing grass and fallen leaves ...

"Phlynt."

"My lord," he said, stretching out his neck to gently touch his forehead to mine. I smiled as warmth bloomed on my skin. "Aerispir summoned me."

I drew a breath through my nose. "I must really need help then."

He ruffled his feathers as he withdrew, showering little sparks onto the ground around him. "Bow your head. Allow me to see."

Obediently, I knelt before him, squeezing my eyes shut, biting my tongue to keep from crying out as he poked under the bandage and kneaded and pinched the skin with his beak. But his methods weren't unfamiliar to me, and as his tears closed the wound again, I felt the pain and pressure slowly ease. As if he stole all the tension from my body, I sank forward until my cheek was wet with the dew of the grass. I splayed over my knees, all the strength I'd gathered for survival abandoning me the moment I had reassurance that I would, indeed, see another sunrise—feel the warmth of it on my skin.

"Thank you," I whispered, and without warning, tears spilled from my eyes, the relief was so great. He observed me in silence, watching my body convulse with little gasps and sobs.

Phlynt cleared his throat, and I sucked in a big breath, holding it, trying to calm myself. For a moment, the night silenced to hear the phoenix speak. The creature's voice, though soft, echoed.

"I wish, my lord," he said, "that my abilities allowed me to heal more than just physical wounds ..." His voice darkened. "But alas, such magic is beyond me."

Pulling my arm out from under me, I stroked the warm feathers of his breast. Automatically, he stepped forward, leaning into my hand.

"My lord, trust in the Spirits as always you have. My dear companions will not lead you astray."

I nodded against the ground. "Never have they before ... nor have you, my friend."

"Rest and recover, sir. This is all I can do for you."

My lips trembled. "It's enough," I whispered. "It's more than enough."

When he didn't answer, I glanced up to find that he'd already gone, though the warmth lingered on my fingertips. I lowered my arm.

"Aery?"

We are here.

"Thank you."

Carefully, I pushed myself up to my hands and knees,

unwinding the bandage from around my temple, letting it fall from my fingertips as I felt the injury. The sutures were still in place, but only a small scab remained of the wound. I moved my head, and there was no shooting pain or dizziness.

"I feel like a weight's been lifted," I said, sitting up against the oak tree again. "Now it feels no worse than normal, like it's just another day."

Animaero's voice was firm. *Except it's not.*

"No," I agreed. "It isn't."

It's different this time.

"I was ... Aery, I really thought—"

We know what you thought, child.

"I shouldn't have provoked her like I did." Groaning, I leaned forward, lacing my fingers behind my neck. "I don't think she'll forgive me this time."

You would ask that woman's forgiveness?

"I—" Glancing down at my feet, I saw the discarded bandage coiled on the ground, frayed and bloody. "I don't know what to do now ... I always go back, but ..."

Then why did you come here?

"I had to get away."

Away from Elenora?

"As far away as I could. I had to—to get out of her reach."

Why?

I jerked my head up, though there was no one there to greet my anger. "You know why!"

What did she do?

"Aery, you know what she did!"

We want to hear you say it.

"Aery, please ..."

Say it.

"She killed him!" I shouted, then gasped, the reality of it hitting me like a blow to the chest. My body seemed to crumple in on itself. I held my stomach, my head pinched between my knees as I retched. Animaero waited for me. "She—she took Soren from me … She killed him. She—"

The Spirit's voice was smooth as silk. *She almost killed you.*

I froze with my mouth open. I thought I'd been prepared to refute, but hearing those words aloud arrested me body and mind because the Spirits never lied. They couldn't. No matter how many lies I told myself, their words were truth.

How close had I been to death that night?

My jaw quivered as I tried to string some words together. "But she—she didn't mean to … It was my fault, Aery. It was." But next to hers, my words were like venom passing through my lips. It felt wicked to speak them.

Sweet boy, Aery whispered. *Child, listen to yourself.*

"She—she didn't mean to …"

Listen to yourself.

"She wouldn't …"

She already did.

"Aery, I—" I bowed my head, unsure what to say when all that I clung to were lies. "Everyone hates her. Why d'you all hate her so much? And why can't I?"

Hatred is of little consequence to beings like us. Rather, we feel she has overstayed her welcome in these worlds. Her presence has disrupted the balance we seek to protect.

I raised my face, confused. "What d'you mean?"

A gust of wind washed over my face, drying my eyes, but she avoided the question.

She has committed the unforgivable against you, child. This, too, we do not take lightly.

My heartbeat quickened because that comment ignited a coal of bitterness I'd long nurtured. How many times had the Spirits watched my peril without interfering, while they claimed that my unhappiness affected them? Why did Animaero choose only now to help me heal my wounds?

"If you care so much, then why didn't you stop her?"

There was a momentary silence, and I pictured her carefully contemplating her response, pondering all the thoughts I'd chosen to keep in my head but that she'd heard anyway.

She was stopped.

I snorted at how simple a reply she'd landed on. "Yeah, by Soren, and look where that got him."

Would you prefer it had been us?

"No, that's not what I'm saying. I mean, she could've been stopped without—without ... l-losing Soren ... I didn't want to lose him."

Soren's death is a catalyst. This is an essential turning point for you.

I felt like my heart dropped out of my chest. "You—you're saying it was necessary? Are you fucking joking?"

It is important for you to understand why and how he died.

I ripped up a handful of grass and threw it into the air. "I already know! Do you think I don't? Do you think I want to think about it? Do you think I'd rather live in a world where he isn't waiting for me when I return? Do you think I'd rather be alone?"

You are not alone. There are many around you. You've an army of allies should you need them.

"Shut up! You know what I mean! You know how I feel! Is me feeling like this necessary? You could've saved me from this! You could've saved *him*! Why didn't you?"

Her voice remained even, unresponsive to my ire. *We beings do not interfere in the affairs of humans nor elves, greeley nor mer. We strive only to assist in maintaining balance.*

"Well, I'm unbalanced."

You will find your footing again.

"And what if I don't? What if I decide to give in?" My heart-beat raced, and the tears felt hot in my eyes. "It's not just Soren. It's everything. I—you know already—I don't want to—to be alive anymore. I don't want to go through my whole life just surviving. That's all I'm doing right now. I'm not living, Aery! I'm just surviving, and I'm fucking tired. He should've just let her—"

How inviting the bed of eternal sleep must seem for someone who is so very tired. We do know. We have seen your efforts, but destroying yourself will only disrupt the balance further. We cannot allow you to do this.

"You won't let me?" I scoffed. "You think you could stop me?"

We will stop you. We cannot let you further the chaos Elenora began.

"What chaos are you talking about? It doesn't matter anymore what she's done to me."

It does matter.

"What chaos?"

For a moment, she seemed to vanish, the gentle breeze of her presence disappearing from the leaves above me. Pressing my hands over my eyes, I shouted into the silence. I screamed—a deep, guttural cry—until my throat burned.

"I don't know what's wrong with me, Aery. I should hate her, but ... I just can't bring myself to. I wish I could. I wish I didn't care, but I—I still ... I still can't hate her. She's my mother, Aery. I can't hate her, and I hate myself for thinking this way."

Is this what you call a mother's love? If so, we are pleased to know that we shall never have to suffer it.

My voice was no more than a murmur of sound. "You don't have to be cruel."

When I lowered my hands, a misty figure knelt before me,

her hair flowing around her face in little wisps of white. There were no true defining characteristics, only a familiar shape, with limbs that seemed to fade in and out in different levels of opaqueness. All of her was in constant motion, cloud and mist shaped into a recognisable being.

Tell me, child. Why did you come to Earth? There are other places beyond her reach.

I watched the cloudy face form and fade and reform again, considering an excuse, but I reminded myself that Animaero would know the truth anyway.

I said, "Because Lily's here."

Why do you not go to her?

"I can't. She told me to go away, so I'm staying away."

Then why did you come?

I thought about it for a moment. "It's sort of ... comforting to know that she's nearby." Shyly, I looked away, clearing my throat. "Somehow, I feel less alone." But that wasn't the only reason, I realised, and I tried to explain it. "I don't want it to be the end. The idea that she could one day become a stranger to me if I don't do or say something now is—"

What was it? Painful?

I shook my head as if it might erase my previous thought and tried again.

"I asked myself all these questions about why it bothered me so much: Can you imagine her being a stranger? Can you imagine passing by each other and her not turning to look at you? Can you imagine your heart not leaping, your stomach not fluttering, when your eyes meet hers?" My exhale was shaky. "Can I imagine not having her in my life?"

When you do, the Spirit asked softly, *does it hurt?*

I stared out at the hazy darkness, then timidly, I nodded.

Perhaps she feels the same.

"Maybe."

Then you will go to her?

"I—I don't know what to do ... She told me to go away, and I'm sad that she did. But neither of us can change what was done or what was said. Maybe it's simply inevitable that we become strangers."

What if she does not want you to stay away?

"I think she made it pretty clear."

One's actions do not always reflect one's true desires.

"It doesn't matter anymore. I'm not going to see her."

Why not? If you do not do or say something now, then ...

"Her mother doesn't want me there."

No, perhaps not.

"Her mother knows what's best for her, right? And it's obviously not me."

Do you think your mother knows what is best for you?

I paused, and I couldn't find the words to answer.

Her misty hand swept over my cheek, streaking moisture across my skin.

Sweet child, she whispered, *never believe that anyone other than yourself knows what is best for you. You are the only one who knows the secret to your happiness.*

"Yeah, me, you, and the other Spirits."

We do not matter in this. The point is that you know it.

Chewing on my bottom lip, I asked, "What if, in pursuit of my own happiness, I encroach on someone else's?"

Then you have a decision to make. That does not mean that you do not know.

I closed my eyes, exhaling deeply.

You are lost.

I nodded.

In your confusion and melancholy, let us tell you this, as it may please you to know: my child, you are not the same as others.

"What?"

Other humans. You worried that we may think you lowly and intrusive. You are not.

It took me a minute to understand why her words felt familiar, and when I did, I held my breath. Somehow, though I knew she was capable of hearing them, it still surprised me when she reiterated my own thoughts to me.

We would not choose someone we do not deem worthy to share our space. We chose you. Do not forget that. If you can only survive now, then survive. Do everything it takes to survive until you find a reason to live.

I felt the warm wisp of a kiss on my cheek, but when I opened my eyes again, Animaero's cloudy figure had dispersed, leaving only the dewy smudge of her lips behind.

I buried my face in my hands. There was something ominous in her words and, again, something familiar and unseemly.

There was a feeling in my gut, something iced with regret and guilt because so much of my time had been wasted on someone who had no intention of ever reciprocating, while I already had the most trustworthy confidantes possible.

Because only I could hear them, and only they could truly know the inner workings of my muddled brain. Only they could filter through the disarray and find someone *worthy*.

"Thank you, Aery," I said softly. "For calling Phlynt ... and for, well, everything else."

She didn't respond.

But the longer the silence lingered, the more the thought bothered me. A tremor ran through my jaw, my voice a dull whisper when I managed to speak again. "Why did she think she could do that to me, Aery?"

Her voice remained level, though it took her a moment to answer. *This is not the first time she has taken advantage of you.*

"B-but—" I fought past the lump in my throat. "But I just

wanted to help her. Why couldn't she see that? Why did she have to do that to me? I did everything for her!"

You did.

"I tried my best, Aery. I tried. I really did, but—but it was too much. I couldn't take it anymore. D-do you think she did that because I gave up? Do you think she thought I gave up on her?"

Sweet boy ...

"It was just so much, Aery. It was too much. It hurt too much ..." I sniffled, mopping the tears and snot from my face with my sleeve. "Don't I deserve to be happy, too?"

The Spirit didn't answer. I coughed and spat out the sputum that had run into the back of my throat.

"Don't I deserve to be happy, too?" I repeated, just to hear the words aloud, to let them sit there in the cold night with me.

A raindrop hit the back of my wrist, and slowly, I drew my hands away from my face, peering upward. I sat still, listening as the sound of the rain grew steadily louder, a few drops slipping through the canopy of branches and leaves above me. I sighed, wiping my face again.

"Why are you crying, Aery?"

LILY

I reclined on the sofa, peeking up from my crochet at Liam, who sat opposite me in an armchair, poring over a book. There'd been almost no communication between us in the last week, and I was beginning to find the silence maddening.

I'd shouted at him, but surely, he understood how distraught I'd been in the moment. He would've been, too, in the same situation, but he still insisted on punishing me for it. Even now that we were alone in the same room, he couldn't be bothered. He sat straight-backed with his feet planted on the floor and a copy of *Alice's Adventures in Wonderland* so close to his face that his nose was probably stuck in the crease.

I tutted at his posture. How much energy was he putting into sitting so properly—as if Mother might appear at any moment to praise him for such perfection? I hadn't so much as caught a glimpse of her all week, and his efforts were wasted on me. Not even Miss Sawyer was available to flatter him.

I had to admit, however, that his dedication to ignoring me was impressive. He'd never been the sort to hold a grudge, but now that he'd decided to, his resolve hadn't wavered.

But I'd been so upset! Couldn't he see that? Look at what Mother had made me do! Liam had lost friends before; he should know.

Then I silently reproached myself because I was downplaying my own attachment. This was different. Jasper wasn't the same as those children, and my relationship with him hadn't been the same as theirs either. I wasn't entirely sure it was accurate to call Jasper simply a friend, though because I didn't know what to call my feelings for him, I thought *friend* seemed the closest allocation.

But how I missed him.

I abandoned my work and scooted the yarn over to the other cushion. It had only been an attempt to distract myself anyway. All I could think about was Jasper. I wanted to see him. I wanted to explain and apologise because he hadn't deserved such a curt farewell. He hadn't deserved one at all.

I wondered if he would come back. Maybe if I just waited a few more days, he'd show up like normal, and we could venture into the woods, talking and smiling like before.

Or maybe ...

Maybe he was the one waiting this time. Maybe it was my turn to go find him.

Abruptly, I got to my feet, my heart already fluttering at the prospect of seeing Jasper again. Liam peeked over the top of his book with one eyebrow arched.

"I—" I cleared my throat, avoiding my brother's eyes. "I'm bored."

His brow lowered.

"I think I'll—um—I think I'll pop down to the garden. Doesn't that sound lovely?"

Liam raised the book again and spoke from behind it. "Mother won't let you. It's late, and it's pouring rain."

I couldn't help the smirk that crept onto my face. Of course,

the only way he would deign to speak was to correct my rebel-
lious ways.

"I'll sneak out then." I shrugged. "It shouldn't be that hard."

Humming, I stepped into the hall and opened the door of
the nearest cupboard, thumbing through the selection of coats
and capes. Then I found some boots and checked the shelves for
my hat. I poked my head back through the doorway, unsuccessful. "Have you seen my hat? You know, the big floppy one?"

"Mother won't approve."

I rolled my eyes, hanging onto the doorframe. "Liam, that
has absolutely nothing to do with the location of my bonnet."

"Mother won't approve," he said again, one finger impatiently tapping the cover of the book.

"I doubt she'll even notice," I mumbled. "Why should it
matter anyway if I want to go outside on our own property? It's
only the garden."

His finger stopped tapping. When, finally, he answered, his
voice was low. "Is that really where you want to go?"

"I've just said it is."

A snort came from behind the novel. "C'mon, Lily, we both
know it's not the garden you're looking for."

I narrowed my eyes, and although he couldn't see my glare,
I hoped, by some chance, he could feel it. "I don't see how it's
any of your business."

"You've just made it my business by announcing it to me."

"I've only said that I'm going to the garden."

At last, he clapped the book shut and dropped it on his lap.
"And I've said that you won't be allowed to. Mother won't—"

"I don't care what Mother thinks!"

"You certainly cared what she thought when you sent Mr.
Behrtram away, so—"

The acidity of his words hit me like a slap in the face, and I
drew my head back in surprise. He stared at me, his own eyes

widening, equally shocked with himself. Never in my life had I heard him utter something so cold.

I felt out of breath. "E-excuse me?"

Immediately, he bowed his head and began apologising. "Lily, I-I'm sorry. I didn't—"

I spotted my hat on an end table and promptly retrieved it, stalking through the room without so much as a glance at my brother. "Good day, Liam," I said at the door.

"Lily, please, Mother won't like it if you—"

"Mother doesn't have to know!" I whipped around to face him again, slapping the hat down at my side. "And you won't tell her either," I warned. Draping my coat over my arm, I grabbed the boots and stuffed my feet into them, squatting in the doorway to lace them.

"Now," I said, straightening up. "If you'll excuse me, I'm going to go to the garden, have a nice soak in the rain, and try to pretend that I don't have an arrogant dick for a brother."

Liam's groan of protest followed me into the corridor.

LIAM

S ighing, I scooted to the edge of my seat and tossed the book onto the table in front of me. I leaned forward, resting my forearms on my knees as I peered out the window. The rain was heavy, sheeting against the glass in a rhythmic symphony, though I listened for Lily's escape. Silently, I hoped she'd be caught before she even left. If she slammed a door in anger, she'd be discovered by one of the staff, but to my dismay, I didn't hear her.

It was obvious she wasn't simply going to the garden, and the forest would be dangerous in this weather all alone in the dark.

I sat, for a moment, in indecision, listening to the rain. Then, grumbling, I ran a hand through my hair. "C'mon, Lily … Don't make me the bad guy again."

"Mother?" I whispered. There was no answer, but the door to her dressing room was ajar. Peering in, I saw her sitting at her vanity, combing her hair and humming softly to herself.

Seeing her like this, it was unmistakable that they were mother and daughter. Because their personalities differed so greatly, it was hard to tell, but when Mother let her hair down, Lily looked very like her. Though I was so used to seeing Mum outside of her room, dressed and ready for company, that this sight felt foreign, like she was another person altogether—perhaps simply an older version of Lily.

There were changes though. Her skin had paled, and she was thinner than before, her limbs long and willowy. Everything about her seemed fragile, from the way she held herself to the expression on her ashen face. But perhaps that was where I saw the greatest similarity; Lily always seemed a little fragile to me, too.

Mother met my eyes in the mirror, and although I didn't think she'd noticed me, she wasn't surprised at all by my appearance. Carefully, she set the brush down. I expected her to scold me for coming into her bedroom unannounced, but she simply asked, "What is it, William?"

"Hello, Mother," I replied, not entirely sure how to answer her question just yet. She seemed oddly dazed, so I asked, "How are you today?"

"Oh, I don't know." Her gaze flickered from my reflection to her own. "It's hard to say sometimes." Then her eyes narrowed. "Do you think your mother beautiful?"

I frowned, confused. I stepped closer and knelt next to her. "Yes, I think you're beautiful," I said, though the strangeness of the question—or the act of having a casual conversation with my mother at all—made me uneasy.

"He still left though," she mumbled. "Your father—he just left us. Why would he do that?"

I swallowed, laying my hand on top of one of hers, which sat delicately on her lap. "He was so ill, Mother ... He couldn't help it."

At last, she turned her head, and for a moment, her eyes widened in alarm. "Oh, it's you, William."

I leaned back a little, fighting the fierce urge to withdraw completely, to leave and close the door and pretend I'd never seen my mother in such a state. But Lily's safety was more important than my discomfort.

"Yes, it's me," I whispered, trying to meet her gaze, but already, her eyes had drifted. "Mother, what's the matter? Can't you see me? Don't you know I'm here?"

Jadedly, she said, "He still left me ... I wish so desperately that I knew why. I thought I was beautiful enough to make him stay."

"You are beautiful, Mother, but Father ... He must've had many demons. He was beyond help, don't you see?" I lifted her hand and wrapped it in both of mine, trying to make her look at me. "Mother, all those years, you survived without him. You were strong without him. Why is now any different?"

There was something brittle about the hand I held, like it might break at any moment. I tried to tread with care, cradling it as gently as I could. "Come back to us."

"Am I not here?"

Hesitantly, I shook my head. "I don't know," I said. "It feels like you're somewhere else ... but we're still here."

"Who is?"

I faltered. She'd said it so genuinely, as if she truly didn't know who sat before her, holding her hand.

"Me," I answered, unable to remove the note of incredulity

that snuck into my voice, though Mother didn't acknowledge it. "And Lily, too. Your children. We're still here, and we need you."

Sighing, she glanced down at me, lifted her free hand, and dragged the back of it lightly across my cheek. "Oh, William ... How much help can I be?"

I drew in a slow breath.

———

JASPER

Tucked beneath the oak tree, I gazed tiredly out at the falling rain, the sounds reminding me of the nights I passed in the library, lulled by Animaero's tears on the windowpane. How gentle it had seemed then with the moonlight streaming in and the warmth of a dying fire in the hearth. But here, it was dark and cold, and there was no lullaby to be heard among the thunder.

I dropped my head back, peering up through the branches at grim patches of sky.

I'd made it to Earth, but my planning hadn't extended beyond leaving Trigon. Already, I could see it unraveling.

How many times had I run away in the past?

It was only a temporary fix.

It was always temporary.

Contemplating it, I realised Earth was a poor choice. Lenore had been the one to show me the Gate. She could easily send someone after me if she suspected my whereabouts.

And I was predictable.

When in danger, I would run for safety, and safety was a familiar person, a familiar place. Where else besides Soren's arms or Quade's clinic would I go? Perhaps the place I'd spent the majority of my time over the last few years.

Sooner or later, I'd have to move on or—I shuddered at the thought—return home. But I knew I couldn't stay in one place, or I'd be found.

It was possible that the news of my absence hadn't yet extended beyond my brothers, Quade, and Penna, but eventually, Gilmer would worry. As time passed, he'd wonder why he hadn't heard his youngest son's voice. He may have been blind, but he had eyes everywhere—informers roaming the castle and streets, always listening, always whispering, always passing information up the ladder until it was hissed, throne-side, into the ear of the king.

I wondered if it had reached him yet. Surely, he was aware there'd been a disturbance in my room that night, but I expected the threat of Lenore's ire would keep the attending guards silent.

I chuckled dryly to myself.

How convenient for her that Quade had been my doctor; if I'd gone to the infirmary and seen the castle's regular physician, the rumours would've spread by now. This way, no one would know about her visit to me, about Soren's interference, about her actions once I'd run away ...

What explanation had been established instead? What lie had been forced down the guards' throats, ready to be regurgitated should the need arise?

I hugged my knees to my chest, my sleeves pulled down over my fingers. My body felt too heavy to move, but the chill in the air was biting.

A familiar person ...

I pictured Noah's face from that night—the fury in his eyes, the panic and horror and tears on his face as he watched my memories and saw what she'd done. I knew his ability allowed him to feel what the other person felt. He, too, had experienced the volatile hatred and lust she reserved for me alone.

Alone.

That's what I was, what I'd always been—alone with this wretched secret.

Until that moment.

That was all it took. A single touch, and the words I could never bring myself to say aloud were no longer secret. He didn't only hear them; he felt them.

But my shame overwhelmed the depth of that connection. I couldn't help wondering if he thought I'd exaggerated the situation—if he'd cried for me simply because of the intensity of the emotions I'd shared. I'd been told many times that I was prone to overreaction.

Did Noah think I was weak for behaving that way? Had I simply humiliated myself? I'd only been hurt a little, and my skin bruised so dramatically. I was fine now, wasn't I? I'd made such a big deal out of—

I dug my fingernails into my scalp.

Stop it.

I squeezed my eyes shut.

Stop it, you bloody idiot.

Quade's voice rang clearly in my mind, reminding me: '*This isn't nothing, Gabriel ...*'

Why couldn't I stop thinking this way?

Noah had held and soothed me. I'd heard his heart racing. I'd seen his tears. Why couldn't I stop thinking he'd belittle or berate me for it? Why couldn't I get these horrible thoughts out of my head?

Get out. Get out. Get out!

My brothers were good people.

They loved me.

They'd protected me.

I felt so ashamed that I'd let myself think otherwise, even for an instant ...

I hid my face in my hands, listening as the rainfall thickened, sheeting down around me, though somehow—perhaps through Animaero's intervention—I remained dry.

"I'm tired, Aery," I whispered to the night. "I'm so tired ..."

If you join us, there is no telling how long you will stay.

"No, not there. I just want to sleep, but every time I close my eyes—"

You feel all memories deeply, child.

"They're so *real*." My voice sounded breathless, detached; I felt as if someone else had spoken the words in my stead. "They never go away. Why do they never go away?" A tear crept slowly down my cheek. "How am I supposed to sleep when I can't escape?"

You cannot flee the confines of your own mind, no matter how far you run.

The wind picked up, pressing through me in a gust of warm air. I whimpered when it passed—when I was reintroduced to the cold.

My child, you may choose which memory to linger on. They need not always be base.

"How?"

You are far more capable than you imagine.

I lifted my face, staring out into the trees, which were hazy through the rain.

'Been outside lately?'

'Just out on the balcony, of course.'

'Of course.'

I closed my eyes, and Soren's face formed in my mind.

Soren, my quiet guardian, who tucked me into bed when I had a hard day, who understood me in a way that only he could, who always waited up for me to return, who gave me a place to return to.

Soren, who'd never been anything but familiar and safe.

Soren, who'd saved me from that woman ... and saved me from myself.

And it was the memory of him tucking me into bed and placing that warm, whiskery kiss on my forehead that finally lulled me to sleep.

'Rest easy, young prince. I'll be right outside.'

PART FOURTEEN
BETWEEN TWO TREES

LILY

I pressed on through the trees, labouring in the rainy dark.

Mother's cry was softer this time, muted by the distance and the downpour. She'd chased me deep into the woods, but I was much faster navigating the boughs and brush.

But my lungs burned. My feet ached.

Tripping to a stop, I flattened myself against a tree, my chest heaving.

No part of my attire was made for this.

I reached up to untie the ribbon on my bonnet and pulled it off. It absorbed too much water, sagging down over my eyes until I could barely see. Without it, I spun in a circle, scanning the surrounding area for something familiar—anything to give me a hint as to my bearings—but I was lost. The oak tree was nowhere in sight.

Every time I'd come here had been with Jasper. I'd followed him wherever he went, trusted that he wouldn't lead me astray, watched him instead of the path we took.

I leaned back on the tree.

What was I doing?

Finding Jasper wouldn't solve anything. Even if seeing him again would satisfy me for a moment, I'd still have to leave him again. Mother would never let it continue.

It wouldn't do either of us any good. I knew that. I knew I shouldn't be looking for him. I knew I shouldn't see him at all. I knew. I did, but ...

But I wanted to.

I really wanted to see him.

Mother could punish me all she liked after—she could lock me in a cupboard for the remainder of my youth if she wanted —but I had to find Jasper first. I had to apologise. If nothing else, I had to give him a proper explanation and a proper goodbye.

But ...

If he'd still have me, I wanted to tell him that I didn't want us to stop being friends, even if continuing our relationship meant—

"Lilith!"

I tensed, my fingers tightening around the brim of my hat. I'd been so preoccupied with my thoughts that I hadn't heard her approach.

Mother stood a few yards away, gasping for breath, her coat and cape looking out of place over her nightgown and bedroom slippers. For a moment, I just stared at her. How strange she was in that outfit with her hair loose and dripping wet around a face that seemed even more gaunt in the dark.

"Lilith, what are you doing?" I could hear the exhaustion in her voice. She coughed against her fist, her other hand clutching her coat at the waist. "Come here!"

Something possessed me then—a frantic need to flee, to get as far from this unfamiliar creature as possible. I shook my head, and Mother's expression hardened. But before she could speak again—before she could beg or order me to return with her—I flung my sopping hat in her direction and took off.

"Lilith!" she cried after me, but I didn't stop. I ran faster, hiking my skirt up to my thighs. I heard the desperation in her voice and felt the unpleasant twinge of guilt, but I didn't slow. Her cries grew weaker, farther apart, and then, at last, ceased altogether, lost under the steady thrum of the rain.

But still, I didn't stop. I didn't feel like I could. I walked briskly when the stitch in my side hurt too badly to keep running.

I had to move to keep warm. I had to move to find Jasper.

Squeezing through a tight copse of trees, I tripped onto an overgrown trail, my eyes half shut against the rain. Branches arched over the path, the trees on either side so closely spaced that it created a natural tunnel. Without a second thought, I flew down it, unimpeded by the obstacles of the forest. I urged myself into a sprint, swinging my arms, wheezing but not stopping. Puddles splashed under my feet as thunder rumbled in the sky above.

A structure rose ahead of me, forcing me to lose pace. Slowing, I came to a halt in front of a tall bronze gate and, staring through the bars, knew immediately where I was. The crumbling building, the cracked courtyard, the rosebushes and peonies that still bloomed late in the season—this was the Atwood House.

Moss and ivy sprouted over the rubble, crawling up the parts that still stood. I grabbed at it as I climbed through a break in the wall, slipping on loose chunks of old brick. The courtyard was slick with rainwater, the stone worn smooth with age and use.

Any other day, it might've been an interesting place to explore, but the rain had grown so dense that even the thunder was muted in the cacophony. I hadn't felt the full magnitude of it in the tunnel of trees; it was far worse than anything I'd expected or prepared for. I shivered, my hands and feet tingling with numbness.

The far wall had collapsed against the back of the house, the two slabs of old masonry propping each other up, and beneath it, veiled by a sheet of rain, was the slim promise of shelter.

I tripped across the courtyard, my legs aching, and when I reached the fallen structure, I took a deep breath, pressed through the rippling curtain, and dropped to my knees. But the ground I landed on was dry. No puddles. No rain. Just damp air and darkness.

I crawled forward a few feet before flopping over onto my backside, breathing heavily, all of the exhaustion from my escape hitting me at once. I pulled my cape closer, twisting my skirt around my legs to try to conserve some warmth. Feeling my way around the dark, I scooted back against the sloped wall, wringing the water from my hair and sleeves.

Then, exhaling, I dropped my head back.

What was I doing?

Had I really expected to find Jasper out here on a night like this? We'd never met in the evening. It was always in the daytime, so if I thought about it logically, the possibility of him waiting for me at this hour in this weather was faint at best. It was unlikely he'd returned to the area at all after what I'd said to him. He was probably long gone, back to Trigon or Iraxhar or whatever he'd called it. Even if, by some miracle, he had come back, he would've been at the oak tree like always ...

I ran my hands through my hair and groaned, my fingers catching in the wet tangles as I listened to a steady drip from farther within.

Drip ... drip ... drip.

The pouring rain outside settled to nothing more than a

hum in my ears, blanketing the silence so that single drip seemed to echo.

Drip ... drip ... drip.

It was almost hypnotizing. I closed my eyes.

A strange quiet stretched between each drop. Unexpected, almost eerie. The blackness around me felt full, as if the spot I occupied was the only one available—as if the very air had weight and could take up space. I curled my body inward to lend more room to the shadows.

Drip ... drip ... drip.

Then I felt it—a shift. A change, a motion, a breeze, but from where? Surely it couldn't have breached that rainy curtain.

Drip ... drip ...

I sat up straighter.

The noise was gone, swallowed up in the span of a moment, and in its place, drifting from the extending darkness, was a smell. I opened my eyes, swiveling my head around, but only shadows greeted me. It hadn't been there before; I would've noticed the pungent musk of age and stasis.

I inhaled, pulling my legs in.

I wasn't mistaken; I couldn't be. Something was there. Something had moved. Something had silenced the raindrop and disturbed whatever vented that horrible scent.

I wasn't mistaken.

There was the scrape of movement, the reluctant groan of waking, the clatter of loose rocks falling away.

Drip ... Drip ... Drip ...

I pressed my hands over my mouth.

There was a slow, ragged exhale, and then a voice from out of the darkness whispered, "Who's there?"

JASPER

"Go away," I mumbled, swatting at the air around my head as the fairy circled. She dodged effortlessly, zipping back and forth and tugging on my hair when she could grab it. I closed my eyes tighter, clinging to the last promise of sleep, but Bridget wouldn't be ignored.

Groaning, I gave in and lifted my head from my knees, blinking at her. It was still dark, still foggy, still raining. It couldn't have been more than a few hours.

"What d'you want?" I whined, my eyes tearing in frustration. I rubbed them, trying to see, but Bridget wouldn't stay still long enough for me to focus. With a swing of my arm, I swept her from the air, holding her in front of my face.

At first disgruntled, she shot me a stern look, and then, as if remembering something important, her tiny face turned fearful. Squirming, she tried to free herself before throwing her arm behind her, pointing at—

I released her, ready to be faced with a threat. Had Lenore sent guards after all? My heart raced as I struggled to rid the drowse of sleep from my mind.

But it wasn't the clunky, armoured uniform of a soldier. It

was the small, lithe body of one person. I sat up straighter, instantly alert because I thought it might be Lily, but it only took me a second to realise it was a boy.

Liam came to an abrupt halt when he saw me. He arched his hand over his eyes, squinting through the rain. "M-Mr. Behrtram? Is that you?"

Settling back against the tree, I waved him over. When he was beside me, he let out a contented sigh and dropped his hood. Cheerfully, he looked around.

"What're you doing out here?" I asked, but he ignored my question and frowned, twisting his body to peer around the tree trunk.

"Lily's not with you?"

I stared back at him blankly. "Sorry?"

"Lily. She's not here?"

Hesitantly, I shook my head. I didn't like the implication of his question. "Why would she be?"

"Well, I just thought—"

"I haven't seen her at all, not since ..." I didn't finish the thought.

"Right." Liam's shoulders slumped. "I thought for sure she'd come looking for you."

"If she did, she didn't look in the most obvious spot." I lowered my eyes to my hands, though I could feel Liam's watchful gaze.

He asked, "You two came here a lot then?"

I nodded.

"Oh."

For a moment, the rain filled the silence, but it felt awkward. I clasped my hands together, squeezing, rolling my shoulders forward, wishing I could sink down into the earth and disappear.

Liam watched me, his eyes never leaving my face. Then I

heard his soft exhale. "She really misses you …"

I scoffed without thinking. "I'm sure she does." Toneless. Indifferent. There was no telling what emotions might surface if I let myself believe him even for a second.

"She does," he insisted. "She really—"

"Look, you don't have to—"

"She misses you."

At last, I gave in, facing him with whatever expression had wormed its way onto my face. "So what? What d'you want me to say to that?"

Liam's face hardened in the dim light. "I want you to say you'll help me find her."

I felt the colour drain from my face. "What?"

"Well—"

"Help you find her? What d'you mean? What happened?"

He raised his hands to my shoulders, gently guiding me backwards; I hadn't realised how close I'd suddenly gotten.

"Nothing happened to her," he said. "She just ran off."

I exhaled in relief.

Absently rubbing the back of his neck, he continued, "But now, we can't find her, and it's late and raining and—"

Before I knew it, I was on my feet.

Bridget slipped off my shoulder, thrown by the movement, and scowling, she flitted over to Liam.

"Mr. Behrtram?"

My face flushed, but I couldn't help the unease I felt. If Lily had come out here to find me, then it would be my fault if she got lost or hurt.

"I-I'll help you look," I said, drawing my hood, starting into the trees without even waiting for a response.

"Huh? Wait up!" Liam called after me.

But I couldn't wait. I couldn't stop my feet. I had to find her.

I sped up, but my body wouldn't let me drive it into more than a jog. Phlynt mending one wound didn't mean I'd fully recovered. I was sore. I felt weak. My stomach protested any amount of activity.

But I couldn't stop until—

"Hey!"

I'd almost forgotten about Liam.

Cursing under my breath, I slowed, but the rainfall was too thick to see very far. Bridget was with him, and she knew these woods better than I did. He wouldn't get lost if I kept going.

But when I wiped the water from my eyes, a shadow flashed past me. I barely caught it.

Spinning around, I snapped to attention.

"Liam?" I said, though I knew it couldn't have been him.

A trick of the light?

No, that wasn't it. The movement was eerily familiar. I'd seen it before.

"There you are!" Liam's voice wheezed from behind me. "You—you're fast."

I turned, careful to keep my eyes moving across the area. Then, again: just a flash of darkness in the corner of my eye. Liam and I both jumped.

"Did—did you see that?" he asked.

Bridget peeked from beneath Liam's hood, her eyes wide as saucers. She scooted closer to the boy's neck, ducking into his collar, shaking her head.

Something else was in the woods with us—something that scared her—and I knew what it was. We'd met briefly before, but there was no way the being would leave us unscathed for a second time.

I stepped slowly backward toward Liam.

"Run," I said.

"What?"

Louder: "Take Bridget and run!"

"But—"

I heard it—a low growl beside me.

"Liam, run!"

LILY

My chest tightened. I held my breath.

Someone was there.

"I heard you," the voice hissed.

I slid my thumb between my teeth, biting softly to keep my teeth from chattering.

It wasn't Jasper. It was a woman's voice but harsh, accusatory.

Carefully, I drew my legs out from under me, crouching and inching my way toward the hazy curtain, praying the downpour would mask the soft shuffle of my boots. I leaned into the wall, sliding across it with my arms outstretched to feel my way.

"Speak!" the voice snarled.

Startled, I collapsed onto my seat, my thigh muscles burning from the squat and the run. But the sudden relief for my legs hindered more than helped. For a moment, I relaxed too much, my breath releasing in a thankful huff. Too loud. Almost a gasp, and I was too late to stifle it.

"I heard you, stranger." The voice lowered. "I know you're there."

The crack of old joints, the grunt of strain, the stomp of a heavy footfall.

I cringed against the ground, shielding my face as dust rained from above.

It wasn't just a footstep; the *ground* shuddered. Loose rocks quaked around me.

I'd already made a grave error. I shouldn't have tried to be quiet and sneaky. I should've run without a second thought.

Whatever filled the darkness couldn't be human.

I could feel the heat radiating from her body. I could feel the air shift as she lumbered closer. I could feel the earth beneath me tremor.

"You can't hide from me forever."

I pushed myself up onto my hands and knees, trembling, breathing as quietly but as quickly as I could. I sat back on my heels, preparing to move, to stand, to run, but then—

Then a puff of warm air kissed the back of my neck.

I felt a trickle of sweat slide down my spine. I felt it bead on chest and stomach as the ripe stench swarmed my nostrils.

"Hello, stranger," the voice crooned so close to my ear that the hot pant of her breath washed over the side of my face—so close that I could feel the moisture in it.

I swallowed my own breath, coughing, choking past the knot in my throat to scream.

I threw my body away from her, scrambling to gain my feet, but my dress was still half twisted around my legs. I hit the ground hard, gasping, trying to kick myself free.

The woman let out a throaty laugh as I burst upward, forward, and through the sheet of rain, but the conditions outside were disorienting. A wave crashed over my head, hitting me with such force that I took one step, stumbled, and fell, crashing into a muddy puddle. The raindrops were sharp pinpricks on my skin, the moonlight glaringly bright after sitting so long in the dark.

I rolled over, wiping my eyes as she emerged after me.

My breath held.

She surpassed all my expectations, but I knew immediately that calling her a woman was wrong. This was a creature, a monster, a beast.

"P-please," I croaked, shoving my feet into the earth, grabbing grass and stones in a desperate effort to push myself backwards. "I-I didn't—I didn't mean to intrude. I lost my way, and—"

One foot thrust forward, falling directly in front of me. I jerked my legs up as mud squished between her scaly grey toes, her talons starkly white against the brown earth.

"And?" the monster asked. "You thought there would be shelter for you here? Is that it, stranger?"

My arms shook. My elbows buckled as I peered up at her gloating face. Then it swept down toward me, wild and wrinkled, her mouth bent nastily. Knotted hair flopped over her shoulders, heavy with rain, long enough to touch me when she inclined her body, the feathery ends of it painting my skin with water.

My pulse raced, and my stomach tightened. Fear gripped my throat, sinking me deeper in the muddy puddle, pinning me down. There was no strength in me to move.

"Please," I begged, bleary-eyed and shivering. "Please, I-I didn't—I don't mean you any harm. Please ..."

"Do not waste your breath, stranger."

"Please, ma'am. Please. I-I'll leave. I'll never return, I swear it!" My jaw trembled. "I beg of you ..."

"Quiet!" Her foot smashed my legs, toes and talons curling around my knees. I shrieked, squeezing my eyes shut.

I couldn't escape.

She had me.

I couldn't escape.

I was dead. This was it, wasn't it?

Please don't let this be it ...

The tears were fresh and hot in my eyes, and the rain against my body was cold. I jammed my legs together, trying to relieve them of the crushing pain.

But then I remembered—

"You're a noisy one, aren't you?" The she-beast screwed up her face, her lips pinched, her pale, cold eyes bearing down on me. "Calm yourself. Wasting energy on tears will only exhaust you more than necessary. They'll not inspire any change in my actions, for we are, together, already on a path from which we cannot stray."

Then I remembered I wasn't helpless.

I wasn't unarmed.

I dug in my jacket pocket, feeling for the handle of Bennet's paring knife that I'd thieved from the kitchen after Liam was attacked by the erlking. I'd wrapped it in a rag and tucked it away in the coat I always wore just in case—

My fingers wrapped around the smooth wooden hilt.

With a wild fury, I ripped the blade from my pocket and drove it between the creature's toes. I screamed, drew back, and stabbed again, trying to find a weak spot, trying to find a flaw or a seam in the armour of her skin, but it wouldn't penetrate.

Again.

Again.

Again, the blade came back clean, the tip chipped off, lodged in the dirt after one of my misses.

I'd done nothing.

I'd drawn no blood and left no mark.

When I finally threw the knife down in defeat, I was wheezing and sobbing, and the beast was howling with laughter so deep it shook her leg. Her grip tightened. I cried out, the bones around my knees grinding against each other.

"Look at this!" she hooted, tossing her head back. "Look at the fight in you!" I shut my eyes, turning my head, but I could feel her dip toward me again. I could feel the air move, feel the rain over my face lessen, feel her rancid breath paw at my skin. "You're a wild little thing, aren't you?"

I hid my face with my arms, the anticipation of her next blow threatening to bury me, but then, I heard a noise. The monster drew back, her attention stolen.

I jerked my hands away and opened my eyes, thinning them against the rain, squinting up at the creature's face.

I was immediately and bafflingly disarmed.

As if a slow wave washed over her body, I watched her muscles relax. The eagerness and hostility in her expression was borne away, leaving behind an air of relief, or perhaps even a peaceful sort of sadness.

"Inah," she whispered, and even her voice lost some of its hardness when she spoke the name. "You've returned to me."

I craned my neck, pulling my shoulders back to rotate my body as much as I could. I had to see what on Earth could instantaneously pacify such a beast.

"And always, I shall," a deep voice replied—a man's voice, though it was an animal that emerged from the trees after it. "I've found him for you."

Its shape grew from the haze, black fur rippling under the rain, and my stomach turned to ice. A new surge of panic screamed through my veins because I recognised it. It was the cat creature from before—the very same one that had fled with the erlking's corpse the day we met Jasper.

"Was the other boy with him?"

The creature stalked toward us, one paw and then the other,

its muscular shoulders rolling with the movement. "He was, but I couldn't catch both at once."

"This is the one though? The one they meant? Are you certain?"

The cat-creature sneered, his teeth sharply white under the silky raven fur. "See for yourself, my love," he said, turned his lanky body, and shoved a thrashing figure into the light.

"Get your bloody paws off me, you feral beast!"

JASPER

Grunting, I fought to untangle myself from the creature's tail, tempted to bite the thing if it would persuade it to release me, but a voice stopped my attempts with a single word.

"Jasper!"

In a second, my heart was in my throat.

I knew that voice.

I felt the animal's grip slacken, but I didn't move. I didn't run. The creature released me as if he knew the person who'd produced that voice would keep me where I was.

And he was right.

I turned, searching, silently pleading that my ears deceived me—that Lily wasn't near enough to speak my name in a downpour and still be heard by me. But she was.

My stomach lurched when I saw her splayed on her back on the ground, a prone figure barely visible in the dark. Her legs were pinched together beneath the talons of a massive, feathery beast, but I could hardly bring myself to look a second time at the monster. My eyes were fixed on Lily: her wet, stringy hair;

her pale, mud-spattered face; her rapidly blinking eyes as they struggled to see me through the rain ...

I wiped the water from my lashes, the hazy image of her clearing for but a moment.

"J-Jasper ..." Her voice quivered with fear, but there was something else, too, something I not only heard in her voice but saw on her face: relief.

At what? At seeing me?

I stood motionless, unable to bring any words to my lips. I didn't know how to react when she looked at me with hope and solace in her eyes, like I was some kind of saviour. Because against two creatures that had already bested and caught us, I didn't know what aid I could bring.

I gazed up at the beast that held her, my eyes sweeping over its feathery legs and bare, sagging breasts, but I didn't react. I'd seen worse than a harpy. Seeing Lily unnerved me more than the creature did.

I wiped my face again, slicking my hair back.

"Lily," I said, stepping toward her, but her capturer spoke over me.

"Quiet!" the beast snapped. I ignored her.

"Lily, are you—" I tried, but again, the creature interrupted.

"Silence!" she howled, and as if in response, a roar of thunder surged through the sky. The rain thickened, a gust of wind blowing it sideways. With widened eyes, the creature peered curiously upward, rounding her wing over her eyes to see.

I was frustrated, and Animaero could feel it. I watched her storm clouds churn and darken, blurring the sky. They rumbled and glowed. This was her response to suffering. It was always her response. It was my anger and sorrow blended with hers, our inner screams snarling through the night with cracks of sound and bursts of lightning.

The harpy's gaze lowered slowly from the sky to me, her voice stolen by the thunder.

But it was too much. This reaction was too much. The torrent worsened as my frustration grew. I could hardly see or hear anything. The rain and wind were biting. I shivered and wiped my eyes and blinked and shoved my hair back again and gripped my head in my hands and pressed my palms against my eyes and—

"Aery!" I bellowed. "Can you please stop crying for five fucking minutes?"

A flash of light. A low murmur of thunder. And then, the rain lifted gradually from a downpour to a light, misty shower, the clouds thinning just enough for the moonlight to press through.

I gasped as my knees hit the ground, all the strength in my legs filched by my demand. I clutched my chest, cursing, trying to catch my breath. I'd shouted without thinking. Every action had a consequence, and now, I had to suffer it.

No one moved, but all eyes were on me.

Lily was the first to speak. "Jasper, are you—?"

"Silence!" The she-beast boomed over her. Then to me: "Who are you, boy?" Her face twisted grimly. "It is quite a talent to command the sky."

Tiredly, I glanced up at her, but I only shook my head. I sat back on my heels, pressing a palm to my forehead as I coughed, but the creature had no patience for me.

"Speak!" she roared, and at once, the long, plumy tail she towed behind her shot to attention. There was a sharp *crack* and a flash of colour before I was blinded by the water that sprayed from the feathers in their movement.

I flinched, raising one hand in surrender as I thumbed the muddy water from my eyes.

"For Spirts' sakes ..." I muttered, but when my sight

was clear and I looked up again, there wasn't a creature at all. In its place was a woman, tall and elegant with smooth skin and full lips, her hair a mane of tight curls. Her eyes shone, glassily reflecting the moonglow, but the light did something else to her, too. It illuminated her dark skin and made the raindrops that clung to it glitter like stars. I stared into the night sky rather than a beastly face.

But even more, it was the colour behind her that held me as if in a trance. The feathers of her tail fanned out above her head, arched like a bejeweled crown, though the ends drooped a little from the rain, casting a shadow that only brightened those gleaming eyes.

But it was only a moment—no more than a breath of time —before she dipped her head closer, and the night sky gave way to a creased face with glaring eyes. I blinked, unsure if I'd seen anything different at all, but I was shaken.

"Explain yourself!" the harpy seethed, and her grip tightened around Lily's legs.

The girl cried out. I leapt to my feet, but the other being moved swiftly. He dashed in front of me and rammed his snout into my stomach. Heaving, I bent double, nearly dropping to my knees again.

"Damn it!" I groaned, wrapping one arm around my waist, cradling what I knew would soon be a tender bruise. "Enough with the—"

The moment I lifted my head, that wrinkled face greeted me. I jumped, startled by the sudden closeness—by the musky stink of wet feathers and sweat—but when our eyes met, she stiffened. I tensed myself, afraid she'd recognised me as Prince Gabriel of Egaldon, but she seemed strangely more concerned than surprised to find royalty on Earth.

"Who—?" Her eyes widened as she studied me, unblinking,

all expression falling from her face. Her voice was low. "It cannot be."

I hunched my shoulders, cringing back, but the moment I did, she leaned closer. I tried to look away, but she turned with me, forcing me to hold her gaze. Then, as if a shadow had fallen upon the world, softening the glare of the moon and stars, her face darkened. She withdrew, her expression settling into a mask of melancholy.

"Oh," she whispered, and even the single syllable seemed solemn. "It's you. Oh, I know you ... Yes, I know you."

Inhaling sharply, I dropped my chin, trying to hide my face. "You have it wrong. I would've remembered our introduction."

She snorted, but it was dry, humourless. "Oh no, we've never met, you and I. I said that I know you, not that you know me ... Child, what is your name?"

My stomach hardened. She had to recognise me. I couldn't give her my real name. "Jasper," I said firmly, glad that Lily had addressed me the same way.

But the harpy's doubt remained, her eyes narrowing. "Jasper what?"

"Jasper Behrtram." The surname left my lips with strong conviction.

But then I balked.

My breath hitched as the name hung in the air.

Don't react, Jasper. Don't react.

"Is that your real name?"

"Yes," I snarled, and there was not even a blink's worth of hesitation. It was a name that didn't belong to anyone anymore —a name that would die if I didn't claim it.

I refused to let it die.

She sighed deeply. "No, I think not." Then, with a thin, embittered smile, she said, more to herself than to me, "Oh, vengeance is sweet ... What a hateful game the Spirits play."

"What?"

The Spirits?

The pitch of her voice leapt up, making me start.

"Just look at your face!" she crowed. "Look at your eyes! Ah! She must hate your eyes. It must torture her!"

A shudder raised the hair on the back of my neck as though light fingertips had brushed my spine. "Who are you? How do you know me?"

She avoided my question. "Y'know, I always wanted eyes like that. My father had eyes like that. If I could but pluck them from your head ..."

I raised my voice, fending off a rising panic. "Who are you?"

"Oh, well, since you are so persistent, I am Almirah, the long lost elven princess of Luvhena, at your service." She threw open her wings, sweeping one down in front of her in a dramatic bow.

I frowned. I knew the name, and it didn't belong to a harpy. Almirah was the late Anim Asaryth's only daughter.

Seeing the confusion on my face, the woman laughed. "Oh, am I not what you'd expect? Ah, we elves are cunning creatures."

No, that's impossible, I thought. *This thing isn't an elf. The elves aren't spiteful like this. They're not—*

And then the foul creature spoke my thoughts as if I'd said them aloud.

"Oh, you don't believe we can be spiteful? Your worship of our kind is sweet, though I imagine you'll be met with disappointment if you ever spend much time among us. We're a tricksy lot."

I hadn't spoken aloud, right? Not yet.

The harpy moved closer, dragging Lily with her. The girl cried out, throwing her arms up to shield her face as she was pulled through the mud, but even I could spare little sympathy in my surprise.

My voice quaked. "W-who are you?"

"I told you. I am one who came before you. Now, I am this, here with my dearest companion. Is he not the loveliest being you've ever beheld?" The cat slunk to her side, nuzzling her hand when she lowered it, letting her smooth the fur between his ears.

"Who are you?"

She pursed her lips. "Why do you keep asking the same question expecting a different answer? I am exactly who I say I am and can only answer in different variations of the truth. Why can you not see this?"

"A harpy can't be an elven princess."

She unfolded the bony, human-like arms she'd had wrapped around her waist and wagged a curled finger at me. "But an elven princess could be a harpy, you see, though it requires certain circumstances."

"Those circumstances don't exist."

She chuckled as if I'd made a joke.

"Well now, I expected an Atwood, but I didn't expect *you*." When I didn't respond, she sneered. "It is indeed a pleasure to meet you, Animosric."

I was completely paralysed, separate from this place and myself. Then sweat began to trickle down my body, slicking my chest, dripping from my brow, embalming me in a cold I'd never felt before.

My voice was barely a rasp when I asked, "What did you say?"

Hers was soft and measured. "Don't pretend you didn't hear."

I shook my head. "That's not real."

"Is it not? Who else calls upon the sky?"

"Many," I hissed.

"Ah, but it's rare for it answer, Lord Anim."

The cold fear swelled within me, exiting my body in a shout. "Don't call me that! It's not me!"

She waited as I gasped, every muscle straining to hold back the darkness that threatened to overtake me. The Void tempted. I gripped my head, driving the heels of my hands into my temples.

No. Stay. I need to stay.

It was something I'd once considered a possibility, only for a fleeting moment. But right now, it was just one more thing, and I couldn't handle another thing.

Don't make me think about this shit right now. Don't add this to the weight that's already crushing me. I can't deal with it. I can't deal with anything. I—

"It's not something for you to challenge."

And just like that, the pull of the Void vanished. The soft invitations silenced. Slowly, I lowered my hands.

This being was right, and she knew it.

It was something that, perhaps deep down, I'd always been aware of. It was something that, in my heart, I knew was true, but I didn't want it to be real. Every part of my being wanted to reject it, but I could see in the woman's eyes that she wasn't going to let me.

For fifteen years, I'd managed to avoid it, and with one look, this being had demolished all of my efforts.

My hands felt numb. I stuttered through words. "H-How d'you—w-who told you that?"

She answered indifferently. "Your eyes told me that."

My eyes ...

Watching the battle of emotion on my face, she said, "Don't panic. Only those who've lived as long as we have could possibly remember. Elves, of course, and perhaps a few of the remaining greeley."

"What're you talking about?"

"They're an odd colour, your eyes. Auric." Her gaze slid across the rubble around us and landed on me. "Those same eyes were last on the face of the former Animosric."

My hands were shaking. My stomach twisted itself in knots. "What d'you want with me?"

But the woman waved my question away. "Nothing at all."

"What?"

"I'm simply returning a favour. I was asked to fetch you."

There it was again. The coldness. The fear that was buried beyond my reach bubbling up to choke me.

Who else but my mother would want to fetch me? Who else was looking for me?

I felt the pressure of hands around my throat, forcing me to swallow. I squished my chin down to my chest, tensing against the dull ache that spread over the bruises that had only just begun to fade.

She must've seen it—the terror that passed over my face, the memory that entered my mind then—because her voice seemed more concerned, more urgent than before.

"It's not who you think."

I lifted my hands to my neck, shuddering, smoothing goose pimples from my skin. "How could you possibly know?" I whispered.

"I make it my business to know." One bony hand stretched out to touch me, and I flinched away, her gnarled fingers cold as death against my cheek. But despite my aversion, her expression was quiet, almost sympathetic. "Oh, you poor child," she muttered. "Look what she's done to your face. How cruel she is to you."

Every bit of my body tensed as I stared into her moonlit eyes, my horrified expression reflected in them.

Her fingers swept down my face as she withdrew her hand. "You know very well of whom I speak. She and I are ... well-acquainted. What is that woman calling herself?"

I swallowed tightly, answering though my voice trembled. "If you're well-acquainted, you should know."

Smirking, she flicked her brows. "Elenora, was it? Lenore the whore, the whore, Lenore." She giggled. "How convenient that it rhymes. Ah, that woman. She is something else, isn't she? The worst sort of something—the kind that would strike someone in their bed."

The processes of my mind were delayed. I couldn't speak. I couldn't think. It took everything I had to keep my feet planted on the ground because I could hear Soren's voice in my head again, screaming for me to run.

Breathe, Jasper. Calm down. Think logically. Catch her in her lie, and you'll feel better.

Squeezing my fists at my sides, I stood up straighter, though my heart hammered uncontrollably in my chest, slamming against my ribcage as if it could break free.

Control your fear. They're not attacking. They're just talking.

You're okay. You can do this.

I raised my face. "If you're an elf, you'll have two names. What's your other one—your true name?" When they were born, elves were given both a public name, known to their whole community and the outside worlds, and a private name, known only to those closest to them, their family or their lover.

"Why should I tell a stranger my name? You know enough about my people to know how sacred a name is."

My reply was ready: "You know who I am. If you are, indeed, the princess Almirah, then we're family."

She grunted and spat. "Distant relatives."

"But family nonetheless."

Amusement played across her face. "Well, I can see that you want to catch me in a lie that does not exist. I can only tell you truthfully what it is, though I can't imagine it will do you any good, unless you know someone who can confirm its legitimacy."

"I might," I spat back. I didn't, of course, but she didn't know that.

"You might," she said without offering an actual answer.

One answer. That's all I wanted. One answer that wasn't vague or avoided.

"Tell me who you are!" I shouted as I charged forward, but the cat's tail whipped around my waist and yanked me back. Struggling, I made it another few steps before the creature's hold tightened again. "Tell me!" I demanded, grabbing at his tail, trying to free myself without success. Tears blurred my vision for just a moment before I blinked them back. "I—I don't understand. I don't understand any of this. Please ..."

It was too much. Everything was too much.

The storm clouds churned again, moving in, blotting out the moonlight as I silently pleaded with Animaero to calm down.

The woman tossed her head back, waving off her companion, who immediately released me, slinking back to her side. Thunder purred around us.

"Aery," I whispered, and petulantly, the Spirit raised the humidity, drawing a fog up out of the ground like ghosts from graves. But I waved my hand, and it dispersed almost immediately, leaving the air thick and moist.

Slowly, quietly, the harpy uncurled her toes and lifted her foot.

I didn't have time to question her actions. I bolted forward, sliding in on my knees and shoving my hands under Lily's arms.

I dragged her back away from the two beings, just far enough to feel the illusion of freedom. It was folly to think I had the strength or energy to actually flee, especially with Lily in tow.

For a moment, the girl sat trembling at my feet. Hair clotted with dirt. Face colourless. Her white-knuckled hand clutched my wrist as I tried to coax her to stand. I'd barely gotten her upright when she swung around and hurled herself at me, all her weight hitting my chest. I staggered, but she held tight. Both of us stumbled backward a few steps before I could find balance.

But I wouldn't have let go even if we'd fallen.

"Lily," I whispered, but she didn't seem to hear me—didn't seem to notice the breath of relief that blanketed the word. "Lily, it's okay." I stroked her wet hair, carefully untangling it. Her breath burst in and out as she buried her face in my shirt, her arms wrapping around my waist, her hands clutching the back of my jacket and shaking.

For a second, I forgot all else, and Lily and I existed, alone, in a world apart from any other. I pulled her closer—as close as our bodies would allow, so close that my bruises hurt. It didn't matter. The pain didn't matter. The last week apart didn't matter.

For a single second, there was only the closeness and warmth of her body.

For a single second, I was transported back to that day we first embraced beneath the oak tree, warmed by the Auric Sun and the flood of emotion Lily didn't know she'd stirred in me.

For a single second, I felt like someone else needed me just as much as I needed them at exactly the same time, regardless of how different our reasons.

Every breath, every smell, every feeling in that second was warm. I wanted to stay there, suspended in time, forever living the same second of my life over and over again.

The thought of letting go didn't cross my mind until—

"I see. My apologies." The harpy's voice was low and contrite. "It seems I may have been too harsh in my dealings with the young lady."

It was the tone of her voice that pulled me from my reverie. I raised my head, seeking her gaze, but she was looking away, down into the eyes of her companion. Gently, her hand caressed the silky fur on his face, and he leaned into her touch. I glanced from one to the other, and I hesitated, almost afraid to speak and interrupt the gaze they shared. I felt like, if I did, I'd be imposing on—what? Their privacy? I wasn't sure, but that stare felt so odd and intimate ...

"Chel ..." The cat breathed, and her brow furrowed mournfully at the way he said her name, though no other words were exchanged. In that stare, I could see that these two beings were so closely entwined that words were not needed to share their thoughts with one another.

Oh, that's it, I thought. *They love each other.*

At last, the harpy woman turned to face me, and when she caught me watching them, she looked away again as if embarrassed—a display that was so uncharacteristically girlish that, for a moment, my fear of her dissolved almost completely. Her companion nudged her and brought her back to herself again.

But the name he'd called her, the way he'd said it ...

'*Chel ...*'

I stared at her, imagining a different face—the younger, beautiful starry sky it had been for but a moment before, the skin smoothed and the hair more tame. And him, a man instead of a cat, grievously, desperately, sorrowfully speaking her name. I'd seen that image before. I knew I had; I just didn't know where. I'd heard the man's voice, but when?

"Have we met before?" I wondered aloud, but the woman seemed surprised.

"We haven't," she said. "I assure you."

"I've seen you before, but not ..." My eyes passed over her large, feathery body. "... not like this. It was in a dream, I think, or a memory." I turned toward the cat. "And you weren't ..."

The harpy's returning smile was sombre. "It is an impossibility for us to have met, my lord. It has been a very long time since we were anything but this." Then, her expression faltered, and I couldn't help wondering what memory had been stirred. I wanted to ask, but she cleared her throat. "It seems that it is nearly time for us to part, sir."

I opened my mouth again, but I couldn't recall enough to contradict her. "You'll let us leave then?" I asked instead, perhaps too eagerly.

The corner of her mouth turned up. "You could've fled already. Why do you linger? Can you not yet bring yourself to abandon your questions now that you know the girl is safe?" When I didn't reply, the harpy woman chuckled. "I, myself, feel torn."

"Why?"

She observed me, pursing her lips. "I cannot decide if I should now advise you as Jasper Berhtram or the Animosric."

I gritted my teeth. "I'll not answer to the second."

"You'll have to someday."

"I can't," I insisted, then more softly, "Not now." I wondered if she could see it in my eyes—the desperation or desolation, the outpouring of emotion or, perhaps, the lack of it. Had she heard the tremor in my voice? Did she understand, even a little, how much I truly could not handle *one more thing*?

"Unfortunately, I fear that day may come sooner than you think." She sighed deeply and bowed her head. "So, to my Lord Anim, I will advise only this: prepare your heart. Doing the right thing is not always the most comfortable."

I opened my mouth, the words sticking in my throat for a

moment before I managed to speak them. "I never claimed morality."

"The Animosric is selected because they will do what they believe is right, no matter how painful it may be. The Spirits saw your heart, and they chose you."

"I don't like pain."

"But you can overcome it."

I didn't have an answer. I stood where I did in conversation with this being because I had endured, and I felt certain she'd spoken knowing that. But really, I had nothing more to say. There was no point inquiring further—no point drawing out more vague responses and explanations I didn't understand.

Lily shivered fiercely and not only from fear.

I nodded exaggeratedly at the girl in my arms. "Whatever you're plotting, I don't have time for it. Let us go."

"Oh, don't worry!" She dipped toward us again, and I flinched back as if I'd been slapped by the stink of her, pressing Lily's face into my shirt to spare her nose. "Do not worry yourself, my lord," she said. "She's going with you."

Lily stiffened against my body.

"No," I cried, the word leaving my lips as quickly as it had before with my mother, and in the very same way, I felt a wash of panic spread through my body. I shielded Lily's head with my arm, turning to put her farther away from them, bracing myself for my punishment.

But no attack came, and when I risked a glance over my shoulder, both creatures watched me in silence. Neither had moved even an inch. The woman tilted her head sympathetically. Her eyes were downcast, and her voice was softly bitter when she spoke. "How wicked of you to liken me to her for even a moment..."

I lowered my arm, my hold on Lily slackening.

Suddenly, I believed them.

Suddenly, I felt cold with guilt instead of fear.

Had I really expected these beings to treat me the same way simply because I'd said *no*? My refusal had far more weight with Lenore than it did with anyone else. I knew that ... didn't I?

The emotion in the creature's voice struck me so deeply that I had to believe she, too, had suffered at the hands of my mother. I didn't know how or why, but the harpy and I were both her victims. We had to be. I heard my own voice when she spoke. I felt the agony and disgust.

I swallowed, trying to relax my tight shoulders. "I—" I began but faltered. Part of me wanted to apologise for my cruel assumption—to ease the bitterness from her voice—but instead, I said, "I can't take Lily there; it isn't safe. I-I don't want her anywhere near—"

"Of course, you don't *want* her to go. She's going regardless."

"No!" I shouted, resisting the urge to cringe away again. I lowered my voice to match hers. "Look, I-I believe you, okay? I'll go with you—anywhere you want to take me—but I'm not bringing her. I don't—"

The woman spoke over me. "Do you want freedom?"

I froze with my mouth open because the question was so far from anything I'd expected her to ask. Then, tightening my jaw, I managed breathily, "Freedom from what?"

Her words were slow and deliberate, as if she wanted to make sure that I listened to each one. "From your chains."

"I don't—" I spoke through my teeth, but I could hear the resolution in my voice deteriorating. "—have any chains ..."

Her eyes tightened. "How terribly unconvincing."

I wanted to say, '*No, you're wrong. You don't know me. I haven't any chains,*' but the words stayed only thoughts. Nothing I could say would satisfy her more than my silent compliance because she already knew the truth. She could see it all—my discomfort, my vulnerability—and as I stared back into her eyes, I saw the guile. She wasn't confused or curious; she knew.

But suddenly, I knew something, too: it wasn't my mother. Lenore hadn't sent these two beings after me. There was no way. There were only a few other people who would be looking for me and only one audacious enough to befriend and trade favours with a harpy.

"It was Noah, wasn't it? The one who sent you after me."

"You have comrades, my Lord Anim—people who are familiar and safe."

What power is this? How could she know the words and sentiments I'd spoken only to myself?

She didn't address the bewilderment I knew she could see on my face. She said simply, "Stay close to them. That is my purpose in being here."

"You said you were returning a favour. What did he do for you?"

"He hasn't done it yet. But ... It will be worth as many favours as he requires. I am in his debt, sir. And yours."

"Was that him, too?"

"What d'you mean?"

"Did he ... tell you who I am—what I am?"

"No," she replied. "I told you; it was your eyes. Your brother is like you, I think, aware to some degree but unwilling to admit it."

Absently, I smoothed Lily's hair. Before I could stop myself, I asked, "What do I do now? Speaking as—" I cleared my throat. "—as the Animosric, I mean."

The two beings shared a glance, and then, the harpy answered, lightly but without humour: "Find my father. Find Asaryth."

LILY

I pressed my forehead against Jasper's collarbone and breathed. It was all I could do. I exhaled against his chest, my breath billowing off his skin and enveloping my face in a little cloud of warmth.

One breath at a time; that was all I could do.

One breath at a time, I slowed the pace of my heartbeat, trying but not entirely succeeding at listening. I couldn't follow. There were too many foreign words and phrases, and the drum in Jasper's chest was too loud to be ignored.

Any poise he displayed was a front. Any ease or aggression was a mask. I knew it was. I could hear the rampant beating of his heart. I could feel the tremor of his hand on my back.

I drew my arms up between us, folding my hands under my chin, savouring the warmth.

But then, a phrase stuck out in the drone of conversation that robbed all the heat from me.

"But I must warn you, my lord. Finding him will not solve everything. It can only provide clarity for you, as I am certain you are lacking in some necessary knowledge. You may choose to follow this advice or not, but if you do nothing, the consequences may be dire." The beast's voice darkened. "There is ... a chance you will not survive the war to come, and your companion, herself, may never find her way back to her true home."

I paled.

'... *the consequences may be dire ...*'

But Jasper sounded unconcerned. "There is no war."

"There are many wars to be fought, my lord, and there are many that have already begun."

'...*you will not survive ... never find her way ... home ...*'

For a moment, his hand stopped its slow path across my back. Finally, he said, "Lord Asaryth is dead."

"Of course, he is," the beast replied—a quiet, private voice. "That doesn't mean he can't be found."

'... *never ...*'

I thrust my hands into Jasper's chest, shoving back. Automatically, his arms broke apart and released me.

"Lily? Are you—?"

I stared back at him, my breath heaving. "W-what's wrong with you?" I shouted, disbelieving. "How—how can you just—"

"Lily, please ..." He reached for my arm, but I jerked away.

"No! Don't touch me!"

"Lily—"

I shook. I staggered back, tripping on loose rock. He rushed forward and grabbed me, wrapping me in his arms again. My lips trembled as I leaned into him, and I sniffled against his chest. "W-why are you s-so calm? I-I can't breathe."

"You can breathe, Lily. You're okay," he whispered, gently stroking my hair. "Don't worry. You're okay. I won't let anything bad happen to you."

Desperately, I attached myself to him, entangling our fingers so it would be harder to separate us. Gently, perhaps without thinking, his thumb moved in a little circle on the back of my hand.

"It's okay," he whispered again, pressing his lips to the top of my head. When he drew back, I looked up at him, at the quiet surety in his face and the gentle smile that tugged at the corner of his mouth. He bent to lean his forehead against mine. "It'll be okay, Lily."

It was the first time I'd actually looked at his face since he'd appeared—really looked at it. I felt as if someone reached into my chest and squeezed my heart. "Jasper, you—"

But he didn't let me finish. "Shh," he said and gently guided my head back to his chest.

"The hour is late, and people will be coming to search for the girl and her brother soon." I peeked behind me at the mention of Liam, but the beast's eyes were on Jasper. "You must go now. We'll lead you to the Gate."

The gate?

I remembered what Jasper had told me. Did she mean the same one? The gate to Iraxhar?

The lanky, cat-like creature dashed toward us so quickly that his movement was little more than a flash of shadow. But he reappeared behind us, nudging Jasper and then flanking left, then right and nudging again until Jasper freed one of his hands and swatted the air.

"Oi, you don't have to bloody herd us. We're not gonna run."

But it was the she-beast that responded. "He won't," she said to her pet, lumbering behind us. "He knows he can't."

Jasper said nothing but walked on obediently, and the cat-creature fell into step beside us.

When we'd crossed the Atwood estate and neared the bronze gate, Jasper steered me toward it, but the cat poked his snout into his ribs, directing him toward the forest instead.

Immediately, Jasper's feet stopped, and he looked behind us at the monster.

"Why're you—?" he began, his confusion drawing a crease between his brows. "The Gate is there." He tossed his head in the direction of the Atwood gate or, perhaps, beyond it.

"*A* gate is there," the beast replied in her low voice. "You'll be using a different one."

"Why?"

"Do you want to return to Gimlon so soon?"

Without a word, Jasper faced forward and we were led onward.

When we finally stopped, we stood before two close-set trees whose branches curved and blended into each other, creating a small archway that looked barely wide enough for one person to pass through. Jasper squeezed my hand.

"This is it then?" he asked.

The she-beast unfurled one of her wings, gesturing toward the space between the two trees. "Your pilgrimage awaits."

"Does this lead to the person who sent you?"

"No, not directly, but he'll find you soon enough."

He?

Jasper drew me a little closer. "And what's stopping us from immediately coming back through a different one?"

"Nothing at all, so long as you know the way." She flicked her bony, long-fingered hand. "As soon as you've passed through, I've completed my task. What you do after is your own choice."

Jasper listened without changing his expression. Then, he asked, "How should I find him? Anim Asaryth, I mean."

Slowly, I watched a sombre smile build on the creature's lips. "I don't know."

"Sorry?"

She inhaled, held her breath, and when she exhaled again to speak, her voice softened. "I've spent decades searching to no avail, though it seems my search ended some fifteen or sixteen years ago ..."

I didn't understand what she meant, but when I peered at Jasper's face, his lips had parted and his brow had creased. He almost seemed ... pained or ashamed in some way. Surely, he grasped some meaning that I couldn't, but his expression returned to its normal set after only a few seconds. He sighed, staring between the two tree trunks.

"The Gates always appear so ordinary. I've surely passed by this one never knowing it was there."

"Many have passed by it."

He faced the woman again, frowning. "This is where we part then. It's been ... very interesting meeting you." He glanced at the cat creature. "And you."

"And you, my lord—" She paused, and Jasper's grip tightened around my hand. Then her face relaxed, and she bent at the waist to meet him eye to eye. "—my Lord Jasper," she finished, and Jasper drew his head back, his eyes wide with disbelief, though I couldn't discern the reason. The monster smiled softly. "That's the right one, isn't it?"

Jasper gazed at her, and she gazed back. He didn't nod or shake his head. He didn't answer in any way at all, but when he made to turn, she stopped him, grabbing his chin in one skeletal hand to force him to look at her again, her fingers curling around his face like a cage. I watched the exchange, confused. She seemed desperate somehow, her eyes boring into his, her jaw nearly trembling. They stayed like that for a full minute, and Jasper didn't move. Then, all at once, she closed her eyes, dropped her arm, and bowed her head.

"It is an honour to know you, my lord," she said, but her voice was different, as though all the acidity had been siphoned from it. "Until we meet again."

Jasper seemed at a loss for words, letting out a forced

chuckle and clearing his throat before dealing a response. "That's assuming we'll ever meet again," he muttered.

"I'm afraid our paths are destined to cross more than you'd like to *assume*." She repeated ominously, "Until we meet again."

Jasper watched her, chewing on his lips. Then, in a voice so soft I wasn't sure he meant to be heard, he said, "Ixchel."

I didn't know the word, but with a glance, I could tell she did. All the colour drained from the beast's face.

Jasper looked down at our linked hands. "So, I was right, then," he whispered. "That's your name, isn't it? Ixchel—" His eyes flashed to the cat creature. "—and Inahteev."

Her words were encased in her exhale. "How did you—?"

"I knew I'd seen you before."

"How?"

"You left a memory behind."

The creature—Ixchel—blanched. "What?"

But the expression on Jasper's face was hesitant, as though suddenly realising he'd made a mistake—as though he shouldn't have said anything at all.

"What d'you mean?" Ixchel pressed.

"There is a room with all the windows bricked up." He cleared the knot from his throat. "And ..."

"Go on," she said.

Jasper swallowed. "And there's a bureau in the corner of the chamber. The edge is chipped."

"Stop," Inahteev snarled, whipping in front of the she-beast, placing himself threateningly between her and Jasper. Ixchel's mouth had fallen open, though her body was stiff. She didn't even blink.

Her breath shuddered when she finally released it.

Jasper licked his lips. "Emotions are a funny thing. If you feel them strongly enough, the memory of them will never go away. They will bleed from you into the floor, into the earth, into whatever space contained your pain for that moment, and the stain they leave will never go away."

There was no emotion in her voice. "It is quite a talent to see such things."

"*I* can see them. I will always see them."

"Then you can see the dead."

Jasper's jaw clenched. "Sometimes the dead speak louder than the living."

The monster lowered to her knees, sinking down until she and Jasper were comfortably at eye level. Her voice was a ghost after his. "What do they say then?"

Jasper didn't answer. His brows pulled together, his lips parting uncertainly.

But before he could say anything and before the woman could question him further, the cat-beast shoved him hard in the stomach. Jasper tripped backwards into me, and together, we passed between the two trees.

***

I walked through a spider's web, the air the tiniest bit resistant to our advance, but with my next step, the change was both immediate and jarring. I felt as if frost bloomed on my skin, the cold was so deep.

I coughed, all the moisture leeched from my mouth. My breath steamed.

The ground gave way beneath my feet, and I stumbled, my boots sinking with every step.

The air felt heavy, like it had thickened, like I breathed invisible smoke. I dizzied and swayed. Jasper gripped my arms.

"Lily, stay with me," his voice whispered from somewhere in the shifting dark.

I cracked my eyes open, following the length of my arm until I could see his hand, his arm, his body, his face …

"Jasper," I tried to say, but my voice was lost. I watched his lips shape around the syllables of my name, but the word didn't reach me.

My eyelids fluttered. I felt tiredness building behind them, urging them to close. My limbs felt heavy.

I shut my eyes, and then—

Silence. Weightlessness. My body relaxed. I felt light as air.

Water splashed across my knees and thighs as I was swallowed by spongey ground. When the wind met my wet skin, the sting of cold opened my eyes again, but only for a moment. My head lolled back. I stared upward, and Jasper's face appeared through mist and sky.

I watched his mouth move with words I couldn't hear, my heart pumping slower as my vision darkened and the world fell away around me. His hands reached for me. I saw his face. I saw his eyes.

His eyes …

APRIL 1912

PART FIFTEEN

THE EDGE OF A STORM

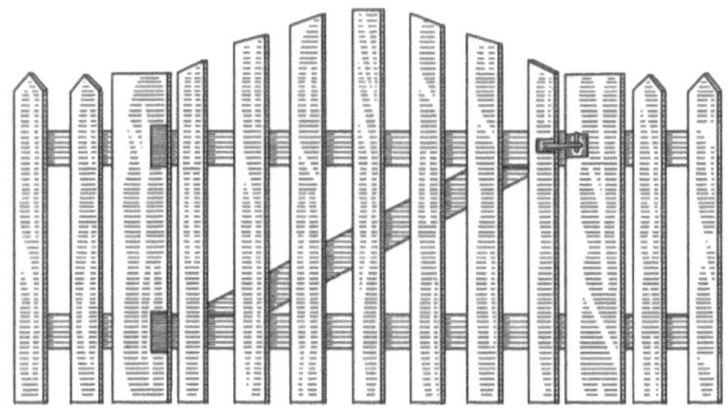

LILY

I woke from a dream or perhaps into one. I felt backwards, disoriented though my surroundings hadn't changed. Shutting my eyes, I inhaled and waited a few moments before surrendering to the morning just in case my dream wanted to resume. But I was awake, and instead of pictures, my eyes closed simply to black.

But what was the dream? Suddenly, I couldn't recall.

It was a maddening thing to never be able to fully remember anything, even a dream.

I opened my eyes haltingly against the rising sun and turned my head, squinting up at the ceiling and blinking away the sunspots. Then I lay still, discontent, my mind wandering up the ladder to the loft—to my little sanctuary of opportunity.

Every morning replicated itself. Every day, I woke and wondered if I was still dreaming because I felt like a stranger in my own body, like even my skin was foreign to me, though I knew it wasn't. I knew it was mine, every dimple and every hair.

And yet, I couldn't tell where it had been, how it had aged, how it had acquired the scars that carved deep grooves or raised welts. That was where the unfamiliarity and aversion stemmed from.

My own body had stories to tell, only I couldn't read them. They were written on my skin in a language I didn't understand.

I peered around when my eyes had fully adjusted. Everything about the room seemed new, though it was the very same room I'd occupied as a child in the same house I'd grown up in. I thought of Alice. She'd described it best—knowing who you are and not knowing at the same time, feeling strange and changed and sometimes like another person altogether—but I could only have been Alice in a dream. The room was quite lacking in rabbits in waistcoats and lobster quadrilles, though the addition of either would certainly have added a touch of vigour.

Heavily, I sighed, exhausted though the day had scarcely begun. The monotony made me feel dead. One needs movement and adventure to be sure they're still alive, or else what are they living for? What was *I* living for?

I glanced sideways, sweeping my arm over the empty space on the bed next to me, grabbing for a hand that wasn't there. Then drawing another deep breath, I slid my legs over the side of the mattress and sat up, pressing my hands into my thighs, rounding my back. I hung my head.

Every morning the floor was cold against my bare feet. It sent a shiver racing up my spine, like an electrical impulse starting me up for the day, reminding me to get up and move because I *was* still alive.

This morning was no different than any other. It was an exact replica of my waking yesterday and the day before. Nothing had changed.

I wanted something to change.

LILY

"How are you feeling today, Miss Lily?"

I could feel Sladen's eyes on me while I stared out the window with my chin in my hand, considering.

"My life repeats itself," I answered dully. "Down to this very hour and this cup of tea I share with you, every day is the same. It's utterly unremarkable." Drawing up my practised smile, I asked, "How could I feel anything but dead?"

Concern drew a line between his brows, and I knew he hadn't expected such a response.

I shifted my position to face him. "Did we not have tea at this hour yesterday, Mr. Ramey? And were we not seated in these very spots in this very parlour? And did you not ask me that very same question?"

He opened his mouth immediately, perhaps to argue, but after a short contemplation, he begrudgingly agreed. "You didn't fight with your brother over breakfast this morning, so if you're looking for a difference, I'd say that's noteworthy."

I shrugged. "I fancied a change."

"And has it done anything to relieve these feelings of—" He frowned. "—dead?"

Snorting, I leaned my head back and tapped my fingers on the armrest. "No, not particularly. To be honest, I'm rather disappointed." I let my gaze drift up to the ceiling. "Sladen, do you ever feel like you just don't want to get out of bed?"

"Are you tired?"

"You could lie there all day, and it wouldn't matter. No one would miss you. No one would need you because you don't really contribute to anything ... You realise that you're not all that necessary, and you only get up out of habit and because the sun is too bright to let you sleep."

He chuckled softly, scratched his head, and asked, "Do you know what gets me out of bed every morning, Lily?"

I shook my head.

"Coming here. Seeing you. That's the best part of my day. It's this little dance we do—this back and forth, bickering, having tea, talking ... Even your rejections motivate me because you never fully reject me, you know. Because you still sit here in this very room in these same seats and talk with me every day."

"Now, that's not true," I challenged, at last lowering my eyes to meet his. "Sometimes we sit in the sunroom or on the terrace."

He tsked and leaned back in his seat, propping one foot up on the opposite knee. "We've already become permanent existences in each other's lives ... Haven't we?" He paused, looking at me with that familiar expression of his that was equal parts stern and pleading. "Do you think about me when I'm not here? Do you expect me to show up? Do you look forward to it if only to tease me? Do you—do you miss me?"

His stare turned so severe that I dropped my eyes to my hands. He wasn't wrong, not entirely. I nodded, though it felt embarrassing to speak it aloud.

"Yes," I said, then clearing my throat, quickly added, "Though I suppose social creatures like humans require interaction and affection. Sometimes I crave it, naturally."

Sladen studied me. He asked, "Lily, do you really think that much would change if we wed? Do you think that we'd suddenly become different people and our interactions would be foreign? Because I assure you, that's not the case. Is this not comfortable enough for you?"

"Is that all you want? To be comfortable? Because I'm quite comfortable with how things are now. Maybe you don't think much will change, but some things will." I faced away. "I'd rather no change at all."

"You've just told me you fancied a change."

"I did this morning, but I don't anymore today."

He groaned. I knew I frustrated him, but I had no intention of changing our usual playful dynamic.

"Lily, please," Sladen said, his voice softening despite his obvious annoyance. "We both know I feel more strongly for you than you do for me, but if I could give you a comfortable life, that would be enough."

"Well, what if I don't want your comfortable life?"

He licked his lips, hesitant. Then he took a breath. "Yesterday, didn't you get out of bed when you heard me knocking? Didn't you fly down the stairs to greet me instead of letting John answer the door? If all you want in life is a reason to get out of bed ... aren't I already that reason?"

I looked up, speechless. Whatever I'd expected him to say, that wasn't it. I didn't know how to answer because that thought had never occurred to me before.

"I—" I gulped. He wasn't wrong, but ... "I-I don't know what to say to that."

"Say you'll think about it. I mean, seriously think about it. My feelings aren't a joke, so please don't treat them like they are." A frown pulled on the corner of his mouth. "I mean, just—just give it some thought. Please."

Swallowing, I observed his expression—both stern and pleading—and nodded.

LIAM

Yawning, I sat up in bed, slumping over my knees. I peered at Sophie, who faced the opposite wall, fast asleep, a soft hum chasing every breath that left her lips. She seemed peaceful, ignorant of my waking. But no matter how long I lay with my eyes closed, my mind wouldn't quiet. The words I'd remembered echoed ceaselessly in my head.

'I do not fear death, Liam ... I do not fear ... I do not ...'

I got up and began to pace the room, but the floorboards creaked. Afraid I might disturb Sophie—and unwilling to explain my restlessness—I lit a chamberstick and went out into the hall. Then, as if urged by some force beyond my grasp, my feet carried me farther. I went to the drawing room, down the stairs, to the sunroom, to the parlour, and finally, without knowing even which door I'd gone through, I found myself standing outside on the lawn.

I blinked as if I'd just woken, the scene around me building with every flutter of my eyes. The dewy grass under that early morning haze, the cobblestone path that wound through it, and at the end of it, directly in front of me: the garden gate washed in pale candlelight.

What was I doing out here?

I hadn't checked the time. I hadn't even bothered to dress or put on boots.

What was I looking for? What was I following?

I didn't know.

It was just a voice—a memory so distant and strange that I couldn't help questioning its validity. It shouldn't matter who'd said those words, if they'd actually been spoken to me at all, and yet …

Those words in that voice that was both familiar and unfamiliar chilled me to my bones, and I stood there in bare feet, shivering in the moonless dark.

How long did I stand inert? How many minutes crept by while I racked my brain, trying to put a face to the voice in my head? He'd said he wouldn't fear death. He'd calmly declared that he'd embrace it, right? It hadn't seemed foreboding at all, so why was I overcome with this horrid feeling of dread? Was it simply because someone I knew had spoken so casually about his own death?

I felt feverish. Frantic. I had to move.

I unlocked the gate, wrenching it open in one swift, desperate movement, the gust of it shaking my candle's flame. But as I did, a tremor crawled up my spine. Tears pricked my eyes. I held my free hand in front of my face, saw how unsteady it already was.

What was wrong with me?

I could feel it—the harrowing fear I'd carried in some dark place in my heart and my mind all these long years. But now, it stirred. It grasped me from within, forcing me to acknowledge its existence, begging me to give it life and power.

I had to move. I had to flee from it.

I stepped onto the soil and walked the rows of vegetables, holding my head, combing my fingers over and over through my hair. I looked left, then right, behind me, in front of me. I spun in a circle and resumed pacing, kicking my feet through mounds of dirt or seedlings without reserve. Shadows of plants danced on the fence around me, an audience to my plight, little spectres created by candlelight and wind. I flinched every time one pulsed into my field of vision.

I tucked my hand under my armpit to warm it. I released it and shook it out. I couldn't stop moving. I didn't know what else to do. I couldn't banish that awful feeling, I couldn't blink fast enough to keep the tears from my eyes, and I couldn't remember that man's Goddamn face!

My head spun. My eyes crossed. My body bumbled and swayed. I had to stop, but the voice screamed louder. I crammed my fists against my eyes, willing it to silence, praying for reprieve. Wax dripped from the chamberstick's reservoir down my arm.

This is just a dream, Liam. That's all this is. This is a dream. Go back to bed. This is just a dream. Go inside. This will all go away.

I spurred, staggering back to the gate, letting it fall shut behind me with the whine of rusty hinges. I fled up the stairs to the terrace, and inside I went, through the French doors, down the hall, up the stairs, and to my bedroom, where my wife still lay asleep.

I paused in the centre of the room, taking in the sudden, strange quietude the space provided. Shakily, I expelled my breath.

At last, the voice had ceased, but for some reason, I hadn't expected to return and find the room untouched. I'd expected some level of disarray to mirror that of my mind. I felt as if a violent storm had ripped through me. There should've been some physical sign of it—some proof of what I'd just experienced. But no such proof existed. I stood in a sanctuary of silence with only the usual hushed noises of night, Sophie's motionless form still a curled lump under the blankets on the bed.

But I felt no relief as I snuffed my candle and climbed carefully in beside her. I couldn't seem to purge the coldness in me, regardless of how many quilts I swaddled myself in. I still felt dizzy and chilled down to my very soul.

But it was only a dream, right?

That was all I could tell myself to slow my frenzied heart—to try to erase whatever ill effect remained of my little passing storm.

Go to sleep, Liam, and when you wake, all will be well. It's only a dream.

Maybe if I said it enough, I'd start to believe it.

When I woke hours after sunrise, there was still dirt on my feet, and inexplicably, I knew two things for certain: the man whose words had plagued my dreams was called Noah, whoever he was, and somehow, sometime in my acquaintance with him, he had died. And although I had no other recollection of him anywhere in my mind, my heart ached.

I covered my face with my hands, stifling my voice as my body shook with sobs.

What ghosts are waiting to haunt us, Lily, and why are you so keen for them to find us again?

I didn't want them to find us again.

I don't want to be found.

I don't …

LILY

My brother arrived late to the breakfast table without acknowledging me, even though I was the only other person in the room. Sophie and Colin had already departed and would be at her sister's house for the remainder of the week, and Sladen hadn't joined us this morning.

I studied him as he stole behind the Herald, his hands gripping the paper so tightly that I didn't think the crinkle would smooth out if I tried. For an hour, we sat in that dour silence, but he never lowered the newspaper or even turned the page.

He didn't speak.

He didn't eat.

And I couldn't help but notice that he was dressed completely in black.

THE WEIGHT OF SILENCE

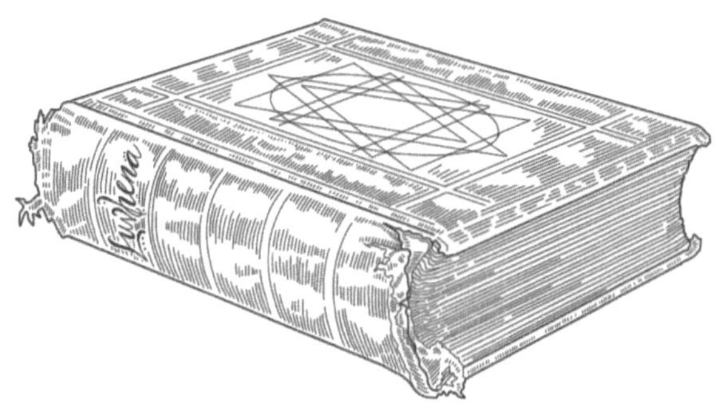

SETH

The creaking door signaled Quade's arrival, but he stayed in the entryway.

"What?" I asked, not bothering to look up from the book I held. I crossed my legs and leaned back in my chair, bobbing my foot as if to a melody.

His voice stretched across the space. "Are you really not gonna leave this room? It's been days."

I avoided giving him my attention, making a show of dragging my eyes from one side of the page to the other, though I retained none of its content. "Mere days are inconsequential to someone like me."

Then I stiffened as the room was swallowed in silence. An intentional silence. A prolonged moment for me to recount what I'd said and feel the full force of my regret. My inability to face him shifted from resistance to shame, just as he intended.

I could see his answering expression without having to look. He loathed when I spoke so trivially of time passing—when I reminded him of my affliction and his mortality. Words like those cut him without even the presence of a knife.

He closed the space between us in three strides and swept the volume from my lap.

I sighed heavily, apologetic but still reluctant.

He dropped the book on the end table and planted himself directly in front of me, leaning forward to grip the arm rests of my chair, caging me. At last, I raised my head, and he moved closer until there were only inches separating our faces. But still, he did not speak.

"What would you have me do—" I hissed, unable to hide my annoyance at being forced to participate in a conversation he knew I didn't want to have. "—besides sit here in this room?" His expression dimmed, and for just a moment, I faltered. But it didn't matter if I was gentle or coarse, I decided; the anxiety wouldn't go away. "I've nothing better to do and many years still left to live."

His mouth twitched, his eyes narrowing as they flicked down to my lips and back up again. His voice was barbed. "You could spend time with me, you prick."

You'll bring up the others, I thought.

Then he said it for me.

"You could go to Earth," he suggested, his voice softly insistent. I peered sideways, but he grabbed my chin, forcing me back to centre, staring hard at my face.

Groaning, I shook myself free of his grasp, pressing my palm against his chest to urge him back as I stood. He didn't resist, though he did place himself between me and the door as if he thought I might flee.

"Just once more," he whispered. "Please."

I met his gaze, defiant. "I already told you, I can't go back anymore ... not unless something changes."

"And what if something has changed in your absence?"

I scoffed. "It's been a few days, Quade. What d'you expect could've happened?"

But again, I was stilled by my own words. They felt sour in my mouth—like I needed to purge any remnants after they left my lips—and the look he returned was grave. He didn't have to answer because we were thinking the same thing.

One day could change everything.

Even an hour or a minute or the third of a second it takes to blink.

How many ways had our lives been altered in short amounts of time? How quickly did each storm come and pass?

But I didn't want to admit it. I didn't want to think about it. Instead, I turned my head with a feigned air of disinterest. "Go yourself if you're so worried."

But Quade knew me too well to be deceived by my acting. His voice was calm, direct. "Are you afraid Colin said something?"

When I didn't respond, he stepped closer.

I wasn't scared of him. There was nothing he could do physically that I couldn't overpower, not that he'd ever try. But there was something to be said about his obstinance. This was a subject he wouldn't abandon.

Quade would never abandon the people he loved, nor had he in all the stages of our acquaintance.

He'd never abandoned me.

I couldn't contend with that. He, at least, was deserving of my honesty.

"Yes!" I threw my arms up, exasperated, though there was a touch of relief in admitting it. "Yes, okay? I *am* afraid. He'd seen me before; they could know about me already!"

"D'you think mentioning a stranger on their property will instantly cure their ignorance?"

"It might!"

Evenly, Quade asked, "And what's wrong with that? I thought you didn't want to be a stranger anymore, Seth."

I felt foolish shouting while he remained passive, but I couldn't ignore how deeply the thought unsettled me. "I don't, but—"

"I miss them, too. You're not the only one. It's been long enough."

The passion in my voice dwindled. I tried to match his rationality. "If they remember on their own, I'll be there for them. Of course, I will, but ..."

"But you don't want to force it. I get that, but you're also seeking to prevent it by running away. Maybe they *want* to remember, Seth. Maybe they've started to already. Maybe your presence could add ease to the process. Have you ever thought about that?" His brows pulled together. "Why're you so reluctant to let them?"

This melancholic expression on his face ... I desired to rid him of it, dry the moisture in his eyes, smooth the wrinkles from his forehead, erase the sadness that seemed to darken the entire room.

But for this matter, his grief could not persuade me.

"I won't go," I said.

"Why?" Quade demanded to know, as if he were not already aware of the answer.

He was. He knew, and it would injure us both to remind him.

Slowly, my eyes drifted back to the door of the little room at the end of the hall. The voice I produced to answer was so soft that I knew he had to read my lips to know what I said.

"Because Lily will remember that it was her fault."

He opened his mouth. He closed it. I knew he didn't want to agree with me, but I could see the struggle on his face as he tried to work out what to say and how to say it—as if she were here, and he was trying to spare her the guilt.

He scratched the back of his neck, bowing his head. His

voice was meek. "You don't actually believe that, do you? Not now after it's been so long. You can't really say ..." His voice trailed off, and he glanced up at me expectantly, waiting for my acquiescence to soften the blow.

But I could only answer with the ambiguity of silence.

Acknowledgments

This story has been more than a decade in the making and has seen many supporters along the way.

So many beautiful people have uplifted, inspired, encouraged, or otherwise assisted me in making this a reality, even if they simply said they wanted to read the story when I was finished.

To my siblings and friends: You are a gift.

To my family, coworkers, and clients: thank you from the bottom of my heart.

To you, the reader: I hope that if you take anything away from this book, it is the knowledge that you are never truly alone in this world. Thank you.

To the musicians, artists, and authors who motivate me every day with their voices and their stories: I am in your debt.

But most of all ... Thank you to all of the people in my life who are familiar and safe. For you, I have not the words to convey my gratitude.

About the Author

H. Dawn Hunter is a licensed tattoo artist and lifelong Alaskan. She enjoys traveling, the band Rush, and singing show tunes to her very unenthusiastic cat.

For more information & updates, please visit hdawnhunter.com

www.ingramcontent.com/pod-product-compliance
Lightning Source LLC
Chambersburg PA
CBHW031232310726
48971CB00004B/976